Printed in the United States of America

First Printing, 2019

ISBN 978-1-7336506-0-1

J.A. Burton
Colorado Springs, CO

www.jaburton.com

FIRSTBORN:
A NOVEL OF
LEONARDO DA VINCI

To Emily and Jacen
Follow your dreams

A painter should begin every canvas with a wash of black, because all things in nature are dark except where exposed by the light.

-Leonardo da Vinci

1

April 15, 1452

Father pulled Piero's farsetto taut against his chest and dragged him closer. "Look what you've done."

Piero traced the outlines of the Vinci countryside made into shadows by moonlight. Nature snared the uneven walls of the sharecropper quarters and oil mill in tangled branches and creeping vines.

Caterina's voice lit the night like a crack of lightning.

Father shook him. "I set you on the right path, and you fouled it."

Father's path was the only path so Piero nodded to please him. "I will make it right."

"Youth and freedom are gone, son. The yoke of manhood is now on your shoulders." Father's face became harsher by the firelight that cast it into an angular shape, unnatural, cutting.

Piero straightened his back. He was the law, a notary, given the title Ser. He wore the black robes of office with a mere twenty-five years to his name. This made him a respectable man. Now Father must see him as one.

"My way is no game," Father said. "You seek distractions in the fields, take your fill, and pack your horse to return to Florence."

"Not anymore." Piero pulled away, but Father's grip gave no slack. "For the love of my own mother, what will it take?" Father should be grateful he knew more restraint than ascribed. "I made my choices and will take responsibility for them. I'm no longer a child."

"No longer, and I thank God for it." Father made the sign of the cross. He pressed on, "Caterina is our servant,

Piero—can you not see what you've done to your family, to your agreement—your future wife?"

"Let me go." Piero knocked his father's hand loose and tugged the bottom of his farsetto to straighten it. "I cannot undo what is done." Piero sat at the outdoor table near the warmth of the fire. He leaned back; his knuckles whitened. His marriage agreement…he picked no woman's lock once he agreed to marry another. "Carlo," he called into the house, "for the love of Santa Maria, bring the wine. We may be here all night."

Piero swallowed hard. Tomorrow everything would change. But the night would end, yet again, with Caterina in mind. Like the heady days in July when he traveled home from the city, she had a pull on him. She lingered in his thoughts and he wished the nights would last.

When he rode into the stable, she was often nearby, working and watching, waiting. Swirls of walnut and honey poked through her bound tresses that wafted in the breeze. Her dark eyes looked as if they held a secret. He tasted soil and sweet basil when he breathed her in and could hardly wait. They ventured out to the edge of the grove and made love beneath the silver tinged olive branches glimmering in the pink and orange sunset.

"I'm so happy," she said, as they lay tangled together.

Soft, and smooth, Caterina melted into him. Piero brushed his thumb across her forehead and down her temple and neck and kissed her again.

"I love you," she said.

Her bronzed skin and round breasts made him smile. "You are so beautiful." His breath caught in his throat. She compelled him to risk everything. He could spend entire nights alone with her, but it felt wrong to lay on the ground naked and hidden in the trees.

Too soon nature would force their confession.

"Signori, I've brought your wine," Carlo said, "I thought you'd like the bottle."

Piero lowered his chair. He nodded and grabbed the two cups set out on the table. "Grazie. You understand this man's need." He poured a cup for his father and one for himself and drank from the bottle instead. "Come, drink with us, Carlo." He offered his cup.

Carlo nodded in thanks. "Of my three boys—the first one was the hardest." He sipped his wine. "My wife says the women who cry out loudest birth strong, healthy boys."

Excellent. How perfect. A son? No. Not for Piero. He could not think of a son now, nor could he see himself as a father. Children and his lack of tolerance for them felt as palatable as eating stones.

Caterina's screams reached them again.

Piero needed Father to relax and pray for a baby girl so the child could remain with her mother until old enough to enter a convent. Mother and daughter would have enough to eat and a place to live. In fact, Caterina should be grateful she worked for a generous family since she had no one else.

"Tell me you have a plan, Piero," Father said. "Caterina must be close now. When your mother birthed you, she sounded the same as Caterina does now, and not long after I could hear your eager cries. You do have a plan?"

"Of course I have a plan." Father's hand would swoop in to solve delicate matters with the utmost finesse, but Piero had refused him.

"Piero, I think—"

Piero thrust his arm out. "Do you want me to tell you or not?" Father always made him stumble and revert to childishness. He pinched his fingers across the top of his nose. "Oh, let me satisfy your doubts."

Father hammered his fingers on the table.

"Caterina and the child will stay here while they recover from the birth and then she will be married. You do know of the man called Antonio di Piero Buti del Vacca? Some of his neighbors call him Accattabriga."

Father's eyebrows lifted. "This "tough guy" is interested in a wife?"

"Though he is a couple years younger than Caterina, he does seek a wife. He understands the woman comes with a child that must be well cared for." Piero needed to convince his father at this moment and on this point. He slammed his fist on the table. The wine cups rattled. "A bastard of mine she or he may be, but the bastard is still my child. Antonio Buti understands that Caterina has a handsome dowry considering her lowly state and his own, and our good family name sits well with him."

"This is the young man—the soldier from Campo Zeppi by the river?"

"Yes, Father. Antonio Buti accepted my offer though I should mention I had a small problem when I brought the documents for him to sign. The mercenary merda refuses to accept her until he can make her his proper wife. You know, he wants carnal knowledge of her. He said she would not be welcome under his roof until the child no longer needs the teat because a married man has nuptial rights. With such eloquent vulgarity he said, "No sex, no marriage, Ser." He told me to keep my money until he has his guarantee. But, I did get his signature." Piero displayed the document like a cat with a fresh caught mouse in its teeth.

He continued, "As for the Amadori woman, I've not forgotten. Father, you were right, she is a good match. Her handsome dowry will honor our family." Not that she lacked a pleasing face. "She can come to live with us in half a year I should think."

Father opened his mouth—

"Do not trouble your mind, Father. Your choice of my betrothed is as secure in my mind as the contract we signed, and in this you know I do not regress. We honor our commitments."

***

Father and Carlo played backgammon while Piero nursed his wine. He heard nothing for some time but kept watch. Caterina's silence tested him. He wanted to know the result, finally, and move on with his plan. Piero nudged Father's arm. "Mother," he said pointing to the pathway.

"Antonio," she called on approach. "You have a grandson."

Piero stared, confused. Father's hands cupped his cheeks, "Piero. You have a son."

"I have a...a son?"

"Yes, a son. It's not every day I become a grandfather. What name will you give him?"

Piero paused. The bastard child would not have the name Antonio. Weeks ago, he heard a name. What was it? "His name will be Leonardo." He tossed the name around in his head. "Leonardo di Ser Piero da Vinci," he said with a sour taste in his mouth.

Father hooked his arm around Piero and led him into the house. Inside, Father opened the old notebook that came from his great grandfather. On the back page, he had written the names of his children, their dates of birth, and their baptisms. At the bottom of the page in the space remaining, Father wrote:

1452 There was born to me a grandson, the son of Ser Piero my son, on the 15th day of April, a Saturday, at the third hour of the night. He bears the name Lionardo.

"Father," Piero said, to correct the spelling error. He waved his hand. "Forget it."

***

Piero pulled the neckline of his shirt and took a deep breath, for he must follow tradition, and a father's first duty was to bring the child before the priest for baptism. Caterina's room consisted of no more than a battered chest, a single stool, a cradle, and a bed. As he drew closer, pitiful infant cries made him wish to turn away. He slowed his steps and peered in from the hall.

The midwife, Maria, lifted the child from his bedside cradle to change his soiled linens. She swaddled the child and placed him in his mother's arms.

Piero rebuked himself for yanking at his collar again. He set his chin firm and approached the women.

They turned to face him.

Caterina smiled. "They said you waited for us." She urged him forward and reached for his hand. "Meet the precious gift of our love, Piero."

Piero stood in place. He knew what needed doing.

But Mother hurried in. "Before we go, let us pray," she said, saving him. She waited for them to fold their hands. "Hail Mary full of grace..."

Piero studied both woman, heads bowed, eyes closed. The midwife waited behind them and held the balled-up child at her chest.

"Amen," Mother said.

Piero cleared his throat to speak to Caterina—

Mother stepped between him and Caterina. "No time for talk else we'll be late."

"Ah," Maria said, "kiss your bambino, Caterina. We're ready to depart." She dipped the child for Caterina's kiss. "You may feel well, but don't rise from bed until I return."

Maria carried the child and walked beside Piero to the church. Halfway there, she halted. "Forgive me, Signore. He's warm and sweet, but not mine." She offered his son to him.

The sleeping baby's wisps of hair shined golden in the sun. Piero made no reach for him. "He's content. Let us not disturb him."

Maria cradled the child against her bosom and continued walking.

A few chosen people gathered at the church: Ser Piero, his parents and younger brother, the soon-to-be godparents, Papino di Nanni Banti and Maria, the daughter of Nanni di Venzo, Arrigo Giovanni Tedesco, and the Monna di Domenico di Brettone. Fra Ferdinand Visconti, the parish priest, baptized the child late in the morning.

Guests visited Caterina in her room and brought simple gifts and well wishes for Leonardo.

Later that night, Piero cornered Maria. "I must talk with Caterina alone." He ignored her stubborn glare. "Grazie," he said waving her out. "No need to fret over her modesty."

"Yes, Ser," she said sighing loud enough to show her disapproval. "I'll gather the bambino and wait in the kitchen."

Piero went to Caterina's bedside. "Caterina, I have important news you must hear."

She studied him and waited.

"You are to be married soon. The contract, written on your behalf, states that your marriage to Antonio Buti will take place once you have weaned Leonardo."

"What?" Caterina fired back. "Did you make such tidy arrangements?" She held a hand to her forehead. "I heard mention of an Amadori woman today—from someone who needed to speak the truth. But how could I believe it?" She dropped her head and wiped tears from her face. "I...I loved you and you know it. We little people of the country have eyes and ears or have you forgotten? You think you're so much better than us?" She crawled out of her blankets and stood to face him. Her finger out, she jabbed him in the chest. "You used me. I'll not go quietly! Don't think I'll go without my son. I want him and will die before I leave him."

"Woman, you would do well for yourself and for your future husband if you held your loose tongue. Fate sits near your side. You will have a home and someone to look after you. A peasant woman could hope for nothing more. The child will go with you. But never forget he is my son. If ever I should wish to call, I have claim of him."

2

June 1457

Leonardo called Campo Zeppi by the Vincio River home. He reached his hand out of the water. "Can Piera come in, Mamma?"

"Your sister can't swim like you, sweetheart. You're a fish. I think you were born with fins." Mamma laughed. "Grab me a few more reeds and we're done."

Leonardo dipped under the water out of the hot sun. He pulled reeds free and handed them up. He wished he could stay in the water all afternoon to find giant rocks, watch little fish, catch frogs and bugs, and look for the big fish, but Mamma called him out once his fingers and toes wrinkled like an old man. When Mamma helped him out he shook his hair at her.

She blocked her face from spray and laughed with him. "Come along," she said carrying reeds and a water filled bucket.

Leonardo slipped on his tunic, grabbed the last pile of reeds, and followed. The skin on his back and neck prickled. He peered over his shoulder and ran to catch up to Mamma.

Mamma poured her water into a basin and sat with Piera under the shade of the big tree next to the house.

Up and down, swish, swoosh went each pass of her strong fingers. Her hands moved like music. More than that, her hands made music. Leonardo closed his eyes to listen.

Mamma reached into the bottom of the basin for a well-soaked shoot and bent it into a circle for a basket. She worked for a long time.

"Leonardo, once I've finished, go run and hide. Me and your sister will count and find you."

Leonardo smiled. "Mamma, I have a new place today. You'll have to look hard to find me."

"That's so?"

Piera stood and ran around the tree. "Piera," Mamma said, "Come, tell me how many reeds your brother has left?"

Piera circled back to the branches. "One, two…" Piera lifted each branch and placed it across Leonardo's lap. "Three like me," she said. "Four, five. He's five," she pointed at Leonardo and tore off in a flurry. She ran toward the house where her cousin, Lisa, sat on an old bench swinging her feet and straw doll.

Auntie Fiore looked after Piera, Lisa, and her two boys, Simone and baby Michele. She chopped artichokes and onion that plopped into the soup pot on the fire.

Mamma held her big baby belly and stretched. "Leonardo, I'm proud of you. You always help your poor mother." She finished her work. "I'm going to count now. Are you ready to hide?"

"Yes, Mamma." He sprang from the ground and waited for her to close her eyes. She started counting.

Leonardo ran as fast as he could. His bare feet made soft thuds on the ground. He ducked under the low tree branches and ran past the house to the small stable behind it. Inside, a hook holding an old horse blanket hung close to the ground. He slipped beneath and stood still as possible.

It was quiet and a little dark. The blanket smelled of horse sweat and dust. "Accchoo!" He peeked out. Mamma didn't hear him. The shady stable had three animal stalls and a ladder to the hayloft. Something moved in the light up there. Mamma's footsteps sounded closer to the door.

Leonardo shoved aside the blanket, ran to the ladder, and climbed.

He waited and watched. "There it is," he said, low. A pile of straw moved again. He snuck along toward it.

A head popped out. "Meow."

Leonardo jumped.

"Leonardo?" Mamma called, "you've hidden so well I can't find you. Where are you?"

"Up here." He giggled. "I found something. Papa told a story about animals in the city. A scary one with big feet and sharp claws and pointy teeth. A lion. Papa says boy lions have long hair around their necks." He grabbed the cat.

"What did you find?"

He lifted the cat. "Look. He poked his face out to scare me but didn't growl. He meowed because he likes me. He's gold and furry. Let's call him Leone."

"Your Papa says we don't name anything we don't mean to keep."

"I mean to keep him," Leonardo said, stuffing his lion into the neck of his tunic. His belt would hold the cat in so he could climb down the ladder. "How did he get up there, Mamma?"

"I don't know. Maybe he wanted a safe place to sleep."

"He couldn't jump down. He looks hungry," Leonardo said. "He's safe now 'cause I saved him and we'll feed him." His bulging shirt shuffled about. Leone's golden head popped out under his chin. "Your hair tickles." He scratched Leone behind his ear.

Auntie cut meaty bits from a plucked chicken. Feathers brushed along the dirt. She looked angry with little Simone. Leonardo understood because Simone was still clumsy and into everything. Auntie told him no again and said, "Lisa, would you pull the feathers out of your brother's mouth?"

Leonardo waited for Auntie to see him. "I have a hungry cat. He needs food. Can we have some? Please?"

She stopped cutting to look at the cat. "Leonardo, you always find things and bring them home." Her eyebrow lifted. "Something killed the chicken."

Leonardo pulled Leone close. "He's too little, Auntie. He didn't do it."

"We can't feed every orphan you find," she said, and tossed a few bits of chicken scrap to the ground.

"Grazie." Leonardo let Leone loose before he clawed him to get at his meal. "Look." He pointed at a rider far out on the road. Trees blocked the view, but once a rider met the clearing, anyone at the house could see him. The rider waved. "Papa."

Papa trotted in on a cloud of dust. "Whoa, Madca." He tightened Madca's reins and removed his straw hat. His short black hair curled. Papa handed Mamma a small sack. "Today's extra earnings."

"Oh, Antonio." Mamma kissed him.

"Papa, look what I found today," Leonardo said lifting his cat in the air.

Leone's feet paddled.

Papa stepped closer to view the cat. He smiled wide at Mamma. "Does it have a name?"

"Leone. Like in your story."

Papa nodded. He lifted Leonardo for a hug and placed him in Madca's saddle. "Madca needs to be brought to stable. Will you tell me how you found the cat on the way?"

"Me. Me," came Piera running to Papa for a ride. He scooped her up and placed her behind Leonardo in the saddle.

***

Leonardo stretched in the grass and found animals in the clouds. When Papa went in the house, he followed.

Papa tied coverings up to the top of the windowsills so the heat would go out. His boots scratched on the mats that covered the dirt floors.

"Papa, can Leone sleep with us?"

"If he'll stay inside."

"Antonio," Uncle said peeking his head inside the house, "Riders come." He pointed in the low spot between the hills.

Papa took Leonardo's hand and went outside to scan the road. "I see them. Only two." He stretched his arms. "I'd say it'll take them time enough to reach the river. I could lay with my wife before they'd be on our doorstep."

"Nah, it doesn't take you as long as that, brother."

Papa shrugged. "I'd take half as long these days, but my wife's not comfortable and the church father says it's a sin."

Uncle nudged him with his elbow and laughed. "A soldier's hands are too quick, huh?"

"Easy for a celibate man to say, I say," Papa said.

"We can agree on that." Uncle grinned and stroked his chin.

Papa lifted Leonardo on his shoulders. "Would it be a sin to injure a man if he comes looking for trouble?"

"Surely they're searching for water." I'd wager they pass by. No one's coming up that hill unless he has business or seeks trouble."

Papa lifted his dagger out of the sheath then slipped it back in. "Good eyes, brother."

3

Piero followed the dusty road marked by horseshoe prints and scattered pebbles. Years since his last visit, he disliked the road as much now as he did then. The hills bordering the valley left riders vulnerable to attack.

Travelers took precautions, and Piero followed sound advice. The first rule: do not take the road alone, especially an unfamiliar road. The second: carry arms, but do not give the appearance of too much armament. Piero carried a sword, a gift from his father, though he never used it, nor would he ever—that he decided long ago. His younger brother, Francesco, carried a sword and a dagger. They may not have the capability to fend-off a strong enemy, but a sword, or in Piero's case, a long stick, could be as much a deterrent as any blade in his hands. The key was to be smarter. Piero believed himself smarter than any rogue, and his brother accompanied him as added protection and discouragement to any brigands along the way.

Francesco was not what Piero would call an imposing figure—not yet; he was only a boy of fifteen years, but one who knew how to avoid the ploys men used to target riders. Despite their age difference, Piero felt safe with him. The boy, the family joked, found his way out of almost anywhere—even in the dark with a sack over his head—a most valuable skill, especially when riding into an unavoidable collision.

Piero doubted his readiness. The past was something to put behind him. Yet, here he went to Campo Zeppi like a beggar. He would not, could not beg Caterina, but he would take what was his. He told her. He was clear.

A son's place was with his father. How else could a boy grow into a proper man? Boys required more than the affection of their mothers. Piero once thought a soldier would ensure the protection of his child, but the experiences of a young soldier offered knowledge of how to kill, destroy, and steal. Lessons yes, but nothing respectable.

Piero took a deep breath. The silence gave him too much time to think. "The cloud cover is inviting." He cleared his throat. "Francesco?" he said, swatting a fly.

Francesco took little notice of the heat. He glanced at Piero. "I see the ridge of the hill. There?" He pointed.

"Yes, past the trees in the clearing you can see the house. We will arrive soon." Piero's saddle creaked when he shifted in his seat. He spotted the rectangular terracotta rooftop. Close now. He unhooked his leather flagon and drank some ale. "Brother." Piero tossed him the corked flagon.

Francesco drank and rode at ease. "We need to water the horses before the return home. The river's close." He paused and held out the flagon. "Better now than after we've disrupted another man's home."

"Disrupted?" Piero said, snatching the flagon back. "We never discussed Leonardo's return, but I want my son in his rightful home. He is old enough to leave his mother. The right time is now, before I return to the city."

Francesco's cheek twinged. He nodded.

Piero clenched his teeth. His brother thought this a bad idea? What did a boy know about fatherhood?

They watered the horses and followed a narrow road lined with golden grain to the ridge of Campo Zeppi. Piero questioned if he waited too long. Things had such clarity and purpose on paper, but in this, there were no rules, no expectations, and he had no experience.

"Francesco, I better go ahead. Accattabriga will recognize me." Piero curved his horse around his brother's and crested the hill.

Accattabriga and another man stood side-by-side, hands on the hilts of their daggers. They met within a good distance from Accattabriga's house. A couple of women and several children watched them. Piero needed to get closer to locate his boy.

Accattabriga spoke first. "Ser Piero, I've not seen you in many years. What could bring you to these humble parts?"

"My son." Piero set his shoulders straight and glared at Accattabriga. What other purpose would he have for coming, fool?

Accattabriga gauged both riders. He clicked his tongue. "What you've come for is no simple trade of goods."

Piero had no time for this dance. "No, but we made an agreement. I have come for my son."

"And who's the boy?" Accattabriga asked, gesturing toward Francesco.

"My brother, Francesco." Piero sensed Accattabriga's hackles rising, so he dismounted his horse. Francesco dismounted and led his horse closer.

Accattabriga grinned and slapped his hand on his companion's shoulder. "This man here, he's my brother. He'll hold your horses and weapons. Me and you," he pointed at Piero, "we'll go to the house. Your brother can stay with my brother."

Francesco looked to the stranger reaching for his property. "I stay with my horse."

"I would have it no other way," Accattabriga said.

Accatabriga wore simple, faded clothes. The scabbard of the dagger hanging at his waist showed fine leather craft with a horse carved around the hilt. Rather than alert Accattabriga to his attention on the dagger, Piero focused ahead.

Piero could make out the children in detail now. He skipped over the babies and spotted Caterina. She looked much the same as he remembered. The boy with golden hair and blue eyes looked old enough to be his son. Leonardo stared at him without recognition. He had his mother's triangular nose and full bottom lip—and his father's eyes. A dirt smudge crossed his plump cheek. He wore a greyish peasant's tunic and no shoes.

Piero looked to Caterina. Her eyes met his in a cold, unwavering challenge.

"Piero? I must say I'm surprised." She crossed her arms over her chest. "You're not welcome here. I left your home an outcast." She looked at her husband for reassurance. "Me, Antonio, and Leonardo have built a good life for ourselves. Leave us in peace."

Piero caught the tremor in her voice. Caterina would take shots at him, so it would be best to get on with his intent and get out of the fire. "I have come for my son. Today I claim him."

Caterina's eyes widened like she might explode. "Your son? When has he ever been your son? You don't even know him."

"Don't think we don't know about you," another woman holding a baby said. "She's a good woman and she loves her boy."

Caterina held her hand up to stop the woman. "You live a short ride away and haven't come to see your son in five years."

Piero readied to grab Caterina's shoulders and command she calm down so they could talk away from Accattabriga's watching family. But he dare not touch her.

Leonardo held his mother's skirt and shook it. "Mamma, Mamma who's that man?"

"He's your father, Leonardo."

The boy cocked his head to the side. First he looked at Piero, then at Accattabriga. "I have a Papa."

Accattabriga smiled at the boy, ruffled his hair, and placed his hand on his wife's shoulder.

Caterina continued, "As you can see Piero, the word father has meaning to my boy, but you mean nothing to him."

Leonardo kicked a stone.

Piero hesitated at the sight of the boy's bare, dirty feet. Caterina made it easy to maintain his hardened edge, but the sight of his son's condition brought him low. What sort of man begged for a poor child? Sweat beaded on his forehead.

He needed Leonardo. Damn it all. He could not look at his son, nor could he look away. He had to fall back on his training. His nerve might slip. Nothing but a transaction, he convinced himself, just business.

He noted Caterina's ripe middle. "He needs his father. I can support him and lessen your burden here. You so accurately spoke of the short ride away." He would turn her words on her. "You can visit Leonardo."

Caterina's reddening face, her posture, everything, indicated she wanted to kill him.

"He has a true father," she said. She took Accattabriga's hand. "This man raised Leonardo with everything he has and knows. He's done a fine job. We're lucky to have him."

Accattabriga stiffened as if ready to throw the first punch.

Piero put up his guard, the one that made him a maestro of business. Washed in a renewed calm, he fought back a grin. "I found the man for you and my son. Accattabriga, Antonio, whatever do I call you, knows it true. He agreed to the arrangement."

Piero knew he had them. Of course he had them. He went so far as to bring the document in his saddlebag. The look on Accattabriga's face told all; he had no argument, no recourse. Piero would leave with Leonardo.

Caterina's face darkened and twisted. She growled. Her hand cracked across Piero's cheek. She swung around and slapped her husband the same.

Piero's face stung.

Caterina begged Accattabriga. "No, he's my baby. He's my boy. Please, Antonio."

Leonardo held his mother's skirts. "Mamma. Don't cry, Mamma. I'm scared. Papa?" Tears left trails down Leonardo's dirty face. His nose ran and snot bubbled at his mouth.

Caterina pulled Leonardo against her. "My boy."

Accattabriga's family, their eyes like daggers, gave warning. One misplaced word and they may attack. Piero staggered to a stump before the undulating hills pulled him down. Here he waited and mustered the resolve to finish what he started.

Accattabriga soothed his wife. "Fiore, please," he called, "Could you gather Leonardo's things? I don't want my son on the road once the sun goes down." Accattabriga whispered, kissed his wife and Leonardo, and led them toward the horses.

Piero followed.

"On your horse Ser," Accattabriga said.

Francesco mounted but Piero waited. After all this, no way would Accattabriga get him on his horse and scare his mount to run before he had the boy.

Accattabriga took the boy's sack and thrust it, hard, into Piero's chest. "Put the boy in your saddle, and off with you before I change my mind."

Caterina bent as best she could to wipe Leonardo's face clean. "Sweetheart, you must go with this man now. He's your father, he'll not harm you," she said clinging to him.

Leonardo looked at Piero and back at his mother again. "Mamma, I want to stay home."

Caterina smiled at Leonardo. "I know you don't understand, but you have to go with him."

"I don't want to." Leonardo paused, "Papa and Uncle say a man has to do things sometimes. Hard things."

"Yes, you're so smart. Be a brave boy. We love you always. This will forever be your home. Nothing can change that."

"Come son," Accattabriga said, "let me introduce you to the men that will take you to a fine house not too far from here. You'll be there in time for supper." Accattabriga pointed. "This man here, his name is Ser Piero."

Piero squatted.

Leonardo held his body upright. "Buongiorno, Signore. My name is Leonardo," he said modeling confidence. He glanced back to his mother and found looks of approval from her and Accattabriga. He offered his small hand.

The boy's courage rattled Piero. Piero willed his hand not to tremble when he extended it to clasp the little hand. "Pleased to meet you, Leonardo," he said, the words thick on his tongue.

Accattabriga hoisted Leonardo into the saddle. "That boy on the horse over there, he's Ser Piero's brother, Francesco."

"Buongiorno, Francesco."

Francesco tipped his hat. "I'm ready to get on the road, Piero. We'll be on our way once we have our swords and my dagger."

"Brother, return their weapons," Accattabriga said. "No bloodshed here. Enough damage's been done."

Piero strapped his sword at his waist, climbed in the saddle, and adjusted Leonardo to sit both of them comfortably. He took up the reins.

Leonardo squeaked. "Mamma, Papa, I want Leone."

Accattabriga smirked. "Son, how will a cat ride in the saddle?" His eyes glimmered. "Ser, you have to bring the cat. You wouldn't want to break a little boy's heart now, would you?"

Piero bit his tongue. They took their shots at him, but he won the spoils.

Caterina handed the cat up to Leonardo. Her hand lingered on his leg while the boy stuffed the cat in his shirt. "Piero, you be sure to feed my son once you arrive."

Francesco left ahead of them.

Piero nodded and nudged his horse.

"Wait," Caterina called.

Leonardo jumped in the saddle at the voice of his mother and twisted around.

In disbelief, Piero found himself circling back.

"I'll be here waiting for him, Piero, when you're ready to move onto better things."

Piero chaffed a little, but he refused to let her see that her strike found its mark again.

"Mamma," Leonardo's voice wavered, "when will I be back?"

"I don't know. But don't be afraid. I'll come to see you tomorrow, the next day, as long as it takes. Mamma will be there."

Piero turned his horse and gave it a light kick. Dust shot up and obscured the road.

4

All eyes fell on Leonardo and he couldn't duck low enough in the saddle to hide from the watchers. "This is home," said the man called Leonardo's father. The land looked the same, but everything was wrong. There were two houses across from each other, a small building down a flowered path, and a large field of grape vines and olive trees. A couple of men sat at a table, and two women came out of the house. No Mamma. No Papa or Uncle, no Fiore or the girls. No Simone or baby Michele.

Leonardo pet Leone. Leone felt warm against his chest and purred. The purr sang the hurt away and made him brave. He wanted Mamma. Papa said every boy needed his mother. Why did Papa send him away from Mamma? He tried to hide his face.

Ser halted his horse. A woman's voice called out, "Piero, just in time. We're ready to meet Leonardo." The sound of a swishing skirt came closer. "What happened to your face?"

"Caterina," Ser said.

In a hushed tone, the woman spoke again, "What an awful...she must be the most unbecoming woman I've ever heard of. What woman touches a man with such lewdness? Dearest, she'll never be in my good graces." She paused, "Thankfully, I can say that once clean, it appears the boy will look much like his handsome father."

Ser shook Leonardo's shoulders but Leonardo couldn't move.

"Leonardo," Ser said, shaking him again.

Ser left him alone in the saddle.

"Son, it seems that things didn't go so well," a man said.

"I brought him back, Father. Your relationship with your grandson awaits you. I no longer want to hear how cheated my parents are of their privileges. Shall we?"

Ser gripped Leonardo under his arms and pulled him from the saddle.

"Leonardo, there are some people I want you to meet."

Leonardo tried to catch his breath. "I want to go home, Ser." Leone rustled around in his shirt and popped his head out of the collar. The woman standing next to Leonardo jumped. She had shiny black hair under a see-through covering. Her eyebrows crinkled together and her lips sucked in.

"This place may be different than what you are used to," she said, "but we have all you need. Welcome to your new home, Leonardo. We're glad to have you." Her hands rubbed and squeezed her bright, clean skirt.

Leonardo stared at her slippery, wormy fingers that wriggled around the same as the ones in the jar Papa used for fishing. She might touch him. He stepped back.

Wormy Fingers looked at Ser and at another woman with gray hair. "Lucia," Wormy Fingers said, "I think he needs a bath." Wormy Fingers put her hand out.

Leonardo snapped his shoulder back hoping to hide behind Ser, but Ser carried his sack of belongings into the house. A different man with brown and white hair studied him. He was tall and had lines at the corners of his gentle brown eyes. He kept his hands by his side.

"I'm Antonio your grandfather. You're my only grandson. I hope we can be friends." A row of straight top teeth peeked through his lips.

Maybe they could be friends.

The lady with gray hair approached. The choppy way she moved, and the way her round belly wobbled up and down, made Leonardo wonder if she had a cat or two in her skirts. She spoke to Wormy Fingers. "Albiera, you're right," she said, "He needs a bath, but not now. You'll fright the poor child half to death. Send for a warm basin and some soap. Piero and Francesco can also use some washing before supper."

As the old woman moved about, Leonardo thought of the mule his Papa warned him about: "Never turn your back on that one, she may bite." Mule lady hunched down to face him.

"You'll not remember, but I held you as a baby. I'm your grandmother, Lucia." She wore a blue dress and matching shoes. "We were your first home, child. You belong here." Her eyes traveled over him. "Your father will take you to the market to buy you some new clothes and have you fitted for shoes."

This woman must be in charge of the place. She was the woman to tell. "Signora, I want my Mamma."

She looked to Ser coming toward them, back to Leonardo, shook her head no, and walked away. Leonardo couldn't hear what she said when she met Ser on his way out of the house.

Ser came to Leonardo and squatted. "Leonardo." Ser wiped his cheeks with his smooth fingers. "I'm sorry, but this is your place. You could not possibly know, but there is nothing for you in Campo Zeppi. I see this now more than ever." Ser's eyes went soft and he waved to Wormy Fingers. "This woman is my wife, Albiera. You are our first son. This is quite an honor. Do you know this to be true?"

Leonardo shook his head. "I have a Papa." He glared at Ser, "I have a Mamma and she'll come for me. You'll see." He needed to get away from the people crowded around him. In the open door of the house, Francesco leaned against the doorway. But he wouldn't run there and get trapped. This place wasn't home.

Leone pounced out of his shirt and he followed him. They cut in front of Ser's horse and ran to a clearing lined with trees and bushes. Leone jumped into some long, dry grass and ducked under a line of large, prickly bushes with small yellow flowers. Leonardo wriggled his way in to find him.

Leone twisted around the low branches. The shade in the bushes smelled like lemons and hid them from those eyes and the wormy fingers that tried to get them. The dirt crunched and poked Leonardo's skin. He turned himself so he could see the house. Someone with little hairs on their legs came close. The hairs shined in the sun.

"Leonardo?" The legs stopped. "It's Francesco. Would you like help finding your cat?"

"No."

Francesco backed away. He grabbed a stick and sat down on a green patch of ground.

Leonardo waited some time before he parted a branch to peek out.

Francesco pulled a dagger out. He scraped it along his stick several times.

"What are you do—?" Leonardo slapped his hand over his mouth. Francesco's turned his head, but Leonardo kept quiet and waited for Francesco to go back to his work.

Before long, the sky turned almost dark. Leonardo yawned. "Is it safe, Leone?"

Leone flicked his ears and trotted out of the bush. He stopped to clean his back leg and moved toward Francesco to catch a wood curl that flung in the air.

Francesco laughed and glanced at the bushes. "I like to sit and listen to the buzz of the cicadas. Hmm, do you like stories?"

Leonardo wasn't sure if Francesco asked Leone or him, but he liked stories.

Francesco continued carving his stick. "One day, a little bird fell out of his nest. Luck was on his side, for his nest was not so far from where he landed, and he was not terribly injured. But, the little bird sat alone, frightened. He'd never seen all these new things before and he couldn't find his mother. He puffed up his feathers to act brave. He stretched his head high above the grass to peek around. Another bird, a handsome bird with strong wings, saw him."

Francesco turned himself toward the bushes and stopped speaking.

"That's a bad story," Leonardo said.

Francesco laughed again, "I'm not yet finished. I had to move this stone from under my bottom." He held the stone up and tossed it. He patted the ground beside him.

Leonardo laughed. His belly hurt from the dirt. He crawled out of the bush, brushed himself off, and looked at the sky. "Would the bird's friend come with him?"

"Well, yes. He would if the little bird wanted him to come."

"I think the little bird would like that." Francesco wasn't a bird. He was a deer with long, skinny legs and large eyes. "Francesco."

"You can call me Francesco or Uncle. You can call me friend too," he said tucking his dagger away.

"I have an uncle at home too. U…Uncle? I'm afraid."

"I know. But I'm your friend, and friends stay together. I can be afraid with you to make us only half afraid." Francesco tucked his chin in and sat upright. "Let's go back to the house together. I have the most courage when a brave friend is with me. How about you? You can make another friend there you might like. He's probably eating his supper so we can find him easily. Are you hungry?"

"Yes. Are you?"

Francesco put his hands on his stomach and rolled his eyes back with his mouth open.

Leonardo smiled.

"My friend's name is Signore Baffi. Leone will like him. He has long whiskers, which is how he got his name."

Leonardo giggled. "I wish to meet him. Can we do it now?"

"Of course."

Leonardo took Francesco's hand. "Will you stay with me?"

"Yes," said Francesco, "We're brave together."

***

Leonardo and Francesco washed their hands and faces in a basin of cold water. They missed supper with the family, but sat in the twilight to share a plate set aside for them. Belly full, Leonardo couldn't keep his eyes open.

"Piero," said Wormy Fingers, "The boy is going to fall asleep sitting up. He hasn't warmed to me. I think it may be best for a man to take him to bed."

Ser looked at Leonardo. "Boy, let me show you where you'll sleep."

Leonardo grabbed Francesco's hand and followed Ser. They entered the dark house with smooth stone floors and wide-open rooms. They passed a low-lit fireplace on the back wall. On the other side, two small windows with wooden shudders remained open. The house smelled of forgotten bread and smoke.

In a bedroom, Ser stopped. The yellow covered bed was bigger than Leonardo had ever seen. Two painted chests lined the walls. The candlelit lamp Ser held showed a hanging painting of Wormy Fingers, Albiera. In the corner, a cushioned chair invited a reader to sit and choose a book from a small desk.

"We sleep here, Leonardo."

Leonardo searched the room for another place. "I sleep with my Mamma, my Papa, and my sister," he said.

Ser put his hands on his knees and he bent toward Leonardo. "Here you also can sleep with your mother and father."

Leonardo yanked on the neck of his shirt and looked for Francesco, who waited on the other side of the bed close to the door. Leonardo placed his hands on his legs and bent toward Ser. "You are not my Papa." He ran to Francesco and hugged his leg.

Ser stared at them then moved smooth and fast like those long speckled fish with mouths full of sharp teeth. He slammed a chest open. The wooden lid hit against the wall with a loud bang. Linens flew through the air and slid across the floor. He pointed at Francesco, "You! What did you do to ingratiate yourself to the boy? He will not sleep with his father and mother, but runs to you of all people."

Wormy Fingers darted into the room and shrieked at the sight of her clean linens messed around the room. "What's all this about?"

Spit shot out of Ser's mouth. "If you do not want to sleep in the bed, you can sleep on the floor."

Leonardo slipped behind Francesco's leg.

"Piero," Francesco said, "You're frightening him. Hell, you're scaring me. I wouldn't come near you if I were a boy."

Francesco placed his hand on Leonardo's head. "You have to be gentle," he said to Ser. "He was taken away from the only home he's ever known. Have some compassion."

Wormy Fingers stood between both men, her hands in the air. "Piero, why are you so angry?"

"Why? I did this for you. You want to be a mother but cannot do what God placed women on earth to do. For years, all I have heard is how you want a child. To no result. You want my son to be our son because he," Ser tossed his hands up and at Leonardo, "he is your only hope." Ser kicked the linens on the floor. "Make his bed,

Mother. He'll not sleep with you." Ser stormed out of the room.

Wormy Fingers and Francesco made Leonardo a place to sleep by Wormy Finger's side of the bed. "Thank you Albiera," said Francesco. "I'm sorry for all this."

Albiera tipped her head toward Leonardo. "Your father can be difficult sometimes. Once you're settled in, all will be well with him. I'm glad you're here. Please child, call me Albiera."

Leonardo pulled a blanket over himself. "Buonanotte, Albiera. Francesco, stay with me?"

"Yes, Leonardo. I'll stay until you sleep. I must go to my own bed later, but I'll be here in the morning."

Francesco sat at Leonardo's side and Leone settled at his feet.

5

Leonardo, Francesco, and Antonio da Vinci walked the vineyard rows thick with twisted trunks. The morning sun sapped dew from the green leaves.

"Each man takes a row. The grapes are made sweet by gentle words or a song," said the man Leonardo should call grandfather.

"Gentle words?" The men entered separate rows of vines. The voice of Antonio, trailed in song.

Leonardo stood at the opening of his row. It cut a straight path through the rolling hills. What should he say? He could think of nothing to sing, but Antonio's song was loud enough for the both of them. He sang of the beautiful grapes and of love, the sun on the rows, "How do you fare?" His voice stopped when riders came up the road.

"Mamma? Papa!" Leonardo ran from the vineyard to meet them on their way to the big house.

Antonio followed and greeted them. "You haven't changed, Caterina," he said, removing his hat.

Mamma took her hand away from her belly shy-like, "Nor you, Signore." She removed her hat and covered her belly with it.

"Mamma, Papa, you came for me." Leonardo crashed into his Papa's open arms.

"Son, you're well?"

Leonardo nodded and rubbed his cheek against Papa's scratchy chin. Papa's hard but gentle arms swallowed him. He could stay like this.

"Antonio, excuse me. This is my husband, Antonio di Piero Buti del Vacca."

"Pleased to meet you, Signore," Antonio said shaking Papa's hand.

Papa kissed Leonardo and stood. "Let me help your mother." He reached up to Mamma. She grabbed his arm as he held her weight under her shoulder and around her back.

"Let me help," Antonio offered. He did the same as Papa.

When Mamma's feet touched the ground, Leonardo squeezed her and buried his face in her skirts. She smelled like sunshine and she held him close. His head rested against her stomach. He wrapped his arms and legs around her.

"I must go to the house and tell my family we have visitors," Antonio said.

"Only one, Signore. We come by invitation, but I'm on my way to work the kiln at Mercantale. I'll return for Caterina at the end of the day. I need only to say goodbye to my boy."

Leonardo knew Papa had to work.

Papa offered Antonio two silver coins. "For the mule. We don't mean to be a burden."

"There's no need to give me money. The mule can stay without cost."

"Signore," Papa said, "I can't go 'til you take it. Please, she can't stay the day without payment."

Antonio tipped his head and closed his hand around the money.

Mamma held Leonardo's head. "My sweetheart, I've missed you."

Leonardo squeezed her. They went with Antonio to the main house. "Mamma, Leone has a new friend." Leonardo called the cats. They came running and he introduced them. "What should we do today?"

Lucia stomped out of the big house doorway. Albiera followed, then Ser, and last, Antonio. Leonardo took his mother's hand.

"Sorry to disturb you, but Piero said I could visit Leonardo. We'll stay out of the way."

Ser's eyebrows crinkled together, Lucia cupped her hips, and Albiera bunched her skirt in her hands. Albiera spoke first. "Well, Caterina, your comfort cannot be assured. Truth told: it's a curious thing that a woman so…so ripe with child rode all this way."

Ser's neck turned pink. He and Antonio looked away.

"No mother I know leaves her home in such condition,"Albiera said.

"I know you not, Signora," Mamma said, "but I'm a woman and a mother, and I am quite able to make my own decisions."

"Shh," Lucia held a firm hand out. "Caterina," she said, "you're no stranger here. We all have our place. Take Leonardo with you to the other house."

Leonardo looked to the other house and back to Ser.

Antonio cleared his throat. "Signore, why don't we all sit for a glass of wine? Caterina is our guest."

Albiera touched Ser's chest and swiped her hands across his shoulders as if brushing dirt away.

"No, grazie," Mamma said. She went to the other house with Leonardo.

***

After Leonardo said goodbye to his parents, Francesco came in from the fields. "I saw your mother came to visit, Leonardo."

"Yes, and she will come tomorrow too. She promised."

Francesco nodded. "Do you know about babies?"

Leonardo thought a moment. "They come from the mother's belly."

Francesco rubbed Leonardo's hair. "They do, but once born, they can't be without their mother, and their mother can't ask too much of them. It's dangerous for a mother to ride soon after having a baby and it's also dangerous for a baby on horseback. Do you understand?"

"Mothers and bambini can't ride horses," Leonardo said in quick answer. "My Mamma rides horses and mules."

Francesco bent close. "Friend, your mother could have her baby any day from the looks of it, and once she does, she'll not visit for some time."

***

The next morning, Papa rode to visit without Mamma. Ser stood nearby. "Your mother's not well today, son," Papa said. "She thinks the child is on the way. She wants to visit." Papa urged Leonardo close and set him on his bent knee. "She sends this," he said kissing his cheek. "But she can't come today, and when the bambino comes, she won't visit for a good while, you see, so they won't get sick."

Leonardo nodded. "Papa, I want to go home with you".

"Yes, if Ser Piero agrees."

They waited for Ser, who shook his head. "We had a deal Accattabriga. You have no claim to him. Do you think that pulling the boy back and forth is good for him? He needs stability in his true home."

"He had it, Ser." Papa shook his head. "If your reasons help you sleep at night, that makes one of us. But this is not about me."

Leonardo hugged his Papa.

Papa placed a folded piece of paper in his hand and squeezed. "Your mother says she'll write until she can see you again. Ser Piero can read it to you." Papa set him on his feet, kissed his head, and jumped in the saddle. He quickly turned his horse and left.

"Wait," called Leonardo, "you forgot me." Leonardo ran as fast as his legs would take him. He bumped into Albiera, took a few steps back, and crawled under the table. Ser searched for him, but Papa was getting away. "No Papa!"

Ser came closer.

Run. Run fast. Leonardo darted out from under the table and ran. His legs moved like a horse. If he went fast enough, maybe he could fly. He ran and ran. Now he was flying. Through the row where Antonio sang, he flew, his chest burning. He wiped dust from his eyes. Catch Papa. Get away.

6

Piero lunged at Leonardo, but the boy ran faster than he thought possible. Leonardo led him across the farm and toward the vineyard. Faster Piero, else you fall behind and will never catch him. The boy squeezed and darted in and out of places he couldn't reach. Piero spotted Francesco in the garden. "Francesco, help me catch Leonardo before he gets away."

Francesco stood with his basket of harvested beans. "Where did he go?" He set the basket on the ground and stretched.

Piero pointed, "That way." He rested his hands on his knees to try and catch his breath. "He's there. Did you see him? He ran into the trees."

"I see him," Francesco said running past.

"Grazie, brother." Sweat rolled down Piero's back. He made his way to the stable for a couple horses.

Piero rode to his brother. "Where is he?"

Francesco bent on hands and knees in the dirt and scanned the vineyard from below and above. "He's gone. We need to go further. You shouldn't have stopped for help."

"He's not gone.'

Francesco's brow lifted. "He may be. Look." He held his hand out to a track in the soil. "There are no others beyond this one facing north. I'll ride that way. You go south."

"One of us had better ride back to the house to tell the others. If everyone is out looking for Leonardo, we should find him soon."

"Be quick about it. He can only run further the more time we give him. Why would he need to run away from his father anyway?"

Piero knew Francesco's method. Francesco asked a question for which he sought no answer. His brother used a roundabout way of passing judgment like Father. Well, here's your answer: Piero rode off.

After his lively summary of Leonardo's evasion, everyone on the property began to search. Albiera and Lucia remained home in case the boy should return. Father kept watch at the vineyard, and Carlo the sharecropper, his wife, and their boys searched the nearby fields. Echoes of "Leonardo" floated on the wind.

Piero rode south and kept his horse at a walking pace to be sure he would not ride past the boy. "Leonardo," he called. He doubted the boy would come to his voice, but what else could he do? A man could sweat standing still. Piero drank from his wine skin and realized that Leonardo had no drink. "God in Heaven look after my boy. Help me find him before either one of us are found by the dishonest." Today was a Sunday, a day mixed with a little work, a little devotion, and rest. And good, for the road would be absent of any souls intending harm, he hoped.

The sun reached its zenith and Piero continued. He circled back on his tracks for certainty that he missed nothing. What is it about you boy?

For such a small one, the boy had much determination. Piero recognized this attribute, for he too knew what it felt like to want; more so, he took action to get what he wanted. Maybe this same force wedged him and his own father apart. Son of mine, we may never see eye-to-eye, but you seem more like me than I am like my father. Yes, the country gentleman lifestyle rotted Father's life away. Piero needed more. Leonardo needed more too. They would not be harnessed to Vinci alone.

Leonardo could be anywhere by now. Could he have made it home to his mother? How would he know the way? Piero rubbed his temples. He had circled the road twice over. His horse needed water and they both needed rest. Lady luck would laugh if Leonardo did get back to his mother. Least of what Piero needed was for Accattabriga and Caterina to know he lost the child.

"Leonnnnnnnardooooooooo," Piero called in desperation. Go further south toward Empoli or return north to Vinci? Piero nudged his horse to a trot, "Let's go home, girl." Francesco probably found the boy and decided to leave him wandering.

Piero recognized the east side of the road where the ground rose to a hill capped with a Cyprus tree at the center. He looked again. The boy! Beneath the shaded side of the tree, which made him difficult to see.

Piero dismounted his horse and brought the reins forward. He led it on foot up the hill. A scattering of scrub bushes and scratchy yellow grasses brushed against his legs. The crusty soil crumbled as he climbed. Leonardo made no movements. So as not to scare him again, Piero made no call.

He dropped the reins and touched the boy's face. "Leonardo," Piero said quietly. He shook him a little. Leonardo made no sound from his cracked lips. His eyes fluttered open and shut a few times. "You need to drink. Here, swallow." He lifted Leonardo's head and placed a flask of mead to the boy's lips. Leonardo drank slowly at first then gulped until he finished the flask.

Piero grinned. "Good ragazzo, good boy. Are you hurt?"

"Ser—my foot." Leonardo pointed to his feet caked with dust. Dried blood clumped over a cut on his heel and his big toe.

Piero dug into his saddlebag and pulled out a piece of cloth. He tied it around the injured foot. "I meant not to upset you. I mean only to make things easier for you, Leonardo." He lifted the boy in his arms and carried him to the horse to place him in the saddle. "Let's go home." Leonardo stared at Piero with blank eyes, his spirit gone.

"Home?"

"We are fine. Hold on. I'll lead the horse down the hill." Piero stepped carefully in the soil that's shifted under his feet. Stones tumbled downhill. Piero peered back.

Leonardo's body slipped sideways in the saddle. He hurried to catch him before he fell.

Leonardo startled. "I'm sleepy, Ser."

"Yes, I know. I'll carry you." Leonardo's head and legs bounced up and down, heavy, almost lifeless. His son's weight pressed into him; it asked for nothing, but took everything. Piero's breath labored and for the first time, he felt like a father.

"Thank you Father in Heaven. Let my son be well." Piero draped Leonardo over the horse's neck and climbed into the saddle behind him. He leaned Leonardo against his chest. "I know not if you hear me Leonardo, but I have business in Chianti before I return to the city, and I will bring you along. Let us use your energy for thinking. This will be better for us all." Piero looked at his sleeping boy, who heard nothing. But he meant what he said.

7
October 1457

The hose squished Leonardo's toes together and tightened his mutande, which made his butt feel like he'd gotten stuck in the ring around the privy stool. Ser's house had many strange things, but his clothes may have been the strangest. Ser said he was old enough for proper dress. Leonardo pulled at the mutande covering his backside again. Smooth and cool when he first pulled the calze up, and now warmer on his skin like an extra fur, he ran his hand from ankle to thigh. He might like calze in the winter if they fit properly. That people would buy them made no sense in warm weather.

"No Ser, these don't fit." Leonardo hid himself from Ser and Albiera, almost strangers.

"Let us see," Albiera said. "Come, step out from behind the bed. Fear not, I'll let no harm come to you."

Leonardo held the calze strings in each hand. "I need help."

Ser waved his arm. "Come here."

Leonardo curved around the bed, each hand attached to a set of strings. Ser and Albiera smiled and made him think he'd done something laughable. "They don't stay up here and here." He lifted his linen tunic and poked his butt. "And these are too tight," he said showing them.

"Have you not seen them before?" Albiera asked.

Leonardo shook his head that he hadn't.

Albiera lifted his chin. "No sad faces. All things are new the first time. New can be good, so smile. Now you know. And, they fit you perfectly," she said sounding pleased.

Ser pulled the strings up and threaded them through the holes at the bottom of what he called the farsetto. Once finished tying, Ser slipped the neck hole of the giornea over Leonardo's head and let it drop.

Children jested or sometimes tossed small stones or nuts at the backsides of animals, so Leonardo wanted no reason to give anyone a target of his backside. Thankfully, the private places linen, the mutande, was no longer visible.

Ser added a belt. "You are ready for business, Leonardo."

"A handsome boy at that," Albiera said.

Leonardo didn't know Ser's business. If it got him a bed in a different place, he'd be happy. Many nights he closed his eyes but didn't fall asleep because he listened to Ser and Albiera. They blew out the lamplight, thumped their bed, and made noises. Ser spoke low last night and said, "Give me a son," and Albiera said, "As you gave me a son, so too will I give you one." When the thumping ended, he could sleep.

Ser bent to face Leonardo. "Some shoes. You wouldn't want to ruin your hose."

Leonardo agreed and slipped his feet into the firm leather shoes with hard bottoms.

"I brought a gift from the city for you. Waiting since you arrived," Ser said. He pulled the gift out from behind his back and swished the covering off to reveal a black hat with a white feather. He placed it on Leonardo's head.

Leonardo shifted his feet. "Grazie, Ser." The shoes pinched his feet. He moved forward. The shoe loosened at his heel. To keep them on, he slid his feet across the floor.

Ser laughed. "You have to lift your feet to walk. Natural, like you've been doing all along."

Leonardo tried. He took one-step, a second, a third. "I won't get anywhere in these."

"For now, you only need to get to the table for your studies," Albiera said. "Piero, smile." She reached for her husband's hand. "It makes us all feel better. Why don't you join us? Leonardo's a smart boy. Your mother and I show him things, and more often than not, he can continue without further instruction."

Leonardo removed the hat and handed it to Ser. He slid his feet from the shoes and went to his chair at the table with Albiera. "Numbers are my favorite."

"We began with numbers since Leonardo likes them. He told us how he could count to fifty because his mother taught him, and in these few weeks, he made it to a thousand."

"My favorite number is one-thousand. It's bigger than the rest. Nonna Lucia says that numbers never end." He rubbed his fingers together and looked at Ser. "Is it true? How many numbers can you count?"

Ser shifted his body side-to-side and looked only at the hat and shoes. "Ah, they do continue without end." Ser counted, "One. On which the future rests." He shook his head.

Leonardo rocked his head side to side like Ser.

Albiera cleared her throat and spoke again, "We started with letters. He practiced each one and makes few mistakes. Leonardo, would you write your name for your father?"

Leonardo grabbed his wooden hornbook and dipped a quill into the inkpot. He began writing his name across the paper.

"Sinistra," Ser blurted. He pulled the quill from Leonardo's hand.

Leonardo froze.

"Albiera, he must use the right hand. No one can trust a hand touched by the devil."

"But he's learning, Piero." She patted Leonardo's back, "We're quite well."

"He must learn the correct way." Ser placed the quill in Leonardo's right hand. "Practice with this hand alone." Ser rolled his hand in quick circles, "Write, write."

Leonardo tried. He would make Ser happy, but the quill felt wrong in his hand and made his letters messy. He dropped it onto the hornbook.

"As your father, I am responsible for finding you a useful skill so that you can be a man of worth." Ser paused, "Look at me, Leonardo. Your instruction with a tutor in Florence shall begin in a few years. We will find something you can do when older. Most boys begin when they reach their eleventh year. We need to find your strengths." He folded his hands.

Leonardo listened and nodded. He scooted closer to Albiera. Ser liked to talk.

"I would love to have a son follow my profession. But not everyone can become a notary. Nor will you become a farmer, illegitimate or not."

"What's illegitimate?"

Ser's eyebrows crinkled into a v-shape. "It means you were born without a married mother. But you can help me with my work. This is good for writing practice, for strength of mind and details, and it will give you invaluable skill."

"Did you want to make my Mamma your wife?"

Ser quieted then answered, "I promised to marry Albiera."

"Will I have brothers and sisters in your house?"

"God willing, yes."

Leonardo turned to Albiera. "When you get your bambino will you keep me?"

"Oh," said Albiera crossing her hands over her chest. She blinked until tears grew in her eyes. "Yes, Leonardo," she said. "I'll keep you. We'll keep you." Albiera and Ser made eyes at each other.

Ser tapped his finger on Leonardo's writing practice. "This will take some time, yes, but practice and you may do great things one day. We all must work hard to find success. Then our father's remember us."

8
May 1460

Antonio, or Nonno, as Leonardo called him, worked in the fields the same as the other men, only better, easier. Nonno finished faster and seemed to take pride in knowing it. Leonardo smiled at him. Men climbed up and down rungs and stretched and twisted on battered ladders set in the olive trees. Clip, clip their blades sounded as the trees shed their overgrowth. Sometimes they sawed and swayed side-to-side with the tree. The pruned branches rested on the bright grass looking silvery white and tangled like a sleeping grandmother's hair. Nonno worked fast. A few cuts, and his feet touched the ground.

Leonardo picked up a branch. "Nonno, why do you cut off the arms?"

Nonno considered his question. "God said, let there be light, did He not? If an arm reaches too high, it casts a shadow too large for the fruit to grow. The best fruit grows close to the tree." He crinkled his eyes and took hold of Leonardo's arms. "So we chop off the arms," he said tugging gently, "and we toss them away." He found the ticklish spot in Leonardo's underarms. They laughed.

Nonno wiped his brow with a sleeve. "When flowers bloom on the tree you'll see we caused no harm." He stretched his arms.

Leonardo reached for Nonno and grabbed his arms as he'd done to him. "I've cut off your arms now too. But Nonno, you don't smell like flowers."

They grinned and sniffed the air between their bodies in agreement.

"You prune the trees to make them thinner so the sun reaches in. But why don't the branches know and do what's good for the tree?"

Nonno chuckled. "Who says they don't? Choose a branch that's been cut away." He took it from Leonardo's outstretched hand and removed the leaves from the bottom half. "Now take it there," he pointed, "and plant it."

Nonno pulled Leonardo close to whisper in his ear. "Nature makes no mistakes." He kissed his thumb and pressed it between Leonardo's eyebrows, started to hum, and grabbed ahold of his ladder.

Leonardo helped him move the ladder to the other side of the big tree. He listened to the song Nonno hummed everyday and waited for him to finish the first part. He hummed it back to him.

Nonno stopped and listened. He shook his head in approval and climbed.

Leonardo went to dig a hole. He pressed the soil. "Nonno says grow."

A few hours later, Leonardo devoured his supper because he hungered but mostly because he wanted to listen to Nonno play his lute like he always did after a long day of work.

Nonno finished eating and nudged his hand at Leonardo. "Inside with you boy. Bring it to me."

Leonardo ran inside and delivered the instrument. "Play the song you hum in the fields, Nonno."

Nonno nodded and played.

The family half listened, but Leonardo sat and watched Nonno's sure hands move across the strings. He wanted to play the song he knew so well. "Can I try?"

Nonno lifted the lute and stood. He offered his seat. "What will you play?"

"Your song." Leonardo sprang up, sat in Nonno's seat, and took the instrument in his hands. He placed his fingers and tucked his thumb under they way he'd seen done.

Nonno waited for him to begin, so he plucked the strings and heard the song. His fingers knew the positions they should make, and it sounded almost perfect.

Surprise lit Nonno's eyes. "Bravo, my boy. Bravo!" he said, which turned Francesco and Nonna Lucia's attentions on him. Ser and the others took notice.

"Father, you taught him to play?" Ser asked.

Leonardo continued by restarting the song. When Ser stood, his finger stumbled and plucked a bad note.

Nonno encouraged him to continue and Albiera joined him. Nonno said, "I didn't teach him. He simply knows, Piero. His hands carry the music in them."

Leonardo looked at his hands and thought having music in them sounded like a marvelous gift. His mother's hands had music in them.

***

Albiera tucked Leonardo's blanket around him the same way she did every night. "Buonanotte," she said rising to reach for the lantern.

"Albiera, do your hands have music in them like my mother's?"

Albiera set the lantern down and considered his question. "No, I don't believe they do."

Leonardo looked at her hands. He wasn't afraid of them anymore. They were smallish and smooth, a little pink, clean, not wormy. "I still like them."

"Well, grazie, Leonardo," she said and held them out. She sat and playfully poked at him. "Will you tell me about your mother? I think she must be a special woman since you are special boy, dear one."

Albiera showed him kindness even when she wanted another child. Leonardo wiggled down in his blankets. He thought of his mother often and tried not to speak of her because he wished not to hurt Albiera. Ser didn't approve either. He looked at Albiera—the two of them, here—alone in the dark by the lamplight. She did say she would keep him.

She smiled softly and waited for him to speak.

"Her hands are bigger than yours, I think. Not as smooth," he said turning her hand over to be sure. "They feel strong and sure and soft and warm. Do you know her name is Caterina?" Saying her name made him strong and sure and soft and warm.

"She plays music?"

Leonardo nodded. "You can hear it when she weaves the reeds we gather at the river." He made the motion with his hand and closed his eyes to hear it. "It goes like this," he said tapping the rhythm on his chest.

"That sounds quite wonderful."

Leonardo nodded. "Albiera, can a boy have a mother and also another?"

Albiera sat up and smoothed his blanket. "A boy is born of one mother, but he can have another." She wriggled her fingers. "Yes, he can have another," she said blinking her eyes and bit her bottom lip.

Leonardo took her hand in his and closed his eyes. "This is good and makes me happy. Buonanotte, Mother."

9

November 1460

Ser led Leonardo into his study and invited him to sit in the cushioned chair that rested a few steps from his bed. Ser spent most of his time here when not in the city. Leonardo approached slowly.

A small wooden table slanted at an angle provided writing space, and above it, Ser's things filled two shelves. The lower shelf held parchment, an inkwell fashioned as a lion with a barrel grasped in its front paws, wax candles, and Ser's insignia. On the top shelf, books laid flat while others stood upright with bits of papers caught between the pages.

Leonardo wondered what the bits might say. Wise words surely, or maybe each one claimed their tight space like a banner posted in a crowded field stating, Here I am. To touch them, open the pages, read their messages…"What are your books about?"

"Ethics, philosophy, law." Ser removed his pricey parchment and set a plain paper on the writing desk. He pulled the inkpot closer and handed Leonardo a quill, which Leonardo took in his right hand. "The only way we can hope to become better is through practice. Copy this property agreement to your best ability, but do not become discouraged should you err. Once you finish, I would like to see." Ser left him to practice.

Leonardo smoothed the agreement and dipped the quill in ink. Though awkward in his right hand, he scrawled each letter slow and steady until they became words, then sentences. After he completed a few sentences, he set the quill on a tray and reached for Ser's insignia. He passed it between his hands and rubbed his thumb over the design. A cloud with a letter P inside it rested in front of a tree. Ser stamped it with pride on all his work. Leonardo pressed it into his palm. The P showed white on his pink skin for a moment before it faded.

Leonardo wondered, if he had an insignia of his own, what it would look like? Leonardo set the insignia aside for the quill. He tapped his chin a few times, dipped the quill in ink, and wrote again. The right hand smudged his letters unless he positioned his hand not to touch the paper. Another sentence, and he saw the line in a new way.

Leonardo peered over his shoulder. He dipped the quill with his left hand and started at the right side of the page forming each letter from right-to-left. In Latin, this document he couldn't read anyway. The lines formed faster. Another line done, he examined his work. Good and similar to the sample. Soon he finished and sprinkled sand on the page. For extra measure, he waved it through the air to dry.

He folded the document into thirds, and where the ends of the paper met, he drew a feathered and winged lion with an L-shape in the mane. "My insignia." This he would hand deliver to Ser.

He searched his palm for any sign of the P and found none. But he could see Ser's face, picture his smile, and hear him say, "Great job. I knew you could do it." Ser would fold him into his arms and hold him with pride in the work he'd done.

***

Nonno, Ser, Francesco, Carlo, his wife, and boys worked together in the olive grove. They hauled thick, wool sacks filled with the harvest of purple and green olives to an oxen cart. Soon the bitter, peppery olives would go into the press.

During last harvest, Leonardo and the other boys tested their strength by attempting to push the handle of the press that would turn the rolling stone around the olive basin. It was hard, but it became fun as the entire family laughed and cheered: "Who's stronger? The boys or the olives?" they teased. "See you this time next year," Nonno said, and played a sad song for the boys until they got the stone rolling—then Nonno played faster and faster. Carlo brought a mule in to do the grinding work, and they jested more, sang, and raced. It was a perfect day.

Today would be perfect too. Leonardo held out his work. "Ser, my document."

Ser looked it over. "What's this here?" he asked pointing to the drawing.

"My insignia so you know it's mine."

Ser looked at it again. "This is notable, Leonardo."

Leonardo's heart beat faster. He yanked at his neckline. "Open it."

Ser lengthened the document. "The first couple of lines can use work, but this is good." He refolded the page and ran his thumb across the drawing. He looked at him and scratched the back of his neck. "Good work." Ser ruffled Leonardo's hair. "Go and run with the boys, Leonardo. You've earned it."

"Yes, Ser," Leonardo said without crying. He turned toward the happy sounds of the other boys. They laughed and tossed olives at Francesco, who ran away before being pelted dead. Leonardo scooped olives from the ground and squeezed them tight in his fists. The juices ran thick and slippery between his fingers.

10
December 1462

"The time has come to move my family to Florence," Piero said. He pushed his chair out from the kitchen table and stood. "I found a house in Santa Maria Sopra Porta." He offered his hand to Albiera. She stood with him as he looked at his mother. "Why do you cry?"

"My baby's leaving home. I knew the day would come. Oh, Piero, a mother can never let go of her son. You're my first child."

Piero smiled. "Well, might I soothe your heart a little mother?" He turned to Albiera's glowing face. "We are pleased to announce: we are expecting a child."

Mother clutched her chest. She found her feet and rushed to Albiera. She placed a hand on Albiera's belly. "Oh son. My daughter. I thought the day would never come."

Delight spread across Father's face. Piero knew this would undo past wrongs. This time he did everything right, and to have a legitimate son meant that the family name would continue with honor. Father would now see him as a man—a man of virtue.

"Congratulations brother," said Francesco, who sat next to Leonardo.

Leonardo pushed his food away. "Uncle, Leone wants to stay home with his friends."

Francesco nodded and gave Leonardo's shoulder a squeeze.

Father embraced Piero. "Wonderful news." He raised his cup, "To our growing family, may the richest blessings flow. Salute."

Piero drank his wine. He eyed Leonardo and breathed easier knowing he acted for the best. To legitimize Leonardo would take from the son of a rightful birth and would break a promise Piero made to his wife. Pressure born out of desperation would not cast down so stark as when he kept Leonardo in wait. The unborn son would fulfill the role intended for a firstborn. Nothing would hold this son back because he would constitute the fruit of a union between husband, wife, and God. But Piero needed to keep Leonardo close until he could be sure of success. One son always counted better than none.

Leonardo attentively watched the reactions of everyone around him.

Piero read the boy's face, which suspected nothing. Albiera's presence would ease his transition, but Piero still questioned if Leonardo would willingly depart with him to Florence. The boy's face shined each time a letter arrived from Caterina. Her letters forged dreams in Leonardo's head. Thus, withholding her letters these last couple months felt a bit criminal, especially when couriers delivered only to disappoint the boy's eager eyes, but Piero determined his act for the greater good. He expected Leonardo to be drawn to the city. He must get the boy there and let the city weave a new dream. Only then he could release the letters. "We leave soon while the weather is passable. I would rather have taken my wife to Florence sooner, but the house was not yet ready."

"We'll not see you and my grandchild, Piero," said Mother. "You can't go. Not now."

"Mother, business is good. I need to live in the city. The days away—to return home—makes things difficult. I'll not live without my wife." Piero opened a pouch strung at his waist and pulled out a gold chain. He placed the delicate necklace on Albiera. "A gift for the mother of my unborn son." He turned to shush his sobbing mother. "While the child is small my wife can travel without issue. The time is right."

Soon thereafter, Piero hired men to cart their household items to Florence. Albiera rode beside him on a gentle horse and Leonardo followed behind them without protest.

11

Leonardo wanted to see Florence after all this time though Ser never took him. And now that they left for the city, he worried he wouldn't find his way back to his mother. They traveled so slow he considered they might never arrive. He wished nothing bad for Albiera, but Ser's overprotection and many stops became far more than even Albiera reasoned necessary.

Ser was generally patient and kind to Albiera, and now that she carried a child, he handled her gentle as a delicate flower. She descended of noble stock and differed from many of the women Leonardo saw around Vinci. Most women in the country her age sweated in the fields and hauled heavy baskets with noticeably large bellies.

The road widened. "When will we arrive, Ser?" Leonardo asked, knowing they'd gone too far to turn back. He breathed deep. Albiera said she'd keep him. He put his trust in her.

"Not long now," Ser said. "Over the next hill you will see the city from a great viewpoint."

The Arno River Valley stretched out before them. Leonardo craned his neck and stretched his body forward and back in in his saddle to see the city between the passing trees. Florence sprawled on both sides of the river. The city sat in a large pocket of land covered in wheat-colored buildings with orange rooftops. "I've never seen anything like it." He found it larger than he pictured in his mind. "What's the big round one in the middle?"

"Il Duomo," Ser said.

Leonardo's belly tingled. "We get to go there?"

Ser nodded. "It is not far from my bottega or our house. Once we get your mother home, I will take you there."

Leonardo couldn't remember Ser ever happier than now. Though far from his mother, Leonardo figured if Ser felt happy then he might be happier too. "Il Duomo. How can man make such a building? Where do they start?"

"At the bottom I would expect." Ser's eyes shined.

"Do you know the man who built it?"

"Everyone knows of him. Brunelleschi did not build the whole church, but he designed and built Il Duomo. Many men helped him."

Leonardo appreciated the view. "You say that a man must make himself many friends. I would like to meet him."

"Yes, but Brunelleschi is no longer of this world. Otherwise, I would have you meet him."

Leonardo considered Ser's words. Il Duomo dwarfed all around it. And anyone could see that Brunelleschi's work left a mark on the city. Dead or alive, this part of Brunelleschi was of the world.

Ser focused on the road in front of him. "If a man should have no heirs as Brunelleschi, then a man should leave as great a legacy for the preservation of his father's name."

"But most men cannot make such grand displays," Leonardo said. "If every man could make something so remarkable with his own hands, the world would be bigger, yes, bigger and diminished." Il Duomo lasted longer than its maker, would last longer than Ser, Ser's children, and perhaps his children's grandchildren.

Ser said that the city began with the ancients of Rome. Leonardo thought it curious that men had the strongest desire to live beyond their years. "Men build and rebuild. Do they do it to prize those who came before them or to use the older stones as steps to trample upon the forgotten and reach higher places?" Leonardo rubbed his chin and locked eyes with Ser. He continued, "Brunelleschi was a clever man. He built large enough to prove his worth and secure a high position. Yes, a mark he made. One no father could forget."

Ser's eyes narrowed.

***

They stabled their horses, except for the wagon, and continued down a long stretch of smooth road. Open land and green gardens lined the river. Homes, workshops called botteghe, and a few small churches bordering the river transformed into crowded streets. The closer they moved toward the center of the Oltrarno, the south side of the river, the more the city closed in on Leonardo. But he took pleasure in the scent of fresh-cut wood from the home goods shops and the savory, spiced torte carried by a man who called, "Pastaccio, pasticcio. One for a quattrino, three for two quattrini." A horse cart laden with grain passed in front of them. People chatted and moved in all directions.

They crossed the river at the Ponte Santa Trinita. Men fished the waters and women washed their clothing. Many narrow streets branched from the bridge into open areas. Leonardo couldn't see any details stretching down the connecting, dim roads. He bumped into an old man who staggered to the side. "Sorry Signore," he said, noticing the man's bloodshot eyes and turned from the stench of soured skin and piss that singed his nostrils.

Much different from the country, sweat and dirt felt hideous here. Animal droppings scattered the walkways and forced people to walk within the piles, for some narrow passages left no choice but to travel elbow-to-elbow. A woman carried a bucket of slop and tossed it to the gutter beside her doorway. Shocked, Leonardo didn't look at the muck that flowed near his feet. Instead, he discovered a young woman dressed in jewels and rich clothes that eyed the street from her high window.

Il Duomo's orange shell of a roof popped out here and there in breaks between buildings and promised an end to the suffocating passages. They turned right down a short street overtaken on one side by a palace with squared battlements lining its top.

"Our home," Ser said edging toward the opposite side of the street. "This is a good neighborhood of the bankers and money changers. Though simple, I hope you find it suitable for bringing a family up within her walls, my love," he told Albiera.

The men unloaded the wagon in the quiet neighborhood. Leonardo set out with Ser to see Il Duomo as promised.

Il Duomo was only a small part of the impressive church that rose skyward. The shadow of its greatness stretched massive across the piazza. Many people stood at the feet of Il Duomo's grand display.

Leonardo studied the odd behavior of a few finely dressed women. Men conversed with them. The women wore bells on their heads and gloves on their hands.

"Those are prostitutes. It is better you know now, Leonardo. Most are women, but there are also men, and they are all dishonorable."

"What's a prostitute?"

A man close by turned at his question.

Ser's neck turned pink. "They take payment for copulation." Ser paused, "You know, a man and a woman come together in the way that should only occur in the marriage bed."

Leonardo nodded. Yes, he knew. Not only from what he heard, but also from what he could see. Not that he wanted to watch. It took him awhile to figure out why Ser and Albiera made such noises in the night until he peeked out from under his blankets. Thankfully, he would get a room of his own in the new house.

They walked toward the front of the church. The lower half displayed massive walls of sculpted figures all different in size. The top half looked plain and unfinished. To the side, stood a tall bell tower mostly in white with pink and green stripes, and next to it, Leonardo found a building similar in color and design, but with many golden doors.

"That is Il Battistero," Ser said. "All the city's babies are baptized inside."

Leonardo walked around it first and determined the shape an octagon. Circling to the front, he focused on the glistening doors. Magnificent. The most beautiful thing he'd ever seen. He extended his arm out to touch the ridges of the figures, animals, and trees with his fingers—so real—too perfect to touch. He hung his hands at the neck of his camicia while he drank in the many scenes.

He could have stood there a few minutes or hours; he wasn't sure. Ser waited for him. If Ser's work felt this way to him, Leonardo could see part of his distraction. But he couldn't do Ser's work and they both knew it. Leonardo wanted to please him but his efforts never worked. Ser saw him as nothing more than a half-son. Ser may have come to Florence to rebuild his life, but Leonardo refused to be forgotten.

Ser tapped Leonardo's arm. "With the move, travel, and work, I forgot to give you these," he said holding out several letters.

Leonardo recognized the writing locked in Ser's grasp. Three? Mamma wrote once or twice a month. To know she hadn't forgotten him filled him with joy...and sadness. He wanted nothing more than to open the letters, but not here, not with the man who kept him from them. A roar caught in Leonardo's chest. Unable to speak in fear of what he might say, he glared at Ser. He wanted him to feel his hurt. He waited to make ready his offense.

They walked to the Mercato for food. Leonardo followed until his response came to him. "Once you have your new son, can I return to my mother's house?" By the look on Ser's face, he could tell he hadn't expected that.

Ser said nothing for a while. They passed a couple of stalls and he spoke, "I'll not stop you from returning to a life of squander if that is what you want." Ser's jaw clenched then he continued, "Your mouth will burden them."

"I never felt like a burden...not there," Leonardo said kicking at a crack in the ground.

"When I thought you were ready for an education and apprenticeship in the city you disappoint me. You want to live your life as a peasant?"

"No. I'll never live as a peasant because I have you. And you can't tolerate others knowing you have a poor boy."

Ser's neck and face turned pink. He raised his hand in a rage-filled look but didn't strike. "Ungrateful boy. You would be nothing without me."

Leonardo's legs weakened, but he didn't flinch. He would show Ser. He would be more than he ever thought possible. Now he needed to figure out how to do it.

"You and your uncle will come with me in a few weeks to Chianti. When we return, I offer you the choice to return to your mother or to take on preparations for your apprenticeship. If you think yourself man enough to make your own decisions, decide, Leonardo. Choose your path wisely, for there's no going back."

12
April 1463

Atop his horse, the sun on his face, these were the times Leonardo felt free. Ser didn't devise ways to bait him while riding the road. But they need not speak to say wicked things, nor did talk center on anything other than anything necessary for business travel. Ser's discomfort showed Leonardo that they felt the same this once. They need not say grazie in praise of Francesco, who, thankfully, rode between them, a divider to keep the peace.

Leonardo closed his eyes. The beast beneath him rocked him rhythmically as he breathed in the cool spring air. Moist and smoky, woodsy, bitter pine, horse, and leather soothed him. Tiny hairs on his arms prickled and he opened his eyes. The land appeared a silent dream of vibrant hills that rolled and bathed in the misty clouds of Chianti country.

The snuffs of horses and hoofbeats, the creaks and thumps of laden carts, and metal clinks filled the air of the familiar yet different land. The soldiers who led them took no notice of the difference because of their arguments and jokes. Before today, Leonardo had never seen a soldier except for his Papa. But Papa was Papa, and he always said his soldiering days were over.

The soldier Ser hired wore a white camicia with billowy upper sleeves beneath a buttoned farsetto in green. His calze were white with a red stripe that ran down the back of each muscled leg. On his left hip, the hilt of a sheathed blade angled away from the buckle at his waist. He looked nothing like Papa.

The soldier gazed back at Leonardo, slowed his horse, and waited for him to ride closer. "You staring at me, boy?"

"No," Leonardo said looking away.

"You were, and I know because I have eyes everywhere." The soldier swung his arm out in a broad swipe to say, my men are watching.

Leonardo hesitated. "Signore, I meant nothing."

"He's never seen a soldier before is all," Francesco said.

"Oh? Well now, feast your eyes, for this be a fine sample." The soldier puffed out his chest and sat upright in his saddle. He grinned. A gap showed in place of a missing tooth.

"Shove off Marco," shouted another soldier in front of them.

"Leave me to my conversation, Horseface," he hollered back.

Leonardo grinned. The other man did have a long toothy face.

"The name is Marco Boccono, boy. And you are?"

"Leonardo da Vinci, Signore."

Marco held out his hand and gave a slight bow. "You're so polite you make me feel like a gentleman, young Leonardo." Another soldier slapped his leg and laughed.

"You go on adventures all the time?" Leonardo asked.

"You could say that." Marco's eyes and mouth crinkled at the edges. "This adventure is good for business."

"We travel on business too. We—"

"We do not have need to tell others our plans," Ser interrupted. "He only need know what he was told. He shall lead us safely to Greve."

Leonardo nodded, paused, and turned his attention back to Marco. "Might I say you don't look vicious?"

Laughter came from Marco, Horseface, and the other soldiers that heard him.

Marco surveyed himself. "Why would you think that?"

"You have a plain hat that makes you look taller, but you, Signore, look most like any other man I've seen. Where's your armor and shiny helmet?"

"An attentive one here," Marco said pointing his thumb at Leonardo. "Boy, as much as I'm sure you favor storytime about fighting and damsels, we're not warring. We're rebuilding, and the place we go has need of the cart there. It's full of supplies and weapons to fortify and help keep the peace. I'll tell you something else." Marco pointed at his hat. "I never liked a shiny helmet. You can't see out the damned things and the sun'll fry your head like a cooked egg in one. Mmm," he said, "eggs."

A soldier at the head of road made hand signals and yelled, "Halt." Marco clucked at his horse and moved ahead. He curved his head back toward Leonardo. "He has the shiny helmet, eh boy?" Marco directed his horse off the road. "Time to eat."

They stopped with the company of soldiers in a valley nestled among hills higher than they had seen in the morning. The soldiers dismounted near a stream.

Ser pulled bundles wrapped in cloth from his saddlebag and handed them to Francesco.

Francesco sniffed them. "Bread and cheese." He opened the other bundle. "Boiled eggs. Your grandmother's doing. She always packs eggs for travel." He gave them each a portion.

Leonardo ate the bread and cheese and considered the cooked egg, but ate none though his stomach growled in protest. His interest centered on the soldiers. The man in the shiny helmet announced, "No fires. We'll not be stopped long enough. Eat what doesn't need cooking, water your horses, then be ready to move."

Leonardo finished his meal and led the three horses to the water. He listened as one soldier told the others how the last time he rode this way the stream flooded with water about forty braccia wide. Big. So big the company further up the hill would have been at the water's edge. Leonardo concluded that if he skipped only a few steps today, he'd reach the other side.

He couldn't understand some of the soldiers because of their strange words. One of them pointed at him. A larger man with thick arms and a thicker tongue said something he didn't understand.

"Take him out of here, Marco," a Florentine soldier said. He pushed the others away. "They're taking bets on the Florenzers."

Marco's familiar voice spoke from the other side of Leonardo's horse.

"Shut your dirty mouths," he said.

Leonardo cut around the front of the horses. His feet splashed in the water.

Marco spit on the ground in front of one man's feet. "Dirty German bastards. We're no Florenzers. You shouldn't speak of such things near the boy." He looked at Leonardo. "Boy, go back to your father. These men are ripe with the devil. Go."

The captain came between Marco and the group of Germans. "What's this?" he asked, his leather face creased. The men went silent. "No one wants to talk now?" He gave each man a hard look. "Good, because it's time to get back on the road. Any man who cannot comply forgoes his pay for the rest of the day. Saddle up."

Leonardo started back to Ser and Francesco until he heard the soldiers' argument resume.

One of the Germans bumped Marco's shoulder.

Marco's fist shot into the man's face so fast Leonardo almost missed it.

Blood ran down the German's lips and chin. "Bastard!" he screeched, "Sie brachen meine nase." He wiped his nose on his sleeve. A thick-armed man held the injured and another back while others took hold of Marco.

"Let him go," said a friend of the one trying to get free. "He's soft as a woman. His fellow Florenzers will sodomize him, not his innocent boy."

Leonardo hurried up the hill thinking it best not to ask about sodomizing Florenzers.

Soon the soldiers were ready to depart. Marco rode up to Ser. "Ready to ride?"

They mounted their horses and fell-in with the soldiers.

***

Ser rubbed his horse's neck. "We are more than halfway and should arrive in good time."

Marco tipped his hat. "No need to worry, Ser da Vinci. You'll arrive as promised. And not a hair shaved from your head."

"Not that we can say as much for you," Ser said.

"Nah, that was a misunderstanding, but I think he got the message."

Francesco tipped his hat at Marco.

"I take my work seriously," Marco said.

Leonardo nodded considering what he witnessed.

Francesco restarted the conversation. "Where do you rebuild, Marco?"

"We go south of Castellina." Marco looked them over. "Being we have nothing but the road ahead, I'll tell you what I know though no answer comes simple." Marco drank from his wineskin and cleared his throat.

"The armies of the Aragonese King of Naples, under the command of his son and another important man of some sort, attacked the important southern outpost of Foiano. See, she's the gateway to the Valdichiana, the heart of Chianti. That bastard army did their work then fled outside Florentine lands into Siena and found their welcome." Marco's face brightened at his listening audience. "As for cities with men," he laughed, "or I should say, men with cities wish to bare their teeth, so does Venice make war on Milan the same the King of Naples wars with Florence. Castellina in Chianti withstood the King's army for more than forty days and those damned Neopolitans gave up. But other places in the Florentine contado didn't survive so fortunate. So we go to repair, build, and toss our shit down the Sienese side of the hill." Marco covered his mouth with his fingers.

Ser's eyebrows pinched together. "No vulgarities around my boy, soldier."

"But Marco, Signore, what made them begin to fight?"

Marco's eyes rounded. "Ah, boy, you ask the right questions. You see," he said, "no one trusts anyone. People make alliances and break them. Promises of marriage to sons or daughters of opposing sides are meant to keep the peace, but enemies like Venice and her allies try to block Florentine trade to northern countries. Yet, Florence's friendship with Milan keeps her trade routes open. Peace is tricky. I would know." Marco looked ahead and laughed. "I may stop soldiering awhile if I had a fair woman with a fat dowry at my bed, but only for so long. Men can't sit idle. An idle man is an addled man, and he'll find trouble." He took a drink. "You see that man there? He's my friend Furbo."

Furbo snickered and smacked his lips.

"Me and him—the way we see it—we found us a way to get paid for finding trouble."

Furbo touched a finger to his head like he was the man with the ideas.

"But Signore, you said you're rebuilding."

"For now. We rebuild to prepare for the next attack. Never doubt there's always the next attack. That's where our services are valued. I've always wondered how people say they want peace and do so little to keep it. When we look inside ourselves we see that man's nature is not peaceful. We thrive on bloodlust, destruction, competition, jealousy, greed. A man fights and kills what he hates, and sometimes what he loves."

Leonardo looked at Marco, Francesco, and then Ser. "I don't understand."

"Poor boy, one day you will."

13

"Thank you Marco. You are a man of your word," Ser said. "I shall remember your name should we need escort again." He held a small bag of coins for Marco. "The final payment."

"I'd like to be at your service again, Ser Piero. You know how to find me." Marco tipped his head, turned, and nudged his heels against his mount. His horse galloped away with Furbo following close behind.

Greve was a small town built around a river in the valley. The town square, as such places were called, formed not a square, but a triangle with buildings lining the street: an apothecary, a basket weaver, a baker, goldsmith, a second-hand clothes dealer, and others. "We go south," Ser pointed. Leonardo located the far end. A church marked the southernmost point where a bell tower sat offset to the right side of one wall. Each building and rooftop had a similar yellow-grayish color throughout the town.

"Let us rest at the tavern and tend to the horses before we go up to Monteficalle," Ser said, leading the way.

The road narrowed on the edge of the piazza, so Leonardo dismounted his horse. He looked over his shoulder with the feeling that someone watched him. An old woman in ragged clothing limped past, a threadbare man labored at his workbench, and three children followed behind their tired looking mother like ducklings. None of them made notice of him.

He couldn't help but notice the man dressed in fine clothes outside the goldsmith's bottega. His overgown

gathered at the neck and had intricate woven, leafy designs
in black overlaid on dark green. Handsome with short hair
and a neat, but unshaven face, the large red jewel on the
man's chest drew the greatest attention. People smiled at
him. The girl next to the man studied Leonardo.

Her rich, colored hair matched her dark brown eyes.
When Leonardo looked into them she didn't shy away. The
way people noticed her lessened her smallness. She floated
alongside the man, who must surely be her father, for he
looked at her with the same shine his jewel reflected in the
sun.

"Leonardo," Francesco called. He touched his shoulder.
"We went to the tavern and you're still here."

After the girl followed her father into the goldsmith's
shop, Leonardo pulled his gaze away.

"I'm sorry. I…" he scratched his temple, "I noticed
something."

Francesco shrugged. "Come along."

***

"Ser, how much further to Monteficalle?"

"Not far. Halfway up the hill."

They sat back in their saddles. Francesco pointed to the
hill and Ser replied, "Yes, that's where we are going."

"Not too far then," Leonardo said. "I can't wait to be
off my horse."

"Your horse can't wait to be rid of you," Francesco
said.

Ser nodded in good humor. "In a week we will be back
on the road to Florence with leg arches wider than the city
gates."

From a distance, Leonardo's eyes followed the upward
snaking road. Monteficalle's circular wall of stone enclosed
the old castle town like a crown.

Now that the journey neared an end, Ser became talkative about Monteficalle. "She has a view and a keep across from the church, but we are not going through her gates. Lapo Attaviano lives on the northern slope. Look for the rows of mulberry trees. They are different from the others."

Leonardo scanned the area. "I see them." Once near, the rows of fat trees with broad tops had new leaves and a few remaining white flowers. They followed the now straight road leading into the Attaviano villa. Two men rode toward them in a courtesy granted to people of importance.

"My friend," Lapo said dismounting his horse the same as Ser. They embraced. Lapo kissed Ser's cheeks. Lapo's groom waited for Francesco and Leonardo, who offered their reins. Lapo smiled at them all and held out his arms.

"Welcome. Shall we walk?"

"We shall, and happily," Ser said. "Let me introduce my brother and my son."

Lapo embraced Francesco and Leonardo and addressed them all. "Surely you're weary from your travels. May I offer a drink? Supper is not yet ready, but surely Cook can find you a bite to eat."

Lapo entered his home and clapped his hands together. A young woman appeared, Lapo requested food, and she whisked away toward the kitchen. Far older than Ser, Lapo could be older than Nonno. Lapo wore heavy wrinkles around his eyes and mouth, but his walk didn't show his age.

Without ever entering a palace, Leonardo imagined one looked similar to this. The tiled floor in the villa's sala pictured a man holding a golden cloth dipped in a river. A large table covered in fine white linen could accommodate many guests. Backed chairs lined the walls. Another seating area with a small table held glasses and a bulbous wine bottle wrapped in straw. Centered opposite the lengthy entryway, Leonardo grinned at the sight of a painted garden scene of lush plants, fruit trees, and small animals.

A woman with black bound hair, a serious face, and a perfect dress entered the sala. "My wife, Serena," said Lapo. He kissed her hand.

"Welcome. How are you?" she asked with utmost politeness.

Ser replied, "Benissimo, Signora, now that we are here."

"Husband, where's Matteo?"

"I know not, but wherever he is we can be sure he's quite occupied. Bring him in."

She frowned. "Excuse me gentleman, but I need to find my son so he can greet you properly. I'm so sorry for his disrespect."

Though splendid, the room size and stiffness unsettled Leonardo. Saddle sore, he stood. "May I come, Signora?"

"Yes, I will enjoy your company. What's your name?"

"Sorry Signora, I'm Leonardo."

The woman's lips curved upward. "Please, call me Serena if you like, child."

"Yes, Signora."

Another woman rushed toward her and placed a large-brimmed hat on her head before they went out of doors.

"Matteo? Matteo," she called.

"How many years has your son?"

"Twelve at the end of August."

"I have eleven," Leonardo said, excited to make a friend.

"Perfect, you'll be good company for each other."

They walked past the house and down the sloping pathway. A boy about Leonardo's size laid on the ground a few lengths away from a propped-up domed basket. A long branch reached from the boy to his trap. "Matteo," called his mother in an annoyed tone.

The boy turned his head, looked at his mother, and turned back to his work. He held out a finger to signal he needed a moment.

"No. Our visitors arrived and you've not been a gentleman. Come now and greet them."

Matteo rose from the ground and slapped his hands together to feign dirt removal.

"A mess," his mother said. "Our guest, Leonardo. He's your age."

Matteo's dark hair flowed to his shoulders in waves that brushed into his thick brows and dark, oval eyes. His full lips stretched into a crooked smile.

"I'm glad to meet you, Leonardo." Matteo reached his hand to shake Leonardo's and clasped his other hand around Leonardo's forearm. He pulled him in shoulder meeting shoulder.

"To the house," his mother said.

The boys walked behind her.

"What are you doing with the basket?" Leonardo asked.

"Setting a trap, of course."

"What are you trying to catch?"

"A weasel."

"What will you do once you catch it?"

Matteo's eyes sparkled. "Do you truly think I can catch one?"

Leonardo hadn't considered catching a weasel before. "Yes."

One side of Matteo's lips turned up. "There are baby rabbits in a hole under my basket, and that weasel chirps its nasty sound once it's dark. I saw it carrying a baby in its mouth early this morning as the sun rose."

"Can I help you catch it?"

"Sure, but you have to be ready tonight. When we catch it, we'll put him in a sack, and when I go back to the river, I'll toss him in."

***

After supper, Matteo led Leonardo to the trap. "I have something I want to show you." Matteo extended his hands, palms up, fingers clasped.

"What is it?"

Matteo opened his fingers. "A sling. You can put anything here in the band, swing it, and it not only hits hard, it goes far. I have to practice, but my mother took it away." He set a finger across his lips.

Leonardo smiled. "I won't tell. Where did you get it?"

Matteo grinned. "My father gave it to me, but Mother took it because she says it is dangerous. Want to do it?"

"Of course."

"Then let's get the weasel first." Matteo tossed the blown-over basket. "It's getting dark and nothing's worked. How do we scare a weasel?" He thought a few moments. "Leonardo, be on the lookout. Here, take this." He handed him a wide tree branch. "If the weasel comes near, whack him."

Leonardo felt a little sick at the thought of the crunch sound whacking bones would make. Their voices would scare the rabbits and the weasel away anyway.

"Walk in a circle around the area with your stick. Weasels are fast devils."

Leonardo walked. He couldn't help but notice Matteo's intense eyes that burrowed into that rabbit hole like, well, a weasel.

"I know," Matteo said, decided on something. He pulled up his tunic, untied a few laces and started peeing in a large circle around the rabbit hole. He looked to Leonardo. "Uh, I might not have enough."

"No way. I'm not doing that. Ser would kill me."

"Ser?"

"My—Piero, my father."

"He'd kill you for taking a piss?"

"No, but he'd be angry that I did it at his friend's house. He's proper and cares about what others think. He says all we do speaks of our family—that people don't forget or forgive often."

Matteo retied his laces. "Do you think any less of my family?"

"No. I'd love to piss freely like you."

"It's not too late." Matteo bit the corner of his lip.

"I can't do it. I just can't."

14

Ser wanted to give Leonardo a skill, a future, he said, but when Leonardo thought about these things his head ached. All the copying dulled his mind and cramped his hand. Where was the honor so valued for a first son? Copy the document. Copy your father, copy, copy, copy. Ser didn't copy his father.

The boys and men sat in the sun. Matteo made a face at Leonardo again, which caused him to have to hide his smile. Francesco coughed to play off his own laugh.

Matteo's father caught on. "Let us to the documents. This old man's mind has little left by day's end. It's best we do it now." He rose from his chair and excused himself to his office. "Please, meet me in my study on the second floor."

Ser retrieved his papers. "Leonardo, come. You can begin the document copies."

Leonardo stood and stretched his back. Matteo gave him a light kick and tapped his fingers on the sling he tied beneath his shirt. Leonardo nodded.

Ser started up the stairs first. "When we go to the city I will introduce you to some good men who might take you as their apprentice if you no longer wish to cling to your mother's skirts. A man can never have too many friends. Connections are a most valuable asset."

Leonardo followed Ser into the dimly lit study. Books and oddities filled floor-to-ceiling shelves, and various ceramic and pricey glass jars gleamed when candlelight bounced off their shiny surfaces. Lapo lit a lamp next to his writing space that held a leather pouch, a pair of shears, and a small box decorated with naked, dancing women. A white bowl filled with nuts weighted Lapo's loose papers.

"Sit," Lapo said, offering them chairs. Ser laid his papers to the side of the table to make room for the documents Lapo pulled from his desk. "Thank you for helping me to settle this property dispute, my friend." Lapo clasped Ser's hand. "You know I have difficulty trusting old men to legalize my matters. They say do this, do that. I have to fight to get what I want."

He let go of Ser. "Piero, you I appreciate. You do what I want the way I ask the first time. My will—my son's livelihood depends on it. My wife, poor lovely woman, perhaps she'll not be unmarried long after I'm gone." Lapo slumped back in his chair.

"Signore, you are not dying yet."

"No, I'm not." Lapo pounded his fist on his desk. "I'm a business man who can manage his own money. Obvious wouldn't you say? It's old money worth far more than a Setaiuloi Minuti could ever hope to earn. My son must have a secure future. He wants to do the same as his father," he said with a gleam in his eye. "I'm too old to help him along when he gets older. My house in Florence is modest. I did that for my son. He needs no vicious tongues to dishonor him. People find more joy in watching a man fall than in seeing him rise to greatness."

"I agree."

Lapo continued, tears in his eyes, "I never thought I'd be blessed with a living son. There's nothing I wouldn't do for him. Something you can surely understand."

Ser eyed the documents, not commenting.

Lapo gestured for him to begin. "I want my wishes made unquestioned. Start with money owed me first."

Ser nodded and sifted through the papers.

While Ser read the first document, Leonardo poked his fingers in the curls of a statue head. The bowl of nuts between Lapo and Ser reminded him of the sling. What could Matteo be doing right now?

Ser finished reading. He made some corrections and added lines. "All is in order here. Would you like any changes?"

"No, as long as everything is clear."

Ser turned to Leonardo. "Copy this. Every page must have a word-for-word copy for the client's protection as well as my own, and if ever a client should lose it, he will be pleased to know there is another safely filed away."

Ser set the document on a small table next to the hearth behind him and Leonardo dipped his quill. Leonardo knew the faster he wrote, the faster he could leave. Awhile later, he tossed sand on the document.

Ser picked it up, examined it, nodded his approval, and gave him the next document.

Three documents later, Leonardo's hand cramped. He'd never finish if he didn't switch hands. On the last line of the document his little finger dropped and smudged an upper line. He stopped and put the quill in the inkpot, licked his right thumb, and tried rubbing ink from his hand. Ser moved toward him.

"Almost finished," Ser said.

Leonardo peeked over his shoulder. He snapped his head back to write. He reached for the quill and missed. The inkpot tipped. Ink spilled down the page, desk, and his hands. "No, no! I'm sorry," he said trying to catch the dripping ink in his tunic. "I'll clean the mess and start again."

Ser's eyes turned dark. "Go then." He snarled. "Your sinistra has ruined it." He crushed Leonardo's offending hand.

"I'll begin again."

Ser shook his head. "I'm sorry Lapo, please excuse us." He pulled Leonardo out of the office by his arm. "You make me a fool."

"It was an accident." Leonardo tried to keep pace with Ser so his fingers wouldn't dig deeper into his skin.

"I will rewrite the document," Ser said, red in the face. "Go. Stay out of my way if you want to be useless." He released Leonardo with a push.

"I can do it. I can, Ser."

"As we see, you cannot. Not today. Maybe never." Ser turned his back on him and left.

Leonardo bolted down the stairs, through the sala, and out the front door before anyone could see him. Don't cry, don't cry, he told himself, but the more he said it, the worse the urge filled him. He went to the darkest corner of the loggia and curled himself into a tight ball. The tighter he folded himself, the less anyone might see him. If he could fold smaller, he might completely disappear. It's easier when he doesn't notice. "Be a bird," he whispered. Be a bird.

A hand cupped his knee. "Are you crying?"

"No. Leave me alone!" Leonardo shoved Matteo's hand away. He wouldn't cry.

Matteo didn't leave.

Leonardo buried his wet face.

"All I know is there's only one man that can bring me to tears."

"Your father," Leonardo said, steady. He wiped his hands on his stained clothes to no good result.

"I know how alone feels. The eye of your father always fixes upon you. Though I have a married sister, I never lived with her, and I'm the only one who falls beneath my father's watchful eye. Let's walk." Matteo offered a hand and pulled Leonardo to his feet.

Leonardo stood. He hardly knew Matteo, but something in him told him he could trust him. "Can I tell you a secret?"

Matteo looked deep into his eyes and considered the question. He nodded.

"I hate copying." Leonardo picked up a stone and tossed it with all his strength. His hands tore into the ground again and again. "I hate him. He brings me close to push me away." He stopped and spit. He lifted his tunic, untied his laces, and pissed. "I hope you'll not think less of me."

Matteo bumped Leonardo's shoulder and pissed with him.

15
March 1463

"Padre, we're going to Greve with Cook and some of the other servants. Mother said yes if you approve."

Padre and Ser Piero eyed Matteo. Leonardo stood next to him.

"And Uncle Francesco is going too," Matteo said directly to Piero, whose eyebrows lifted so high they might fly off his head.

Lapo held his small wine glass in mid-air and swished the liquid around. "Yes, you may go, but listen to Cook and Francesco."

"Grazie, Padre." Matteo turned to Leonardo, who seemed to be waiting for his father to speak, but the man said nothing.

Lapo called, "Son, no loans from any person."

Matteo put his hand on his heart, bowed, and yanked Leonardo's sleeve, "Let's go. We can ride in the wagon."

They bumped along in the wagon ride down to Greve. Cook told them they might have to walk the way back since the wagon would be laden with food and goods.

Matteo talked about his father, his married half-sister, and the place he called home. "The town meets in the middle of three main roads, and there are many travelers and people who live in the area that visit the market to buy, sell, meet, and all that, but the performers are my favorite. You never know what you'll find."

"I'm glad you invited us," Leonardo said. He examined his ink stained hands. "My father hasn't forgiven me. Some things don't wash away."

Francesco placed his hand on Leonardo's arm. "It was an accident, and Matteo's father told you all is forgiven."

Matteo agreed, but he made note of Ser Piero's volatile nature.

"All forgiven? No, not all. Ser will never forget it." He held his palms out. "Look. Can't you see?"

"I'm sorry. He can be difficult. He cares and that's why he angers." Francesco squeezed Leonardo's shoulder. "I'd be grateful for a son like you if ever I become a father. You've done nothing wrong." He shook Leonardo. "Listen to me."

"I've done nothing right."

"You're a boy. This is not for you to do right."

"Then why am I here?" Leonardo pulled a piece of straw stuck from between two slats. "I don't understand him and I don't want to like him."

"The market," Matteo said, jumping from the wagon still in motion. Cook slowed the mule and flung his hat on the wagon bench. "Are you trying to cause me trouble, Matteo? Cook'll not go home with you broken, young signore. No, no." Cook turned to Francesco. "Master Francesco, watch this one well. Does he look for trouble or does it find him? How's Cook to know? Cook has work, and work he shall."

"Calm yourself, Cook. We'll find the performers Matteo told us about," Francesco said.

"Good for me," Cook said, "Work's easier when there's no children." He placed his hat back on his head with force and turned his attention. "What's the chitter ladies?"

"Signori," said one of the servant women, "would it please you if we meet back here upon the ringing of the midday bells?"

Francesco waved them on. "Yes, meet here."

Matteo, Leonardo, and Francesco made their way through the crowd of local people and travelers. The stink of humans and beasts, manure, and fish stagnated the air. Chatter buzzed, men tossed dice, and working women sold their vegetables and bread. Further up the market, away from the church in the piazza, people crowded in circles around street performers. "I love Saturdays. I wonder what feats or jokes we will see today," Matteo said.

They first happened upon two men who swallowed swords. After applause, the performers juggled nuts and fruits while pelting one another between catches to the delight of the crowd. They tossed daggers and cloth bundles. Each bundle burst into colorful showers of seeds when caught on the blades of the daggers. "I've never seen anything like it before," Leonardo said, his face in wonder.

"Look, another," Matteo said. "Are you well now?"

Leonardo grinned.

"Good. A little fun before we ride to the city, right?" Nearby, a man sat plucking the strings of his lute and sang of his betrothed's vast beauties and gifts while another performer, a man dressed like a woman, flitted around him. The crowd was large, the laughter loud. Matteo grabbed Leonardo's sleeve and wove a way for them to the front.

The man sat on his stool and paused to encourage the crowd to sing the main verse:

> *She gave him her heart*
> *But he'd rather she fart*
> *For the maiden had lost her flower.*

The man-woman placed her hairy leg on the singer's knee. He pushed her away and made disgusted faces. A younger man paraded himself along the front row of the crowd and swished a flower around in his hands to cheers.

Matteo didn't understand it, but he and Leonardo laughed as members of the all male spectacle. Matteo grabbed Leonardo again. "I smell bread." They nudged their way through the crowd to find the bread woman.

"Ah, the boy of Messer Lapo. Fresh bread for you and your friend?" The woman shifted her large basket to the crook of her arm to wait for him to open the purse hung at his waist.

"One for me and one for him," he said with a quick glance Leonardo's way. Matteo took a bite and noticed Lucrezia and her father coming toward him. He swallowed and stood straight. "Buongiorno Signore and Signorina," he said properly. "Let me introduce my friend, Leonardo da Vinci."

"Buongiorno, pleased to meet you," Lucrezia's said.

"This is Messer Galeotto del Caccia and his daughter Lucrezia, Leonardo."

"Pleased to meet you, Leonardo," her distracted father said. "Excuse me, gentleman, I'm meeting a friend. Wait here, Dove." Her father walked a few steps away.

Lucrezia faced Leonardo. "Hello," she said looking in Leonardo's eyes and quickly to the ground. She twisted a bit making her dress swish sideways. "You're the boy that stood in the middle of the piazza with his horse."

"Yes, no—"

"You two have met?" Matteo asked.

"No," Leonardo hurried to say. "I saw her on the way to your house. I walked through the piazza and she stared at me."

Lucrezia bored into Leonardo's eyes. "I'd never seen you before. I wondered what a strange boy was doing alone in town. You're different from that day though. Your eyes are sadder."

Matteo noticed Lucrezia eyeing Leonardo from head to foot. She differed from the other girls. She may act it, but she wasn't shy. Matteo liked looking at her.

Leonardo turned pink. "I wasn't alo—"

"What's wrong with your hands?"

Leonardo clasped them together. "I spilled ink."

I'll help you make a good first impression, Leonardo. "While writing a legal document, ink spilled on his hands," Matteo said. "He's here on business with his father. He writes well as a notary and he's not yet begun an apprenticeship." Matteo smirked. "He'll be a notary and I'll be a silk merchant. What will you be, Lucrezia?"

She held her hands at her hips. "I'll be whatever my father wishes me to be. A good wife. I'll marry a wealthy man with *good* manners. I'll be a nun if it pleases him."

The boys turned to walk away, but she hadn't finished. "My mother says that men would not be born but by a woman. A mother does the most important work."

"Yes, we all love our mother's," Matteo said with his most impatient face.

"Some mothers have to love the unlovable, *Matteo*." She tossed her bread, which hit him in the chest and dropped to the piazza cobblestones. Her cheeks turned red.

The girl looked light as a lute but tasted harsh as a cup of gall. He'd love to shove that roll in her mouth.

"Here take mine." Leonardo offered the bread Matteo bought for him. He waved it a bit. "Come then, somebody's mother made it."

She smiled not showing her teeth but held out her hand.

"Take it in honor of our mothers."

Smooth—the way Leonardo handled Lucrezia—he made her smile, and not because she bettered him with her wit. Matteo shrugged though he was impressed.

***

The boys left.

"You're hard on her. One day, she'll make a respectable lady," Leonardo said.

Matteo couldn't contain his laugh. "But she's not one now."

"She can't know what she'll do anymore than me or you."

"But your father wants you to be successful. Of course you'll be a notary."

"No," Leonardo said. "I cannot. I'm his illegitimate son. He wants my success only to honor him. If I could bring him honor by carrying the Medici's golden turds on a platter, then, I may be a worthy son. And I want to return to the city?" he didn't ask to have an answer.

***

"Now's as good a time as any to practice our throws. Come on. I'll let you go first," Matteo said to urge Leonardo out of the piazza. He arched his arm through the air in encouragement.

Leonardo waved to Francesco and pointed the direction he intended to go.

Francesco nodded and waved back at them, and they tore-off.

"First one to the water wins," Matteo called with a head start. Leonardo clipped at his heels. They pushed and shoved each other close to the finish. They tried to keep the other's feet from touching the water. Locked arms and eyes, Matteo caught Leonardo angling his long leg out. It hovered mid-air above the water's edge. When he slackened a little for a better grip to pull him in, Leonardo took advantage and dipped his toes in.

Satisfaction set upon Leonardo's face but he gloated none. He only asked, "Do I still get to go first?"

Matteo bit the inside of his lip. He didn't know what to say since he expected Leonardo to gloat like he would've. "What are friends for?" He untied the sling at his waist and gave it to Leonardo. "Here, your pellet," he said setting a stone in his hand.

Leonardo knew how the sling should be used, but his throw needed loads of practice. He used his arm, not the force of his body, and he swung the sling at his side.

Matteo stepped up for his turn. "The big tree across the water," he indicated as his target. "Do it like this," he said to show him. He swung circles above his head until he felt a rhythm. Using his left arm as a counter balance and target guide, he stepped wide when the sling swung forward, and moved into the toss with a sharp snap of the wrist.

The stone hit a small tree, which caused an echoing thunk. "Yeaaasss," he crowed at the sound though he missed his exact mark.

Leonardo skipped over some rocks to the other side of the water and examined the hit tree. He stood smiling, his eyes determined. "You left a mark. Tore right into it." Leonardo held his arm out in-line with where they stood. He took counted steps and tipped his head to the side in thought. "Wait," he said, "I have an idea." He crossed back over. "Can I try again?"

Interested, Matteo gave him the sling and Leonardo tried again to no good effect. His miserable toss sunk in the water, which made him even happier.

Leonardo hurried back. "Do it again," he said excited, without moving away. "I see the angles." Leonardo ducked low enough to see over his shoulder.

"No way." Leonardo must think him amusing. "I could hit you or something."

"I have to see. Do it. I think the next one will hit your target." He placed a stone in Matteo's hand. "Aim for the tree you already hit."

Matteo shrugged. "It's your head. At least take a step back." He swung, tossed, and missed. "Argh, so close."

Leonardo grabbed him and pulled him back to where he started. "Swing but don't toss right away." He moved to a safe location and watched.

Matteo swung until the whirring of the straps made the right rhythm. He looked to Leonardo in question.

"You bank left. Take a step that way," he shouted. "A little more. Good. Put your arm out and aim to the right of your target when you step into it."

Matteo nodded. He felt the rhythm and tossed. Thunk. He hit it.

They both splashed through the water to the tree. The rock stuck in it.

Matteo scratched his head. "How'd you do that?"

"You did it," Leonardo said massaging his shoulders.

Matteo bumped fists with him. Never did he hit the same target twice until today. "We did it."

16

Lapo and Matteo, Ser Piero and Leonardo, and their traveling companions rode all day and neared Florence. "To the right!" Francesco yelled startling them out of their pace. He pulled his dagger free. The group of travelers quieted and stilled. "Damn, I see them coming around the hill." He waved his arm for everyone to prepare.

Lapo's two guards pulled out their weapons in answer to the three riders that shot out from the tree line at full speed.

"What do they want?" Leonardo asked to anyone who would answer. He froze in his saddle. His heart raced in his ears.

Galloping footfalls struck the ground in rhythmic time.

"Stay calm, everyone," Lapo told them. He shoved the hood of his mantello back.

Leonardo's horse jolted forward. He pulled back on the reins. "Whoa."

"Protect the boys," Francesco said as the men drew their weapons.

"They've not come for injury. They want our money and we shall give it to them," Lapo said. "Serena," he shouted toward the enclosed wagon.

One of the Lapo's guards stood, feet wide, with his crossbow aimed, and he fired. Caathack.

"No." Lapo held his hand out too late.

The brigand's arm jolted back. An arrow stuck in his shoulder.

The sound of rapid hoof beats rumbled behind them.

"Serena, stay in the wagon. Brigands block our way," Lapo shouted.

The guard tossed his crossbow underneath the wagon before the scraggly middle-aged one circled behind them and entered the wagon.

Matteo's mother screamed.

One brigand held the guards at sword point while the one with the arrow in him dismounted his horse. His partner, the leader, yelled, "Drop your weapons if you want to live. Dismount. Now, I say."

Everyone but Lapo scrambled off his horse.

The injured brigand tried to remove the arrow in his shoulder. "Damned t'ing hurts," he said with a lisp. "I should kill you," he told the guard who shot him. His mouth contorted in pain and revealed missing front teeth. He put his good hand in the guard's hair, jerked his head back, and forced him to his knees.

"Weapons. Hurry along," the leader told Matteo. He turned to Leonardo. "You too, boy."

"Ouch." Leonardo said to the prick in his back. He unlatched the small blade from his belt and handed it over.

"Don't you dare touch the boys," Ser said.

The leader approached Ser. "We got a man who wants to be a hero." He pointed the tip of his sword at Ser's chest. "Hero, I'll take that."

Ser moved cautiously. He unsheathed his sword.

"Slow and steady. Toss it in the pile there." He pointed to the middle of the road.

The injured brigand steadied the guard with a chokehold, kicked him in the belly, and thrust him to the ground.

The guard dropped forward gasping for breath.

"That wasn't so difficult gentleman, was it?" The leader signaled for his partner to gather the weapons. "We'll be having your purses, jewelry, and horses." He whistled to his men. "Not the carriage. It draws too much notice." He stood before Lapo. "Old man, why so stubborn? Move."

Signore Lapo kept his seat. "Take our money and go. A carriage would look suspicious, but three men with all these saddled mounts and bags will draw no notice?" He straightened his back. "I'll have you know I never forget a face."

"You threatening me?" The brigand rushed at him and fisted his mantello. "Off your horse, fool." Signore Lapo made no move. "Maybe you're stupid and deaf?" He pulled him from his saddle.

Matteo lunged at the man threatening Lapo. "Take your hands off my father." His eyes turned crazy. His fists flew.

Ser pulled him in and held him tight, but his arms and legs flailed around. "No Matteo, you will make it worse."

Signore Lapo hung in his mantello red-faced. He coughed and sputtered, and they could do nothing but watch the brigand punch him. Blood bubbled from Signore Lapo's lips. Lapo wiped his mouth on his sleeve.

The brigand jerked him to his feet. "Get in line." He ran his dirty hand across Lapo's mantello. "Wait. I'll take this first, you old bag of bones." He kicked Lapo hard in the leg and loosed him of his long mantello.

The injured brigand forced them to the opposite side of the road. "I told you t'was a bad idea. An' I'm the one bleeding." He turned back and stabbed his sword through the guard's foot.

The guard screamed.

"Blood for blood," the brigand cursed. He held the arm that dotted the ground red.

"Take what you must, but injure no one further," Ser said.

Francesco tended to the injured guard's foot. The uninjured guard examined Matteo's father's leg.

Matteo stood. "Where's my mother?" he asked when they could hear her cries.

Leonardo trembled. He reached out for Ser, who placed an arm around him. A shriek startled them all. Matteo's mother emerged from the carriage with her fingers spread about her neck. A red mark swelled where she'd worn a necklace.

The third brigand pushed her along. "A fine dress, Madonna. I'll be having it."

"How dare you." She made to rush to her family.

The brigand caught her arm. "Tsk, tsk."

"You awful, dishonorable men, burn in hell." She clawed his face.

He slapped her. "Your dress," he said, amused and pointed at Ser. "He can help you undress or I will." He licked his lips.

Ser shook his head. "This is madness. We have the money to pay you. Drop your spoils and let us go. I can write you an agreement that entitles you to further payment. It would be far easier money than all this work. Walk away. We can part as if nothing happened."

"Yap, yap, yap, you say. We don't make agreements. Too complicated. Too many ways to be cheated. Our way is the money now way."

Ser tipped his head a moment and tried again. "Take all the purses now, and the weapons, whatever you gathered, but leave us the horses so we can go home in peace."

"Do we make deals?" the brigand asked his partners.

"No," they answered. "Not with the losing side, we don't." He pointed at Matteo's mother. "Give me the dress now, or I'll cut it from her and sell it for scrap."

Matteo kept an outward calm, but when his mother cried out, his face showed how he could burn the brigand dead.

"For shame," Matteo's mother whimpered. She untied her sleeves, and placed one, then the other across Ser's arm. Eyes closed, she lifted the outer skirt above her waist.

"I'm sorry, Signora. Please forgive me," Ser said when he put his hands on her to raise the dress over her head.

Leonardo turned away when he saw her legs through her camisa.

She ran behind her husband and son and covered herself by ducking and pulling her legs in at her chest. Matteo hugged her against him for further protection.

The third brigand turned back to the carriage and climbed underneath it for the crossbow. The leader collected the horses. The injured one packed the weapons.

Lapo looked to his guard. "Now," he whispered. The guard pulled a hidden dagger from Lapo's back. He slipped the blade free and charged the injured brigand. Hands positioned above his head, the guard stabbed the man between the neck and shoulder on his uninjured side.

"Son of whore," the brigand said through a moan. He slumped to the ground.

Signore Lapo's guard ran to the brigand leader. The guard twisted away before a slice struck him. Each man's blade thrusts wooshed and clanged.

Ser retrieved weapons from the pile and tossed a couple to Francesco. He didn't join the fight, but guarded the injured, Matteo's mother, and the boys.

Soon the brigand leader surrendered.

"One is getting away," Signore Lapo called. He pointed to the third brigand, who ran for the tree line.

"Matteo—here," Leonardo said holding a rock at the ready.

Matteo hurried to untie the sling at his waist. His possessed eyes and lips curled tighter when he swung the sling. After a few turns, he stepped a bit to the right like before, released, and roared. The rock flung through the air and found its target knocking the brigand to the ground.

Matteo's fist thudded against his chest.

"You're amazing," Leonardo said.

"No one hurts my father," Matteo said in a shaky voice. "No one shames my mother. They're all I have."

Matteo's mother ran her trembling fingers along the sling. "Son, I'll never take it away again."

Leonardo pulled the dress from the brigand's sack. "Signora." He held it across his arms and looked away like an honorable man should.

Signore Lapo's guard dragged the runaway back by his leg. "Signori, the boy hit him square in the head." He dropped the leg. "Matteo, you're a perfect shot. Knocked the light right out of him."

Francesco nudged the toothless brigand with his foot. "This one's almost dead."

They dragged the knocked out brigand and placed him beside his dying partner. Lapo's guard held the third man at sword point.

"Please, decent men," the leader said, "You have your belongings. Let me go."

Ser rushed him and took hold of his filthy clothes. "You refused a better offer. We will suffer you as far as the Stinche."

"I can't go to prison."

Ser kicked his legs. "On your knees you poor excuse of a man. You dishonored us and took the innocence of a respectable woman and children. Die here or die in prison."

"Here. I'll die here."

"No," Ser said. "I am not a killer. Tie him up," he told the uninjured guard.

Ser went to his friend's side. "Messer Lapo, can you ride?"

"Not with this battered body." A hole showed where Lapo's tooth should have been. He limped on his leg. "Take me to the pageant wagon," he said in jest.

Leonardo flung his arm rapidly toward the horizon. "Trouble. More riders."

Ser looked north. "No. Fate may be late, but she is on our side. The city patrollers have arrived." He released the brigand, "You stink." He turned to address the others, "I will give them a full account and clear us to enter the city. Let them deal with these treacherous men."

17

Courage was never Leonardo's strength; rather, it squealed out of him like a mewling newborn. He could hear his fading mother's voice saying, "The first breath is the hardest, but the babe knows he must breathe."

"Are you well, Leonardo?" Matteo asked, slowing his horse. "Your skin is pale. You look like you might faint."

Leonardo sipped from his wineskin and swallowed hard. He wiped his mouth and looked to the road ahead, which led straight to the southern gate of Florence, the Porta San Piero Gattolino. "I'm well," he said, unsure.

Leonardo located the heart of the city. As much as he wished to go back to his mother, he couldn't ignore his desire to return to the treasures he recently discovered. The compass at his center turned him back toward Florence, which turned him back toward Ser. Devil take him, he couldn't let go of the need to prove himself, not that he knew what he was trying to prove.

Decision made, and none too soon. A large, imposing tower stood in the middle of tall brick walls at the gate, and beneath it, the main entrance arched open like a great, guarded mouth. Each side had two similar, smaller entryways. Once night came, the mouths closed and held the inhabitants inside the bulging belly of the beast.

Many people awaited entrance at the gate. Matteo's family had the only carriage. Some people rode or led horses, others had mules or wagons packed with goods, and many carried their goods on their backs. Two well dressed men a few paces in front of them rode striking horses adorned with padded pommels, studded harnesses, and stirrups with designs of the sun. Another man wore a threadbare tunic covered on one shoulder with a mostly empty sack. He held the hand of a small boy with bare feet.

Ser turned toward Leonardo and Francesco. "They will search for illegal weapons and such. I will pay the tariff." Leonardo and Francesco nodded and waited behind him.

Matteo waited beside one of his father's guards, who held a document from the city's patrol officers to allow them to gain entrance without suspicion. Behind them, the carriage held his parents and the injured guard.

"Once through the gate, are we going to stable the horses straight away?" Francesco asked.

"We lack enough fodder for all three. We take mine alone," Ser said.

Francesco nodded and rummaged through his saddlebag.

Large iron doors rested open against the fortified walls. At each entry point of the gate, guards stood identifiable by their striped hose in the city colors of red and white. Some stood watch at the tower lookout while others walked along the walls. Ser paid and the gate guards let them pass.

They walked bearing left into a cramped street. Leonardo found it difficult to see where one home ended and another began. Many roads turned at sharp angles. He smelled the damp straw and manure of the stables. Further down and to the right, the air lightened to open gardens.

"Too bad for you old girl," Leonardo said to his mount. "I wish you could graze in the open green." He patted his horse. Freedom denied to her so near a place that could provide happiness.

Signore Lapo hobbled out of the carriage and stood beside Matteo and Ser.

"My friend, I'm grateful for all you've done for me and my family." He embraced Ser and shook Leonardo's hand. "Thank you. After our travel ordeal, we're ready to be home. Though my Florentine house is a far humbler a place, you're welcome to join us any time."

Matteo embraced Leonardo. "I never had a brother but I am glad I found one. Our houses are not far from one another I hope."

"I hope we're close too." Leonardo's breath caught in his throat at the thought of Matteo leaving his side—in part, because he was good company, but more so because he accepted him without conditions. Confident, brave, strong, Matteo charged forth without fear or thoughts of rejection.

They didn't live far from the other after all. Together Leonardo and Matteo walked the via Romana through the Oltrarno. Men filled the workshops mixing business and pleasure. They chatted over their worktables. Old men sat on benches and watched the world pass them by.

"The Ponte Vecchio," Matteo said. "Ugh, the meat reeks today."

Butcher shops lined the sides of the bridge, and before they crossed, a man popped out an open back window. He scraped animal bits off a platter that dropped to the water below.

Leonardo recoiled. "The city's not what I thought it would be."

"What, the bridge?"

"The bridge. The whole city."

"What did you expect?"

Leonardo shrugged and thought a moment. "More but less."

Matteo considered what he said. "Wherever there's more, I agree, there's also less." He smiled and brushed his hair from his eyes. "All this." He looked at Leonardo with a questioning face not serious at all. "What's not to like?"

"Right," Leonardo said, "We can't say there's nothing to offer." He looked ahead to draw courage. Whatever he said to Ser would always leave a mark.

Leonardo dropped his voice low enough that Matteo alone could hear him. "I'm going with Ser to show my drawings to some of the masters in the city. If one of them will accept me, I'm going to leave my father's house."

Matteo waited for him to continue.

"But I'll go to my mother's house before I'll do anymore copying." He didn't say how he'd almost forgotten the sound of his mother's voice, the color of her hair, the shape of her hands. He couldn't breathe if he didn't return to her. Afterall, she was the source of his first breath.

18

Once alone with Ser, Leonardo straightened his back and approached him. "I will accept your offer if you accept mine." His legs trembled a little.

Ser's full attention rested on him.

"I can't focus on an apprenticeship until I return to my mother. She labors much with the written word. I must go to her." Leonardo intended to go whether Ser approved or not, but he thought it wise to ask, make a good appeal, to do his best so he'd have a way back.

Ser's face appeared none pleased.

"You've shown me the possibilities. I want to make you proud—" He couldn't use the word. He couldn't call him father. Doing that would give him no escape. Ser could crush him.

"Tell me your decision, Leonardo. Let us understand the other. What offer do you accept?"

"I'll do what's required for an apprenticeship in the city." Leonardo shifted his feet. He didn't want to commit as much until he made certain he could continue without his mother close.

Ser agreed. "I accept because you chose like a man. A boy of eleven cannot take on a maestro and responsibilities if he has no mastery of his mind." Ser lifted his flask and drank. His eyes flashed worry. "There's no time to loose. While you're gone, I will arrange for a tutor. Mind first, all else follows." Ser removed his riding clothes. "You depart in three or four days. Remember this: If you fail to meet your escorts on the thirtieth, the last day of the month, they will be instructed to leave." He thought for a moment. "You should meet where the road at Campo Zeppi meets the Vincio River. This should be sufficient."

"I understand, Ser. Grazie."

"No exceptions."

"Yes, Ser."

***

Leonardo remembered the land, which looked much the same as it did in Vinci. He spotted the long terracotta rooftop between the dips in the hills. His stomach knotted and his mouth dried. He recalled the tree with the long branches he sat under with his mother. He looked hard for it, found it, and rode forth with his two escorts.

At the top of the hill, the women and children appeared shadowy. He spotted the open windows of the house and the stable off to the side. The long grasses on the edge of the hill rippled like a river of green and gold in the gentle breeze that welcomed him. He remembered how dust billowed in clouds above the ground when no rain had come for days.

"Leonardo? My son?" mother called from a distance. She dropped her basket and ran closer.

He slowed his horse and dismounted.

Mother's hands curved around his face. Tears filled her eyes.

Her voice flowed through him in a warmth and comfort he thought he'd lost. "Mamma," he answered back embracing her. A few of his tears collected on the fabric of her dress, crisp, yet soft against his cheek. "Mamma." Home. He closed his eyes to smell her the way he used to, but his head rested above her breast. He couldn't roll his face in the folds of her skirts that once surrounded him in her scent of sunshine and herbs. Taps thumped against Leonardo's side. He raised his head.

"Leonardo," said a girl with hair so dark he almost didn't recognize her. She looked like Papa. "You're my mother's Leonardo?"

"My sister, Piera?"

Piera's face scrunched into a laugh. She nodded and wriggled her loose eyetooth with her tongue for him. She held the hand of a younger girl, who looked like his mother, but with black hair. "It's your brother, Maria," Piera said leading the girl forward.

Mamma bent for her. "Come here, child." She took Maria in her arm and stood. She wiped the girl's hair from her face and told her she was too old to suck her thumb.

So this was the one Leonardo never met, the one born after he went with Ser, the reason Mamma stopped her visits. The girl clung to his mother, their mother. She stared as if to say she'd accept no stranger. Mother's swirled hair changed colors in the sunlight, but Maria ran her wet fingers through it and made it dull. The girl's legs wrapped high around Mamma's waist and tightened Mamma's gown over her half swollen belly.

"Come my son." Mother hooked her loose arm over Leonardo's shoulder and led them, joined together, toward the house.

Aunt Fiore crushed Leonardo in joy. Lisa, he could tell, remembered him, but she shyly watched her mother while tending the bread on the outdoor oven. Simone, they said, went to help his father plant in the garden with Federigo. "You remember Federigo?" Mother asked shaking her head when she realized he did not. Mamma introduced him to his littlest sister, Lisabetta, and his toddling brother, Francesco.

Startled, Leonardo called to one he recognized. "Baby Michele?"

The boy, not much older than he must have been when he left this place, squinted and looked up at him.

Michele tipped his head back. "He don't look like us."

The boy spoke the truth. Leonardo's heartbeat quickened. His new hat, his blonde hair…his white, clean sleeves and deep blue tunic, leather belt, hose and shoes, the way he carried himself upright, the way he felt wrong because they looked different—everything that made him acceptable to Ser made him a stranger here. Leonardo looked to the others for relief, but they all paused to consider what Michele said.

Ser told him he would be a burden. Now he understood. He wanted to hate Ser for being right, but he couldn't. And he wanted to love this poverty, but he hated it. He wished he could take it all away and make them people, just people.

Mother set Maria down and took his hands.

He weighed them against what he could remember of the way they moved, comforted, made music in his thoughts and dreams. He squeezed then released.

Fiore stepped in. "He's your cousin, Michele. Your Auntie's oldest son."

Leonardo moved to unclasp the top of his farsetto out of habit but stopped before he made more aware his difference. He glanced back at his horse. "Mother, I'll get my things," he said and returned to his mount. His two escorts waited near the end of the road that led up to the house. They repeated the date of their return as he and Ser agreed to and left.

Leonardo led his horse to Papa's stable. He stole a glance back at his family and questioned if he made the right choice coming here.

***

Not long after, Papa led his old mare into the stable.

Leonardo paused his brush strokes. He craned his head around his horse's neck a hooked his hand under the halter. He sized up Papa's old horse. If Papa tried to leave him now, he wouldn't get away so easily, he thought, as he sized up the man.

"Leonardo," came Papa's cheerful voice.

Leonardo stepped out from behind his horse. "Antonio," he said in a formality that seemed proper given the way they ended.

Papa's face straightened. He wiped his palm on his tunic and held out his hand. "Welcome home, son."

Papa's large, calloused hand smothered his.

"Should I move my horse, uh…" Leonardo brushed his hair from his face. He shook his head.

Papa took hold of his arm. "Call me what you will. You'll always be my son, Leonardo. If I had the power to do what I wanted, you would've never left. But you've returned to us," he said cupping Leonardo's shoulders.

Leonardo nodded and blinked back his tears. Yes, he returned. He got what he wanted all this time. It saddened him.

Papa pulled him into his arms without asking. He held him too tight and kissed him on his head.

Leonardo twisted to free himself and focused on tending to his horse. When finished, he grabbed his belongings and headed for the house.

Mother trailed inside behind him. The clay oven in the center of the room oriented him. He looked down the dark stretch of the house where Mother, Papa, and his sisters slept. "Can I sleep here?" He plopped his bags on the floor against the far wall behind the oven. "I always sleep alone now."

Mother reached for his face and nodded that he could. She busied herself with finding bedding.

Sleeping here would be easier. He couldn't sleep with others close by. After all, in two weeks he'd leave; knowing this was a great burden.

***

Leonardo ran in the fields with his sisters and cousins and played their games. They thought him strange to buy food he didn't grow and he could tell they regarded his city living soft. But the questions came nonetheless and he answered them honestly. He sought out ways to show them he didn't lack the strength for country work.

There were no servants to bring in water, so he took his horse to the river for it to drink while he filled buckets. His horse carried back a few buckets and he carried the others by yoke. He spent days in the fields of flowering trees, red poppies, purple wildflowers, and pruned olive trees with the family. They spent days hoeing to prepare the ground for summer seeds, and in the afternoons, he helped chop firewood to burn for cooking and keep out the overnight chill. His hands blistered. He made no complaints. At night they sat around the oven, full from supper, with the fire's orange glow alight on their faces.

His last night, they competed to see who could tell the best story ending before the fire burned low.

"But what did the man and woman hear crushing the long grass so close it could eat them?" Simone asked, his hands like claws in the air and his eyes big for effect.

Piera giggled. "A dumb ol' goat."

"A goat?" Simone groaned. He groaned again when everyone laughed.

"No, no, Aunt Fiore said. She added to the story she started, "The boy and the girl heard nothing but the wind whispering of their love."

"Ehhhhhhh," Simone said. He looked at Leonardo who agreed. Simone slapped his head and dropped on his back to show his pain. "You ruined it."

Leonardo burrowed down in his blankets. "But the wind told them only what their ears wished to hear," he said. "The boy knew that if he stood there long enough, something would eat him. It could be a large beast. Maybe it was the goat," he said and turned his head to the men, "or the girl." They laughed. "So he covered himself in his robe dark as night, and before birds could peck his eyes, he vanished." Leonardo covered his head with his blanket.

The fire crackled and hissed a response.

"That's an ending," Simone said before his mother told them to scatter for bed.

Mother bent to kiss Leonardo's head. She sat on the floor next to him and tugged on his blanket. "Before you leave us tomorrow, I want to show you something."

How did she know he was leaving? Leonardo raised himself on his elbows. "Mamma, how can I leave you?"

Mother waited until they sat alone. She lifted the floor mat and pulled out a bundle wrapped in cloth. She replaced the mat and settled next to him.

He watched her beautiful hands open the cloth.

"Your letters. Every one I ever got. Here," she said pointing to her heart. "You make us proud. Don't be ashamed for wanting better. You're bigger than Campo Zeppi, Leonardo. Do what makes you happy. I've loved you since before you were born and always will."

Leonardo wrapped his arms around his mother and rested his head on her shoulder. "Mamma." His letters slipped into the folds of her skirts where he couldn't remain. In a few months, another child would come and tangle in them. Mother would copy the same page over and over.

***

Papa woke Leonardo to say goodbye before he left to work. Leonardo ate and washed and went to pack. He shoved his clothes in his bag and thought to tear out unused pages from his notebook. He wrapped them inside his blankets for Mother to discover later. He wouldn't ask her to write him since he could tell her effort came with difficulty, but if she wanted, she could.

He said goodbye quickly before the farewells made him feel bad. He shifted his pack and went to the stables to do the same with his horse. "Be good," he told his mare feeding her a fistful of grass he plucked on the way in. "Old Madca will grow out of good use soon. And I...I want to walk."

So he walked away when they weren't looking. He turned back when he heard his name and waved once more, but hurried down the hill toward the river before they could return his horse. He wouldn't take his escort's reins, so they could forget rebuking him. Though the two men may not like it, they agreed to bring him back. He hoped his feet would bleed.

19

May 1463

Piero sat at the long counter of the bottega with his associates. Finish the document, Piero. Finish so you can be on your way. "Damn the distractions." Piero signed the document, poured wax on it, and sealed it with the stamp of his insignia. He stood to unhook his keys hanging on the wall, grabbed the lantern, and held the light close to the door lock.

The wooden door creaked open to the strongboxes arranged perpendicular to the wall in alphabetical order. He went to the first box to file under A. The walnut wood of the chest, reinforced with iron strips, made a square pattern. He jiggled the key in the lock, gave it a turn, and hefted the lid.

The wood and parchment combined in a smooth, buttery scent. Piero placed Lapo's documents in the file and pulled out Alessandro Amadori's document. He set it on the lid of a nearby chest so he could relock the strongbox. He rolled the document and placed it in a barrel-shaped, wooden holder about half his arm's length. The snug lid of the holder screwed on tight. He hooked it across his shoulder and relocked the storeroom.

"Gentleman, I will be gone the rest of the day," he said to his associates, Ser Antonio and Ser Bartolomeo. They tended to their scribal duties by lamplight. The front window of the bottega provided sunlight bright enough to illuminate the workspace in the late afternoons, but bad weather called for closed shutters.

Piero hung his robe on a hook behind the counter. He grabbed his wool mantello for protection from the pouring rain, flung it over his shoulders, and clasped it at the neck. It reached to his ankles providing full coverage, but days like today made him wish he had a horse in residence. Before he reached the end of the block, he may need a paddle anyway. He slipped his arm through the strap of the document holder, chose a wide-brimmed hat, and made haste down the street.

The rain lessened the street's foot traffic. Loggias and overhanging extensions of homes provided shelter from the rain. Many men congregated beneath them. A few of the popular artist workshops were more crowded than usual. Piero noted how the artisan shops proudly called their gatherings "collaboration," but today the gathering made more a creation of noise and the possibility of things only God himself would know. For the love of God, workshop rigors did keep the boys from darker mischief; despite all the fooling around, the artisans were far better off than the gypsies and pickpockets. Leonardo would join these artisans. Piero decided Leonardo's studies would take him no further than the few months given to them.

Piero felt for the purse strings near his groin out of habit. He readjusted the strap at his shoulder and dipped his head down to drain the excess water from his hat. The weather made him more determined.

He knocked on Signore Uberto's door and waited.

Uberto opened the door. "Ser Piero, welcome." He ushered him inside.

Piero dripped water on the stone floor in the entryway. He removed his hat and held it out unsure of where to place it. Near the fireplace on the far side of the sala, sat two small boys and three older ones. They held wooden boards and chalk and gathered in a semi-circle around Signore

Uberto's chair. All but one, Piero's one, looked up from their studies. Of course, now that he decided to pull Leonardo from school, the boy showed concentration in his studies.

Uberto held out his hands. "Shall I help you remove your mantello, Ser?"

"No grazie. Forgive the intrusion, Signore."

Uberto looked relieved at not having to attempt to dry the clothes of a man who appeared to have been swimming in them.

Uberto lowered his voice. "Leonardo had a better day today, Ser. He's intelligent and has great potential if he would only keep focus." He looked at Leonardo. "Moments like these, his work can be consistent. He asks the most marvelous questions." Uberto let out a nasally chuckle. "When he tries," Uberto paused, "I hope not to cast doubt on my authority…" He clasped his hands in front of him. "I must confess that he sometimes confounds me. His mind is capable, but he lacks diligence."

"Yes, I know what you mean, Signore. I intend to find him an apprenticeship as soon as possible."

"Oh? Yes, Ser." Uberto's eyes flickered down with a look of regret. "Perhaps working his hands will help his focus. Some boys need a more active approach. Give Leonardo a piece of paper and his drawings come alive. You can see the wheels turning in his head." Uberto glanced back to Leonardo. "I'll miss his presence in class."

One of the boys next to Leonardo tapped him on the shoulder and pointed toward the door. Leonardo looked up. He set his writing board and abbaco book aside, and gathered his papers.

"Ser, I have more to show the masters today," Leonardo said with enthusiasm. He rolled his drawings in preparation to place them in the document holder. "Do you have my other drawings?"

"I do."

Leonardo prepared himself for the rain and said goodbye to Signore Uberto.

"Arriverderci, Leonardo, and good luck," Signore Uberto said.

Back on the street in the pouring rain, Piero and Leonardo walked down the via Ghibbelina past the imposing Stinche, a building of neither beauty nor pride that stood at the center of an open area where it touched nothing else. After all, no man, woman, or child could afford association with the disgrace of the place.

Several blocks away, the rain stopped. None too soon, the road reverted to the usual inflow of people. Two men shot out of a doorway. One clawed the other down and punched him while a woman, probably the wife of one of the men, burst out the door. She poked and whacked both men with her raging broomstick.

Women, Piero said to himself, always interfering. Not that he could say much. His wife nagged him more than he could bear. "Leonardo knows that I love him, does he not, Piero? He seems sad. Does he think we are trying to replace him? What should we do? Piero, reassure him. Piero, take him to work with you. Piero, he wants to spend all his time with Matteo. Piero, he seems lost." Enough. The boy needs discipline. He has enough skill to learn a trade and earn his keep.

He knew Leonardo wanted to please him, and Leonardo would find him well pleased once he knew the family possessions were secure by lawful lineage. Taken together, what mattered was the obligation to one's father, and Leonardo would please Piero by committing to an apprenticeship.

Piero knew himself too realistic to pretend himself an ideal father. He made a mistake and the consequences would follow him the rest of his days. No apology would be sufficient. In fact, it would make things worse, for if he said sorry, his words would imply that he wished he could take everything back. But he needed the boy, a son. He told himself years ago that he took Leonardo to give his wife a child, but sometimes he choked on his pride knowing he also did it as a hypocrite for the love of his father.

To unburden himself and Leonardo from the mounting pressure and frustration they could never seem to navigate seemed the best option. Leonardo's face told Piero that he understood far more than ever spoken of. Piero was no more ready to become Leonardo's father than Leonardo was ready to be his son.

Nothing in the world gave Piero reason to think life fair. He could not help but reject any idea of restraining his and Albiera's joy at the birth of the first legitimate son. Thoughts of his unborn child offered some relief. The correction of his misdeeds would set him in on the right path. Thank you Mother Mary and all the Saints.

"Leonardo, if there is a bottega of good reputation and quality work in the city, Andrea del Verrocchio's workshop is the place. If Maestro Verrocchio likes your drawings, he may take you on as his garzone." He didn't say they would try another shop if need be. Not that he wanted to try another shop. This was the only one where he personally knew the maestro and his family.

They arrived at Verrocchio's workshop on the eastern edge of the city close to the Porta alla Croce. Piero and Leonardo entered the doorway and into a hive of activity. Boys, and some closer to the age of men, created a buzz in all their activity. Some constructed wooden panels and marble sculptures. Others chattered in "collaboration" around their clay figures or in front of their paintings resting on A-frames. A few of the younger boys sat at tables with paper and applied metal points with ink, chalk, and charcoal.

"Good day, Signori," chirped a lanky young man in his middle teens. How can I help you?" He set a small jar down and walked toward them.

"I am looking for your Maestro. Where may I find him?"

"He's back by the kiln." The boy stopped moving and held out his arm. "I'll take your hats and mantelli," he offered ending in more of a question. He frowned a bit at the weight of the wet wool in his arms. "I'll show you the way. Oh, I'm Dante di Domenico."

Quite tall compared to the other boys, Dante stood a head or so shorter than Piero. Piero frowned at Dante's short tunic that covered none of his too small farsetto, which exposed his backside only covered in blue hose. "Grazie, Dante."

Along one side of the bottega, shelves held jars, terracotta busts, clay heads, paintbrushes, rolls of parchment, palette boards, wood, and various tools. On another table, the clay head of a child with ringleted hair and round, fat cheeks sat on a wooden base. Dante arranged the soaked garments over a grate in front of the fire. Piero inhaled. The fire offered a welcome scent from the pungent mix they walked through. The further they wound their way around the back of the bottega, the less the air assaulted Piero's senses.

A shaft of sunlight cut through a double doorway, which led into an outdoor courtyard. Boys placed clay figures on a table to dry in the sun. Three gathered around a large, rectangular, brick oven of sorts, presumably the kiln.

Dante nudged Andrea, whose head and shoulders disappeared in the kiln. "Maestro, a visitor asking for you."

Andrea pulled his head out, stood, and recognized the familiar face. "Ser Piero," he said embracing him. "What brought you to my bottega?" Andrea smoothed his black hair and placed his snug cap on his head.

"My son, Leonardo, has many drawings. Could you tell us if he might have a future in your workshop?"

"Straight to the point, Ser. Of course." Andrea's strong eyebrows lifted in wait. His one and a half chins, short fingers, and the hint of excess in his middle gave him a stumpy appearance. However, he had an excellent reputation and an easy smile.

Piero pulled the document holder from his shoulder and removed the contents.

"Boys," Andrea said, "tend to the fire in the kiln. Now that the rain stopped it should stay hot enough." He reached his hand out and grasped the edge of Dante's arm. "The name given by your father does not mean you should tend to the fire." Andrea and Dante smiled at one another. "Go on. Tell them," encouraged the maestro.

Dante took a breath. "My father named me Dante because he said my mother put him through several stages of hell to have me." He put his hands out in front of him like a performer finishing a trick. The maestro mildly slapped him on the back with one hand and slapped his knee with the other. "I can't help but love this one."

Piero found himself smiling at the relationship Andrea displayed with the boy. They waited while Leonardo sifted through his papers one by one trying to decide which would show best. "Leonardo, give him the papers." Piero wanted to waste none of Andrea's time.

Leonardo gave no indication that he felt pressured. He flipped through two more sheets and pulled one out. "Maestro, this is my best," he said holding the page out for judgment.

Andrea examined it. "I see you like animals."

Piero glanced at the page filled with birds, cats, horses, a cow, and a few flowers.

Andrea smiled. "This is an extraordinary beginning. I'm pleased to offer you an apprenticeship in my bottega if you're willing to learn. Humor me, Leonardo, may I view the rest of your pages?"

"Yes, Maestro." Leonardo hurried to offer them.

Andrea finished thumbing through the drawings. "Follow me if you will."

The maestro walked them back through the workshop and introduced them to the boys. They walked up the stairs that led to second and third floors. Andrea led them into a large, elongated room with beds lined the length of the wall. Beside the single beds, a small side table held a lamp and a drawer. Each bed had a trunk under it. Three pegs jutted out from the open wall on the left side of each section.

"The boys in my shop sleep here. A few of the older boys that work hard advance to their own room down the hall. I stay on the third floor."

"When can I move in?"

The maestro smiled wide. "I like an eager student. Once we have an agreement drawn up you can begin."

Piero stood between them wondering how it could be so simple. Leonardo and Andrea looked quite pleased with themselves.

***

Leonardo followed behind Piero, who opened the door to their house. A familiar, soft-spoken voice greeted them before their eyes could adjust to the dark interior. "Uncle?" Leonardo said rushing toward Albiera's brother, Alessandro. "I didn't know you were coming." They embraced.

"You've grown, Leonardo. Your head reaches my shoulder," he said and placed his hand on the top of Leonardo's head to mark his height. Alessandro always had a gentle touch and warm smile. "My sister deserves a visit from her favorite brother, wouldn't you say?"

Albiera swatted Alessandro. "You're my only brother."

Piero and Leonardo hung their mantelli and hats on the hooks next to the door.

Alessandro rubbed his hands together a few times while he waited for them. "Sister, family, I bring news."

"Yes?" Albiera leaned forward.

Alessandro's perfectly white, straight teeth showed in a broad grin, which added to the anticipation of his news. "I thought it fitting to bring my sister a gift for her unborn son since I, the proud uncle, have no desire for earthly riches. Your husband already knows father's lands have passed from my hands."

Albiera gasped. She looked to Piero and then to her brother. "I, I don't believe it. You were to be a man of the law."

"I intend to be a man of the law, but cannot do what's not in my heart." Alessandro waited for his sister to look at him. "Forgive my long absence. I've sworn my vows to God and my Augustinian brothers. My postulate time has past. I'll wear my habit in May. God willing, one day I'll be ordained."

Albiera stood to pull him to her. "Then come, let me touch your beautiful hair before it's gone." She held his head to study him. "To think—my brother—a priest."

"Don't cry," he said wiping her eyes, "This is a moment of celebration for us all."

"Uncle, will we see you again?"

"Fiesole's not far away. Think of me as looking down on you from above. I'll show you the place. You can see it on the hill above Florence. Please, all of you, a monk's life may be simple, but it is not a curse."

Piero cleared his throat. "Leonardo has news as well."

"Mother, Uncle, I'm Andrea del Verrocchio's newest garzone." He cracked a grin.

"Wonderful news!" Albiera took his hands.

"God smiles on the da Vinci and the Amadori this day," Alessandro said.

Piero clapped his hands together. "Albiera, bring out the best wine to celebrate."

She left the sala for the kitchen with Leonardo.

"Alessandro, Ser Cavalli delivered the document to me yesterday. I read through it. Here," he said producing the agreement. "Look it over. With your approval, we can call the notary of your choice to finalize the property transfer."

"I thank you, brother. But one addition for the eternal rest of my father, please understand."

Ser nodded and waited.

"If my sister doesn't bear a son, the lands must remain within the Amadori's possession. Succession shall pass back to my father's brother."

"Of course," Piero said. "I understand." He ran a finger around the inner edge of his collar and tugged down. "We will have a son."

20

In Maestro's bottega, Leonardo sat tapping his foot to the song in his head and pinched a bit of the bone he spent hours grinding yesterday. He spit into the dust, worked it with his fingers until it made a paste, and spread it across a small wood panel. He set it aside to dry and prepared another panel, each of which would serve for the practice of drawing.

The more advanced boys gathered around the front window in preparation for drawing a human figure. Maestro commanded a firm but kind authority. His confident voice reached far enough from the window that Leonardo could hear his instruction.

"Dare you think to form drapery as real as the clothes on his back?" he asked. The pupils gave a small laugh. "No. I challenge you to perfect the human body before you try to clothe it. No amount of fine robes will save you from yourself oh, poor, poor artisan, until you know the body."

Maestro signaled to a handsome boy older than Leonardo. Without delay, the boy opened his robe and let it slip to the floor. He stood tall and proud like the Adonis from Ser's hidden book. Leonardo looked away.

"Show me his bones, his muscles. Let me see the hairs on his head and chest. Draw the shadows," Maestro said.

Leonardo moved to the edge of his stool to look again. The boy appeared relaxed. His brown hair flowed in waves to his shoulders and framed his smooth face and neck. He puffed his chest out. His arms were not too thick or thin, a waist well-muscled and...

"The light is perfect," Maestro said like a purr.

Did they draw everything? Leonardo shifted in his seat and flicked some paste from his fingers. His face flushed with heat. Maestro said beautiful gifts of nature should be studied, admired. Leonardo glanced around the room and questioned if nakedness was a vice or a virtue. Even priests were born naked into the world. He rose from his stool. The only way to know was to look. He stepped closer.

There, the dark patch of hair at the boy's genitals—the nearest drawing showed it. Yes, they drew everything.

Satisfied, he returned to his stool. Ser would have something to say about this. But what did he know about art? A shadow shifted the light when a man crossed in front of the window. Leonardo whipped his head around to view the doorway. Wouldn't it be his luck for Ser to walk in at this moment? Ser did think the methods of art simple.

"Can I help you?" Maestro asked.

The man removed his hat. "A message for…" he looked at his list, "A message for Leonardo da Vinci." He held the letter out.

"No, not me. Him," Maestro said. He and the boys pointed at Leonardo.

Leonardo took the letter. From Ser Piero—he recognized the writing. He walked to the stairway, sat on the bottom step, and cracked open the seal.

Thursday, June 18, 1463

Son,

I hope this letter finds you well. I assume you adjusted to your workplace and new home? We have not heard from you in some time. As my money is not accepted as a mere offering, I trust your apprenticeship is of equal value or more to the cost of your training. Andrea is a good man who can teach you much. At the next leave from your maestro, please, I ask, of your own volition to return home,

if not for me, than for your mother, who has given birth and asks for you. Your presence will bring her much joy.
    Your Father,
    Piero da Vinci

Two months or so past since Ser helped Leonardo bring his trunk to the bottega and they'd not seen each other since. Ser paid for him to live in Maestro's house for now, but as soon as he was able, Leonardo would pay his own keep. He worked hard and held no debts to his maestro save loyalty and respect for the man, so when he wished to leave the bottega after work, he did.

That night, the church bells of Santa Croce tolled for the end of the workday. Leonardo cleaned his workspace and made his way to the far end of the piazza. He scanned the area and paused at the shop of the candle-maker across from Santa Croce that lent the piazza its name. This was the right meeting place. Where was Matteo? A peddler draped clothes over his arms and rushed off down a side street full of noise.

Cheers and grumbles bounced off tall buildings that echoed up the narrow passageway. Leonardo followed the sound. His best chance of finding Matteo would be to search close to the action.

A group of men and boys massed together. The street smelled like cooked vegetables and feces. He grimaced thinking of his best friend here. "The things a boy will do for friendship."

"Twelve," said a seedy man shaking his fisted hand. A burst of curses rolled off his tongue.

"Matteo," Leonardo yelled when he located him.

Matteo lifted his head, saw Leonardo, and waved his hand. But he didn't approach as Leonardo indicated, so Leonardo went to him.

Matteo and the men gathered around an overturned crate lined with coins arranged along its border. Matteo thumbed a stack of coins in front of him and scooped three dice into his palm. He raised his hand to his lips and kissed it. "Eighteen," he called out with confidence.

The group roared. "Boy," said an old man, "we'll take your money if you want to give it away." Another man sat on a crate beside Matteo. He encouraged him, "Do it, boy." The man's yellow teeth and fat belly probably added to the stink of the place. "Soon enough you'll learn," he said. "It may take you running home to mamma naked, but you'll learn." He licked his lips. "We'll take it all. Even if you bet the skin off your back."

They placed their coins against Matteo, who grinned and sauntered back a step. He tossed the dice from his hand and called, "Eighteen! And that's how a man bets." The group became louder and burst into an uproar at the sight of three sixes.

A man across from Matteo shouted, "Boy, you may be dumb as a stone, but you have balls of a bull." He reached across the crate and shook his arm in awe.

Matteo collected the coins scattered about the table. "Gentleman," he said bending to the ear of the fat man, " I leave you lighter." He poured his fist of money into the coin pouch hung at his waist and stepped out of the fray.

"Come back again," called the old man, "Fortune is a fickle bitch." The group roared their agreements. Another man called, "Watch yourself, pretty boy."

Matteo cinched his purse tight and screwed his face up at them.

"Leonardo," he said waving off his betting companions. What should we do tonight?"

Leonardo shrugged. He held Ser's letter crumpled in his hand, unfolded it, and flicked it out. "I'm summoned. Albiera had the baby. Ser didn't say if it's a boy or a girl."

"We should go then," Matteo said glancing over his shoulder. He lifted the edge of the letter in Leonardo's hands. "Your presence will bring her much joy," he said, his voice dripping in mockery.

Leonardo laughed a hollow laugh. The joke was on him.

***

His eyes couldn't adjust in the darkened space before he heard movement in front of him. "My son," Ser said, an arm's reach away. "Oh, and Matteo. Welcome." Both boys looked at each other in question.

Leonardo blinked a couple times. My son—so welcoming, what's this? Footsteps clacked on the floor above them. "I got your letter today." He tapped his fingers against his leg and waited.

They stood without anything more to say.

"Come. Come in. This is your home." Ser chose the first chair in the sala. He sat and smoothed his hand down his chest.

Matteo raised an eyebrow. He swiped a finger across his chin and spoke to break the silence. "How are you Ser?" He didn't get a reply so continued, "I rejoice with you on the occasion of your newborn child."

"Grazie, Matteo."

Matteo sat next to Ser. "You can sit, Leonardo."

Leonardo remained standing. Now was no time for play. The muffled cry of an infant sounded from upstairs. He'd rather go directly to Albiera.

Ser stood and approached Leonardo. "Son, you have a sister. We would like you to meet her."

A daughter. Leonardo nodded, "Of course." Behind Ser, Matteo stood and punched his fists into the air for victory. "A sister. What's her name?"

"Born two days ago, she has no name. Your mother wished to give her only son the honor of naming the child.

Let's visit then." Ser led the way up the stairs toward the bedroom where the bambina's cries grew louder.

Matteo stopped halfway down the hall. "I'll wait here. Your daughter sounds hungry and I do not want to uh…" He waved his hand. "Give the signora my blessing."

Ser knocked on the door and cracked it open. "Albiera, your son."

She squeaked. "Leonardo, come in."

Albiera combed her fingers through her hair and flattened her bed sheet. She held the bambina in her arms. "Thank you, that will be all I need for now," she told her servant.

"Yes, Signora." The girl departed.

The bambina's fuzzy black head poked out from Albiera's arms. "She has your hair, Mother." Guilt gnawed Leonardo for staying away, but the only way to Abiera was through Ser.

Albiera invited them bedside. "What fine men I have," she said pulling Leonardo in. "I've missed you," she said and kissed his cheek.

"I've missed you too."

The bambina whimpered. Albiera moved the child closer and unwound her blanket. "Look. She's so beautiful." She placed her finger in the babe's mouth.

"Your father agreed to give you his honor. As my son, you'll protect her second only to her father." Albiera smiled at Ser then focused on Leonardo. "We all need our family. I want you to remember us. We haven't forgotten you." Her face saddened.

"I've forgotten no one. I've been busy. Forgive me, Mother. I'll visit more often. I promise."

"Will you hold her?'

Nooo. Leonardo shook his head. "I might hurt her."

"How would you hurt her?" She wrapped the bambina in her blanket. "You're the gentlest boy I know."

She placed his sister in his arms before he could refuse again. The bambina wiggled, but Leonardo kept his arms locked.

"Here, put your hand under her head," Mother instructed positioning his hand.

Soft and small, the bambina's dark, round eyes stared at him.

"She likes you. Perhaps she wonders what her name will be."

"I don't know anything about naming babies."

Ser came close. "Some babies are given the name of their grandfather or grandmother. Others are given names that have special meaning or are fitting for the child."

Leonardo always liked his mother's name best, but Caterina wouldn't fit. "Albiera, your father was Giovanni?"

"Yes, you're right."

"Then her name shall be Giovanna in remembrance of him."

"Beautiful." Albiera and Ser smiled their approval.

***

Leonardo said his goodbyes and assured Albiera he would return within two weeks. He left with Matteo.

Matteo stretched once outside. "You're alive."

"It went well enough."

"At least she'll not fight you for your inheritance." Matteo said.

"I must protect her."

"You're her brother."

"If her father is unable, I'll be the one to defend her and pay her dowry one day. I'll protect her purity and honor." Leonardo sighed. Ser had caught him once again.

21
July 1463

Ser's servant woman cracked the front door open and peeked through the gap. "Signore? Young Signore," she said with urgency and ushered Leonardo inside.

Terrible wailing drowned out the rest of the servant woman's words. "What's happened? Mother. Is that my mother?" Leonardo asked, breathless. The servant tugged on his arm. She weighted him down but he had to keep moving. She dropped to the sala floor. "Oh, Signore."

"Mother? Mother," Leonardo called rushing up the stairs. He tripped in the darkness and realized no one opened any windows. Pathetic sobs filled the hot house. He flung the bedroom door open.

Albiera's back faced him. Sunlight parceled the floor in strips between the window slats. Mother sat in a heap of tangled bedclothes on the floor.

"Mother?" She didn't respond. Clumps of her long, black hair formed mounds at her side. "What happened?" Leonardo's knees weakened.

Mother twisted her body to look at him. Her lips trembled. She didn't answer.

Then he saw his sister. "No, no, no." Giovanna lay on the floor at Albiera's knees, blankets undone, her small body clothed, and her face blue. "God help us. Albiera?"

Leonardo lifted Giovanna and felt no movement. He gave her a slight shake.

Albiera wailed.

"Someone go for Ser Piero. Now," he shouted down the hall. He held the small body cradled in his arms. "There's nothing I can do. She's gone. She's—" his entire body trembled. He searched Albiera's face. "She's dead."

Albiera's eyes turned dark.

"How long mother?"

Albiera caught her breath. "I was tired, so tired. I rocked her." She closed her eyes and moved her arms as if rocking the child. "I placed her in the cradle." Albiera's arms shot out and she glared at Leonardo. "Give her back to me."

Leonardo held the bambina out, and when he passed her to Albiera, Giovanna's arm flopped lifeless in the air. Soured saliva flooded Leonardo's mouth. He ran for the chamber pot.

No longer heaving, but still hugging the pot, he made his way to the window and opened it for fresh air.

"She's cold. She needs her blanket," Albiera said. She held her hand out for Leonardo to fetch her one.

Leonardo set the chamber pot by the door and returned. "Mother, can I sit you by the window?" He pulled up the rocking chair and helped her stand.

"Careful of the child," she told him.

"Gentle now, Mother." Albiera held the bambina's face at her neck. She whispered.

"Mother, what did you say?"

"This is all a bad dream. I must try and wake." She nuzzled the small head of hair.

Leonardo stared at her. He couldn't be her only child. The air sucked out of him. "I'm sorry, so sorry." He kissed her head and quietly left the room.

Once downstairs, he searched the house. "Where's Ser Piero?" he asked, his voice thundering. "You, there in the kitchen. Open the windows. This place feels like a tomb."

A scared woman bowed her head and hurried to do what he told her.

He opened the front door in wait and searched both sides of the street for Ser.

A servant cleared her throat. "Signore, I'll bring you a drink?"

"Yes, white wine."

The servant gritted her teeth and shook her head. "No white, Signore."

"Do any of us ever get what we want? Bring me what you please." His legs felt too tired to stand. He pushed his back against the open door frame, fisted his hair in his hands, and slid until he reached the floor. "I can't do this." He stayed like this until he heard footfalls.

Ser's legs moved faster than ever down the street. He dripped with sweat. "Leonardo," he panted, "Your mother? Giovanna?"

Leonardo shook his head in answer and stood.

A pitiful groan escaped Ser's lips.

"Breathe, just breathe." Leonardo pulled Ser's large body into his arms. The man shuddered and wet Leonardo's neck with his tears. He waited for Ser to calm. "Mother lost her wits. She thinks she's having a nightmare."

Ser wiped his face and looked at him.

"She must be sleeping now. My sister is with her."

"This is not the way life should be," Ser said. "A newborn child taken. Why?"

Leonardo wiped his eyes. "Maybe we are all living a nightmare."

22
October 1463

For as long as Matteo could remember, the land never changed. Flooding rains, snow, fire, or even changing leaves, the land never truly changed. People changed.

He was no longer a child, nor did he feel like one. It felt good, no; it felt great to be home. Florence tingled in Matteo like flashes of lightening, but home warmed him like a burning ember bright as the changing leaves that displayed their best reds, yellows, and oranges. He took in the colorful landscape.

Rooted here, he could return to the city. Home always waited, but city living? It made him soft. He stretched his sore arms and watched the women. Prime views when they leaned over to snip grapes from the vine. He smiled. Perhaps city living also softened his mind.

Padre whacked Matteo upside his head with his hat. "Get your head out of the clouds and back to the picking."

"Grazie for the acknowledgment, Padre," he said and grabbed an empty crate. He carried it down the vineyard.

A group of loud women didn't notice him within listening distance. He chose a patch of lush vines to conceal himself and returned to the grapes. Snip, snip, the place grew sticky with juices and stickier with conversation.

Few women lacked conversation or opinions. One could learn much from what they heard by listening to them. Matteo kept out of the way, his ears attuned. He worked a little so his crate wouldn't be empty. He laughed to himself. The quiet Magdalena with child? Oh, Niccolo, that lazy lover. No more laughing he insisted—he might miss the names. A couple of girls lingered in the square too long and looked Tino, the baker, in his eyes.

"I swear the youngest strumpet winked at him when she flounced her skirt," said one woman. "And her sister! Have you seen her neckline? The child grew breasts and thinks she can hook him too."

Matteo hadn't seen such things, but the next time he saw those sisters, he would pay attention.

"He'll be putting more than bread in her basket." The women chuckled. "Poor Tulia had to sell her best linens to feed all those children. Her husband could be a father if he stepped his foot out the tavern long enough." Another added, "For shame. What about the young del Caccia girl's father? He does her no favors. Has the man any thought in his head?" The women agreed.

Lucrezia? Matteo stood, surprised. Vicious women. He moved closer.

"He treats the girl like a son, but forgets she's missing the vital part." They exploded into laughter. "Won't her future wife be shocked to find her looker of a husband a woman?" said the fat one with dull eyes and a big nose. She continued, "The child needs her mother to lead with the rod and lock her in if that's what it takes. She'll never marry. My husband says he'd never accept the fattest dowry of a compromised girl. He'd never be called a cuckold."

"Shh," said a woman named Simona, "she'll never make a respectable lady."

Matteo couldn't listen any longer. He stepped out from the opposite side of the vines.

Simona jumped when he crossed over. "Aggh."

Matteo could take a rod to all of them. His chest grew hotter. He eyed Simona. Surely she wished for bigger breasts and less moustache. She swiped the back of her hand across her mouth.

"That's right, cover your ugly tongues, for it's not respectable to slander your neighbors. Mother of Christ, Lucrezia's little more than a child," he said for greater effect. Wide eyes held him in contempt of his curse, but their grins, now humbled, faded. "You grind her good name in your teeth. Shame on you." His words tasted sweet as the juice on the vine.

The women carried their buckets away without further word. He must find Lucrezia. She needed to know the evil things the women said about her. Rumors contained lies, but these had truth in them.

Maybe he'd find Lucrezia at market. He could ride to her house, but his appearance wouldn't remain quiet and her reputation could only fall further from grace by his call. Plus, he needed no questions about his intentions.

***

The next day he arrived early at the market to the sellers laying out their wares. Matteo walked down the square past the spice seller's baskets filled with roots and powders. The saddler waved. Smoke carried the scent of hot iron and burning wood out the blacksmith's doors. Across the way, the goldsmith's workshop, a collector's dream, tempted the passerby to behold the treasures within. He entered and admired the details on small figures, jewelry, crosses, coins and numerous other items worked in fine metals.

"Buongiorno, Signore Matteo," greeted the short goldsmith. "You've come for the chain? I've held it many months. We wait for our customers," he said with pride.

"I have, grazie. I've been in Florence, Signore."

Another man entered the shop. Matteo didn't recognize him.

"Matteo, Gaddea will get your chain in the back." He waved his arm to point the way.

"Gaddea girl, fetch the Attaviano boy's chain."

"Yes, Papa," came Gaddea's voice from the back of the shop.

Matteo hadn't seen Gaddea in a few years—not since she grew little lumps for breasts at her chest. His best guess would give her sixteen years now—an older woman. He turned a corner and stopped. "Gaddea?" No girlish figure anymore, Matteo understood why her father kept her inside. His tongue went dry at the sight of her curves.

"Matteo?" She smiled.

Dong, dong, a bell rang in his mind. The last he remembered, she claimed to drink a love potion each morning. He thought it dumb at the time, but now...

"Matteo, I can't find it. Help me look? What does it look like?" she asked ducking below the high counter.

He heard her rummaging and hesitated. "I'll find it." He went behind the counter.

Gaddea knelt on a small stool and giggled. "You've found it." She turned and faced him. She traced the chain hung around her neck in a downward motion to reveal loosened laces. His crucifix rested between her plump breasts.

His breath caught in his throat. He couldn't speak. Christ in heaven. Help me... Thank you, God...he reached out his hand. With the other, he pulled on his tunic but couldn't hide his excitement. Both hands in pillowy heaven, he caught himself. Mother Mary and all the Saints. "Gaddea. Your father..." he whispered, labored. He couldn't look away. Her breasts so soft and tender filled his hands with warmth and made him want to taste. "I'll die if I don't leave this place." He closed his eyes and took a deep breath. "You want to be locked away the rest of your life?" He turned away. "You want me dead? Gaddea, you're thoughtless!" He ran from behind the counter and darted out of the shop.

Far enough away, he caught his breath. Crazy girl. Every one of them. His body trembled from seduction? From fear? If anyone discovered what happened he'd be in a mess, and for Gaddea, it could be worse. Forget them all. Forget Lucrezia. He wouldn't wager anything on them.

But he couldn't forget. That night he startled awake. The last image in his mind, breasts. It was a sin. A torture brought upon him by the devil. To think of her and to see the destruction brought on by breasts seemed reason enough to keep women indoors. Or perhaps he should be locked away for protection. He needed to be taken from the enemy. Breasts could mean the end of him.

23

Piero's wife shriveled more each day. Albiera's sunken eyes and pale body wretched into the goblet she carried about the house—a sick reminder of her condition, their condition. Drained empty, they waited for someone to fill their cup, and it filled and filled with bile and dregs.

Piero pulled a cloth from his vest and offered it, but Albiera didn't see him anymore. Her sour stench gagged him. He dabbed her mouth. "It will get better, my love. We will…" What? Live another day in hell? Survive until tomorrow? Have another child? No, not that. He tried comforting her, but she sobbed until sleep finally gave her rest. He found none.

Many nights he woke sweating and shouting in belief that the walls had fallen in on them. Last night, he wished it so.

He pulled Albiera softly to him. "Walk with me, sweet wife." They reached the stairs and he grasped her arm to have her follow.

"No," she begged, "Piero, no. Please." She pulled away. "Not the room. My baby. Our baby." Her body trembled and she turned white.

"Shh," he said holding her against him. "How can I help you? Albiera, I know not what to do."

He already sent for the physician, who fed her aniseed and cassia to purge her yellow choler and gave her drinks to balance her humors of melancholy. The barber bled her. Nothing could bring her back, and now he could think of no better choice than to heed the advice of those who knew. Get her with child, and soon, they said.

He could not stay home any longer than the night. Was it not enough to lose the child? He slept alone. He lost everything. Albiera would not leave the house but to step out of doors a few short moments, lost to another place. She was gone, far gone.

The days grew shorter and the nights darker, colder. He stoked the fire while Albiera arranged her bed linens on the lettuccio in a room not meant to house a wife, a room not meant for permanence.

"Stay with me, Piero?"

He nodded as he did for weeks, and she held his hand and he would stay until she fell asleep. He would rise from her bedside chair and drag himself upstairs to their marriage bed. No other bed would hold them both. Tonight it was no matter.

"Let me love you," he said and kissed her lips after she washed. "Albiera, my love," he said sliding a tendril of hair from her cheek, "Be with me."

He untied her stained sleeves. Lifting her over gown, then the other, he laid them beside her. She sat in her camisa, still and silent and staring into the fire, while he removed his clothes.

"I love you. Please, come back to me." He wet his fingers in his mouth, and lifted her thin linen skirt.

***

Piero kissed Albiera's forehead, placed another log on the fire, and dressed. He closed the door and stood in the sala. "I cannot be alone again in this wretched dark," he said into the night.

He crossed the room to the hearthside with no flame, only embers. Their low, orange glow offered dim protection from the demons that thrashed him. He searched the mantle for his small keepsake box, opened it, and felt around until his fingers found the knotted rope of his childhood rosary. He placed it around his neck and made the sign of the cross. "I'm not worthy to ask," he said dropping to his knees. "I beg you." He found the first knot with his thumb and recited the Apostles Creed. "We need a child. My wife will not survive without one, and you know that I need my wife. I want my wife. I love her. Give us a child."

Piero jerked awake. He sat up and ran his hands ran along the cold, stone surface beneath him. The fire had gone out. Shivering, he turned to see daylight peeking through the window shutters. He rose and opened them. Sunlight filled the hollow house. It had been so long since he smiled. "Thank you for a dreamless night," he said to the heavens.

A knock at the door startled him. "Who knocks so early in the morning?"

"Leonardo," came the answer. "Early? Ser, the second bell past prime rang some time ago."

Piero unlatched the door. "The house is silent. I just woke."

"Are you ill?" Leonardo asked, his voice suspicious.

"No, not ill. I feel good." Better at least.

"I suppose you and Mother are not ready to travel?" Leonardo set his bag on the floor next to the door. "Is she worse?"

"Yes." Piero rubbed his hand across his unshaven face. How could he forget about the farm and harvest?

"Ser, you do want me to come with you? We've delayed twice. It's part of your agree—"

"Of course," he cut in, "We can bring in what is left of your grandfather's grapes and start on the olives." Albiera's condition meant he would not work a full day away anyway. They both needed a break from this place. Life lost all its sweetness, but going away would bring it back again. Going away may be his last hope.

***

A couple months later, Piero gave thanks for his answered prayer. Albiera carried a child again. But sadness followed through her nine months. She sobbed without end when her labor began on the 15 of June, the year of our Lord, 1464.

Piero sent for Leonardo, whose presence calmed and quieted her. When her pains deepened, only the women stayed at her bedside.

The midwife found Piero and Leonardo pacing in the sala. "Excuse me, Signori," she said. "She makes no more efforts to help the child out." She wiped her hands on her apron and tugged the cloth in a sort of desperate complaint. " 'Tis been more than two days and a night. She's made an effort more than she can bear. "I, I..." her wide eyes spoke the rest.

Piero pushed past her and opened the door. Two of Albiera's ladies backed away from the bed where she laid and waited for him to right what went wrong. "Albiera? My God, my God." Her color drained Piero cold. Piero sat beside her and brushed her matted hair from her face. He repeated her name to call her to awareness. Her lips moved ever so slightly, which gave the only indication that she lived. "Albiera. Wake up. You have to push the child out."

She gave no response. Her eyes fixed on the wall.

He turned her head to face him. "You have been gone long enough. Wake."

She made no response.

He slapped her hard. "No, I say. You shall not perish." But she had, slowly, and he might have known if he accepted that she gave up long ago, that he alone kept her alive.

"Oh, Signori" said the midwife, "I'm sorry. What can I do?"

Piero shook his head and found Leonardo, who stood at the foot of the bed.

Leonardo's face screwed up red and tormented. "You did this to her. I loved her as my mother. You forced her by your will and now she's gone." He stormed out of the room.

Piero buried Albiera and the unborn child in the church of Santa Maria Sopra Porta.

Almost nine months later, a letter arrived to call Piero home: Father died in the night.

24
March 1465

Leonardo smelled the smoke in Nonno's sala before he glanced into the room where Nonno's body rested. Candle wax dripped off a ledge nearby. The flames shined bright and would keep Nonno out darkness. Leonardo puzzled over keeping light on a person whose life light went out. The family sat together and kept watch, but as he learned with Albiera, no one should say the deceased's name else the dead lose their way. If Nonno could wake, shouldn't they shout his name and call him back?

Leonardo sat in the back of the sala along the wall to watch people enter the house. Visitors dressed all in black, carried food and packed into the place where Nonno's body laid. Leonardo approached for one last look and to say goodbye.

An old woman stood next to him. She dabbed her eyes. "He looks like he's sleeping, child."

"He's not sleeping." Leonardo kissed his thumb and pressed it between Nonno's eyes. "He's dead." His voice raised, "Dead. He'll not open his eyes again."

"Leonardo da Ser Piero da Vinci!" Nonna Lucia said, and led him away by the arm as she marched him to Ser.

"Let him go," Ser said. "Let him work through it like the rest of us."

Leonardo yanked free from his grandmother and wiped his tears away. "I'm sorry about your father," he said touching Ser's arm. "I'm sorry for…" Albiera he wanted to say, "I'm sorry for everything."

Leonardo wound his way out the door past the visitors and found his way in the olive grove. He located the little tree that grew from Nonno's clipping. It lived but had yet to make fruit. He wished Nonno could see it. "Nonno," he called with no one to stop him from speaking, "Nonno." If he closed his eyes, he could see his grandfather in the trees and hear his songs. He wondered if Ser would take Nonno's place. Would he love and tend the lands of his father? Leonardo gathered his mantello tight under his chin for warmth.

He sat until he shivered from cold. Down the way from the house, boys postured and ran about for their stick tossing game while a few girls watched and cheered. They waved for him to come over, but he didn't want to join them.

Inside, people sat and talked. He crossed the sala to the fire. Many made no notice of him while others looked on him with pity.

"You must be hungry," said a kind neighbor woman holding a sleeping bambino. "Your father and uncle went to the kitchen. You should go eat too."

Leonardo nodded. The kitchen held the makings of a feast and the food smelled good, but he didn't want to eat alone.

Francesco's voice carried from Nonno's little room. He shouted, "That's not what I said."

Ser replied, but Leonardo couldn't hear his words. He moved closer and listened through the crack in the open door.

"My work is in the city," said Ser. "Father well knew, as should you. Never could I please him, Francesco. And you still take his side?" Ser paused. His voice went higher. "Even with him gone? Christ in Heaven! All of you are alike."

"I've never not been on your side," Francesco answered. "Father loved you, but you pressed him to do and give as you wanted, not how he wanted." Francesco's voice flattened. "As you say, he's gone. Now you're the one to decide for the family."

"I decide, yes. Oh, the freedom. No longer must I act to gain his love," Ser's voice trembled. "Only in his death am I granted my freedom."

Leonardo wished he never heard them. He kicked the door open and stood facing them, daring them to say more, waiting for Ser to speak badly of his Nonno.

Ser fixed his hands at his hips.

Francesco held his hand frozen in the air and looked between them. "With Father gone now, you have no one you can blame but yourself."

25
June 1465

The Feast of St. John stretched vast as the cloth canopy that covered the Piazza di San Giovanni. For the Feast, the city cleaned the streets and draped her buildings in colorful cloths and silks adorned with trimmings in silver, gold, and jewels. The women dressed much the same and prized their children as gems worthy of all the glory and conceit of the men, who flaunted their treasures in the open.

Ser and his bride, Francesca, exchanged rings two days ago. Ser led his wife along the route he chose to announce their completion as man and wife. Behind the wedded couple, the bride's trousseau consisted of a large basket and a wooden chest pulled by cart. Francesca's family, merrymakers, and Ser's friends followed the paraded couple. Leonardo and Matteo held the rear of the procession.

Leonardo laughed.

Matteo smiled. "Did I miss something?"

"Only Ser's heated argument with the stable master yesterday morning." Leonardo grinned. "The master told him he kept the horses at livery or wages for the Palio racers and those in the tournaments. He showed Ser what little he could offer. You know, a few old horses and some mules. The best one was a well-bred ass." He laughed again. "Ser turned red and said, "I cannot lead my bride with an ass! For the love of God in heaven, man, I'm a widower and will take enough pains for it. The Feast days are as ribald as Carnival!"

Matteo laughed. "How did he come to get his horse?" he asked pointing at the cart.

"First the stable master advised he take the mule for a good price." Leonardo held his hand at his chest to gather himself. "Then Ser asked me..." His shoulders shook and he blurted, "I told him a fine ass would do."

Matteo bumped his fist on Leonardo's arm. "They say a fine ass helps in the marriage bed."

"Ser asked around to borrow a horse. A shame he got one," Leonardo said. "But tonight there'll be plenty of asses. We're not waiting until morning to bristle Ser's."

"Asses everywhere." Matteo stretched his arms wide as if to pull everything to him. "I love this time of year." He smiled at Leonardo. "I wouldn't miss the Mattinata for money. How much mockery do you think your father can take?"

They continued and turned down via Proconsolo past the Palace of the Judges and Notaries. Surrounded by workshops of the stationers, the passed the abbey across the way that made parchment, copies, and bound books. Merry-makers, emboldened by the spirit of the Feast, made jokes, and a few men added vulgar gestures.

A man placed his hands like horns on his head while two younger men sitting with him stood and shouted, "Signore, your wife looks very tender." The other added, "Good meat." The older man formed his cuckold horns again.

Francesca pulled away from Ser, but Ser acknowledged the men and bowed. As a widower, he'd take some abuse for his second marriage, but to celebrate a marriage during Feast days, he couldn't take offense. Francesca's weary face suggested otherwise.

Leonardo pitied her. So young and innocent, her family set her out into the foolish world for great honor and commitment made stronger by the blessed day of the patron

Saint, and she obeyed. A good girl always obeyed. Good sons did the same.

Once the procession reached the Piazza della Signora, its grand, erect tower set the mood for performance and frivolity. Countless golden towers decorated with jousting men, dancing girls, and a number of other figures danced around them. "Blessed be the Saint," they cheered. Banners trimmed in velvets, silk, or furs hung by iron rings around the dais—each given by representatives of outlying cities that paid tribute to the Florentine commune.

In the same way, each person performed for the brotherhood of his confraternity, in loyalty to his kin, neighborhood, and government during the celebration days. The organized processions honored all aspects of society through generous offerings. There was no choice, only duty, and each citizen had a role. How one could know true devotion this way, Leonardo didn't know; yet, everyone proved his or her fidelity to the city as they did in marriage. Leonardo decided, never would he marry. Marriage: another way to smother freedom.

The marriage procession reached close to Ser's home.

Leonardo's heart weighed heavy. He committed to being a good son, but with Francesca he felt nothing. "Albiera was the one who kept us together."

Matteo's brow lifted. "No, Albiera smoothed the waters. Blood binds you to your father." He softened his expression. "This you cannot change."

"Albiera's gone. Change happens if we will it or not, but some things we can change by choice." Leonardo pointed to Ser for his example. "Ser has a new bride. I chose not to take her as my mother. She's not my blood." He lifted his hat, smoothed his hair, and set it back on his head. "Look at her."

Matteo focused on Francesca.

"She could be my sister," Leonardo said stepping clear of costumed men dressed as theatrical towers who twirled across the piazza. A tower decorated as a dancing girl twisted after a tower jousting boy. Leonardo considered what else he might change. He unclasped his farsetto at the neck.

Matteo's face lit-up each time he saw a pretty girl— even the married ones. Often, they pretended not to notice him though Leonardo would catch their stolen glances. Matteo was the boy the artists should paint. His embroidered tunic lay arranged in neat folds and reached from his shoulders to his seat. He belted it at the waist for a fitted, flattering effect. His lush hair brushed across his eyes in the breeze. Matteo, his best friend, his brother… He watched Matteo rub his hand across his chin to reveal his perfectly crooked grin.

Matteo said, "Franceca's young and not unappealing. Your father has a pearl not in need of polishing."

Leonardo shrugged then tapped his shoe against a loose cobblestone. "Let us to feast so we can watch the races."

"Yes. To the races after we eat."

***

At Ser's house, some older men awaited the procession's arrival and welcomed them. Matteo's father raised himself by cane to kiss Ser on each cheek. "If I could walk, I would have been honored to join you, but my foot's never been the same since our adventure. Well, we grow no younger." They embraced. "Quite the affair you have on your wedding day, Piero. I never knew you as a man for the festa. My family's blessings upon you, my friend."

Ser bent close to him. "The festa is for her." His eyes sparkled. "A beautiful, young bride will make a man do many irrational deeds, yes?" They chuckled together. "Not a man can say I have not embraced the spirit of celebration."

Ser's marriage celebration came after the usual time of the morning meal. A servant woman provided a small basin for hand washing while a youthful musician played a few songs on his flute. They drank wine and ate sweetmeats. Guests passed bread around the table. A second musician filed into the sala behind the first and held a lute. The two began their boisterous playing of what they introduced as The Hunt. Ser's friends laughed, well pleased with their joke. Ser offered a bounty of summer vegetables, melon, goat cheese, sweet-crusted pies, and trays of pasta to the bride first, then his guests. He indulged them with lamb at the feast table and received many compliments.

Later, Ser rose from the table, wine goblet in hand. "I thank you all for celebrating our marriage with us." He raised his goblet to drink.

A man called Noriano interrupted, "Piero, the day is young. Try not to labor yourself or you'll miss the Palio."

The men laughed together. "He needs no races. First the ring, the nuptials won, soon the bedding must be done," announced Cione, a neighbor to the men who had a glass or two too many. Another man added advice. Cione motioned his hand for Leonardo to come close. "Four strokes of the bell past nones we meet at Oransmichele." He winked, hiccupped, and waved him away.

Francesca's cheeks flushed pink. She poured another full glass of wine.

"Pace yourself, Piero," Signore Lapo said. "It's not always easy to get back into the saddle."

Francesca no longer took lady-like sips from her goblet; she gulped her wine. Her expression revealed a desire to escape under the table or perhaps to run away.

"Signori," Ser said. A large grin set on his face and he held his hands in a loose praying position at his chest, "I thank you all for your concern. She is in good hands. I shall require no further instructions."

His profession received hearty applause.

***

The guests departed before the heat of the day peaked. Ser, Francesca, Leonardo, and Matteo remained in the sala. The kitchen servants busied themselves cleaning.

"Husband?" Francesca said in a low, meek voice. She held a hand at her forehead. "Signore, would you escort me to my room?"

"I will," answered Ser rising from his seat. He placed his hand on hers and raised it to his lips. "There is plenty of time. I wish for your comfort first."

Her flushed face relaxed. "Grazie," she said. "Forgive me, but I think I've had too much drink."

"Wife, this is your wedding day. Surely I can forgive your celebration if you can forgive mine. Rest awhile then unpack your belongings and make this place feel like home."

Ser walked her to the room next to the sala and opened the door. "The house needs a woman's touch. It has not felt like a proper home until you entered." He released her hand and stood in the doorway. "Martina," he called, "Your lady wishes to rest. Help her make the lettuccio."

Ser turned his attentions toward the boys and paused. A few awkward moments passed where nobody moved. They looked from one to the other. Ser shooed his hands. "Leonardo, Matteo, off with you. Nothing to see here."

***

Late that afternoon, the streets filled with people making their way to the Palio. Leonardo nudged Matteo. "Let's find ourselves a place close to the finish line."

They made their way by following the crowd east to the piazza of San Piero Maggiore. People lined the streets on either side. Boys their age gathered in groups and blocked the narrow passages leading to the piazza with large branches. "Pay your dues to pass," they yelled. People cursed them and complained, but they could do nothing but pay and continue moving forward.

Matteo and Leonardo dropped their silver denari into one of the boy's plumed hats. "Giuliano?"

Giuliano waved Matteo closer. "You want to help? We share the money." He wiped his brow, "You know, make it even after the last man passes. We'll all have coins for the last Feast days and a few more bets. I'll have a full purse by the end of the day." A few boys pushed a grown man back. "One denaro is the price for this one," said Giuliano holding out his hat.

A man a few paces back yelled, "You, boys, I know your faces. Your fathers will hear my complaint."

"I have no father," an older boy replied, but by your generous hand, I'll have a meal. Do unto your brother…Wait, your brother came through our street."

The man hitched his long tunic up in a fist. "This is not your street, and generosity is a gift freely given. This game you boys play is thievery. I'll call the authorities to arrest you."

"The debts of your banished brother have no shame today thanks to the generous citizens of Florence. He's been granted entrance to the city, forgiven of his crimes, and wants to celebrate," the boy said, "As do we. Go another way if you cannot pay, Signore. We mean not to take from the poor." The man growled aloud, "I'm not poor." The crowd mumbled and commented on their exchange.

"I'll not take your insult you worthless, filthy child." The man charged through the crowd pushing and cursing. His hands thrust for the boy, who ducked under a few arms and ran. The man tore off after him.

"Too many people," Leonardo said urging Matteo away by tugging his tunic. He yanked again to get him moving.

Matteo stepped backwards. "No, we can't help today," he called, "We want to see the winner of the race. Buona fortuna, Giuliano. Ciao."

***

Men, women, and children of all ages claimed their place to watch the spectacle on the road. Others viewed from their windows above, and at the end of the course, officials awaited the winner, who would be presented with the finest of cloths, the palii, offered to the city that morning. The crowd cheered and chanted for their favorite horses and riders.

"Leonardo, I'll be back. There's something important. Wait here," Matteo said. He wound his way out of the onlookers and back into the street.

"Where are you going?"

Matteo didn't respond.

Leonardo waited. More time passed and Matteo hadn't returned. The fool. Leonardo made his way back the way they came; he knew where his friend went. He found Matteo in an alcove between two buildings where men set a makeshift table for placing bets.

Matteo hurried out of the alcove. He held a small scrap in his hand. "I asked you to wait."

"And I waited."

"I don't need another mother."

Leonardo shoved Matteo. "You have money to spend as you please, but I didn't realize you find placing bets more important than your friends. You're a stupid ass." Leonardo turned to walk away.

"You can't call me an ass and leave."

Leonardo cocked his head. "I can and I did."

Matteo grabbed him to stop him from moving. "It's just a game."

The clacking of hoof beats on the cobblestones sounded behind them. A loud voice called, "Clear a wide path. Off the road! The race is about to begin."

People on the street moved to the side viewing areas, Leonardo and Matteo included. "Get behind," shouted the people who arrived early enough to claim the front. Hands gripped Leonardo and Matteo by the shoulders and steered them back. Leonardo shot Matteo a look. "See? We lost our place." By the time the boys reached the back of the crowd, the race started. Noise echoed through the streets some distance away and grew louder as the racers approached.

Many beautiful horses ran at full speed. Each rider showed great strength and horsemanship in his ability to stay on while riding bareback and keeping control of his horse. A rider dressed in blue with white hose turned the corner wide on his white mount as another rider lost control. They slammed together in a sickening crunch. The horses screamed. The riders tumbled onto the street.

The crowd across the road shouted, shifted, and tried to avoid becoming part of the collision. A few men grabbed a rider that rolled close to their position to pull him off the racecourse. The other rider rolled and got trampled by a horse that had no choice but to ride over him. A riderless horse veered close to the sight of the collision. The crowd worked into frenzy. More cheers erupted until the blast of trumpets signaled the end of the race.

"Should we go see who won?"

"No, I've lost my bet." Matteo tossed his scrap to the ground. "I can't win if the horse finishes the race without his rider."

They bumped into people scattering all directions. "Why do you bet? Matteo, you're too smart to be so foolish."

Matteo jaw tightened. "I decide what I do," he said jabbing himself in the chest. "I win, I lose. It's a game. You never play Leonardo. So how would you know?" He tossed him a frustrated look. "We can't all be perfect like you, the boy who never does wrong."

Leonardo growled. "You lie through your throat."

Matteo took hold of Leonardo's clothes and tried pushing him down.

"I don't want to fight you," Leonardo said, but Matteo continued, so he fisted Matteo's clothes and they slammed to the ground.

"Fight, fight," yelled some passing boys. "Punch him in the teeth," encouraged another. "That's Matteo. Pull him off," another said. "Off I tell you. He owes me money. Before you beat him, I want my money." They lifted Leonardo from the ground.

Matteo sat up, wiped his head, and spit. "Guido."

"Where's my money?" the boy called Guido said.

Guido dressed in fine clothes like Matteo; well, before Matteo's clothes became rumpled and soiled from the fight.

Guido's dark eyes seemed to glimmer. He lifted his chin a bit higher and glared at Matteo. "How favorable the day to find you in your place."

"And you in yours." Matteo scrambled off the street and swung at him.

Leonardo jerked his arm free from the boys holding him.

Matteo missed, but continued. "Don't think you're better than the rest of us because you turn a handsome ankle. We know that once your clothes come off, you're as inadequate as the next cock," he said, smiling wide.

Guido jumped forward and snapped his fingers. A couple of the boys seized Matteo. One punched him hard in the gut. Matteo dropped to the ground gasping. The other boy cut his purse from his waist and tossed it to Guido.

Leonardo fisted his hands at his sides. "Don't you touch him again," he warned crouching beside Matteo. Leonardo glared Guido's way.

Guido shuffled the purse in his palm to weigh the contents. "Yes, I would say you've paid your debt." He jabbed his elbows at his partners. "We leave you lovers to your quarrel."

Lovers! They were not lovers! Leonardo rushed at Guido and punched him in the jaw.

Guido's eyes grew huge. His partners ran from his side. Guido staggered back a few steps and touched his face.

Leonardo held his arms ready to strike again, but Guido's confusion left Leonardo confused. Tears stung Leonardo's eyes, but he willed them back so they wouldn't think him weak. He helped Matteo to stand and turned to find Guido gone.

Matteo straightened his clothing. "Would you say they only like me for my money?"

"No more jests. They could have done much worse. Are you hurt?"

"I'll live. My pride's injured most." Matteo placed a hand on his arm. "I'm sorry. You're my best friend. Grazie for that."

"Let's go." Leonardo turned his hand over front to back, shook it, and stretched his fingers. The poison of the fight still pumped through him. Not lovers!

"Really Leonardo, most friends would rather stuff a man with sweets and run him through with a sword as soon as he turns his back. Too often they ready their greedy hands to dip into another man's purse. The trick is finding the honest friends." He avoided Leonardo's face and asked, "Can you forgive me?"

"I forgive you. I do, but tell me, is there any honest man who gambles?"

Matteo's face contorted for a brief moment then he hid his feelings behind a straight face. "I—how do we know when we're ready?"

Leonardo kept walking. "What do you ask?"

"It's no secret. My father's old." His eyebrows pinched together. "He has an illness most of the time these days. It's only a matter of time before I'll be alone—the head of my family. It's not much since I'll have only my mother. No one will respect me. No one will see me as a man until I have near to thirty years. They'll say I'm not worthy."

"Your father is a good, respectable man. You're your father's son," Leonardo said. He shook Matteo. "Your father knows you're enough." He paused, "You are enough. Your father has given what you need." He smiled. "And money never hurt a man. Man hurts man. We're all idiots."

***

After supper, Leonardo and Matteo ran to the meeting place. Ser's neighbor from the morning procession and feast waited near the front of Oransmichele with other men they recognized from earlier in the day. Cione held the reins of five donkeys and greeted them. "Ah, Piero's boy has come to roast his father. Glad to have you boys."

Once a group of eight or nine men arrived, they made their way to Ser's house near dusk. The street remained quiet until they began. One of the men sounded his horn with an obnoxious, single blow, which he held for a long count until it ended in the sound of a flat fart. Three men began their rehearsed song. The best voice sang the lyrics and the other two repeated the last words.

> *Oh, the marriage of the notary. The notary.*
> *Has written here a lovely decree. Lovely decree.*
> *The beginning of fruitful nights. Fruitful nights.*
> *Worry not maiden. He won't bite. He won't bite.*

Ser's room window lit-up and the shutters came open.

> *Forget your words and set them free. Set*
> *them free.*
> *Otherwise give her to me. Her to me.*
> *Give your bride plenty of good wines. Goo-*
> *od wines.*
> *She'll think you a knight who shines. Knight*
> *who shines.*
> *Then she'll make no mistake. No mistake.*
> *Was it the ass or snake? Ass or snake?*

They applauded the singers and shouted a few more jests. Cione threw his leg over one of the last donkeys and held the remaining one by the reins. "Piero," he called, "The last ass is for you. Come down so we can show you how to ride."

"Friends, your asses shall please you plenty, of this I am sure. I shall not leave my beautiful bride for the prettiest one of you."

"Please yourself then, as I am sure you will," hollered another man named Piero. He gave his donkey a kick to the starting line. "The poor bastard with the worst ride wins," he said. The horn blasted and the men rode off in a flurry of noise.

When Matteo tugged Leonardo's sleeve and grinned, Leonardo's stomach fluttered.

26
November 1466

Matteo approached Maestro Gherado, who carried an account book in his hands. "I counted and rechecked the silk bundles again, Maestro, and everything's ready for our departure."

"First, Matteo, you must go to the bottega of Bartolo di Duccio. You do know the place?"

Matteo nodded.

"He has several bundles of silk to deliver. I told him my garzone needs practice in all matters and that you'd get the bundles and deliver them to me." Maestro looked down his long nose at him. "I trust you can do this important task?" His bony fingers came up between them. "You've given me no reason to doubt your integrity. Your father raised a good son."

That made one man outside his house who thought so.

Maestro focused on his account book. "Eh, Matteo?"

"Yes, Maestro?"

"I've called for a groom to bring a horse. My merchandise will be most secure by good transport. Take care. It's more than you'll make in all your time as a garzone. You understand?"

"Yes Maestro," Matteo repeated. He waited for other words likely to follow.

"Off you go," Maestro said. "Once you return, get your affairs in order. We leave in two days." He called again, "Matteo, do this well, and Maestro will have a reward for your efforts."

Matteo hurried to fetch his mantello and hat and found a groom waiting outside Maestro's door.

"Signore Gherardo's garzone?" the groom asked.

"I am."

The groom offered an arm to help Matteo into the saddle then handed him the reins. "A good day to you," Matteo said, tipping his hat. He made his way down the road.

Many workshops and houses, large and small, melded together along the Silk Lane. Along the Lane, the whirring sounds of the squared beams of spinning wool came from many of the workshops. In the doorways of other botteghe, woven textiles of delicate birds, flowers, leaves, and vines as beautiful as in nature, showed workmanship intricate as a jeweler's brooch. The city kept her profitable ventures under strict control down the Lane, and the Silk Guild monitored and measured all things pertaining to such business. Any man in the silk trade could make good money so long as he followed the rules of his trade.

Matteo's mind cleared in the crisp autumn air and his senses livened this time of the morning. If the breeze blew right, the odor of wet wool, set out to dry, made the city smell like a farm. Remnant smoke from the night's hearth fires lingered to combine an earthy taste in his mouth. Horse carts and messengers wove their way up and down the Silk Lane. In the same fashion, the random comings and goings created a sort of pattern as complex as any quality brocade created within a local workshop.

He turned his horse left before the street of the red door. As he tied the horse reins to the iron ring on the bottega's wall, feminine voices pricked his ears.

More than one girlish laugh came from inside. He smiled and thought his maestro brilliant in sending him on this task. Was it a test?

"Give me a boy any day over a superior man. A boy is eager to please. A man brings me to my knees," said a single voice carried on the breeze.

The girls clucked like chickens. Matteo cocked his head. If that wasn't an answer to his question, he should take himself straight away to the nearest monastery. Rarely did he turn from a challenge. He inspected himself, straightened his face, and showed himself in the doorway.

Four girls stared back at him and a fifth girl knelt on the floor in prayer. Odd, and not what he expected. He removed his hat and traced the rim with his fingers.

"Anastasia," called one of the girls, "Your prayer is answered."

"What?" She opened her eyes.

Her cheeks flushed. Matteo's face might look the same. He stood there gaping at the girls. They sat around baskets filled with rolled silk. One of them continued winding her threads. To the back of the small bottega, the room steamed from the two large pots of boiling water that killed the silk worm and loosened its threads. The girls dressed in light linens. Their skirts clung to their legs.

"Buongiorno," Matteo said with a bow. "I've come for the packages of my maestro, Mariano Gherardo."

"Look at him ladies," said the voice he heard outside. "How his halo shines. He must be sent from heaven."

Matteo glanced up at the sunlight shining through the doorway onto his head. "Not from heaven my ladies," he said bearing a wicked smile. "I could not pass your happy sound unnoticed. Fortunate for me, I'm sent to do my maestro's bidding and it led me here. Did I hear you have you need of a boy?"

The girls looked at each other, smiled, and giggled in a way most girls did. But their smiles turned cold. They sucked their joy back inside themselves, self-conscious toward one another and him. He thought it such an offensive crime to suffocate such joy and beauty. "My name is Matteo. I'll help you if I can."

Anastasia drew Matteo's name out on her tongue and finished by introducing herself. "I'm Anastasia," she said with a lift of her brow that teased him. While the other girls played coy, Anastasia continued her direct approach. She pointed to a busty girl with wide hips. "That's Ghita, and there on the stool is her sister, Stella."

The sisters wore the brown smocks of the children of the Ospedale degli Innocenti, the dress of orphans. The smallest girl swished a paddle in one of the boiling pots.

"Chloa is the one with the darkest hair, and Margherita there is the oldest." Anastasia went to Margherita, the wide one, and kissed her forehead. "She needs a husband. She's twenty-three. Do you have an unmarried father, uncle, brother, anyone?" The girl pulled at Anastasia and shot her a dirty eye.

"Is there no match for her?"

Margherita shook her head but Anastasia continued, "She has no dowry. The owner of the shop, Uncle, tells her she's too valuable to enter a convent. We call him Uncle, but there's no relation." Anastasia moved closer to Matteo and lowered her voice. "He doesn't want to pay for her keep when he makes more profits by her labors here."

Matteo shifted his weight from one foot to the other. A boy couldn't offer much assistance in these matters. Moments like these called for a light touch, and a boy learned first from his mother. He would share her wisdom. "Margherita, worry not. You have a roof over your head, someone to feed you, and friends around you. My mother always tells me to remember that a woman may have many husbands, but she only has one heart. A good husband will come for you. If not, you've not lost." The ladies eyes softened on him.

"You see?" Anastasia asked holding out her hand, "A boy listens to his mother's wise words. He's not too convinced of his own worth." She grumbled, "I shall never marry. My father was the first man I loved, and he shall be the last."

"Then you'll never leave this place. You'll die alone, childless, and poor," Margherita said. "Without a husband, what regard does a woman have?"

They all jumped at the sound of creaking stairs and footsteps. "Uncle comes," Margherita said. The girls rushed back to their work.

Matteo tried to recall his business. What was the name of the man? Antol—Gregorio—

Bartolo. Yes, Bartolo di Duccio.

Reaching the last step, the man Bartolo wheezed. "Girls, how many hanks have you made? You shriek on and on. Ahead in your work?" He made a tortured noise from his mouth with every movement. His body resembled an overstuffed sack of grain and his shirt clasps strained as if ready to pop.

Matteo approached him. "I've come for the merchandise of Maestro Gherardo, Signore."

Signore di Duccio turned toward him with a critical eye. "Are you in the habit of conversing so and such to lead the girls to temptations?" He eyed him. "I know the mind of a boy."

Matteo wasn't sure if he needed to answer the man's question, but the man need not offend. Matteo shook his head and scrutinized the floor.

"The father of any girl would have the hide of a lecher."

Matteo jerked his head up. No need for rudeness. If of age, he'd put the bastard in his place. "Forgive me Signore. I'm no lecher," Matteo said in an even tone. Best to play calm so the man wouldn't see his resentment. "I've come in the name of my maestro and nothing more." He placed his hat back on his head, all too willing to leave, and hoped Bartolo got the message.

Bartolo stuffed his broad hands where his hips should be. "Come around to the door on the side of the building, and I'll consult the ledger."

Matteo untied the horse and led it to the side of the bottega.

The gruff man opened the door. "Maestro Gherardo has four bundles. And your name again, boy?"

"Matteo Attaviano, garzone of Maestro Mariano Gherardo."

Signore di Duccio wrote the name in the ledger. "Your maestro must think you a trustworthy boy to place this much value in your hands." He tossed his hands in the air and grumbled, "As he asks, I shall give. Once the silk leaves my shop, I have no responsibility for what happens to it."

Bartolo di Duccio brought the bundles to the entrance. "I've packed it well—tight and dry with abundance of matting." His lips twisted like a wet slug. "If the silk is rubbed too hard or pulled, you'll damage it. Tie it correctly, for your maestro knows that I never delivered bad merchandise."

The spittle resting on the man's lip made Matteo cringe. "Yes Signore. He's shown me how to do it many times." Now go away. "Grazie."

***

Matteo took care to bring the packages back to his maestro.

"Maestro, I've returned with your silk," he called.

No answer.

He walked further into the bottega. "Maestro?" A messenger almost knocked into Matteo when he turned the corner from Maestro's bookkeeping room.

"Come in. Sit down," Maestro said, holding an open letter in his hand and directed Matteo to a chair in front of his desk.

"Maestro, I've accomplished my task. Your silk is here in perfect condition, as you'll see," he said, prepared to rise and show him.

"Never mind that for now, my boy—"

"But Maestro, you can trust me—"

"Let me finish what I was saying," Maestro said, "I've opened a letter from your mother. She asks for your swift return home." He sat forward in his chair.

"My mother?"

"Stubborn boy, let me tell you that your father has taken to his bed with illness. Two days ago. She writes, "My son, the physician and priest say a healthy man will die within seven days from an incurable pleuritic. Your father is no healthy man, bless his soul. Come quickly. Waste not a moment. Signed, your mother, Serena Attaviano.""

Matteo stood with such force he knocked his chair backward. "Maestro, I beg your consent to go." His throat tightened. "I must leave now."

"You must. Pack your bag and let me send for an escort. I'll not leave you to find your way back to Chianti alone."

"Grazie, Maestro. I know not when I'll return," Matteo said in rapid breath.

"Send correspondence the first of December if you've not yet made your way back to Florence. I return late in November." Maestro squeezed Matteo's shoulders. "I wish you well and shall pray for your father. Now go. My horse will await outside and so shall a companion for your travels." He held the letter out for Matteo.

Matteo took it and ran to gather his possessions.

27

Leonardo raised his head from his drawing paper covering his knees, pinched the charcoal between his fingers, and waited for Ser's house servant to answer the door.

"Buongiorno, Signore," rattled the servant.

"Signorina, I carry a message for your head of house— a Ser Piero da Vinci."

"Yes, this is the house of Signore da Vinci." The servant held her hand out.

"There's no note. It's from a woman," he said in a condescending tone. "Do understand, it's not my usual manner of delivery. I have precise instructions from her, who spared no expense to see the message delivered."

Martina gathered her hands in her apron clicked her tongue at him, her annoyance obvious in the way she pursed her lips together when she crossed the room. Leonardo set his papers and charcoal down and waited for Ser to come. Martina turned to him. "Young Signore, your father, he's in his study?"

Leonardo shrugged. "I'd look there first," he said. He stayed home two days as Ser requested so he and Francesca could get acquainted, but he and Francesca busied themselves in their own matters. Leonardo wanted only to get back to work in his maestro's bottega.

"Please, come in and wait," Martina said, "I'll tell my maestro."

"Grazie." The messenger entered the sala and removed his hat. He assessed the space and sat on a stool nearest the door. The older man carried a large leather side bag strapped across his chest. He drummed his fingers on his legs and tipped his chin in a silent hello to Leonardo, who disregarded him and returned to his papers. They both raised their heads when movement sounded down the hall.

Ser entered the sala. "I am the head of house. You have a message for me?"

The messenger stood. "Yes Signore. No note, only words from Madonna Serena Attaviano di Monteficalle."

Leonardo shoved his papers aside.

"No letter? I do know the Attaviano family. Very well, give me the message."

"Madonna Serena Attaviano, wife of Signore Lapo Attaviano di Monteficalle, regretfully wishes to inform you of her husband's failing health. He has few days remaining on this earth, and implores you pray for your friend." The messenger paused and held his finger in the air tilting it at a side angle similar to the turn of a crank. "He cannot lift his head and she fears the message will have arrived past his final breath. Please, Ser da Vinci, my husband asks you to pull your papers of his last will and testament and attest to his departing commands so no man may find dispute under the eyes of the authorities. Your copy will show his wishes without contest."

Ser ran his hand along the sides of his face and down his chin. "When did she send the message?"

"Not even two days gone from today. I rode straight as an arrow."

Ser went to the mantle and removed a few coins from the ledge. "I thank you for your efforts and more directly, your speed."

"My pleasure, Signore," the messenger said. He pocketed his coins and departed.

Leonardo pounced at Ser. "Matteo. Matteo knows? He's with his maestro, not home in Chianti."

"I should hope his own mother had the sense to tell him. Before Lapo was my friend, he trusted me with his business, his documents, and his family. He always paid me well. God give him rest. Because he is my friend, I am avouched to help him." Ser called to the house servants, "I depart at first light tomorrow." He went to the front door and placed his hat on his head and his mantello over his shoulders. "Leonardo, pack your bag. I'm off to arrange escort to Chianti." He stepped outside and poked his head back in the open door, "Stop at Matteo's master's bottega. Also, inform your maestro. Tell Signore Verrocchio I know not when we return."

"Yes, Ser," Leonardo said relieved. No way would Ser leave for Chianti without him. Matteo needed him. Leonardo dressed for the cool weather and set to his tasks.

***

They arrived in Chianti before supper the next day. Their tired bodies pressed them to ride faster and reach shelter from the rain and chill, but the unknown fate of Signore Lapo made their arrival less than welcome. An unfamiliar face greeted them at the Attaviano door.

They removed their hats. "Piero da Vinci and Leonardo, Signora, by request of our lady Attaviano," Ser said.

"Thank you for coming, Signori, my lady will be grateful." The servant woman held the door open wide and collected their soaked garments. "You must be chilled to the bone. Here, rest yourselves by the fire."

"We thank you," Ser said.

Leonardo nodded in agreement and groaned with his hands held to the fire's warmth.

The servant bowed and hurried up the stairs.

While they waited, Leonardo looked for anything to hint at Signore Lapo's condition. "Ser, the house appears no different than our last visit. Do you suppose Signore Lapo has improved?"

Ser didn't answer right away. "We cannot suppose anything. So many times we have thoughts in our mind that are different than the truth of what is real."

Matteo staggered down the stairs toward them.

Ser's words rang true. Matteo moved like a stranger who lost his way. Dark circles shadowed his swollen eyes. A woman followed behind him. "Serena asks if you would follow me, Ser Piero?"

Ser followed her up the stairs while Matteo paced the sala without acknowledging anyone.

Leonardo rose from his chair, cautiously, and waited for Matteo to pass. "Matteo?" He waited for a response that never came. "We left as soon as your mother's message arrived." He wanted to embrace him, make something right.

Matteo halted and reached his elbows into the air. His hands formed around his head and he tore at his hair. He squatted to the ground and howled.

"He's gone," he sobbed. "In the night." He rocked on the balls of his feet. "Gone."

Leonardo bent beside him. He reached a shaky hand out and placed it on Matteo's head. Tears filled his eyes. Leonardo remembered the hopelessness he felt at the loss of his sister and the pain and disbelief at his grandfather's passing. "I'm sorry for your loss." Words wouldn't help.

He squatted beside Matteo so long the muscles in his legs burned.

Matteo raised his head. "I'm not ready." He searched Leonardo's face. "I can't do it."

Leonardo stood and nodded his head. "No one's ready to say goodbye to someone they love." Agreeing with him seemed the proper action. It didn't mean Matteo had it right.

Matteo charged him. "I'm not ready!" His hot breath blasted onto Leonardo's face and made Leonardo flinch. He turned and pulled at his clothes; red marks formed across his arms.

Leonardo managed to pull him close. He squeezed him tight. "Stop hurting yourself." He tried holding his arms still, but Matteo thrashed about. "Stop hurting yourself and I'll let go." Matteo fought him a bit longer. "Hurting yourself won't help."

"It doesn't matter."

"It matters. It matters to everyone who cares about you and it should matter to you." Matteo settled, so Leonardo released him. But Matteo's fingers hooked in the folds of Leonardo's sleeves.

Matteo rested his head on his shoulder.

Leonardo sighed. He could hold him. Friends embrace. They weren't in public view. No wrong impressions. Friends, friends…Liar, shouted the voice in his head. A stab shot through his gut.

Matteo mumbled. "What did you say?"

Leonardo couldn't pull away from his daydream. Matteo's hair smelled like lemons and his heaving chest pressed against him. Leonardo forced himself to admit that it felt good but wasn't real. He closed his eyes. Shameless. How could he take advantage? If only Matteo would release him, please. Tell him he was no good friend and no brother. He was worse—like a dog that bites the hand of his maestro. A knock at the door interrupted his dream.

Matteo disentangled from their embrace and wiped his face on his sleeves before answering. "Fra Angelo. Come in." Matteo held the door open for him and another hooded man. "Warm yourselves by the fire. I'll tell my mother you've arrived."

The Friar nodded, removed his wet mantello, and hung it on a peg by the door. He wore the gray habit of the Franciscan's. On his way to the fire, he stopped and introduced himself to Leonardo. "I'm glad to know the family is not alone. You're a friend of Matteo's?"

"Yes, Father," he said guilty as a sinner. The friar's companion dressed in black and lacked conversation. He made no noise when he moved. A crack of his knees made the only sound to give away his position. When the undertaker leaned closer to the fire, Leonardo clasped his hands between his knees. Here he sat between a man of God and a man who courted death. His skin itched. He had nowhere to hide.

Ser entered the sala with Matteo. "I'll take you to him, Father, Signore." Ser followed them upstairs.

Matteo rushed to the hanging mantelli and hats by the door. "I can't be here when they take his body from the house. Come with me?"

"No need to convince me to leave. Where are we going?" Leonardo pulled his wet mantello over his shoulders.

"Anywhere."

"I'll follow you wherever you wish to go, but we have to come back before nightfall or our parents will beat us."

"My father was the only one who ever beat me. There'll be no more beatings when I've disobeyed." He regarded Leonardo. "Before nightfall. I give you my word. We could sit in the stables. The smell of shit on a miserable day is fitting, wouldn't you agree?"

Signoria Attaviano scheduled a mass for Lapo the following day, a Monday, the 12th of November, 1465. The friar preached long and included meditations and prayers for all souls departed. He reminded his congregation, using the vernacular, that November was a time for devotions in remembrance of the dead. To represent Signore Lapo's honor within the community, many pounds of wax illuminated the church, and people from the neighboring areas of Montficalle and beyond attended and expressed their condolences to his family.

***

Five days later the rain abated and Leonardo rushed out of Lapo's—no, Matteo's house. He stepped out from under the loggia and lifted his face to the sun. Not far behind him, Matteo followed and did the same. Soon, all persons inside the house made their way out of doors. Two of the servant women carried a large basket of linens that needed washing.

"Lady Serena," one called, "if you're well, we must tend to the washing. Too many days gone by and with one thing and another, we've not been able to wash. Many garments need attention and," she hesitated, "we will go to the river to wash the bed linens."

Serena's mouth twitched at the mention of the bed linens of her departed husband. "Yes, grazie. I'm feeling far better under the warmth of the sun. Perhaps tonight I'll rest in my bed after all."

Matteo's mother maintained a quiet composure despite her sunken face. Cook pulled a stool up and lifted her feet onto it. "Rest, Signora."

The women wrestled with the linen basket and tried to lift it in the cart. Matteo approached them, "Let me help," he said, and lifted the bottom of the basket. He slipped on the muddied ground, steadied himself, and proceeded to climb into the cart. "Mother, I need to get away for awhile. The women could use my help bringing the laundry back too."

Mother blocked the sun from her eyes. "We have people enough to help, but if you need to go, go. Refresh yourself."

Matteo removed his boot and whacked mud from the sole. "They may need help if the cart should get stuck."

"Ladies," Serena said, "the bed linens can wait. The rain has made a mess."

"No, Mona Serena. We have few days to tend to the washing before the cold sets in. My lady will not go into winter without her linens," the servant woman said.

Leonardo jumped in the cart beside Matteo.

The women drove down the winding road to Greve. Matteo eyed Leonardo in a way that said he wanted to speak, but he held back.

Leonardo turned his attention to a roadside farmer inspecting his pooled fields. Leonardo cringed at the thought of Matteo's anger falling upon him. He knows, he told himself in a panic. He knows I'm false.

Matteo cleared his throat.

Leonardo peered out of the corner of his eye.

"I've spent so much time trying to act like a man, or at least to make myself think I'm a man." Matteo paused, "A true man has to make choices. But not always consider himself first."

Leonardo's throat choked like he swallowed a turnip whole.

"Father granted my independence in his will." Matteo jabbed his chest. "I'm a boy of fifteen with a man's power," he said, ending in more of a question. "But I've learned my lesson. For love, family, for friendship, I have to make an effort to be wise. Father was wise. I had him to lead me to the right choices."

Leonardo nodded. He hoped his face didn't give anything away. He deserved to be pummeled, cursed, but the thought of losing his best friend he couldn't accept. No amount of embarrassment or hidden affection could hurt him more than the loss of Matteo.

"Now I have to discover for myself how to be a man and gather the shadow of my father close in all that I do." Matteo's face contorted. "I've played too hard for wanting what could not be given, and now that I have the power to make my own decisions, there's no joy in it."

Leonardo nodded as relief washed over him. He tossed about what he meant to say all along until his throat unclenched. "Your father was a good, wise man. The greatest gift he gave was his love and belief in you. He left this world with great confidence in his son." He wanted to punch himself for being a coward. The burden of love, yes, love, weighted his words inside him. Such love was a sinking ship better left to the depths that claimed it. He prodded himself for hope of redemption. Make yourself honest.

Through sheer will, Leonardo looked Matteo straight in the eye. "Every man, young or old, needs someone to believe in him when he stops believing in himself. Never forget you have friends to help." Leonardo glimpsed a slight upturn on Matteo's lips. That smile could bring him to weep. But he'd bury those thoughts. He'd be the best-damned friend—the friend Matteo needed.

The cart slid to a halt. "Be with us Mother Mary and all the Saints," said one of the servant women. "Fionda, have you ever seen such a sight?"

The rains marked the hillsides with gashes and pulled the earth away from its resting place to expose roots and spew stones. Water in the river expanded many times wider than usual and would have covered half a piazza. Several women labored in the shallow waters. Most tended to their household linens.

"Step carefully boys," Fionda said. "There's nothing to do for the muddy pits about the ground."

Leonardo and Matteo climbed out of the cart and helped the women remove the basket.

"Matteo, please be gracious to your mother's ladies? It would be kind if you'd not wander far so once the washing is done, so we can leave straight away. Our priority is to tend your mother." The other servant shoved Fionda with her elbow. "No. Signore," she corrected, "our priority is to tend to our Maestro and his mother. We shall leave when Maestro desires."

"Grazie," Matteo said with sincerity. "I'll not wander far and will leave with you once you have finished the washing. Can I help you bring the basket to the river?"

"If Maestro would like to assist, a lady will not deny him."

Leonardo watched for Matteo's usual eye glimmer or his enticing, crooked grin made by the trappings of a pretty face, but they never came.

Matteo and Leonardo lowered the basket and carried it riverside for the women. Their efforts didn't go unnoticed by the other woman who glared at them in suspicion. Not that they could blame them. This was women's work, and they violated the dividing line. Their good intentions didn't matter. Few people tolerated this sort of muddied waters well.

They placed the basket on a tuft of grass on drier ground.

"Grazie," said the servants.

Matteo stood there a few moments. He looked around the area and scratched his chin. "Good," he said waiting for nothing.

"Shall we go into town?" Leonardo asked as unsure as Matteo.

"We'll go to the tavern."

***

Fed and watered and tired of wandering, they made their way back to the river.

Women waded in the shallows while others draped their clean garments across bushes and branches. Some hauled their garments to the fig trees on the downward slope of the hillside. A girl bent over her wash lost her linen and stumbled in the water. Her white garment floated downstream and caught on a stick protruding in the water's middle.

The girl lifted her skirts higher and ran waterside to where her garment churned in the fast-flowing river. She waded in past her knees bunching her skirts in one hand. She reached with the other. Not even close.

"That's Lucrezia is it not?" Leonardo asked, as the girl waded deeper. "The girl there," he said pointing in alarm. He ran. "No! Lucrezia," he called sprinting to her location.

She didn't hear him, but some of the other women did, and they too yelled and tried to get her attention. She turned her head and made another reach.

Lucrezia's head centered in a circle of her floating skirts, and suddenly, she disappeared.

Leonardo flung his boots from his feet, pulled his mantello from his shoulders, and plunged in. Cold water stunned the breath from him. The current pulled strong. He fought his way to where Lucrezia went under. Where did she go? Why wasn't she surfacing? He took a deep breath and dropped below. He groped around in hope of feeling her. His arms searched in wide arcs. Nothing. He resurfaced.

"There yelled the women."

Matteo ran downstream and pointed at her arms thrashing above the water. "There."

Leonardo shook his hair from his eyes and swam toward Lucrezia's frantic arms. He took another deep breath and reached for her as her hands went under. He couldn't see her, but he could feel her.

She hit and clawed at him.

He tried to grab her from behind so she wouldn't drown the both of them, but he couldn't get hold of her.

Not wanting to lose her again, he thrust himself forward and found her. He fisted her clothing in one hand and tried paddling with the other. When he pulled, she wouldn't rise toward the surface. He panicked and tasted the murky water.

They dropped like stones.

Don't drown, he begged. Kick harder.

He reached below her arm, around her back, and pulled with all his strength. His lungs screamed for air. He was taking too long.

His face breeched the surface, and he gasped and sputtered, but her weight dragged him back down. Right before she pulled him under, he took another deep breath.

He grasped her so hard he felt like he could break her. He tugged, kicked, tried to force them upward, but she fought no more.

No, no—he wouldn't let her go. Not in my hands you won't.

He thrust his legs in vigorous kicks, but they didn't rise far enough. Bubbles escaped from his mouth.

With another kick, he felt something hard under his feet. He pressed against it and pushed. Don't fight the current he told himself. Get above the water. He bent at the knees and pushed off.

His head emerged to glorious air. He held Lucrezia against his chest with trembling arms. Her head bobbed on the surface.

Exhausted, he back floated and guided them to the shallow waters. Soon the shallows gritted against his back. He collapsed with her body resting atop his.

Matteo and several women cleared them from the water's edge. "My Signorina, Lucrezia. She's blue. I…" The cries of a woman pierced through the crowd.

"My baby. Lucrezia, my child." Lucrezia's mother cradled her daughter's head. Fear strained her mother's face. "Move away," she yelled, "she's my child."

Leonardo rolled Lucrezia off him with the help of her mother and Matteo.

Lucrezia thumped in the mud like driftwood. Her blue lips gushed open. She wheezed, coughed, and vomited water.

Matteo shook Leonardo's shoulders and smiled. "You're a hero, Leonardo. She's alive." Matteo kissed him on his forehead, kissed Lucrezia's mother's head, and pumped his fists while strutting around them.

Leonardo tried to lift himself off the ground, but violent shivers made the task difficult.

Lucrezia blinked several times. Her hair was tangled, her dress clumped and filthy. She coughed again and her lips pinked. She placed a hand on Leonardo's chest.

He smiled. "I'mmmm frrrrrfrrrfrreezing."

Matteo pulled Leonardo to a sitting position and removed his dry mantello to cover him. "I'll bring the cart. Wait here," Matteo said.

"IIII prommmise nottt to rrrrun aaaway," Leonardo said.

"Bring me dry clothes, ladies. My daughter and this brave boy need to get warm."

The women wrapped Lucrezia and Leonardo in a collection of mixed wardrobes. Matteo arrived with the cart.

"Her first," Leonardo said.

Matteo bent at Lucrezia's side. "Signora, may I lift your daughter into my cart?"

"By all means."

Matteo scooped her into his arms. He grunted. "You've been eating, Lucrezia?"

Her eyes widened in response.

Matteo returned to Leonardo's side.

"I'llll walk on mmmy own."

"What, you think I can't lift you?" Matteo asked holding his hands at the ready.

"Help mmme stand."

Matteo helped Leonardo to the cart and took the reins. The servants from his house rode in the back with Leonardo, Lucrezia, and her mother. Matteo assured them he would pay for wine at the tavern.

Leonardo waited for Lucrezia to speak, but she said nothing. Was she damaged somehow? Lucrezia's mother held her in her lap and smoothed her hair. Lucrezia stared at the road behind them.

Matteo stopped the cart near the tavern entrance. The women climbed out, Lucrezia last. Her mother held her hands and Leonardo held her under her arms to ease her to the ground. The servant women reloaded the cart.

Matteo and Leonardo entered the tavern. Lucrezia and Leonardo sat in stools arranged in front of the hearth. The woman of the tavern brought wine and stoked the fire for them.

"Leonardo," Matteo said, "I'll ride home to tell what's happened. I'll ask your father to gather clothes for you, then I'll return."

Leonardo sipped his wine. The warmth of it snaked down his chest. "Grazie, Matteo."

Matteo went to pay the tavern woman. "I'll return shortly," he said ready to depart.

Lucrezia's mother rushed after him. "Matteo, my daughter needs fresh clothes. Could you...?"

"Signora, I would be glad to help you, but I cannot go to your house and demand clothes for Lucrezia. Her father would beat me or your servants would distrust me." He rested a hand at his chest. "I can escort you home?"

The signora parted hair from her face. "Though I don't want to leave her, I have little reason to believe I cannot trust your friend. He saved my daughter." She turned her attention to Lucrezia. "Mother will go and return if you're well?"

Lucrezia nodded. "Go mother," her voice croaked, "I'll be here when you return."

Once her mother left, Leonardo said, "You can speak."

Lucrezia shifted beneath her coverings. "Yes. How can I thank you?"

"No need. I'm glad you breathe. That's thanks enough for me."

She gave a weak smile and drank from her cup. "If not for you I'd be gone. It all happened so fast." She whimpered and coughed but continued, "I slipped and my dress weighed me down. I lost my father's shirt."

"I screamed as loud as I could," Leonardo said. "I called your name. You didn't hear me." He noticed tears shimmering on Lucrezia's cheeks when she gazed into the fire.

"I heard you," she said. "But I was too stubborn to listen. You shouldn't have saved me. I was a fool." Her bare arm showed red marks.

"Your arm. I meant not to hurt you. Your head wouldn't rise above the water, so I had to pull. I couldn't let you go."

She offered a weak smile. "I can live with bruises. Grazie for saving me." She pulled her upper body out from the linens. "All this for a shirt."

"Your father can buy another."

"He may never let me out again," she said forlorn. "He always wanted a son. He got me."

Leonardo held his wrinkled hands closer to the fire. "You're a girl of position. You need not tend to the washing like other women."

She shook her head. "Because I don't have to leave my father's house doesn't mean I don't want to. You know nothing of it," she said in a huff.

28

These Chianti hills, the people declared, were blessed with a hero, and the hero's father? "A good quality grape cannot grow without the vigor of the vine," claimed the saved girl's mother. The local's adopted Piero and his brave son as family. Though Piero was proud, Leonardo's act soured his belly.

The boy did honor his family; yet, Piero's thoughts centered on the fact that Leonardo could have died. Francesco looked after mother now—they had each other. Piero rubbed his eyes. Who did he have? He must not overlook his wife, but a wife was not bound to the same vine until she birthed a child, and even then, she would always be her father's daughter.

He clicked his tongue and led his horse to where Leonardo stood along the line of mulberry trees close to the Attaviano house. Alone with his son, he could talk to him about what happened. "Leonardo, you've made a name for yourself here," he said rubbing his chilled hands together.

Leonardo turned his head. "You know how fast news travels," he said dismissing the idea.

Piero stuffed some wrapped food in his saddlebag. "You are my only son. I doubt not your intentions, but it is prudent to stop in the heat of the moment and think with your God-given mind. You could have—"

"Please, Ser. I'm tired." Leonardo's voice quieted as he went back to checking his horse's saddle straps. "I did the right thing."

Leonardo seemed on edge. Piero wanted only to speak of his concern. "I do not deny that saving the girl was a noble act, but I nearly lost you. You could have drowned."

Leonardo's eyes narrowed. "Yes, I could've, and for a moment, I thought I was drowning." His nostrils flared and his face turned red. "I'll not sit and watch another flail as she prays for someone to save her." Leonardo clenched his jaw and glared at him. "And if I did drown? Yes Ser, if I drowned you'd no longer suffer from my flailing, would you?"

Piero fisted his hands as Leonardo sharpened his tongue to lunge again.

"You can't control me. Why did you bother to take me from my mother? Admit that I'm your burden. Tell me you wish you left me with my mother to never see me again. Say it, Ser! Say that I'm your only hope. Admit how it burns you."

"Shut your spiteful lips. I'll not listen to this outrage any longer."

"If you wanted to be my father—"

Piero's insides vibrated. "I am your father." He opened his hand and swung. It cracked across Leonardo's mouth. "No more of this." He turned to his horse but swore he heard a chuckle. Did Leonardo mock him?

Leonardo wiped his face. "I'm glad to know you can act without thinking." Leonardo jumped on his horse and turned it away in the enclosure.

Piero turned his hand over to follow the sting at his fingertips, which traveled up his arm and into his chest. All this time his son never once called him father. "Damn you boy," he said, his arms jabbed into the cold air, "I will suffer you as my burden. That's what fathers do." His words formed clouds, "Your adolescent passion knows little gratitude." He continued to shout, "I give you more than many children can hope to receive. I see to your needs. I do what is best." Leave him. You argue on deaf ears.

Piero tightened the straps around his horse and led it on foot. Before showing his face, he would walk-off his anger and let the morning air clear his head.

Around the bend, the del Caccia girl and her father approached Leonardo. They must have been close enough to hear the argument. Did the Attaviano household hear him screeching like a whipped child? Regardless of what anyone saw or heard, no man wished to get involved in another family's battles. Piero headed toward them.

"Buongiorno, Ser Piero," Signore del Caccia said.

The girl and her father made weak eye contact so as not to intrude or acknowledge notice of what they witnessed. Galeotto looked at them and cleared his throat. "Pardon us Ser Piero, if this is a bad time," he said trying not to focus on Leonardo's face. "We came to thank you again and to say farewell before you return to Florence." His voice softened, "How can a father repay the saving of his child's life?" He shook Leonardo's hand. "Grazie, Leonardo."

"My son acted with no reward in mind, I assure you," Piero said.

Leonardo raised his chin. "That she's alive and well is reward enough, Signore."

***

Piero and Leonardo said their final goodbyes to their hosts. If anyone heard or suspected anything, they did not speak of it. Piero mounted his horse then tipped his hat to Signora Attaviano and Lucrezia. Leonardo rode in front of him. They reached the main road. A familiar soldier whistled their direction.

Piero gave a cursory wave. Marco had gotten his message. "Small mercies," he whispered. Before they departed Florence, he returned to the S. Piero Gattolino's outlying stables. The stable master's ways Piero found cloaked in some sort of crooked mystery, of that he was sure, but the crooked always found a way to make good on profitable ventures.

"Ser Piero, I'm honored you called on me again," Marco said.

"The stable master told me he would send word. He made no promises you would be able or willing to escort us."

"I do my best," Marco said.

Piero made note of Marco's examining eye. He was no fool. Indeed, a man who fought for a living recognized the stench of conflict.

"What battle is this?" Marco asked.

"The kind not of your concern."

"At ease men. I'm not poking my sword in your armor." Marco rode behind them without uttering further sound.

The absence of voices gave Piero peace.

Marco burped.

Piero took a deep breath and stretched his neck. Breaking the silence seemed Marco's greater purpose.

"It's been so long since I ate a proper meal. All the travelling 'round makes a man dream of savoring a succulent roast. I've tired of fish and rabbit. Pig, goat, mmm, I'd love a spiced capon."

"Signore Marco? I'm surprised to see you," Leonardo said. He offered a bit of bread.

"No, no," Marco refused after some consideration. "I'm not surprised to see you though you look different. You're more man than boy now." Marco hummed a few moments. "Boy, don't think me harsh to say your arms and legs remind me of a youngling deer." Marco chuckled. "You'll be tall like your father. Hmm, how long since the first time I saw you?"

"Long," Leonardo said. "But you look the same as I remember."

"Dirty and mean?" Marco asked.

Leonardo laughed. "Yes, I think so."

"At least two years," Ser said.

Marco whistled. "Just like that. Two years gone. Here I am. Still drawing breath in this land."

"This land? Marco, can I ask where you're from?"

"Boy, you can ask whatever you want. You should ask if I want to tell you where I'm from."

Piero pushed ahead of them to let them have their entertainment side-by-side. Let him talk easily with Leonardo—such a simple idea.

"Signore, do you want to tell me?"

"Haha, my boy. I'll tell you if you give me your name again. You see, once a man gets older, he starts to lose his mind."

"Leon—"

"Ah, yes, Leonardo. To answer your question, my home was Venice. I left when I was no more than a boy."

"Marco is a mercenary," Piero called back. He didn't mean to let it slip that way, but there it was. "He's a soldier," he corrected so as not to be petty. "He travels wherever his employer requires his skills."

"He's right. I'm a mercenary."

Piero glanced back at Marco. Marco held his hands up like claws and growled. Leonardo seemed unmoved by knowing the truth, but rather, took it all in play.

"Call me what you will. I have no shame in making my living the best I can."

"You left your home as a boy?"

"All of twenty years I had. Battle will turn any boy into a man, and I was no different."

"You battled in Venice?"

"I did, in a battle at Caravaggio. I'll never forget it. I don't think a man ever forgets his first battle. It changes him all the rest of his days."

"Did you win?"

"Don't get too excited. I didn't win," Marco said with a firm finality that ended the conversation about Venice.

29

Leonardo licked his sore bottom lip again and grunted to himself. Grateful to have Marco as a travel companion, he wanted to get back to the city and away from Ser. Too many times today Leonardo's anger tried to claw its way out. To coax it down, he thought it easiest to forget Ser. But the welt on his lip gave a reminder of a father's willingness to listen and it showed no love, only discipline. He wanted to spit fire every time he looked at the man.

They approached the city gates, and he had no intention of continuing any further with Ser. When Ser stopped to pay Marco, Leonardo pulled his coin purse out from beneath his mantello and continued without a backward glance.

The Porta S. Piero Gattolino congested with people on the way out of the city, but a side entrance had a short line in. Leonardo directed his horse to it, paid his toll, and made his way back to his maestro's workshop. His time in the river weakened his arms, back, and legs, and the long ride didn't help, but time in the city baths would. He arrived not long before the nones bell sounded from each tower and bounced wall to wall throughout Florence to mark the end of the workday.

The bath must wait, for the shortened days of November left him no time except to return home for rest. He couldn't recall his last full night of sleep, but a warm meal and his own bed promised oblivion.

"Leonardo," Dante said, "you're back."

Leonardo removed his mantello and draped it over his arm. "I'm back." He smiled at Dante and assessed the room. From the high-beamed roof to the dusty floors at day's end, all stayed the same. This, his place, filled the air with the smell of damp clay and fresh cut wood, solvents, and paints. When he breathed it in, the bottega was life. From conception to completion, no decay happened here. Order, beauty, fortitude, continuation, this was the interior of the bottega.

Dante stood in front of him. His square chin jutted forward waiting for an answer to a question Leonardo didn't hear him ask.

Dante pulled the side of his mouth into a sort of half-smile of annoyance. "I asked what happened to your face?" He pointed to his lip as a hint.

Leonardo ran a finger across his swollen lip. "My father didn't want to hear the truth."

"A hard truth from the looks of it," Dante said with an apologetic look.

Maestro Verrocchio entered from the back door. He set his tools down and pulled Leonardo in for an embrace. "I'm glad to have you back." His eyes lingered on Leonardo's lip. "Are you well?"

Leonardo averted eye contact under Maestro's scrutiny. "Yes and I'm glad to be back. I need to work."

"I have work for you." Maestro examined him from head to foot. With his hands on Leonardo's shoulders, he searched his eyes.

Maybe Maestro understood he didn't want to talk about his appearance. Did he wait for a response? A confession?

"You look taller," he said. A massive grin stretched across his face. "I have news to make you thankful for having a most excellent maestro."

Leonardo smiled back. "I do have a most excellent maestro."

Maestro handled his upper arms and prodded a bit. "Strong as I thought." He held his forefinger in front of his face. "Lorenzo de' Medici commissioned a bronze David, and here I have the boy who defeated Goliath," he said, eyes gleaming.

"A commission of de' Medici? Maestro, they've come to the right place." Leonardo ran his hand through his hair. "I'm no David." People talked about Donatello's David statue. If he heard right, David was nude.

"You'll be the perfect David. You have a graceful bearing." Maestro rubbed his hands together like a man eager for a gift.

"But, Maestro…" Models posed nude for payment. They showed themselves, all of themselves. "I can't be David. I don't know how to be what you ask."

"You're David, Leonardo. You're my garzone. I know you're a quiet boy and my request pulls you from the back of the room to the center." Maestro took hold of him again. "Do you not trust your maestro? I'd never harm you." He gave Leonardo's arm a shake.

"Maestro, I'll help you anyway I can if you're certain."

"I'm certain," Maestro said. "You're a handsome boy, my son. I'm glad to have you back. The bottega hasn't been the same with you gone."

Leonardo couldn't help but smile at his maestro's enthusiasm. He pulled Maestro in. "It's good to be home."

Maestro and the bottega boys gathered and washed for supper. Maestro sat at the head of the rectangular table. The others sat on long benches on either side. A basket of bread and butter passed from hand to hand. At the other end of the table, a boy named Giorgio spooned soup into bowls, which he handed to the boy nearest him. They passed the bowl until Maestro received his supper first. A platter of chicken followed. Leonardo and Giorgio refused it.

"I can clean it," Giorgio said, "but I can't eat it."

"I can't live with an animal one day and send it for slaughter the next," agreed Leonardo.

Across from them sat Lorenzo, a boy of fourteen, with dull brown hair and a caterpillar moustache. He snatched a piece of chicken from the plate and bit it between his teeth, tore the meat from the bone, chewed, and swallowed. "You two wouldn't be alive if your fathers and those before them were so particular. Man needs meat to survive. It's a way of life." He gave them a disappointed look and pulled another chicken thigh from the platter resting in front of him.

"You may be right. But now the day has come when a man can choose what he'll eat," Leonardo said, "and the minestrone soup is delicious."

Maestro called from the other end of the table. "Yes, delicious soup, Giorgio. With cook sick today, I agree, you've done well."

"Maestro, the cook should be worried, he may be out of a job," Francesco, a boy with a hooked nose said. He laughed and elbowed the older boys next to him. "Have you seen Giorgio's drapery sketches?" he asked the group.

Giorgio pointed his finger out to make an accusation and began to laugh, which sent several boys laughing. "I may not be able to sketch drapery well, but if someone should have need to see pigs humping under a blanket, then we can present him my drawing."

"Easy now," corrected Maestro, "if he could do all things I ask of him so well, he'd have no reason to be here." He tossed a chicken bone aside. His eyes danced. They all waited for him to share what he found amusing. "Sometimes a maestro needs to laugh. Your sketches can make a maestro feel young again." He laughed boisterously with his boys. "But before one of you dare comment, I'll have you know that pigs are entertaining, yes, but they're not for anyone who intends to find a patron." His voice dropped to a serious tone. "If I find that you're wasting your time trying to please yourself or anyone else with such worthless work, I'll have a thankless job waiting for your special talents." Maestro drained his ale. "Giorgio will learn."

Giorgio lifted his goblet and toasted, "To no clothes."

The boys held up their goblets. "To no clothes."

The candle flames danced from their movements and cheers.

"Whatever you do without your clothes is private business, boys. Keep it that way. Make good choices and don't disappoint me, your families, or yourselves," Maestro said. He stood, patted his belly, and left the dining room.

Leonardo tipped his goblet back and swallowed. Maestro faded into the darkened stairwell. And what happens when a group of boys come together? Learning of the highest order. He laughed to himself. Maestro wouldn't have him pose naked, would he?

***

Leonardo woke before daybreak. A sliver of moonlight cast on the floor across from his bed. He sat under his blankets and peered through the darkness, breathless. His member throbbed. He rubbed his eyes. The dreams wouldn't stop. Bodies tangled together, the same grinning mouth, wet lips on his lips, his ear, his neck and fingers. They touched so lightly he burned under their sweetness. He wished he could let them go, but the harder he tried to escape the dream, the more it surged against him.

He dropped back onto his mattress, pulled his pillow over his face, and moaned. Hating himself, he stuffed his pillow back under his head with a couple of punches. How long before he'd be saved from temptation? Where was the sun?

Boys slept in beds next to him. No one moved or made a sound, except for one boy on the far end who snored. It couldn't be too long until morning. He stared at the black ceiling searching for distraction, but all of his attention focused on one thing. The ache robbed him of his rest and threatened his resolve. It made him crazy. He thought of anything—anything plain, dull, the darkness, wood, rocks, cold water, knives, storm clouds, hot pokers, pinchers, burning flesh, blood...

No longer could he ignore it. He reached his hand beneath his blankets. If he let himself release, then the dreams might stop haunting him. As soon as he touched it, there was no going back. With his free hand, he fisted his bedding to keep from crying out. He stroked more and grunted. His toes tingled, his legs tightened, and he exploded. His vision turned white to stars in brown eyes and a crooked grin. Let me rest. Please, go away, Matteo. Leonardo let the waves soothe his distress.

He rose from bed and quickly poured water from basin to bowl on the side table. Cool water splashed against his sweaty face. He scrubbed his hands, rinsed his mouth, and ran back to his bedside trunk. The trunk's creak might wake someone, so he took care opening it, and removed a clean tunic and hose.

A clean tunic dropped below his waist and he sat on the edge of the bed to put on his hose. Giorgio, two beds down from him, stirred and popped his head up. Leonardo pulled on his hose and waved.

"It's early," said Giorgio in a loud whisper. "What are you doing?"

Leonardo held his hands up in answer. He didn't know. Think, think.

Giorgio got up and sat beside him.

He could tell Giorgio thought him up to no good. "I'm going to the baths when the prime bell rings so I can be back by the morning meal," he said quickly.

"Sure," said Giorgio.

Leonardo eyed him. Yes, he's suspicious. Distract him. "I'll be the first to get hot water."

Giorgio's eyes popped wide. "I'm coming too." He stood.

Leonardo grabbed his purse out of habit then realized someone could steal his money at the baths. Distractions make you hopeless, he told himself. He set a few coins out on his pillow and shoved his purse under his mattress.

By the time Giorgio dressed, washed, and gathered his money, the prime bells rang to mark the start of a new day. The other boys woke. Leonardo and Giorgio told them they'd return before the morning meal and left the bottega for the city center.

"I don't know if you've ever been to the San Michele Berteldi baths on the via dei Pucci, but that's where I intend to go."

"I follow, you lead," Giorgio said. "If you know where to find hot bath water, I'm interested in going to the place."

Never before had Leonardo been inside one of the city's bathhouses. Some of the older boys deemed the San Michele baths pleasant and social, and no surprise why, the bathhouses were reputed locations for prostitutes and their clients. But these couldn't be the only people who wished to bathe. His housemates claimed that a priest bathed there, so he found no reason to worry.

A skinny but clean man stood in the entrance to the building. He announced the baths open. He took payment and directed the boys to a room on the left.

Giorgio went first. "Signore, how hot is the water?"

"I know not, but you can start in the vapor baths. It's warm in there."

Light-colored squares decorated the tile floors, and on the walls, innocent bathing scenes of men, women, and children talking, playing, and washing embellished the walkways. Serving maids dressed in simple, knee long tunics carried trays with jars of pleasant smelling herb mixes and oils for applying to the skin. They turned right into a smaller room used for changing. Benches and hooks lined the walls.

The boys began to undress. A man entered the room. He removed his clothes fast. Leonardo and Giorgio smiled at each other. They stood in their mutande while the man jiggled out of the changing room naked as the day he was born. The plume on his velvet hat bounced in rhythm to his strides. They laughed.

Giorgio slapped his belly. "See you in there."

Leonardo pulled back the heavy felt curtain that sealed the sweat room shut. A man dressed in a tunic and leather apron entered behind him carrying pails by yoke. He ladled a scoop of water over the heated rocks. Steam hissed and whirled around the hatted man and Giorgio. Leonardo sat on a bench across from them closest to the steaming rocks. He closed his eyes and let the sweat beads roll over his body.

Awhile later, Leonardo stood to leave the curtained tent. "If I stay any longer, I'll faint, and I don't need you telling all the bottega boys about it."

Giorgio wiped his upper lip. "I'll leave with you in the event you weaken in the knees on the way out." Giorgio wavered a bit and caught himself by gripping the curtain. "Ha, I wouldn't want to miss a good story to tell."

They exited the vapor bath and Leonardo found a serving maid. "Could you tell us where to find the pool?"

The maid led them down the hall past the changing room. Straight on, a double entry opened into a great pool with a bubbling fountain in the middle. "Would you like anything else?" asked the serving maid. She held her finger out and pointed at them, "A private room?"

"No," blurted Leonardo crossing his hands in front of him, "We're not together, not like that." The painted ceiling depicted a sky filled with cherubs. "I would like a sponge," he said, attention back on the maid. He glanced around the pool again. Several men and younger boys sat in small groupings enjoying drinks and conversation. Two men nestled in a more discreet corner; one leaned his back against the other's chest. Another man held bunched leaves and beat the bundle against his skin. "What are those?"

"Good for the blood." She held one out. Giorgio took it and whapped Leonardo's back.

Leonardo smiled at her. "I'll take one, grazie." He gripped it hard in his hand, spun around, and whacked Giorgio behind his knees.

"Owwww." Girogio howled and laughed.

"How's the blood now?" Leonardo grinned. He thought of how his blood thinned when Maestro thrust David upon him, and until he tested his meddle, he couldn't know the response he'd receive from others. No one wore garments in the pool. Leonardo casually walked to a poolside stool that rested in front of a beautiful wall hanging full of sea nymphs. He removed his mutande, took a few deep breaths, and turned to face his fear. They couldn't know his desire for Matteo.

No one took much notice of him. Giorgio sat in the water scrubbing his arms with a sponge. An older boy approached and sat next to him.

Leonardo climbed into the pool and rested beneath the fountain. The water poured over his shoulders as he washed and rubbed lavender oil over his skin. Giorgio and his friend waved to another boy who walked into the pool area. Giorgio must have told them he came with Leonardo because the three of them looked his direction at the same time.

Leonardo finished washing and dunked under one last time. The boy with black hair looked his way when he rose from the water. Leonardo couldn't duck now, for the surface hit only above his knees. He approached Giorgio and his friends. Water sloshed between his legs.

"This is Leonardo da Vinci, friend from the same bottega as me," Giorgio told his friends. "Leonardo, this is Lionardo Tornabuoni called Il Teri, and his friend, Pietro."

Leonardo sat. "Pleased to meet you, Signore," Leonardo said, all too aware of the prestigious man, albeit, a boy from a leading family of the city. Il Teri was the boy with the black hair who watched him. His nose turned upward at the tip, which fit the arrogance that dripped off him like rivulets of water. The boy wore a delicate gold chain about his neck. The way his dark eyes lingered on Leonardo made him uncomfortable.

"My pleasure meeting you, Leonardo. That name should be easy to remember," he said with a cursory smile.

Leonardo turned to see what caused the laughter that erupted from the group of men at the other end of the pool. When he turned back, Il Teri caressed Giorgio's shoulder and ran his fingers down his side. He pulled away when he noticed Leonardo watching.

Il Teri dipped his hand in the water and splashed Giorgio and Pietro. "Do you come here often?"

"No, we've never been here before today."

Il Teri and Pietro looked at each other and found something between them amusing.

Leonardo refused to play into their tricks. "Please excuse us, but we need to be getting back to work." He stepped out of the pool, covered himself, and looked for Giorgio. Giorgio stood beneath Il Teri's overhanging head, which bent to kiss him on the mouth.

Giorgio turned and searched for Leonardo. He carried something shiny in his hands.

They hurried to the changing room and dressed. Giorgio stopped in the doorway. "I have to confess something."

Leonardo slipped on his shoes and waited for him to speak.

Giorgio held a chain in his hands and placed it over his head. "I've been here before. Only once. With Lionardo. He told me that he loves me months ago. And I love him." Giorgio smoothed his hair. "I beg you, tell no one. It's not that I'm ashamed. I just don't want any trouble."

"I'll tell no one. What's there to tell?"

"There are people throughout the city who wish to persecute people like me." Giorgio's faced paled. "We're not hurting anyone. He brings me pleasure, and his gifts are generous."

"Your secret is safe with me."

30
December 1466

The next day, Maestro Verrocchio returned to his bottega with a boy called Il Secchio. "Cosimo de' Medici's tomb is near to perfection," the boy said. He carried Maestro's box of chisels, hammers, and other tools to a workbench while Maestro walked from one garzone to the next. "Though I've been gone most of the day, your maestro will see the work done beneath his roof." He approached Giorgio, who sat next to Leonardo.

"Maestro," Giorgio said, "Leonardo showed me how he does his metal point etchings. Here, look." He lifted the small panel at an angle on the tabletop. "Already better. Wouldn't you say?"

Maestro patted Giorgio's shoulder. "I agree. It's much improved." He ruffled Giorgio's hair.

Leonardo set his silver-pointed style down and sat upright so Maestro could view his work. "I added white to the drawing to show the light."

Maestro lifted the panel to look. He held it a long while then nodded. "Leonardo, when I look at this, it's true to life. It says to me...soft and hard, quiet yet forceful, beautiful." Maestro pinched his forefinger and thumb together pulling his hand sideways across his chest. "Perfetto."

"Perfetto?" Leonardo's breath caught in his throat. The praise struck him like lightning. In the bright light, he envisioned his grandfather who gave him sweets when he was little. He popped one into his mouth. "Do you taste it?"

Nonno asked, his voice thick and sticky. Leonardo rubbed his belly in delight. "Mmm, now you know the sweet life, my boy." Nonno talked in simple words that made no sense then. Yes, Nonno, now I understand. I can taste it. I can truly taste it.

The boys sitting nearby turned when they heard the elusive word spoken by their maestro. Leonardo searched in disbelief for the source of its mystery. Everyone in the artist's botteghe talked around perfetto, but few discovered its sweetness. It wasn't something one grasped in his hands; rather, perfetto slid inside the skin and spread its majesty out like rays of the sun.

"Write your name on the page. For your esteem," Maestro told him. He wrapped his arm around Leonardo's back and turned the panel for all to see. Maestro removed a sketch from the wall to hang Leonardo's in its place. "When you surpass the work hanging on this wall, you too will have a place to display the best of the best," he told the boys. "Learn from those before you." He held his arm out wide in introduction to his challenge. "Surpass them I tell you. For I'm no maestro if you can do no better than the one who taught you."

Maestro handed Leonardo the drawing that once rested on the wall. "Tomorrow, Leonardo, you're ready to paint." Maestro walked away.

The boys crowded around Leonardo to congratulate him with bumps and shakes. "You may be the first we know of, but you'll not be the only one to get your work on that wall," said one of the older boys.

Once the festa-like moment ended, Leonardo examined the picture Maestro removed from the display wall. The drapery's highlights came from the absence of charcoal, not white. On the bottom, in small lettering, he read the name A. Verrocchio.

Perfetto. A proclamation. Proof he belonged here.

***

"Leonardo will sit here, next to Il Secchio." Maestro waited for Leonardo to take his seat next to the four boys by the window. He draped a linen cloth across the top of a chair, arranged branches of leaves, a glass orb, a woman's necklace, and several books. "Make a sketch many times in many ways. You may think you know it well by the time you finish. But don't be fooled. Close your eyes and see it in your mind. When it comes to you as clear in your mind as you see with your eyes, draw it again. This is the way of excellence."

"Maestro?" Domenico said.

Maestro held his hand up to show he wasn't ready for questions. "If you wish to paint, you can't be lazy. No twiddle here, twiddle there. Painting's not your midnight mistress, she's your wife. If you place your brush wrong or dip into a bad color, ugliness will come upon you." Maestro slapped his hands together and the boys laughed with him. "You reach for the brush only once you see her beauty in your mind and eyes." Maestro sat on his stool and pulled his paper closer. "In this bottega, there is no other way." He began to draw, and they did the same.

The sunlight spilling through the window shifted many times before Leonardo closed his eyes. He pictured the lay of wrinkles in the cloth, folds, the glint of the necklace draped across a large book, and the two smaller books stacked on top. The orb he could see, bright when the light struck it, smoky on the inside. A branch of dried leaves rested against the backbone of the large book. Leaves covered the title of the topmost book bound in reddish leather; a single leaf curled and hung over the edge of the seat. His eye, his mind, his hand, this was seeing. Little hairs on his arms rose. He opened his eyes and started drawing the scene again from memory.

A hand touched his arm. "Leonardo," he heard somewhere on the surface. Leonardo finished the last bit of shading and set his charcoal down.

"Leonardo?" said the voice again.

Leonardo turned away from his work to see that everyone had gone. "Yes?" he asked, unsure of who called him.

"I need your measurements," Maestro said.

He missed something. "What?"

Maestro waved him over. He held a ribbon-like spool in his hand.

"Maestro, I don't understand."

"You're David. I need to measure you for your costume."

A costume?

"We talked about this. Don't look surprised." Maestro flicked his wrist and his ribbon unspooled. He stretched it across Leonardo's shoulders, around his chest, waist, legs, and took his height. After each measure, he called out a number to Giorgio, who wrote it down in a small notebook.

"What am I to wear?"

"I hoped you could help me figure that out. Do you have any ideas?"

No. "Something with trim. A breastplate?"

"Good," Maestro said. "Keep an eye out for the head of Goliath."

"No need, Maestro. I know where to find him."

31
January 1470

Could two months have gone by? Two months without a father made Matteo more responsible than fifteen years with one? What cruel joke was this? As master of the house, Matteo stayed busier than he thought possible. Everyone under his roof consulted him in all things, numerous, but necessary. The allocation of monies for payments, expenses, charity, and the payments due him resided in his father's ledger. Thankfully father kept it well tended.

Matteo sat at his father's desk and let his attention wander from the ledger. He remembered a time when his feet dangled at the supper table and he kicked them about carefree, but now, Father's chair simply swallowed him.

He turned the chair to the familiar crack near the floor that crept up the wall to the window. Outside, snow, smooth and untouched, covered the ground. Frost painted the trees blinding white. He never liked winter. Its frigid cloak hid the living behind a wretched white masked as something pure that could freeze one to death.

He stood and walked to warm his hands by the fire. Father's fur-lined cloak wafted the sweet musk of sage. He pulled it to his face. "I can smell you, Padre. Are you with me?" A shadow stretched long outside the door, but no one answered.

Every day, Matteo studied the stained floor in thought—a gift that saw him through these long days and nights. No one could remove it. He wanted to believe it a foresight of God to remind him he wasn't alone. Like the salutation of a letter, the inkblot ended in a flourish. Matteo smiled. In the firelight, he thought it a mangled sea creature caught in a torrent, and at another angle, it morphed into a sea nymph. When he studied it, he considered life, as it should be, with a father and a son, together.

His apprenticeship required he return to Florence, and he must carry on father's vision. The last night they had together, Padre grasped his face with trembling hands and said, "Our blood's wrapped in silk. It's strong. Stronger than death."

Mother, he knew, could manage the household without him. But if he left, she had to stay. Who else could they trust to protect all father achieved? Matteo hung his head. No matter his choice, he'd fail one or all of his duties as a son and a head of household. He couldn't forfeit his training, nor he could skip his duties at home. He climbed the stairs to find his mother.

He knocked and cracked open the creaky door. "Mother, we have to talk."

"Come in. You can help me."

Mother reached into father's chest. Her canopy curtains had been opened and small piles of clothes lay separated on the foot of her bed. She rubbed her lips together and eyed him, "You're becoming a fine young man, son," she said. "I decided to go through your father's clothes." She set a finger against her cheek. "A few things may not fit you for sometime, but I think you'll wear them well like your father."

"We can't rummage through them like they don't matter. I...I want them all."

Mother turned to look at him. "You can't hold onto everything. He's gone." She reached her hand out to him. "You have to accept it."

"I know he's gone." He held his breath to keep his composure. "But if we remove his things, one day will become another and another until there's nothing left."

Mother's posture wilted. "You can't hold onto material pieces of him forever." She started to cry. "There are men here who have worked for your father half their lives. I thought it would be a kindness to give them something."

"Don't cry, please. It is kind of you to think of them." Matteo pulled her into his chest. "I try, I do, and seem to think only of myself."

"You want to give nothing away, and I can't live with the reminder. It saddens my heart."

"Then I'll take only what I need. But tell Father's men it was your doing. Give me no credit for your kindness. I want to do what's right. You know better than I." He hesitated and sat bedside. "Mother, when the weather turns favorable, I must return to Florence."

Mother didn't show surprise or fear. Instead, she wiped her eyes and regarded him in the way he'd seen her do with his father so many times before. "I agree. You must finish your training. As head of the household, you have obligations. But you're too young to give your dreams away." She sat next to him and waited for his reply.

"It was father's dream before it was my own. Everything weighs heavy in my mind." He paused. "I want the right answer."

"Beautiful boy, there's no right answer. Not everything comes with a book or philosopher. You have to find some answers for yourself." Mother ran her hand through the strands of hair that dipped in his eyes. "You have a year left of your apprenticeship?"

"That's right. The work is worthwhile, but the pay's a pittance. Thank you Lord for giving us the virtuous Lapo Attaviano. Without him we would be beggars." He made the sign of the cross. "Father said that as a maestro's son, I soon would be a master workman. But I'll still be able to fill my duties here." He grasped Mother's hand. "While I'm away, I need you to do what I cannot."

Mother folded her hand over his and squeezed. "I'll do whatever it takes to give you the chance you need and deserve."

Matteo pulled his mother to him again. "Mamma, grazie."

They held each other a few moments. "Mamma, what do you need?"

Her lips trembled and she sighed. "I need you to continue to make me proud. And I want you to come home often. A widowed woman needs her son."

32

Did a happily wedded man flee from his bedside and wife? Piero could only blame himself for the past eight months. Francesca made a good match and came with a handsome dowry. Facts aside, her undeniably girlish face searched his for understanding, direction, perhaps a connection? She confounded even the wisest of men. Her body, fresh as spring morning, left him flaccid as an autumn twig. He was far from old. For the love of God, he must be crazy. Pull yourself together! Many a man would willingly have her.

His bowels clenched at the thought of her youth. She could outlive him, or worse, they might have a long life together without passion. But all saw their coupling well wedded, for rarely did one find a marriage consummated in love. She didn't have to love him, but she did have to please him if they were to live together the rest of their days. His first marriage counted more blessed than many. Piero looked to heaven. Perhaps living came easier in the terms of a contract. A contract made no demands for love, and as written, Francesca fulfilled her portion.

Try, you desperate ass. And he did, but his wife was built different. If voluptuous women were cathedrals, women like Francesca were the private chapels. The intrigue of what he could not yet see led him close, and she gave entrance when he could pry open the gate. How proud her mother would be to know she continued to close her eyes and remain still and rigid, meek and passive beneath him—cloyingly innocent. So much so that his sex went soft, and when he failed to proceed, she peeked her eyes open as if waking from sleep.

So she didn't understand when he flipped her onto her stomach to fondle his cock. It was the only way, and if she watched, he did not rise beyond thoughts of defect and failed manhood. She could touch him anywhere, and he would rise like the tide—if she would touch him.

"No," she cried, and pushed him off. "It's a sin, Piero. It's the way of the sodomites."

"I would never." Piero removed himself from her and tried to stay calm. "I will never sodomize you, Francesca." He helped her sit up and ran a hand across his forehead. "There are many ways to…" He moved his hand in a circle. "To get it in the right place."

She held her hands in her lap and stared at them. "Why must you touch yourself?"

Because you will not, he wanted to say. Piero folded his hands in his lap for concealment. "I cannot enter…if it's…not firm." He could see her outline in the darkening room. If she were to look at his face, he would be blood red. He bent forward, his elbows on his knees. "It may help if you could relax." If she received him, touched him, encouraged him with her body, held him, he knew he would respond.

"I'm sorry," she said, voice quivering.

"I can put my clothes on and touch you gently until we find what you like."

She said nothing.

His chest pounded. If she knew how he felt, she need not fear. He reached for her hand and placed it on his chest so she could understand. But when her hand brushed against his hair, she yanked it back, rolled across the bed, and covered herself.

How could he be with a woman who revolted against his body? He sat staring at the wall and ran his hand around and down his chest. Was he unattractive? He had a little bit of a gut, but everything else was muscular and firm. Ah, everything? Everything but one thing. He looked at it hanging, useless.

He could forget about fathering children with her. He produced a single son in fifteen years. Once he had passion, felt free and lustful. Then he made a son. Now he reflected a stranger of his younger self. He watched his shadow contort on the wall and soon heard the slow, rhythmic breathing of his sleeping wife.

How long could he play the eunuch? Not any longer. His last days with Albeira continued to haunt him and newer days brought more sadness. Never in his life did his cock shrink with such an ache in his balls.

Piero tightened his belt under cover of darkness. He crept away from his room to keep from waking Francesca. He glanced back at her sleeping face. Bellisima Francesca with the flowing light hair that curled around her big eyes and small breasts. On her pillow, beside her head, laid her hand, ringside up. It reminded him of his commitment. He slid out the bedroom door. You must reclaim your manhood.

***

If he arrived in time, he could order a strong drink to drown his better judgment. Piero hurried to reach Del Buco before the bells tolled and met curfew violators with fines. Aptly named The Hole, the small, tucked away tavern provided discretion not far from home or the Ponte Vecchio. Street noise distracted notice of his personal business.

Inside, several men sat at small tables drinking and gambling. In a curtained corner, a woman led a man by his hand, pushed him down on a chair, and tugged the curtain shut. Piero chose a table to the side with no candle. A man approached.

"A drink, Signore?"

"Yes, I want the strongest wine you have."

"You plan to stay upstairs?"

Piero nodded. "I have never been here before, Signore. Could you tell me where I choose a woman?"

The man pointed to a side counter next to the stairs. "When you're ready, you come to me and I'll take you there. We'll see what you can afford."

Piero swallowed his heady drink. The bells tolled. No going back now. The head below his belt whimpered. If he waited too long, he would have to choose from hags. He finished his drink in a few large gulps. When he rose, his head floated in slow motion. He went to the counter.

The man who approached earlier made marks in a ledger. He peered up from his work. "Business-minded. I like that. We're alike, Signore. Business, pleasure, for some it's all the same."

Piero lifted his purse. "How much for the best woman you have?"

The panderer's cheek lifted and a click sounded from his mouth. He measured Piero. "That depends on what you like. The older ones know some tricks that'll not disappoint."

"No, not old. Young, pretty." He needed to pound something warm, but he had to be able to look at her and feel arousal. "Signore, I have money. Could I see them and choose? See, I have particular tastes." He jangled his full purse on the counter.

The man's upturned lips betrayed him. Piero knew better than most how everyone had a price. He saw it daily.

"For a decent man, I'll show you. Follow me."

The panderer led him up the creaky stairs slick with candle wax. They reached a sala of sorts. Many women and two men turned their attentions on them. The women ranged from gray-haired to what Piero considered girls. Their clothes varied from bright to drab. Their strong smells mingled together like overpowering herbs at the apothecaries shop.

An older woman slinked over and rested her breasts against her maestro. She held Piero's chin with her fingers. The panderer shoved her away. "No, you're too old for his tastes and too cheap for his purse." She shrieked and thrust her arm out with a rude gesture, but the panderer waved her away. "Anyone older than twenty-five or younger than seventeen, step aside."

"But I don't know how old I am," said a younger girl neither pretty nor ugly.

Piero cringed. He shook his head when the panderer looked at him to determine her chance.

The panderer shrugged. "Step aside, stupid girl."

Four remained. A young man made the cut. "Only women," Piero said. If a man touched him they way he wanted to be touched, he would beat him and report him to the authorities.

"No such luck," the panderer said to the harlot. "I know he's what you like. Tall and dark. Soft hands. Too bad. Not tonight."

A short woman with ringlets in her hair and a round face waited. Her sizeable breasts could topple her over. No. A woman with brown waves cascading down her back held her hands at her hips and watched him with dark eyes, long lashes, and pouty lips. The third and youngest reminded Piero of a mouse. Small with skittish eyes and thinness at her neck made him think of the poor. No. "Her," Piero said pointing at the woman in the middle.

The panderer smiled. He snapped his fingers at Piero's choice and led Piero into the hallway. "Never talk money in front of a woman, especially a whore." The panderer drummed his fingers on the windowsill. "She comes at the highest price, but for you, since it's your first visit, I'll give you a deal."

Piero held his purse ready.

The woman eyed him over her shoulder and prowled down the hall.

"Fifteen soldi for the whole night, but you get her for twelve."

Now he knew why desperate men chose older women. He hesitated. How could anyone afford it? Men often took a mistress—too messy. They may have them, but they couldn't afford them. And this is why you have a wife, he thought, but the pull in his balls cared not.

"If she's too high, you can have another. If you need the cheapest fuck, cover the old one with her skirt and pay me three soldi."

"No," said Piero, "I am not that desperate." Below them something shattered. Men yelled.

The panderer shrugged. "You have excellent taste." He made a lascivious sound with his tongue. "You're in for a night, Signore. Only men of means get my top-price ladies. I think you'll not be disappointed in your choice."

"Twelve soldi?"

The panderer tapped his finger again. "They'll do whatever you ask if you treat them well." He could tell the man grew impatient. "Twelve soldi," he said setting the coins out in two stacks. "And I was never here."

The panderer laughed, "No one ever is." He pocketed the coins and led him to her room. "If you want to eat or drink in the morning, you pay more." He opened the door. "Meet La Viola."

Piero stepped into the room. The man shut the door.

La Viola already removed her dress and wore nothing but a linen camisa, which veiled the darkened circles of her nipples beneath. Candles lit the room in a hazy glow. The room had one shuttered window offset from a bed in the corner. Next to the bed, a table held various jars and oils. A stool sat in front of the table. A worn chair filled the opposite corner, and a line strung from one wall to the other held a few hanging garments.

La Viola smiled and fluttered past Piero to lock the door. She ran her fingers along his neckline at the back of his head. Her eyelashes blinked and she brought her mouth close to his ear. "What do you like?"

Piero's skin prickled beneath her warm breath that wafted sweet grass under his nose. He cleared his throat. "First I want to look at you."

"Yes," she purred. "You look and I'll wash you."

He gave no answer but she took his hand. She may not have realized she need not guide him to make him follow. Or maybe she did, but he couldn't take his eyes off her now. He sat on a stool next to the bed. La Viola pulled a basin from behind him and poured water into it. She removed his shoes and slid her hands up from his feet, his calves, knees, and thighs. He moaned. The slowness of her hands made him hot on the way up, and she removed his hose and mutande with the same finesse on the way down.

She dropped a sponge into the basin, loosened the neck of her camisa, and slid her body out. Her curves plumped in all the right places. He took in the site of his cock. It stood erect and proud. Asking to look first may have been undue torture, but he had to be sure he was still a man. The whole night he could have as much he wanted or needed to test his desire to feel the passion that once filled him, to see a beautiful woman who encouraged him.

La Viola stood and turned for him to behold the view. She licked her lips and ran her hands down his body to lift his clothes at the waist.

Her warm skin brushed against his as she worked. His camicia cleared from his head, and her breasts surrounded his face. He held them in his hands and kissed one then the other.

She waited for him to finish and bent for the sponge. Straddling one leg across his lap, then the other, she brought the sponge above his groin. Her eyes softened and her lips parted open.

He prayed not to come when she lifted the sponge between her hands and squeezed. He bit his lip hard and tasted blood. The water spread over him as she gently rubbed, a confident look upon her face. He watched and waited, not limp, holding his blow. He placed his hands on her hips and ran them down the curve of her ass while she placed the sponge between her legs. His fingers dug into her flesh as she washed.

"You have a name, handsome?" she asked dropping the sponge to the floor. Her finger ran down his chest and she leaned her breasts against his.

"Marco. My name is Marco."

"Tell me what you like, Marco," she whispered in his ear.

"I want to take you here," he said, his breath jagged.

"Yes, take me how you like, Marco."

He licked his fingers and moved to wet her, but she caught his hand.

She raised her eyebrows. "You're a good lover. Not like other men." Her pouty bottom lip puckered. "I reward kindness." She sucked his finger into her mouth then lifted her hips. With her other hand, she guided him into her wetness.

He thrust hard.

***

After the morning bells tolled, Piero woke and clothed himself. He found something regrettable in leaving a sleeping lover without saying goodbye, but he knew nothing of her. He wanted to tangle himself in the bed linens wrapped about her waist. Though exhausted, he knew he could perform again.

Instead, he cinched his belt tight to yank his mind back to reality. If you linger, you will be seen. He unlatched the room door and stepped into the hallway. Downstairs, he swaggered to the counter and bought wine to quench his thirst. The final sip down, he heard a familiar voice.

The panderer drew near. "So ready to leave. Was she not to your liking?"

Piero knew he grinned like a schoolboy. "She was all I wanted and more."

The panderer slapped the countertop. "Satisfied fuckers bring good business. Come back and you can have her again."

The thought of it sent a twinge down Piero's spine straight to his cock. "I have to go." Too much of this could not be good for him. He pulled his hat snug over his head and hurried down the via Lambertesca. One more street to reach the Piazza della Signoria, and he would escape detection. He hurried away.

"Ser Piero?"

Piero thought he recognized the voice but decided it a trick of his mind, so he continued his brisk walk.

"Ser," said the voice again.

Once obscured by the shadow of a building, Piero glanced back. Matteo. The boy jogged closer. Piero turned away quickly and shook his hand to signal the boy mistaken. He walked with haste, and though he feared being caught, another part of him reveled in his latest identity. "Marco's the name," he called. Don't poke your sword in my armor, he thought. Laughter welled up from within him. The meat was succulent.

***

Piero passed his workplace to the east side of the city, and why not? His continued exertions drained negativity and invigorated him thoroughly. He could keep last night burned in his memory and call upon it when he needed motivation. The thought of last night might bring him as good a return as the initial investment. He filed his Marco identity away as an afterthought, but the thrill of his deviance pinged below his belt. An afterthought? He always created files to open more than once.

His excessive activities left him half starved. He bought two spiced raisin pastries and wolfed them down. For some men, the houses of harlots served as a lesser evil, but not for him. His livelihood depended on honesty, consistency, and a credible face. A man had nothing if he lacked good face. Now he must retreat to what seemed mundane, and put on the face that brought him respectable work and everyday comfort.

In a mature frame of mind, he berated himself a damned fool and realized where he headed. He and Leonardo were not much different. Piero remembered his youth—wanting to please his father—having things he would not, could not share with him. His thoughts hit him like shards of crumbling stones. Son, I acted without thought. Can you forgive me? He could call himself the lesser. Tell Leonardo of his sinister passions. Son, my only son.

Leonardo's purity showed Piero his false dignity and made him envious. And Francesca? If ever he found a living penance, he discovered it by carrying these upstanding people at his side. His poisonous trap of a soul rotted the pastries in his stomach.

"Buongiorno Signore, Maestro Verrocchio is not in."

"I am looking for my son, Leonardo." Piero peered around the workshop.

"He's gone with my maestro."

Piero pulled his hat from his head. "Gone? Where have they gone?"

"To the San Silva monastery." The boy pointed. "Outside the city gates."

"When should they return?"

The boy shrugged. "They left right after prime."

Piero pulled open his purse strung at his belt. "I need to pay for my son's keep." He poured coins into his hand, counted payment, and looked for ink. He tore off the upper portion of the paper tracking his expenses, and made show of keeping a count for his records. He wrote the identifying information on the larger piece of paper and folded the coins in the small one. "Give this to your maestro when he returns," he said. "I should leave a message for my son who I've not seen in many months."

The boy nodded. "I'll give him your message."

Piero searched for something else to write on but found none. "Tell him his father came to speak with him and requests he respond without delay." Piero paused, "Tell him I apologize." He placed his hat back on his head. "Grazie." He walked to the doorway, stopped, and added, "Tell him I will be working or at home."

On the way home, and for good measure, Piero stopped in La Badia chapel to light a candle for those he hurt most.

33

"Maestro Verrocchio, a payment arrived today and I have a message.

"Thank you, Lorenzo," said Maestro handing his notebook to Leonardo.

"Maestro, how was your day?"

"The monastery is well pleased with the sketches for Tobias and the Angel." Maestro wiped his forehead. "All went well during my absence today?"

Lorenzo nodded and handed him the folded paper. "Ser Piero da Vinci's payment for Leonardo. He brought it this morning."

Leonardo thought his father had forgotten him all together. He squirmed under Ser's looming reach. "Maestro, I want to pay for myself. I don't need my father's money. Please, send it back."

Maestro set the coins on the table in front of him, studied Leonardo's face, and set the money aside.

Lorenzo added, "Leonardo, your father left no letter, but he did come to speak with you not long after you left this morning. He said he was sorry and to respond soon. You can find him at work or home."

"The harvest. He must have need of my hands on his land. Ser gives nothing freely. I know no other reason." Maestro and Lorenzo waited for him. He didn't mean to rattle aloud.

"No matter your father's reasons, you have money to pay for yourself?" Maestro said in a tone that cast doubt on sound reasoning.

"I do, and I'll get it now." Leonardo ran up the stairs to his bed and lifted the mattress. He opened his purse. Many would say a father had a duty to provide for his son, and Leonardo agreed, but one less tie to Ser let him breathe a little more free. Ser taught him planning and forethought, which now allowed him to refuse further support. He counted the amount owed, shoved the purse under his mattress, and returned to his maestro.

Maestro smiled when Leonardo set the coins on the tabletop. "I admire your ambition," he said, "If this is what you want, I'll return your father's money." Maestro pushed the money back and waited.

Leonardo didn't waver. He pushed the money across the tabletop. "Return it."

Maestro wrote an explanation at the bottom of the letter, refolded the coins inside the paper, and set it aside. "Tomorrow I'll send it."

"Grazie. Maestro I can't thank you enough for respecting my request." Leonardo took a deep breath and thumbed his lip. File that, Ser.

***

Matteo sat across from Leonardo in the Inn. He hoped, as a friend, Matteo would go along with his plan. Leonardo took another bite of vegetable soup then swallowed the rest of his wine. Knowing Matteo, the exciting prospect of trouble would outweigh the consequences of any actions he proposed. "I'm glad we could meet for dinner. I have something important to ask you."

Matteo gave him his full attention.

"Under the latest turn of events, would you like to return home with a friend?" Leonardo gave a weak smile.

Matteo set his drink down. He bent inward scooting his plate forward and grinned. "No need to ask." Surprise brightened his eyes. "How do you not have to go to Vinci?"

"I sent Ser's contribution toward my education back. The messenger took it this afternoon." Leonardo sat back in his chair and folded his arms across his chest. "I'm not going with him this year. He's not had interest in me for so long. I thought he released me—forgot me, but now he wants me back."

Matteo shook his head. "He'll not allow it. You know it. I know it."

Leonardo nodded.

Matteo wiped his lips. "How soon do we need to leave?"

"Soon. Before he can stop us. And Maestro insists I leave according to the contract Ser signed. He'll not violate it." Leonardo bent forward and lowered his voice. "My plan is to tell Maestro that Ser's message is as suspected—that I need to depart for Vinci." He thought a moment. "Do you think Maestro will forgive me?"

Matteo pointed at him. "You've never talk to your maestro about your father. He'll forgive you if you tell him true."

"I never thought I'd lie to him," Leonardo said.

"A lie that protects a person is not always bad. You have what, almost sixteen years now? Your father should be proud that his son is capable of living without him."

Matteo grinned, which pained Leonardo's heart, but was meant to set him at ease.

Matteo continued, "You know, this is a sound plan considering you just made it. The men and I already made most of the provisions for our departure." He finished his last bite of stew. "I'll talk to my maestro and ask if I can leave a little early. But you have to give me at least a day. I need to tell my escorts that we leave tomorrow or Thursday."

They stood to leave. Leonardo placed his hand on Matteo's shoulder. "One more thing. For the plan to work, you must send a letter to tell me when we depart."

"Sure," Matteo squeezed Leonardo's shoulder. His eyes glimmered. "I'm going to lose sleep from excitement."

***

Leonardo made his first stop at the Stationer's for parchment of the same kind Ser used. That night, he delayed his retreat to bed. The last person awake in the bottega, he worked to forge Ser's hand. To the last detail, he dripped wax from his candle onto the folded edges, and pressed it with his thumb. No matter the improper seal. They cracked off sometimes when opened. If not, he'd scrape it off before giving it to his maestro.

He tucked the letter in his tunic and started up the stairs. Carry the letter at all times for the moment of opportunity, he told himself. He awaited Matteo's readiness now, and when word came, he'd give the letter to Maestro and pack his bag.

The next morning, a message arrived for him. He couldn't back down now. Read it then bring it straight to Maestro, and don't look him in the face. He tried to calm himself. It must have been Marco who once said it was good that soldiers were long dead when the bugs and worms writhed inside their guts. Leonardo wasn't dead, but he felt them. He checked the area around him. Away from the bottega boys, he opened the letter.

Leonardo,

All is ready. Meet me at the Oltrarno side of the Ponte Vecchio tomorrow morning after the toll at prime. Look for four riders and an unmanned horse, which is your mount for travel. Food provisions are packed. Travel light and swift before anyone grows wise to our deception.

Don't forget to say your prayers,

Matteo

Leonardo walked behind a table stacked full of panels and wood. While concealed, he quickly swapped Matteo's letter with the one he forged. To act like he forgot something, he gave a punctuated stop, turned around, and changed course toward Maestro. "A letter arrived from my father." He held it out and looked only at the back of the open parchment. He knew he must look Maestro in the eye else he'd know he played him false.

Maestro finished reading and returned the letter. "Your father takes his contracts serious, and so do I," he said looking up to recall information. "He wants you earlier than usual." Maestro tapped the letter. "I can't say no, but do let me say that I eagerly await the day when you can decide to stay and work with me."

"I do too, Maestro."

Maestro let out a deep breath. "I'll wait to continue work on David until you return."

Leonardo shook his head and thanked his luck that his head didn't burst. The hair at the back of his neck dampened with sweat. "I'll return in a few weeks." He prayed Maestro would forgive him.

Leonardo packed that night, ate a filling supper, and went to bed early. The next morning he woke to the sounding of the bells. He sprang from bed, washed, dressed, and found Matteo according to plan. They arrived at Matteo's house late that afternoon.

***

Matteo's household required additional food and drink for the unanticipated arrival. Cook prepared the wagon for market the next day. Bitter faced, Cook said nothing when

Matteo suggested he and Leonardo ride behind the wagon and follow him the entire way.

Cook directed the wagon past them and further into the market.

"Now he's happy," Matteo said. He held up his hands and waved Cook off. "I never thought us bad company." Matteo tied up his horse.

Leonardo shrugged and watched Cook go about his business. "As a weed needs water, old men need their traditions."

"Speaking of traditions—" Matteo tipped his head. "I don't think she's seen us. Let's surprise her."

They wove their way around and behind horses, women with wide skirts, between market stalls, and rushed toward Lucrezia, Matteo in the lead. She must have heard their descending footfalls because she whipped around ready to strike. Matteo ducked away from her fists.

Lucrezia's wide eyes returned to their normal size and she glared at them. "I felt your evil eyes on me. Do you make a habit of chasing girls in the company of their fathers?"

Leonardo, now in the center, shook his head no, but looked to Matteo to answer.

Matteo's mouth curved into an evil grin. "Not a habit, no. Where's your father?"

She pointed at him in the blacksmith's bottega. "I know what you do, Matteo." She shook her head with half closed eyes and sighed. "I'm asking Leonardo if he chases girls." She brushed a wavy lock from her face, "Well?"

"No Signorina," Leonardo said. "But I am in the habit of noticing people who stand out in a crowd." He shook his head realizing what he said.

Lucrezia pinched her lips together to hide her smile.

"No, I didn't mean in that way. I—" Leonardo swatted the air and hoped his face wasn't pink.

Lucrezia focused on Matteo. "I was this close to hitting you," she said lifting her fist close to his face. "And maybe I should."

Matteo leaned his head forward to touch her hand.

She pulled away.

"Once you marry me, you can hit me all you want," said Matteo, "it could be our game." He seemed proud of himself and added, "Not to worry. I'll play fair and not lock you away like a proper woman."

"Matteo Attaviano, I am a proper woman!" Her face reddened.

"No," he considered, "not yet."

She jutted her chin out. "Have you found your goldsmith's girl?"

Matteo's spirited face went flat. His lip snarled. "You know nothing of it. I've not seen her. I'm not looking for her." He rubbed his hands together and fired, "Why? Are you jealous?"

"Why I—" She straightened her skirts. "I've never met a ruder boy than you."

"I've never met a girl like you who walks in public like a common woman. I know why you do it. Do you?" Matteo looked at Leonardo to help her answer his question.

Leonardo shook his head. He couldn't help but watch the two of them take their stabs back and forth. Marriage between them? A terrible idea.

"I hate you," Lucrezia said, calm and sharp. She swished her skirts and turned to walk away.

Matteo struck again. "You think you're a boy." He laughed. "The fairest boy here, but still you want to be a boy." He jabbed Leonardo in the arm to try and bring him in on his prod.

Leonardo backed up. No way would he get in the middle of this thing that they did.

Matteo smirked. "Maybe you wish to be a countrywoman selling her goods at market?"

Lucrezia stomped her foot and rushed at him. "Only you would know what they sell," she said blushing. "Girls talk, Matteo, especially about ignorant boys like you." She poked her finger between them.

"You're not as wise as you think," Matteo said breathing down her face. "Let's go, Leonardo."

The boys turned to depart from Lucrezia. Leonardo glanced over his shoulder expecting her to be gone, but she stood watching them.

Matteo glanced back and growled. "Look at her. The devil beast actually smiles. Why do I think I like her?" He hit himself upside his head. "Steer around that one."

"Yes. She's small, but she has bite. What about the goldsmith's girl?"

Matteo stopped walking. "The goldsmith's daughter tricked me. Gaddea offered me her plump breasts." He made an approximation of size with his hands. "Well, you look sympathetic."

Leonardo did feel something. "Are you well, Matteo?" It shouldn't matter, but he had to ask, "Did you touch her?"

"I swear on the Virgin." Matteo shrugged. He looked at Leonardo and changed his tune. "Yes, I touched her. I couldn't help myself. She startled me."

"Oh," Leonardo said, not surprised, but disappointed and worried. He stopped thinking about the way Matteo could've touched Gaddea. "Matteo, if girls talk as Lucrezia said, then you may find yourself in a bad position. Why would girls want to spread information like this? It can only hurt them."

"Because they're foolish and dangerous."

"I don't like it."

"Nor do I," Matteo said.

"Lucrezia wouldn't tell anyone, would she?"

"I think not. I hope not, but she did say she hates me. If they told the wrong person, I would've already heard about it, or worse, I could be condemned to marry Gaddea." He thought a moment. "That was near what, three years ago. Lucrezia heard it from someone. I hope the goldsmith's girl. Then it's not spread across the countryside. Girls more than anyone know to be careful of what they say because others will use it against them." Matteo rubbed his face. "Gaddea knows that I like Lucrezia. Troublesome. All of them are jealous creatures. No wonder their fathers keep them inside." Matteo started back from where they came. "What in hell?"

A man ran down the piazza followed by a young woman, another man in close pursuit behind her, Lucrezia's father behind him, and Lucrezia chasing her father. Lucrezia's father shouted, "No. Brunello."

"That's Gaddea," Matteo said surprise on his face.

Matteo and Leonardo made chase. They ran close to the edge of town and caught up to the turmoil. Soon, many people in the piazza followed.

"You ugly, rotten, whoreson!" yelled the man named Brunello, who cornered a young man. "And you," he shouted again focusing on the girl, Gaddea.

Lucrezia's father grabbed hold of Brunello causing him to fling his arms about.

Gaddea sobbed. "Papa, please."

"You have no right to ask anything of me. I call you daughter no more. You're worse than a whore. You shame me. Your family is ruined." The man's face turned purple. "Release me, damn you. Damn you all! This is none of your business," he yelled to the many people now crowded around.

Lucrezia's father held tight though Brunello bucked like a madman. "There's a way. He'll marry her."

"One of her lovers jumped out her window and ran for his life," Brunello said, "Worthless whore that she is! Another man, this piece of shit cowering in the corner, he too entered beneath my roof."

The cowering man stood, broke the purse strings from his belt, and tossed it at Brunello. "For her dowry," he said.

Brunello spit his direction. "You owe eighteen Florins. One for each year of her life you've turned to dust."

"Signore," replied the man, "I don't have that kind of money."

"But you will marry her," Lucrezia's father said. "There's no other option for your dishonor or hers. And you'll pay your new father a Florin each year until your debt is paid in full. Take her under your roof and pray for forgiveness from your sins."

Gaddea looked at her father and her lover, closed her eyes, and prayed.

"Let me go so I can count the money," Brunello said, no longer raging. "If we're to have a deal that saves them, I want it to be known what he owes me."

Lucrezia's father released him.

Brunello opened the purse and counted two Florins and small coins. "This is an insult I can no longer bear." He turned toward the man. "You'll find your bride in hell." In a couple strides, Brunello tossed the purse, pulled a dagger, and reached unsuccessfully for his daughter's lover. "Who else touched her?" he screeched.

Leonardo looked away and spotted Lucrezia balled-up in her gown on the ground. Tears poured from her eyes and she mouthed, no. Her attention focused somewhere behind him. He craned his head back to see Matteo, pale, and hidden on the fringes of the crowd.

But Lucrezia didn't tell.

A gasp thundered through the crowd followed by a female shriek, which echoed off the town walls. Leonardo couldn't see because the crowd hemmed in.

"It's all I could do." Brunello wailed. "For my family."

"Brunello, have no further shame," a man told him.

The crowd broke up and stayed clear of Brunello. A few people ran ahead for the authorities.

Leonardo located Lucrezia's father. He scooped his daughter into his arms and carried her away. Matteo must have moved again. Leonardo looked behind him to make sure he hadn't circled around, but instead, he saw a blood bath. Brunello held the body of his murdered daughter. He wore her blood like Satan and covered the slit across her neck by lifting the outer portion of her skirt.

Brunello would go to prison until he could explain. In no time the authorities would probably absolve him of his deed in the name of honor, as these things went.

Leonardo's own blood boiled from the madness. No amount of shame should force the hand of any father to shed the blood of his loins.

34

"How will he live with himself? He killed his own daughter. We all stood there, helpless, guilty of doing nothing to stop it," Leonardo said, his words ash on his tongue. The vision of what he witnessed woke him many nights. Instead, he urged his horse forward and tried to focus on the road lined with cypress and pine trees that stretched tall among the scattered underbrush.

Matteo clicked to encourage his horse up the final hill to Florence. "We could do nothing to save Gaddea. Be mad, scream if you must. Brunello should have taken the money and swallowed his pride, but it was too much to ask of him. Gaddea brought on her own shame. You think she's above her actions?"

"No, but she shouldn't have been murdered," Leonardo said loud enough his horse's ears flicked back. "Her father asked too much of his daughter."

"And what would you have done to change what happened?" Matteo raised his voice, "Don't you realize it could have been me there next to her? I didn't do anything she didn't invite. The blame lies with her."

"No one did anything right. Every one made bad choices, but Gaddea paid the highest price. Under guard of their male relatives, why are women blamed when their purity becomes dishonored? It's easier to point the finger rather than accept the father's deficiency," Leonardo said as fact. "Some decisions people make are deplorable. They're meant to injure, to oppress, to violate, and it sickens me." He waited for Matteo to look his direction. "I never wish harm upon you. Please, just be careful."

Matteo nodded. "Lucrezia chose to spare my name, and I'll not forget her mercy."

"Nor will I. Real honor has many faces," Leonardo said, "and it manifests before anyone is watching." He thought of the tears streaming down Lucrezia's face. If she hated Matteo, she could have done away with him. "She's proven herself a woman of virtue and a true friend. You have to protect that bond."

Sometimes Leonardo thought Matteo his only friend, and he knew why. Trusting people was hard. Dangerous. No one could go a lifetime without placing his trust in someone, but was it fair to rely on one person to fulfill his needs? He knew where he'd he be without Matteo. Not to see him caused an ache far worse than when he did see him. To have no one cast a worse fate.

Now he must face the punishment for his lies. He regretted them but had to know if anything changed between him and Ser. Until now, he didn't realize he acted to test him, and he had his answer: Ser didn't come for him.

***

Leonardo entered Maestro's bottega. He barely reached the stairs when Maestro's stern voice shouted his name.

"Turn yourself around and get out until you settle the deceit you inflicted on your father. I've nothing more to say until you make it right."

"Maestro, I'm sorry I lied to you, but there was no other way. I—"

Maestro barreled toward him. "Out. I'm more than disappointed."

The bottega boys gained renewed interest in their work. Leonardo cringed. He became a plague in his home?

Maestro's hands pressed his back and pushed every few steps to force him out the door.

Leonardo swung his head around before Maestro dumped him on the street. "What if Ser Piero does the same as you?"

Maestro didn't answer.

"Where then will I go? You know I belong here, Maestro."

Still he didn't answer.

Leonardo's heart raced. "Maestro? I want to be here."

Maestro shoved a small piece of paper into his hand. "Take it. So you can find him."

Leonardo's feet slid into the street. "Maestro?" Maestro no longer faced him, but planted his feet in the doorway so that Leonardo viewed his back. Soon Maestro faded into the darkness and Leonardo stood motionless for some time. He read the paper. The neighborhood of the Piazza della Signoria? Of course Ser chose to reside in the seat of the government.

Leonardo couldn't have guessed the outcome of his return. His mind raced from one thought to the next as he made his way to Ser's house on the via delle Prestanze. An apology, though right, meant admitting guilt, and he'd not apologize for his existence.

He found Ser's house and knocked on the door. Knotted thoughts filled his head. Do it. Apologize.

A house servant opened the door. "Please, tell Ser Piero Leonardo has arrived." He waited in the doorway, a stranger by choice.

Francesca entered the sala, glanced around the room, and located him in the entryway. "Leonardo, your father has business, but if you'd like, I can keep you company until he's finished. Come inside and wait with me." Her violet dress tucked in at her thin waist formed perfect folds. She sat in a chair oriented to view out the window. "Sit, please."

He didn't want to sit, but avoided rude behavior so as not to make his situation worse. He sat in the chair beside Francesca. She looked at him and twisted a curl of blonde hair resting against her elbow. "This is one thing we have in common."

Leonardo didn't want to play bond with your mother, so he looked out the window.

Francesca's skirts swished and her oversweet scent wafted in Leonardo's face. She fondled the rings on her fingers. "Your father delayed the trip to Vinci because of your trick." She sighed and placed her hand on his forearm. "As your mother..."

So taken aback by her lead-in, he heard nothing more that spilled from her lips. She was not his mother and he would never see her as one.

Ser escorted a man to the front door and said goodbye. He shut the door and his cheerful tone shifted. "Leonardo, I wondered how long it would take for you to return and show your face. Your deception hurt more than the people beneath this roof. Your family in Vinci—they know who is to blame. How could you do such a thing to us?"

Leonardo stood. "I'm sorry," he said and waited for a blink, a twitch, something to let him know that Ser accepted his apology, but Ser continued his glower. "I'm not the sole person to blame, and you know it," Leonardo said, undoing his apology.

"And your Maestro? You lied to him. Did you see him when I came for you? The look on his face said everything." Ser pushed the pins in deeper. "Maestro Verrocchio apologized for you. The misunderstanding as he called it, was a slight foremost against me, he said, and he asked that I not think bad of him for falling into your trap."

"I never meant to hurt him."

"But you did, Leonardo. And now you hurt others and yourself further because you must return to Vinci. We have work to do. The family relies on me as its head, and you as its son." Ser's hands firmly cupped Leonardo's shoulders. "Fidelity to family is the cornerstone of life."

"If the family needs you, why did you not go to them?"

Ser released his grip. His eye squinted whether he realized or not. He searched for an answer meant to cause pain. "I waited on you because your Maestro said you would not be welcome under his roof until you came here. How then could I leave?"

"Take your hands off me," Leonardo said wanting to get away from the skilled talker that could turn everything back on him. Ser was no mystic, but his clever moves concealed his cruel ways like smoke. The closer Ser pulled him in, the worse the pain he caused when he pulled away. "I could have been gone longer. How did you know when I'd return?"

Ser's eyes widened. "I am more resourceful than you think. Prepare to leave in the morning." He brushed past Francesca and walked away. "Oh, and the money you sent back went to good use in your absence. I sent it to my brother so they could hire workers to help them when we could not." Ser left.

***

About a month later, Leonardo returned to Florence. He'd beg on his knees, outside, in front of all the bottega boys, in a hair shirt, naked, beaten, if Maestro would take him back. He recited his apology one last time and entered the bottega to find his maestro.

"Leonardo." Giorgio welcomed him in an embrace. "We thought you gone for good. Il Secchio searched for you. No one knew where you went."

"I hope to come back to work. Forgive me, but I have to go straight to Maestro."

"He's working on the bell in the back."

Leonardo went to find him. He nodded and waved to more familiar faces, which seemed happy enough to see him. Maestro poured plaster into a large wax mold, set down his bucket, and shook the mold side to side. He lifted his head, noticed him, and hurried over while wiping his hands. Maestro pulled him close.

"Maestro, I never meant to hurt you or drag you into my lie. I know it wasn't right, and I know you expect better of me. I'm sorry." Leonardo paused and continued, "When you sent me away, I knew more than ever what I should be doing. I want to be successful. I want to make you proud. I want to love something for its sake and no other reason. Please, can I come back to work?"

"You're a son to me. Where have you been? You never sent word, and your father never responded. I searched for you," He shook him. "I've worried that I abandoned you until now." Maestro looked him over. "You went to your father? You settled things with him? You're well?"

Leonardo shrugged. "I did go to him and I apologized. We went to Vinci and I labored hard. I ran because I needed to get away from him. He'll never hear what I have to say. He's difficult and confusing. Can you understand?"

"Of course," Maestro said. "Whatever your problems, you can talk to me. You can trust me, but, you can't decide who your father will be any more than the next boy. We all have to tailor our clothes sometime or another for a better fit."

"I was desperate and angry. We're bad for each other."

35
May 1471

The day Leonardo went to the cathedral workshop with Maestro, the rector unrolled the cupola plans and told them to use them well. "Brunelleschi's hoists and cranes will be used again?" Maestro nodded, and from that moment on, the plans possessed Leonardo. Maestro brought the plans back to his bottega, and Leonardo couldn't help but pour over them. He knew he must take part in Maestro's commission, and the way to do it was to understand the devices that would carry him all the way to the top. So he studied the plans morning and night and knew how to assemble the scaffolding better than anyone.

***

He worked unhurried today, the thirtieth of May, the final day on high. He closed his eyes and waited for the view to replay in his mind. This, the well of memory would swell like water to nourish him when he needed it.

Laughter spilled forth from the hopes and dreams of the child. It was the nature of a boy to change himself into anything, to believe, to be unfettered by his grown visions. The boy sometimes carried the man. No longer did Leonardo stand in the shadow of Il Duomo; he stood at the heights of Brunelleschi. The view was magnificent.

The wind caressed Leonardo's face and flapped his clothes like wings of a bird. Below, the crowd reminded him of flowing leaves caught in torrential waters. He could see far beyond the city gates, over the valley hills, to where earth and sky became one. Here he peered into the mind of a great man, who did build high enough to touch heaven.

Maestro's men finished their bread and wine and readied the ropes holding the lantern and cross. Leonardo steadied himself on the platform, tugged on his harness, and gave two thumbs up. He helped hoist the lantern and cross to Maestro and the men waiting to solder them in place.

Soon cheers and song reached his ears from the crowd gathered below.

Canons blasted, trumpets blared, and Maestro joined with, "Blessed be the day!" He and the men lowered themselves from the top-most point. Maestro thanked his assistants for their efforts and embraced Leonardo.

"You make it difficult for me to consider leaving your bottega, Maestro. How could I ever do better than this?"

"I never said I'd make it easy for you." Maestro placed his hands on his waist and took in the view. He hooted and turned to Leonardo. "Let us laugh in the face of those Greek Gods. This is a worthy challenge."

They laughed and shouted into the wind of their victory. If only Ser could see him now.

***

The next summer, Leonardo went with Maestro, Sandro, and Filippino Lippi to the church of Santissima Annunziata. A representative for The Company of St. Luke wrote Leonardo's name in the red covered ledger. Next to his name he read his title: Painter.

"Thirty two soldi for your membership," the representative said.

Leonardo set his money on the table. He'd officially call himself a painter once he stepped out the church doors.

Maestro smiled and tapped him on the back. "Now you're a member of the confraternity. You have many brothers listed in his book." The four men acknowledged one another.

The representative offered a congratulatory hand. "Signore, I welcome you to the Company."

The men stopped for drinks at the nearest inn. Maestro and Sandro discussed their commissions while Leonardo and Filippino added a comment here or there in response to their maestri. Given Leonardo and Filippino's positions next to their maestri, they eyed one another's success. They too could rise to distinction. Filippino had more time to wait, for his sixteen years, meant far less practice with a brush, though his father may have set him toward painting before he could walk. Filippino's illegitimacy mattered not; he shared the name of his talented father. Leonardo took pity on him that would forever walk in the shadow of a father's great name. He gave silent thanks for living without this struggle.

Maestro stood. "We must return to work. The day is young, but never for the man who grows old. Buongiorno, Sandro." Maestro tipped his head at Filippino, placed his hat on his head, and walked back to the bottega with Leonardo.

Leonardo returned his notebook to the small desk in his room above the bottega. He went downstairs and pulled up his stool. In front of Maestro's commission, the Annunciation painting, Leonardo examined his progress. As a student and maestro collaboration, they never finished the work before Leonardo gained the privilege to call himself painter. Early 1473, more than a year since commissioned, Maestro must deliver it to the monks, whose patience did have limits. Leonardo gazed over his shoulder then back to the painting. Someone stared at him. He looked again and focused on the bronze statue of his younger self, Maestro's David.

The Leonardo. That's how he thought of it. The boy's upturned mouth mocked him. Leonardo sneered back. You're forever stuck in time, and I'm on my way to freedom.

A familiar voice slithered across the bottega. Ser smiled and made small talk with the boys he passed. He carried a bundle of cloth in his hand.

"One day in, the next day out," said Leonardo wondering the purpose of Ser's visit. Ser had no reason to come when his son flew back to him like a moth to flame. Leonardo wished he could chisel the smile off The Leonardo's face.

Ser reached an arm out for him the way friends did. "Everyone on the farm asks how your painting goes?" Ser lifted a bundle. "Carlo and his boys made good on their threats and chopped down the fig tree that kept trying to grow in their window." He unwrapped the bundle and held it out. "From it, Carlo made the buckler. He asked if I could bring it to the city to have it painted by the family artisan." Ser's single eyebrow rose in question.

Leonardo took the buckler and examined it. Warped, it lacked skilled construction. "I'll do what I can with it. It's not the best cut of wood." He swallowed hard. "When do you need it?" Never did Ser ask him to make anything not related to notary duties. This could be their olive branch.

"Whenever you can get to it."

Carlo, a man of good humor, would enjoy the thought of him painting creatures of fantasy. Leonardo would show the family what Ser's son could do. "I'll call when it is ready."

36

Summer 1473

Matteo's itch needed scratching and he couldn't relieve it at home—not after what happened to Gaddea. Who wanted his private life open as the mouth of the town crier? He heard the malicious women's words and took what Lucrezia once said as warning: girls did talk. But every man had certain needs, and none more so than a man in his prime.

Matteo guided the horse wagon along the cobbled city street and replayed his conversation with his mother. She mentioned this girl and that girl from good families and asked him what he thought most important.

"Dowry or the girth of her hips?"

A young man should have this conversation with his father. He ignored his mother until her list of names ended with Lucrezia.

"Ah, I know she holds your attention." Mother balled her hands at her chest. "You have some time, but since you have much, many parents have their eyes on you as a match for their daughters. Lucrezia's of age."

Matteo closed his eyes and shook his head in frustration. "I'd make a premature husband now. Do you want me to remain in the cradle of men's minds for another ten years of my life? I've had enough of the jokes about undescended testicles." He glanced at his mother, whose cheeks blushed. "I need time, Mother. Let me earn my merits." He kissed her cheeks. "I leave in the morning. When I return, can we not talk about brides?"

He didn't want a bride. He wanted to continue his visits to Vanni's tavern. Every time he thought of marriage he couldn't breathe. Inhale the free air while you can, he told himself, taking a few deep breaths.

He arrived at the church stables of the Florentine Palazzo and halted the horses to lead them in by foot. Blinded by the darkened entry, he paused to let his eyes adjust.

The stable boy with the curly hair he'd seen many times before approached and held his small hand out for payment.

Matteo held his money ready. He liked the dirty boy well enough though he never asked his name. He set the coins and a sweetmeat in the boy's hand.

"Grazie, Signore," came a squeal of surprise.

Matteo smiled. "Boy, I must take my silk to the Inspector. If you come with me to deliver it, there will be more to squeal about. Once I make my delivery, you are to return the wagon here until I return. Can you do this?"

The boy shrugged. "My sister could do it."

"Would you like me to ask her instead of you?" Matteo scanned the stables for her. "Sister of the dirty boy? Where are you?"

The boy gave him a nasty eye and snuffed. "They call me Massimo."

"That's a strong name," Matteo said in appreciation. "I can see it fits you. Well, perhaps when you grow a bit more and brush your hair," he teased. Matteo tugged his purse strings. "Help me Massimo, and when I return, you'll have your reward."

"I'll do it." Massimo climbed into the wagon and grabbed the reins.

"No, not yet," Matteo said climbing after him. He slapped Massimo's hands from the reins. "This here," he said pointing at the padded bundles tied tight in the back, "is too valuable to trust to over-eager hands. You take the reins after I unload."

The boy nodded and sat beside him. They turned the wagon, rounded the corner, and rode onto the street.

They passed the Palazzo de' Lamberti, of the Silk Guild Consuls, with its yellowed walls of stucco, glassed windows, and lavish frescoes representing the work of good men. The arms of the guild on the tower of the residence displayed two closed doors at the center surrounded by a wreath and putti. Matteo stopped in front of the large workshop. "You keep the horses here until I remove my goods."

Massimo's face pinched.

Matteo repressed a laugh. He could almost see himself younger, staring back. He removed a load of the bundled silk and lifted the awkward mass onto his shoulder with a grunt. He turned to Massimo, "Don't move and don't touch anything, understood?" The boy answered by raising his hands to show him he did nothing but stand next to the horses.

Once Matteo removed the last bundle from the wagon, he called to the boy, who tossed stones down the street. "You've done well, boy. Off you go. I'll return before day's end."

Massimo sprang to life, hopped into the wagon, tapped the reins, and rode away.

Matteo hoped the price list posted by the Consul would be higher than last year. "Where's the price list?" he asked the inspector, who pointed to the wall behind him. Matteo studied it. "Better than the insult of spring." He helped unpack the silk cocoons.

The inspector weighed them and kept count. "The total weight today is five hundred and forty one pounds." He showed Matteo his calculations.

This part of Matteo's work tried his patience. "I have no need for credit, Inspector. Give me the money so I can leave this insufferable place."

The inspector's face puffed out like a knotted sleeve hung on a drying line, and he thought the man's face might flatten if he poked a finger in his cheek. Sadly, the inspector exhaled and counted the money out on the counter.

The inspector annotated the amount in his ledger book along with all information regarding their transaction.

Matteo opened his purse, held it up to the counter, and slid the money in.

"Signore Attaviano. Enjoy your day."

Business finished, money in his purse, Matteo walked to the city center. Across from Il Duomo, stretched a representation of Florentine private and commercial interests: the piazza, botteghe, houses, inns, and taverns bulging with foreigners, merchants, travelers, peddlers, priests, servants, porters and carriers, beggars, gamblers, pickpockets, children, whores, and the like.

On Matteo's first visit to the tavern, he asked for Vanni and heard laughter from the men around him. He'd never forget his grotesque fascination with the old drunk, who lifted his head when laughter jolted him awake. The man waved his hand to the right corner. He hiss-laughed. "If you want food, go there. If you want to eat, go there," he said wobbling on his stool and pointing to the other side. His directions were confusing. The old bastard. He gripped Matteo's arm and kissed his cheek with his acrid lips. "A handsome boy like you. Stay away from the doors at the back. Those fields are plowed all day and night."

No longer new to Vanni's tavern, Matteo went to the left and paid a high price for more privacy and a fresh face. The first time, la Chiavetta told him he had soft hands, and now that he knew how to use them, he had the confidence to make demands in choosing his woman. It would be la Chiavetta, his favorite, or the one called Cera. And because they came at a high cost, they worked no more than a few times a week—"to keep them attractive and valuable," according to Vanni, who "understands value."

Why would he want a wife unseen? It wasn't right of him, but he had to know if the woman he took under his roof would be compatible in more than his eyes. Damned itch. A man might count himself fortunate to see his betrothed's face before her family pushed her to accept the nuptial ring.

37

Piero left La Viola early to return home and change his clothes before work. He turned his key in the lock and jumped when the door swung open. Francesca waited on the other side.

She wore her dark mantello hooded and wrapped about her cloistered body. The edges of her white nightgown rimmed her bare feet. She lifted her legs onto her chair, drew her knees up under her chin, and sniffed the air. "You smell like a woman." She glared at him and embraced her legs. "A man may have his mistress," she said, "but a wife can divorce her husband for his failure in the marriage bed."

Piero closed the door and turned to face her. "My failure? Do continue, wife. I want you to get the attention you think you deserve." He knew not what, but something made her proud.

Her chin set hard. She rose from her seat. "You underestimate people, Piero," she said raising her chin higher to see his face. "Well, we do have one thing in common."

He latched the door lock. Curious, he waited for her opinion of their commonality.

She stood firm. "Neither of us could care less how many bastards you bring into the world."

He blinked, slow. No woman would threaten him—especially one who rejected him. How he despised this woman. He smacked her across the cheek.

She screeched and held her hand to her face.

Piero snarled and bent to meet her eye-to-eye. "You will never speak to me this way."

She shook her head and hid her face in her unbound hair.

He lifted her chin so she would look at him. "Your mouth is such a weak line of defense. Thin as the slit that separates your cold, hard lips." Piero burrowed into her tear-filled eyes and felt nothing but hatred. "I have never abused my conjugal rights with you, you ungrateful woman." He fisted the front of her clothing in his hands and pulled her closer. The tip of his nose trailed down her chin, neck, and back up to her ear. "I could take you day and night if that is what I desired," he whispered.

Francesca whimpered.

He inhaled her scent and shoved her away. "But you please me none."

Francesca tried to flee, but he stopped her with an outstretched arm. She cowered against the wall.

"I have not failed you, Francesca. You know not what you speak. Maybe you have forgotten. Shall I remind you?" He ran his hand down a lock of her hair. "Your maidenhead is mine. But your womb is barren by choice. Is it not your duty to birth my children?" He waited for her answer, but she said nothing. "Tell me, what becomes of a woman who fails to please her husband?" His teeth ground together the same way Francesca's hair smashed between his fingers.

Francesca's glazed eyes and tamed confidence allowed him to back away from her.

"Forgive me, husband," Francesca said dropping to her knees.

"Never again will you forget your place. I am your maestro, and you will obey me. Now leave me and speak no more."

Francesca got up and ran from him.

Piero punched the wall. His marriage? A damned failure. He could find no betrayal in the agreement. Bitter barbs of regret, yes, but he could not betray one who never gained his confidence.

There were many ways to manage a woman who thought she found her head. Now that Francesca knew she lacked the faculty for cleverness, he would finish her. Piero went to his studiolo and wrote the document before she made her morning visit to the chamber pot. He sent for her to meet him at his desk.

She looked at the floor. "What does this mean?"

"It means you have the status of a married woman, but you will live chaste as a nun. Therefore, you hold no ill-will against your husband, who intends not to take advantage of you, and you will not take advantage of your husband in any way that degrades him in his generous conduct of you." Piero pressed his palm flat on the edge of the parchment. "Sign," he said.

Francesca read the remainder of the document. She glanced from the document to him and back again with a dazed look on her face.

Piero dipped the quill and placed it in her hand. "Sign," he insisted.

Francesca's bottom lip trembled. "If this pleases my husband." She signed on the line.

From then on, she lived sheltered and quiet as a ghost under his roof.

More than ever, the nights stretched long and wide in the shadows of the painful wife? Life? What mattered the difference? All ghosts haunted Piero. Francesca's presence reminded Piero of charitable giving he could not afford. He wriggled under the pinning of another poor decision. Poor decisions make a poor man. To pay for them, he sold bits and pieces, then more, until his soul became smaller while the expanding anger in his chest gouged out the remaining light. He wished to regress time and find easier days, but when he searched those records he found the truth: his anger and fear became his weapon and shield.

Years passed in separate beds, separate rooms, separate lives, and once the doctor spoke of influenza, Piero treated Francesca like a plague—not far removed from their routine living condition. As her wretched husband, he paid and paid for those who brought his wife comfort. He decided it a kindness to maintain the distance that sustained them over their marriage.

He should be sorry for many things, but not Francesca's passing. Fever, and coughing wracked her frail body, so he comforted once her malaise ended.

For the sake of them both, he spent no effort in asking why she was taken from the world. No matter the reason, he was chosen to stay—maybe to honor her memory and redeem a shard of his soul. Never again would he be enticed by foolish eyes or restless loins.

***

He carried a pitiful candle flame to light his way through the bottega's darkness to the lockboxes. Perhaps his lot in life was to sidle alone in the dark. Many a man would say he could start again, but Piero thought the idea ill-conceived. Man found no fresh starts unless he could cleave out pieces of his mind. But no, he carried his anger, his sins, and his fears on his shoulders like Atlas. Piero laughed aloud. He was no god. He was hardly a man. Francesca what have you done to me? He would remove the last evidence of his rejection from the records inside the lockboxes.

He set the written corner of Francesca's signature in the flame and watched their final agreement burn. It smelled sweet and lit the room in a bright blaze before turning to ash.

He unlatched all the locks and opened every lid. As his candle flame swayed to and fro, he found the records without gain for his sickness and frowned at the irony of his position. You barter, sell, write, and speak from the affliction of self-preservation. He thumbed through the documents and returned to his personal file. Do not be afraid, he told himself scanning the parchment rows around him. As proof is your witness, you are not alone.

His file held so little, and what it did contain was incomplete; the final page, a Transfer of Property. Written in his hand at the top it read, "Upon death…and to my son…" Blank. No name, no appointment.

He gathered his documents and noticed the one at the front. An agreement he made half a lifetime ago. How he loved Albiera and wanted her back, but what if he had the balls to go back on the arrangement? What if he told his Father no and followed the path he started on—a proven one at that? What if he married Caterina? Would he have a house filled with sons? Would he feel joy? He could not deny the poor woman had little to offer him but her love, which he now recognized as greater than a dowry built on bought alliances and affections.

Do what needs to be done. Do what is right, he told himself. Fill the hole. Piero set the candle as a weight on top of the document, uncorked his inkpot, and added: Upon my death and to my son, Leonardo di Ser Piero da Vinci…

For as long as he could remember, he hid behind the damned laws to protect him. They made him untouchable. He wanted his wives to be better than him. None remained, only Leonardo, and this hope must carry him.

He shuddered. If his life showed truth, the truth ripened him ugly, bloodied, and naked as the day he met evil and was used in the worst way. These thoughts he buried deepest.

38
February 1476

Leonardo smoothed the juniper tree branches with his finger and highlighted the last of Signora de' Benci's curls. The Signora requested the painting, a gift for her husband, and wanted her portrait no later than the first of March. No time remained to work. He must deliver it before week's end. He set down his brush and stepped away from the painting for one last judgment.

Sufficient and not like any before it. The Signora's youth and beauty he deemed a delight not unusual in theme. Rare, though was it to find a woman who looked a man in the eye without apology. Ginevra's eyes would speak volumes if only they had lips. Leonardo smiled. He'd never know her mysteries. In the portrait she peered back at anyone who attempted to discover them and another woman came to mind.

Lucrezia always had plenty to say but never gave away her secrets. The constraint of good women, so unlike the bravado of men, showed well in the painting. Satisfied, Leonardo accepted it as complete.

Loose floorboards creaked down the hall leading to Leonardo's room. "Ser?" he asked backing up to look through the doorway.

"Not even close." Matteo entered and busied himself by looking around.

Leonardo smoothed his tunic and blew his breath into his hand. Bravado displayed striking on some. Matteo's movements enhanced his athletic build, which caused ripples to form beneath his well-fitted clothes.

"Where have you been hiding? Here, Leonardo?"

"Hiding?"

"I've never been in your room. It's good to be the maestro's right-hand man from the look sof it."

"I've found a place where I belong. Left or right has no bearing on my position," Leonardo said. But the curve of Matteo's ass did. His hose gripped the perfect curvature in profile. Matteo went sour-faced as if he could somehow hear his thoughts. Coward that he was, Leonardo looked away.

Matteo continued his assessment of the room.

Leonardo couldn't stand without drawing notice to his arousal. He shuffled papers on his bedside desk. "Has your lady life become so dull that you've come to visit me in my humble quarters?"

Matteo laughed and shrugged.

The last time Matteo entered his room, they were boys. Then life flowed easier and they were free from their lusts.

Matteo removed his mantello and tossed it on the bed. His lemon scent swished through the air.

Leonardo inhaled and hoped it would linger. "I'll not be too hard on you," he said, and then bit his tongue and wanted to crawl under his blanket. "I've been enticed by a woman."

Matteo's head snapped to attention. "What woman?"

"There she is," Leonardo said directing Matteo's attention to the painting.

"I've worried for you—always alone." Matteo's lips turned upward. "I can see she has an effect on you." Matteo moved across the room to view her. "She's beautiful. How fortunate to be a man who gets to spend time in the presence of a woman like her." Matteo's face brightened before he asked the question.

"She's married," Leonardo answered.

Matteo smirked. "If a married woman like her should wish to pose for me, I'd not complain." He winked and nodded. "Not a bad room at all with the exception of the hideous smell." He sniffed about the room in search of the offensive odor. It didn't take long for him to find the source.

"No—"

"Ugh," Matteo said. He lifted the cloth set over Leonardo's worktable, groaned, and pinched his nose. He squinted his eyes and spoke still holding his nose. "What's this? Some sort of animal necromancy?" Matteo dropped the cloth and went to open the window. "It may be miserable outside, but you can't live like this." He waved his hands to direct the pungent air out. "Explain yourself, Leonardo. Has this been here since the summer? Is this why you never leave this place anymore?"

I leave this place all the time. "I apologize for the smell and regret your discovery of my 'animal necromancy.'" Leonardo laughed. "I don't notice the smell anymore." He went to the side of the table holding his collection of man-made creatures from the body parts of lizards, geckos, crickets, butterflies, locusts, a bat, and such, and lifted the covered buckler from the floor. He glanced back at Matteo, who didn't look amused.

"I can promise you'll never find love if you live like this, Leonardo. Your room may be clean, but the scent will send—" He swiped his hand to the side. "You'll send visitors fleeing."

They both turned to the sound of the creaking floorboards.

"Well, someone's come for the rotting body," Matteo said. "The undertaker's nose surely led him here as soon as I opened the window."

Ser rapped his knuckles on the doorframe. "Leonardo?"

"Wait a moment." Leonardo propped the wrapped buckler up against the wall, covered the table of creatures, and invited him in.

Ser hesitated in the doorway. "Leonardo, living like a bachelor is no excuse not to bathe. Your room stinks."

Leonardo sighed. "I've heard. So the sooner you see the buckler and carry it away, the sooner I can remove the offensive source."

Matteo reached Ser in three long strides. "Ser Piero," he said in greeting and pulled him in. "Hurry along. Come. See before we choke."

"I must admit, I forgot all about the buckler. Carlo must have as well," Ser said.

Leonardo uncovered his work. "I give you a monster fearsome enough to terrify Medusa." From a dark cave, the monstrous dragon-like creature emerged with venom dripping from its mouth, fire burning in its eyes, and smoke wafting out its nostrils. Leonardo looked away from the monster to Ser and Matteo who stepped back. "Ah! My work has served its purpose and did what I expected. Now you can take it away."

"Marvelous creativity," Ser said. "Carlo will display it proudly, or he would if it was not bound to frighten his little daughter in the night."

Matteo placed his arm around Leonardo's shoulder and squeezed him. "Yes, well done. Take it away, Ser Piero, but do it fast so you escape the smell."

Ser nodded in agreement and picked up the buckler. "Your mother says she has such fright within her that our child must be a girl. I'll not show her this. I pray that God not take Margherita or the child away."

Leonardo never spent much time around Ser's wives after Albiera, but he could say something kind. "You're not yet married a year and have a child on the way. What cruelty would befall you for such a blessing to be taken away again? Margherita seems a strong woman and will birth a strong a daughter."

"She is a strong woman," said Ser. He looked frustrated. "I must leave for work." He took the buckler. "Grazie," he said and departed.

Matteo punched Leonardo's arm. "I'll carry your carcasses out because I'm your friend you sick, sick painter. A word of advice: keep with your women." He pointed at the painting. "They'll keep you from other mischief. Now, let's clear the table of terrors." He held his hands above the creatures, grabbed an insect first, and tossed it onto the cloth cover. "Tell me that you'll never value dead things so much that you avoid me in the future, Leonardo."

"Dead things have not taken your place." Leonardo sighed. But women have taken mine. He dropped the bat onto the cloth. The more he worked the less time he wasted hoping for impossibilities. He loved Matteo. He may love him his entire life. He didn't know how to be with him without fighting against his desire. A day may come when he could fight no more, and in his weakness, he would ruin them with a kiss.

"Now your creatures make you ill?"

"No." Leonardo sat on the edge of his bed. "I'm not a good friend. I want you to find happiness, and for you, that's not in or around this bottega. We move in different directions."

Matteo tossed his hands out to his sides in a hostile way. "That's not us, Leonardo. Tell me you're working, or tell me it's none of my damn business. Say you have other plans. Don't avoid me like I am a stranger not worth your time."

Leonardo couldn't speak. Cowards never act. No. No! He couldn't tell him how he felt. He tried to find something else to say.

Matteo waited a long time for him to speak. "Tell me when you find time, brother," he said, and waited one more moment before he stormed out of the room.

Leonardo couldn't take it anymore. He lied to everyone including himself, but he couldn't call Matteo back. Not yet. He groaned. Once he gathered enough courage, he would go to Giorgio, whose lover, Il Teri, knew the ways of discretion.

39
Spring 1476

Laughter erupted from Leonardo and his companions in the back of the inn. Leonardo and Giorgio sat on stools around a scuffed table of toppled goblets. The conversations between Il Teri and Baccino never grew old.

Baccino placed a hand over his heart and bowed; his bushy hair swished forward and his square chin tipped into the crevice of his fine doublet. "Your words are brave, Il Teri," he said, and gulped his wine. "Yet I find them lacking ambition."

They all laughed harder. A Tornabuoni with no ambition was a bold assertion. Il Teri's lineage reached all the way to the city's princes, thus, Lorenzo de' Medici's mother. The Medici family stood for many things, but not a lack of ambition. Leonardo knew the dangers of drink were many, yet he took part in the loosening of male morals and tongues. That was the idea. Loosen the wheels. But one must speak carefully.

Il Teri took no offense but countered, "Baccino, I think you speak what you couldn't possibly know. You wobble down the road. Your rod like a homing pigeon." He sucked back his laughter and stood with his legs tight together and thrust his hips forward in imitation. "It always leads you to the same place." He thrust rapidly. "I've seen the hole in your wall."

Il Teri wiped tears from his eyes and placed a sympathetic hand on Baccino's sleeve, "I understand," he added full of sarcasm, then addressed Leonardo and

Giorgio. "Can we not help but picture his discomfiture at the presentation of Pandora's box? Legs open and glaring at him with her Cyclops eye." He stomped his foot and caught his breath. "Dearest Baccino, doubt not my ambition, for I have visited the Cyclops once. She's not worth the stop."

Peals of laughter emanated from the two, and the more they jested, the more they drank.

Baccino stood, placed his arm around Il Teri's neck, and spoke to his drinking companions. "Forget Pandora and her beast." He faced Il Teri, straightened his friend's misaligned collar, and nodded. "Come men, I'll show you the way to redemption," he said slamming his goblet down.

Giorgio stood and looped his arm in his lover's. They waited on Leonardo.

Leonardo held a finger up as he finished the last of his wine. When he stood, he released his goblet. It toppled and rolled on the tabletop. Everything moved in whirling motion. Leonardo weaved between the tavern's tables locked in the crook of his friend's arms. He stumbled and they laughed together. Baccino righted him on his feet with the bolster of the other's bodies. It might have been easier to navigate his departure alone, but as many men said, that ship already sailed. Companions stuck together. They ambled out of the tavern and into the piazza.

Baccino released Il Teri, whose hold on Giorgio became a half embrace. "Come along you two," Baccino called. "Can't you keep your hands off the other? Give no one reason to send the Night Officers your way." Baccino pulled on Il Teri's sleeve and led the way. Soon they turned at the southwest corner of the Vacchereccia.

It was a good neighborhood not unlike the rest of the city, but cleaner, distinct, more noble. Most of the marked entryways had family coats of arms and doors carved with flowers or knobbed heads—some with lion-headed knockers. The masses didn't congregate on the street. In this sort of neighborhood, unwelcome guests found stern escort out.

"Bartolomeo expects us," Baccino said. He cocked his head to the side and leaned into Leonardo. "Giorgio told us you're worthy of our confidence. Il Teri assured those you'll meet he finds you true." Baccino swung his arm out. "With pride, count yourself among men of worth." He nearly lost his balance and laughed. "Fair young men are we of the noble arts of love and virtue," he announced to anyone who would hear. "There," he held his hand up to direct Leonardo, "Bartolomeo."

Bartolomeo, a man standing outside his door, looked their direction. In the dusky light, he appeared a handsome man with dark hair and prominent muscles.

Baccino called on approach, "You wait for us outside your door? What a greeting."

Bartolomeo glanced down the Vacchereccia and back again. "Come friends," he said waving them in. "Across the street, Antonio bickers like a child in complaint of the noise. What noise I ask? Do you hear anything at my door?" He grumbled. "I'll remember those del Pollaiuolo brothers." Bartolomeo waved his fist in the air then addressed his arrivals. "Please friends, come in before he grows more jealous. The musician is here and the other men have arrived. Make me wait no longer for you else my guests think I left them." Bartolomeo kissed Baccino on his cheek.

Baccino returned his affection by kissing him lightly on the mouth.

"And how was the vino, Baccino?" he asked kissing him again to taste.

Leonardo cleared his throat.

Baccino turned to Leonardo. "Let me introduce you to my friend, Leonardo."

"Thank you for your gracious invitation, Bartolomeo," Leonardo said in quick greeting as the host ushered them inside.

Baccino followed behind Leonardo. "Up the stairs to the right. Follow the music."

Before Leonardo reached the top of the stairs, the music ended and the sound of conversations filled his ears. In the sala, several men lounged on intricately woven carpets furnished with cushions. Many held drinks.

Baccino introduced him around the room. "And with that, I leave you to your own devices. All's fair in the game of love," he concluded with an eyebrow waggle.

A card table had no players, so Leonardo turned the chair outward and sat. Sheer draperies flitted in the breeze of open balcony doors that obscured a man or two behind them. The musician, lute in his lap, sipped his wine then stood to perform a new song.

A thin, bird-nosed man led his younger, graceful partner to the center of the room. They danced. The man had no care for his awkward movements, but his boy partner turned many heads as he glided across the floor. Something familiar about the boy struck Leonardo.

The boy appeared tender, yet older than his years. His angular, green eyes blinked in surprise when they met Leonardo's from across the room. The wine slowed Leonardo's mind, but he remembered now. He drew and sculpted the striking Jacopo Saltarelli as the Christ in Maestro's bottega some years ago. The representation, however, began and ended with Jacopo's face. The boy came across too abrasive for some, but Leonardo took delight in him. Undeniable was Jacopo's self-assured bearing then, and apparently now, for time traded his cherubim features for lustier forms.

Jacopo floated toward Leonardo, bowed, grabbed his hand, and pulled him up. "Dance with me," he said as a command and caused them to twirl about.

With each turn, Leonardo's head swam. His feet found each step, and his enjoyment mirrored the grin on Jacopo's face. Odd—that vino—to cause him to stumble when walking, but able to make him dance. Jacopo slid his hand across Leonardo's back. When they crossed center, Jacopo's hand brushed his ass. Startled, Leonardo craned his head and waited to see if Jacopo also assigned his errant hands to the birdman. He didn't. Encouraging.

Heat rose on Leonardo's face and neck. He hoped his onlookers would think it from his dancing exertions. Virginity aside, the partner tonight mattered less than the diversion. On their next pass, Leonardo brushed a lock of the boy's hair from his eye. "Jacopo, how long since last I saw you?"

Jacopo's lips parted and they spun again.

"You remember me," stated quite-full-of-himself.

Many a male lacked sufficient reason for arrogance, but Jacopo mastered the attribute. Leonardo laughed under his breath. Desperation made him far too easy. He closed in on Jacopo, "I never forget a magnificent face."

"Nor I, Leonardo." He flung his foot out in perfect time to the music.

Lustier in all ways, Jacopo moved too bold to look away. His eyes persuaded.

He drew near again. "Tell me, how many years have you now?"

The boy smirked but didn't answer. Jacopo clasped the birdman's hand and his own. He led them close again. "Seventeen."

They swung out and turned a final time. "As many as I need to choose my partner," he said, passing shoulder-to-shoulder.

"You chose the birdman," Leonardo said.

Jacopo looked at the birdman and chuckled. "That's good," he said enjoying the comment. Rather than preparing to bow at the end of the song, Jacopo clasped their hands and spun. The room had no focus save their faces, which giggled like children.

"Jacopo," Leonardo said, "I drank more than my share of wine and will loose my feet."

"But a bird must fly." He released his partners and spun into the final bow.

Leonardo sidestepped and fell to a knee while the birdman mocked him. This one failed move may force him to spend the night alone.

Jacopo shoved Leonardo's rival aside. "Have care." He offered his hand.

"You find me at a disadvantage." Steadied, Leonardo rose. Not graceful. Not attractive. "I'll go for some air."

Like a continuation of the dance, Jacopo's fingers glided beneath Leonardo's palm. Their fingers hooked fingertip to fingertip. A spark set Leonardo's nerves taut. He wanted to proceed, and why not? The men here shared similar desires. Why else did they stay, if not to find solace inside these walls? Leonardo raised Jacopo's fingers to his lips and kissed them.

The boy ran his fingers along his lips, turned, and walked away.

So, he lacked the skills of a proper seducer—clumsy and ridiculous. That never mattered with Matteo, who would tell him something encouraging like at least he garnered points by not vomiting. He wanted to laugh, but then he may vomit.

Alone, Leonardo entered the balcony. As tempting as drowning himself seemed, it wouldn't be prudent to have more wine. He glanced over his shoulder to see if Jacopo followed. Earlier, an agreeable man found company no sooner than he set foot on the balcony, but no one approached Leonardo. Perhaps he wasn't agreeable. His remaining pride leeched more darkness into the night.

He'd grown used to solitude. Solitude lent some personal freedom, but he didn't really belong to himself.

Time alone scattered his thoughts and set his imagination on fire. Matteo battered his mind day and night, and he tried to move on, but he couldn't let him go. He rubbed his brow to try to clear the soup of love and lust inside his skull. Most irrational pits of man! His groan rose from the marrow of his bones.

"Are you sick?"

Leonardo startled. "I'm sick of frustration."

Jacopo's voice he recognized, but the boy's face distorted from the light cast behind him. He lifted two goblets, drank from one, and offered the other.

Leonardo refused him. Unfulfilled desire could exhaust man to despair. Rather than longing for the impossible, he needed the possible. Sick with love he blurted, "Love is a miserable state. No one can escape the disease."

"And so you danced with me." Jacopo's voice sounded amused. "Most of us come here to forget our troubles and find comfort. It's obvious to me that you wish to purge this love. Am I mistaken?"

"No, you're not mistaken."

"Why is he not here with you?"

Loosened enough to talk about his love life with a half-stranger, Leonardo could bear his restraint no longer. "The day he knows the truth he will abandon me." He couldn't see Jacopo's reaction.

"I see. Deny your love then. You can be sure you'll never attain it."

Jacopo's blunt words hurt because of the truth in them. How could a boy of seventeen command such wisdom? Astonished, Leonardo found himself eager to listen.

"If you refuse to try, you can't know if your love is returned." Jacopo sipped his wine and turned to face the light spilling out the balcony door. "Does true love not endure once the truth's set free? Act, and you'll discover your commitment to this supposed love." Jacopo stood prepared to leave. "I have nothing I wish to hide. I come here for the sex," he said as a matter of fact and placed a hand on Leonardo's.

Leonardo licked his lips. The boy stirred him. "And so I've come, but," he hesitated, "I've not done this before."

Jacopo unbuttoned his farsetto. "Please, don't let that stop you."

Leonardo reached for the wine Jacopo first offered. He drank deeply, set the empty cup down, and stepped forward to kiss him. He held the balcony handrail to steady himself.

Warm lips melded together; first soft and gentle, then harder, searching and aching. Leonardo's breath caught when he opened his mouth to taste. Sweet and bitter, the warmth radiated from his lips to the rest of his body. He brought his fingers to the bared skin at Jacopo's neck and felt his pulse pounding against his thumb. Jacopo's hands moved across his sides to his back and scooped up toward his shoulders. Leonardo bent to cup Jacopo's ass with both hands. Smooth and firm. Chills pricked along his spine.

The boy moaned when their bodies pressed against one another in the cloak of darkness.

Jacopo's erection lay against his thigh. "Is there another place we can go?" Leonardo asked panting.

Jacopo folded his fingers into Leonardo's. "Follow me." They walked with purpose past the dance area, into the sala, and made a left turn down a hallway lit by lanterns. The third door down was open. Jacopo took an unlit lamp on a table and set the wick to flame.

Leonardo clasped his free hand and followed him into the room. He closed the door.

Jacopo set the lamp aside. He stared at Leonardo and unbuckled his belt, unbuttoned his farsetto, then slipped everything off above his waist. His green eyes glowed. "Your turn." The boy encouraged with a lewd grin.

But before Leonardo finished, Jacopo stunned him by removing all his clothing. He approached Leonardo in confidence. "I want to help you."

40

A thunderous knock rattled Matteo's door and shook the walls. He stopped his housemaid on her way to answer. "No, let me. I'll stop he who attempts to beat down my door." Matteo slipped a velvet giornea over his bedclothes. The door took a beating again. "Raging fool, how dare you." A face peered through the window closest to the door. "Matteo Attaviano," it called.

Matteo swung the door open ready to thump the intolerant knocker. "State your business and lay not another finger upon my door."

The knocker gripped the front of Matteo's clothes. "Matteo. You must come. Now."

"Giorgio? From Verrocchio's bottega?"

Giorgio nodded and pulled Matteo closer to his reddened face. "It's Leonardo. They led him away—he told me to come here—he begs you help him. He's accused." Giorgio took in a jagged breath of air. "The Night Officer's pulled his name from the tamburo on the Vacchereccia."

"A denunciation?" Matteo yanked himself from Giorgio's grip. "Who would have reason to accuse Leonardo? It's not possible."

"You're wrong," Giorgio said. "An officer came to the bottega with the citation. Maestro told him to get out with his false accusations, but the officer warned us all. He said when charges are ignored, the inquisitors assume the accused's guilt." Giorgio swallowed hard. "Failure to appear before the court when summoned leads to the harshest penalties."

"I'll not believe it. How many a man has found his name dropped in a tamburo because his competitor wanted to inconvenience him?"

Giorgio's cheeks sucked in and out.

"Calm yourself or you'll piss your shoes." He invited Giorgio inside. Strung tight enough for plucking, one touch and Giorgio would screech. Matteo doubted his tolerance for a puddle of piss on his floor but needed to know what happened. "Come. Sit, no matter the early hour. The state of your choler insists that I offer you a valiant drink."

Giorgio refused. "You come. I gave Leonardo my word." He shifted his feet and pointed in accusation. "Why do you not make haste? You more than anyone should know Leonardo went quietly. The officer came for him. That was enough to make him leave and avoid drawing more unwanted attention. He left without a fight."

"Of course he did," Matteo said. "Now get inside. I must dress to present myself in front of the Podestà."

Relief washed over Giorgio's face and he entered. "You'll go then?" He placed a hand on Matteo's shoulder and squeezed. "I shouldn't have doubted you."

Matteo shook his head. "What are the charges against our friend?"

"The officer didn't say."

"If nothing else, I'll slap sense into Leonardo when I see him." He called down the corridor, "Joanna, bring my green tunic with the gold trim, the matching giornea, fresh hose, and my favorite belt." Turning back to Giorgio he asked, "The man couldn't or wouldn't tell him his crime?"

Giorgio shrugged. "He's accused. Perhaps there's no crime to mention until found guilty." He chewed on his words and continued, "If I were him, I would look to you to secure my bond..." his voice quieted, "that is, if he should find himself in route to the Stinche."

Matteo swung around to see Giorgio biting his lip. Now he would take his turn at fisting clothes. "Don't play games with me. First you pound on my door like a child rushing to relieve his bladder, and now you jump from no guilt or crime to condemnation in the Stinche? Tell me what you know. Now is no time for secrets."

Giorgio squeaked, diverted his eyes, and said nothing.

"Haven't you any faith in your friend?" Matteo thumped Giorgio's chest and released him. "Perhaps I need the drink." His clothes arrived. He yanked his lopsided giornea over his head and removed his soiled tunic. "Giorgio, you've shown faith enough to come on his behalf. That's more than anyone else." He sat to change his hose and questioned why Leonardo called for him when his father would have more influence in these matters.

Giorgio stood. "I've accomplished my task. Buongiornio," he said and made for the door.

"No." Matteo tossed his dirty, balled-up hose hitting Giorgio in the center of his back. "No buongiorno. You're coming with me. We'll both find the truth and speak on Leonardo's behalf."

***

The main floor of the Palace of the Podestà consisted of a great hall. Rectangular in shape, the hall's dual-leveled windows and vaulted ceilings provided openness and light. Would the accused find his hearing in similar, attractive surroundings? Matteo and Giorgio crossed the long hall to the far side where an official stood behind a full-length lectern. The official was a boar of a man with dark wooly hair, eyes close together, and a prominent nose.

He held his hand up at their approach. "The Judges will not address those who have not been called to the bench today. Come tomorrow if your business warrants a return visit."

Not wanting to be provoked, Matteo took a deep breath. The way the official spoke and the way he looked down on those who waited would take Matteo's best effort to maintain calm. Matteo crooked his finger for Giorgio to stand at his side. "We've not come for any judge." Annoyed, he waited for the official to give him his full attention. "We've come to defend our friend."

"You and all the rest," said the official. "I follow orders, Signore. You've not been called to the bench." The official pursed his lips together, removed his hands from the register, and crossed his hands at his chest.

"Signore, please could you tell me the charges against my friend? His name is Leonardo. Leonardo da Vinci." Matteo reached a finger forward to scan the register.

"Step away from the lectern." The official shoved Matteo's arm.

Matteo's hand formed a fist. "Ah, how thoughtless of me." Some men took their simple jobs far too serious, while those with greater duties so often failed their post. How dirty would he have to play the game? He lifted his purse. "Name your price."

The official snorted. "Bribes will buy you nothing here."

Matteo yanked his head back. "Truer words were never abused so much as those," he said. "And given the conceit so displayed by the way you position your snout, Signore, I would not advise you force those before you to distraction by viewing straight into that ghastly thicket of hair in those holes on your face."

The official's eyes narrowed and his jaw twitched.

Damn. He displayed far more restraint than expected.

Giorgio stepped in, concern written across his face. "We ask nothing of you, Signore. It's as simple as reading from a page that I assume you've written."

The official remained uncooperative. "Then we'll wait for his release here," Matteo said moving closer to agitate the man further. If he focused his attentions on the entrance to the judges and twitched unpredictable like a wild animal, the protector of the post would have to decide between the register and the door. Matteo hoped he'd choose the door.

"Leonardo will come. Let's sit and wait," Giorgio said. "Matteo?"

Matteo didn't respond. He didn't know how to wait around helpless, but he did know how to fight. He studied the grain of the door, traced the outline of the frame, and stared at the handle. Twitch some more, rub the hands together, lick the lips, and slink forward. He took care not to seem aware that the official viewed his every move out the corner of his eye.

Finally, he stepped out from behind the lectern to block Matteo's entrance.

Like a lamb to the slaughter, Matteo laughed to himself. Before the official could read his move, he sprang to the lectern and searched for Leonardo's name.

The official shot over and tried to tug it away. "That's not for the eyes of the likes of you." He grunted.

Matteo pulled back. "You'll have to cut my hands from the pages."

Giorgio attempted to separate them.

"Whose side are you on?" Matteo asked.

Giorgio's eyes bulged in his head. "Stop. Think of where you are."

"I know where I am. And I know that if this ass kisser has balls enough to report me, then he will have gained some respect, and I will have gained entrance to approach the bench." He strained his neck further to find Leonardo's name. "This is a place to represent the people? How a man can be deceived." Matteo yanked hard. "What—are—the—charges?"

Others who waited in the hall pressed forward. "For the love of God, tell him," called one voice. Another chiding voice said, "What ever happened to the civilization of good men?"

"Quiet in the halls," shouted the official with a twist of his torso. "This is a place of order and respect."

"Respect?" When Matteo tugged, the official's head rocked like hits from a battering ram.

The official lowered his voice, "Release the register and I'll tell you."

Matteo laughed. "I'm no fool. I have no reason to trust you." He spoke loud to address the people. "He'll not tell me or you until we make him."

The people agreed with Matteo. They moved closer to the scuffle.

Matteo held tight to the register.

"Order. Order!" The official's hands trembled and loosened. "In turn, I shall give you the information. Quiet now, quiet." He glanced over his shoulder toward the door where he refused Matteo entrance. "Do no more to disturb the proceedings now in session." He gasped. "Back away and I'll tell you." He tugged on the register and almost fell when Matteo released it.

Matteo scrambled up to be first in line. He drummed a finger on the edge of the lectern. "Leonardo da Vinci."

The official straightened his clothes then searched the register. He took his time. A foul smile set upon his loathsome face. "Accused of, ooh—"

"Yes?" Matteo prepared to attack again. The bastard stalled for effect to harass him. Matteo's fingers clawed into the wood.

"Cited by The Officers of the Night for sodomy," the official said for all to hear. "Next."

One word sucked all air from the hall.

"I must go," Giorgio said. He backed up apologetically. "I cannot do what you ask." His words rushed from his mouth, and he fled from the lectern and bolted down the hall.

Matteo waited in front of the official unwilling to accept the charge. He viewed the ceiling to send a prayer after the official pushed him aside. How the awe-inspiring majesty of the palace lifted the eyes and spirits—until it didn't. Lulled into a false security, poor souls soon discovered the palace foundation crumbling beneath their feet. Matteo stumbled to find his seat for support.

No decision yet made, Leonardo may walk out freer than he walked in. But instinct gnawed at Matteo's gut. And Giorgio, that betrayer, weakened any thoughts of Leonardo's innocence. No stranger to the sodomites, Florentines turned a blind eye at one moment then moved to persecute them the next. But the court would not, could not dismiss crimes against religion. At least not without a mild form of punishment, perhaps a fine, which may be why he sat in wait. And what if the judges had evidence beyond the slip dropped in the tamburo? He hoped he wasn't right, but given the time that past for the proceedings, he felt sure that there must be evidence. At worst, sodomites burned for their transgressions. Leonardo, what have you done?

He may have known all along, or at least suspected the way Leonardo's gaze lingered upon men. Have I not seen him appreciate a handsome woman? No one answer fit, but all served a possible indication.

He pictured Leonardo's blue eyes. Always they held pleasure and pain as inseparable twins. As much as he worked to divide them, they were one and the same for Leonardo, trapped. Now his friend made sense. Leonardo lived everyday caught in the shadows, a prisoner inside a shell. Afraid to let anyone see him. He wanted to live free from persecution like every man.

How many times did Leonardo stare at him, a shroud of words hanging unspoken from his lips? Leonardo held back, and why? He must have known his friends would fail him. Leonardo didn't speak out of consideration for those who feared to look beyond the surface. For the love of God, could there be greater pain than acknowledging the truth about one's own deception?

Matteo sucked back his emotion and looked to be sure no one noticed him. Imagine a man who wished not to have strangers see his grief? And what of Leonardo's? Whether he lusted for men or both sexes alike, Leonardo's restraint chained him down and the world around him stomped him further into the pit. Matteo set his chin firm. I'll deny you no more.

A creak sounded from the door. Matteo looked to see the official move and hold it open wide. First came a judge, marked by his dark robe trimmed in white. Two men followed behind him. One wore a meticulous doublet, the other, younger, dressed similar to Matteo, but in the color of wine. Matteo stood to look for Leonardo. He spotted his blaze of blonde hair first. Leonardo took a few steps more and emerged from the hall. None of the men's appearances offered a positive outcome.

Tension stretched across Leonardo's face. "You came," he said, sadness in his eyes. "Giorgio—thank him for me."

Matteo nodded. "Of course I came. Where are we going?"

An armed official followed behind Leonardo. He carried a sheathed dagger at one side of his waist, and a whip on the other, which whapped against his thigh when he walked. "Keep moving," said the armed man with a jab in Leonardo's back.

Leonardo clutched Matteo's arm. "I wish not to drag you into my mess. You were the only one I thought would come to help me. I thank you for your efforts."

"How can I help? Tell me and I'll do it."

Leonardo shook his head. "When I was led away, I didn't know what to expect. Knowing someone might come gave me hope." His face looked defeated. "I thought you'd pay my bail."

"Yes, I'll pay it. You know I will."

Leonardo lowered his voice, "The Night Officer's mostly let a man pay a fine for their denunciation and go with a warning. But there are complications. Matteo, I'm sorry I pulled you into this." His face hardened, "I want you to go."

"You don't mean it. What complications do you speak of?"

"Go. Now," he said, his tongue sharp as a blade.

They reached a door that led the opposite direction of the door Matteo used to enter the hall. Matteo's blood turned cold. "Where do you take them?"

"Where you can't follow." The official in the lead opened a heavy wooden door and held it for the accused to pass through.

"He'll take his lashes in the Podestà courtyard," said the impersonal judge pointing at the youngest boy. "A courtesy for noble blood. You can find his foul lovers at the whipping post in the Palazzo della Signoria." The official behind barred Matteo's path.

"Captain," said the lead official, "the lesser two would benefit from watching the boy receive his lashes before they have their own."

"They would," he said, and stepped through the door.

A whipping in the Palazzo della Signoria stripped a man of honor more than anything else Matteo could think of. The punishment would be bad enough, but while the whole city looked on and hurled insults at his friend? No, Leonardo deserved better. Matteo caught the door with his hand. "Those two men may not be of noble birth, Signori," he said, "but I'll pay you handsome coin if you spare them further humiliation." Matteo doubted that anything save bribery could seal a better outcome. "Give them their lashings in this courtyard. I humbly beg you." The officials seemed unmoved by his petition. "I'll pay one Florin." The door shut. Matteo waited. He moved to a window to see if they'd gone.

The Captain reopened the door. "Two Florins. One for each man, and it's done." He thumbed his whip. "You have the money or you don't."

A steep price. Matteo loosened his purse strings and shifted his coin around in search for the gold Florins. He pulled them out, and held them in his hand.

The official took the money.

"Where should I look for my friend after?"

"The Stinche." The door boomed shut.

Leonardo would be led down the via Ghibellina to the sole entrance of the Stinche. Though not far, Matteo's path to the place took effort on legs that had only begun to truly walk. He feared for the condition of his friend. What if the lashes tore into Leonardo's skin and bloodied him?

People stared and whispered while Matteo waited. No sane man lingered here to smell the rotten stink that seeped from the place. The Stinche was a most dismal assembly of brick upon filthy brick. The tall structure loomed dark from the three guard towers above and from the absence of windows on the outer walls. The entrance consisted of a small doorway that stooped lower than street level. He couldn't understand why or how Leonardo became a target for this kind of abuse. Matteo smelled another filth, and it didn't come from the Stinche. How long would Leonardo's confinement last? Would he emerge a stranger?

***

From the corner of the via Ghibellina, Leonardo and the others arrived on foot to the Stinche. The men were bound together by rope at their wrists, which looped and knotted around their hands. The Captain on horseback held the lines. That Leonardo walked gave Matteo a bit of relief. On approach, Leonardo noticed Matteo, and rather than showing relief, he shook his head in disapproval. Welt marks lined the side of Leonardo's neck, but Matteo saw no blood, just a humped posture.

The Captain stepped from his horse and adjusted the ropes to lead the men inside the prison.

"Matteo, you've done all you can. Grazie, but go. Please go," Leonardo said.

Matteo didn't budge.

"Can you not see my shame?"

Matteo moved closer. "I see it. Does that make you feel any different? I'm here, and I care not a donkey's ass for whatever you've done or not done."

The Captain clicked his tongue the way one urged a horse to signal they move.

"Wait. What crime of his is so vile that he must be held in the Stinche? Captain, tell me that you and other government officials refuse fruits of pleasure behind closed doors, and I'll see your logic."

The whipped boy stepped into the downward sloping entrance first.

Matteo tossed all caution away. He moved to block further passage by holding the rope in place.

"I follow orders, Signore," the Captain said. "They tell me to lead them to the Stinche, and that's what I'll do. Now move aside or you may well find yourself walking the same path."

Leonardo took Matteo's hand and lifted it from the rope. "You can't save us. You can only save yourself, Matteo. Let me go."

"How long should he be in prison?" Matteo asked to anyone that would answer.

Leonardo gripped him tight. "Until another accused man is located. Once he's been put to the question, our fate will fall into place. Will you tell my Maestro what's happened?"

Matteo nodded but knew he held back information.

"Il Teri, Lionardo Tornabuoni's the name of the other," the man spared public beating said. He spoke the Tornabuoni name with such venom.

"Ah," Matteo said to the foul smell.

The Captain got his prisoners moving through the door again.

"Remember, Leonardo, there are people who wait for your return."

Leonardo gave one backward glance. He closed his eyes a moment and ducked to avoid hitting the sloped entrance.

 Matteo yelled, "I'll not rest until you're free from this place. Believe my words, brother."

Leonardo faded into the darkness.

41

Leonardo ducked his head and upper body to fit through the short doorway of the Stinche. His bow of reverence, they called it, held no veneration. Immediate darkness enveloped him. His most reliable sense gone, strong smells struck him with force—stagnant, sour, sick. The thumping inside his chest quickened for want of clawing a way back into the light, but a tug on the line attached to Baccino and Jacopo pulled him along. The rope that bound him carved an unforgettable message in his wrists: you will not depart.

Down a narrow, rectangular hallway a faint orange light glowed.

"Halt," the Captain said inside the receiving room. He tugged the rope to get the full attention of the prisoners. "Line-up there," he said pointing to a solid wall. "The warden will speak first."

They followed the Captain's orders. A notary of sorts sat at a battered desk and wrote in his notebook without looking up. To the side of the desk, a messy shelf held a couple inkpots, a stack of registers, and a basket of candles. The warden entered the room, scrutinized them, folded his arms at his chest, and waited for the notary to finish. Both Stinche men wore dark clothes and twitched about like rats in a tunnel. The Captain stepped forward and produced folded papers from his pouch. He handed them to the notary. They all stood silent.

A slow plink, plink came from a corner puddled with water. The furious scratching of the notary's quill offered

Leonardo little comfort. Smooth, slick stone beneath his feet marked the passage of many who came before him— quite different from the unforgiving walls so jagged, harsh, and heavy they could have been here five or five-hundred years. Thousands of candles must have burned to form the low, blemished ceiling able to boast of one vile accomplishment: the decay of time. Leonardo fixated on the single, precious flame that lit the room. It swayed perilously under the breath of the busy notary. One snuff, and they'd become entombed in the blackest of darkness.

The notary ceased his writing and waited for the warden. "Turn and face the wall," the warden said. "You'll remain where you stand until we call your name."

Leonardo faced the wall. One torment led to another and caused him to fall deeper into the abyss. Have I asked too much by wanting to forget? He closed his eyes and dropped his chin to his chest.

The warden called his prisoners in turn. He untied Jacopo, then Baccino, and the notary made his annotations. A heavy door groaned with each swing open and shut.

Last called, Leonardo answered the notary's questions. "I see you are guilty of sodomy, Signore da Vinci. Need I remind you of the duration of your imprisonment?"

How could he forget?

The notary held his quill in mid-air, the tip of the feather brushed against his chest. "I am inclined to ease your stay, but," the man referred back to his register, "a painter of your standing is not likely to have additional soldi to pay an agevolatura fee for a better room, is he?"

Leonardo bristled from the man's slight, but he appreciated his direct approach. All the time he'd spent saving his money would be lost in this pit. The humiliation, his struggle, would have no end. Though Maestro encouraged him to begin his own bottega, he felt sure he wouldn't refuse him a longer stay under the circumstances. Some comfort was better than none. "I'll pay."

The notary sat stoic. "A small room in the malevato for thirteen soldi per day."

Leonardo nodded. His stomach churned.

"Very well. You must pay your first day now, and we will keep an account of your debt to the Stinche each day hereafter."

Leonardo paid his initial fees with the money Matteo gave him. The warden removed the rope from his hands and waist and directed him through the groaning door. Leonardo squinted when they entered an inner courtyard open to the bright sky and savagely sucked the sweet air in.

They passed stairs, and to one side of the courtyard a lunette of the Virgin and Christ child centered on the wall. Opposite the lunette, a stone lion marked a small chapel. Past the chapel, a barred window, followed by a great wooden door, and another barred window held some of the prison cells. Here they turned left. The warden unlocked the door and indicated Leonardo should enter first.

"The malevato," the warden said following with a torch.

Whistles sounded from a couple of prisoners when Leonardo made his way across the center walkway of the ward. Men rose from their beds and peered out over their shoulders, from beneath blankets, and behind unshaven faces. "What man is this who has the distinguished escort of the warden?" an unseen voice asked.

The entry and rear windows gave a glimpse of natural light into the otherwise dark ward. Two simple columns centered the open room. Beds more like benches bordered the walls and stuck out like fingers in long rows. The scent of piss and merde increased in the darkest part of the malevato, the privy center. Leonardo shuddered to think of his situation had he not paid for a better room. Of all places, he couldn't survive next to this stench, he recited like a prayer. They hadn't reached the windowed end before the warden stopped.

"Look there," he said directing Leonardo's attention to a bed. "You have fresh straw."

Far from joy, his bed did have fresh straw with no coverings. A shelf hung above it and a chipped washbasin rested under it. A sliver of light angled across the end of his bed to offer a little comfort.

The warden held his torch between them. "You're free to move around the room at will, but you'll not use any part of yourself or any of your possessions as a weapon. Sexual pleasures of any kind are forbidden." The warden paused with a stern eye and continued by rote with his rules. "There'll be no gambling, no drinking or excessive noise, no destruction of the grounds, and all lights go out when the vespers toll rings. Any violation of the rules results in a punishment, fine, or both." He turned to take his leave.

"Oh yes, one of the friars will see to your needs. Good fortune for you," the warden said, "he's not arrived for the day."

Leonardo stood in place. Out of the darkness someone approached with a guarded gait.

"Thank the Virgin for a familiar face," Baccino said crossing a sunbeam on the floor. Baccino embraced him.

"Let me alone," Leonardo said, "I desire no further condemnation. I'm not your companion. I'm not your brother. I'm…I'm nothing." He knocked him away and dropped to his pitiful bed.

He counted a few candles and some paper and ink on some of the men's shelves. The man next to him had the same but better—a book and a small desk with an unlit lamp. Drawn out flat on his bed, a chain cuffed the man's ankle.

The man grunted and sat up in bed. "What's your name?"

Leonardo answered.

"Well, Leonardo," the man said, " I've been here two years, one-hundred and fifteen days." His wrinkled face

turned into the last bit of light that shone across his bed.
White hair framed his head and age spots dotted his nose.
He spoke in a deliberate way. "I've told many men my
crimes, and my sorrows. I've talked of my family, my
friends, my desires, my hopes, and I've nothing more to
say." The man coughed and tried to settle again.

"Have you silenced yourself long?"

"Yes." He waved his arms back and forth to indicate he
would say no more. "No comforts for old men. Now you
know I want to be left alone." He hacked so hard his chain
rattled. "I'm forgotten and left to rot."

"Forgive me, Signore. I cannot help but wonder how a
man who says he has nothing to say can say so much."

The man's eyes crinkled and he bit his lip. He cracked a
smile then began to laugh. His laugh grew louder. The
other prisoners gathered around the cheerful sound until the
most unlikely of sounds echoed around them. His laugh
ended in a huh, huh. He turned to the others. Fear flashed
across his face. "Go on. Back to your own business," he
told them.

The sound died and they dispersed.

The man offered his hand. "Call me Papi. And grazie, I
have no remembrance of the last time laughter touched my
lips. I used to keep count of my days, but now I don't want
to remember." Papi sat in thought. "Marks on the wall
showed me I'm still alive." He placed his hands on the edge
of his bed and pushed to stand. His chains clanked. He
waddled to his desk, retrieved something, and returned to
his sitting place. "Here, take it." Papi set a charcoal stick in
Leonardo's hand.

"No, I can't accept."

"I insist. It pains me more to know the passing of my
days. You're young. You have a life to live upon your
release."

Leonardo refused.

Papi slapped Leonardo's knee. His finger poked out like a knife. "You'll get out. Use it to count your days, for you have many to live."

Leonardo shook his head to disagree.

"Damn you. You'll learn how numerous the days you have yet to spend in the light once you count how few you spent in darkness." Papi rolled Leonardo's fingers around the gift. "I'd say don't look so forlorn, but to what end? We're all forlorn. Enough time spent in a flat note, and a man numbs to the sound until he hears nothing. I've earned the right to forget and I want to die. I've lived my life."

An awful sound assaulted Leonardo's ears. When he struggled for air, he realized he made it. He wanted to forget the pain of never feeling the love of the man who should love him most, and he wanted to profess his amore for the one who loved him only as a friend. Neither could he do, and here it led him.

"Release it, Leonardo else you wear my chains." Papi looked on him with kindness before he stretched across his bed. "When you're ready, speak young man, and I'll listen. I enjoy a good story. Thousands of places we'd rather be." Papi pulled his blanket up. "Now I have nothing more to say."

Leonardo gathered himself. "Papi, why are you in chains?"

"Leave me to my silence today. Tell me your stories, and one day I will tell you how I got my chains."

42

Matteo kicked his blankets off, staggered through his dark room, slipped on a camicia, and hobbled down the stairs. It did him no good to lay restless in bed. All night he turned over a thousand questions. Bits of well-chosen words stewed in his head on a repeat pattern. In the room of convenience, he lifted the wooden lid and pulled his camicia up. If the call of his morning piss provided any indication, dawn should break within the hour.

He washed, dressed, and returned downstairs. "Ring worthless bells, ring," he said, pacing at his front door. Perhaps if he closed his eyes, the shuffling of his feet could trick him into thinking he went somewhere. He convinced himself of the importance of an early morning call: so as not to miss Leonardo's father and to keep the man's volatile nature at bay.

Matteo knew of no efforts Leonardo made to notify Ser Piero of his arrest. Not that he could blame him. When Leonardo woke yesterday morn, Matteo doubted that he or anyone could have guessed the misfortune that would strike him by midday. Thus, today, tomorrow, and the next, he'd wait for the turn of the wheel to deliver Leonardo up. But no one ever said waiting meant sitting idle. When a man lost hope he set one foot in the grave. Never would Matteo lie down quietly to accept his punishments, so why should he expect otherwise for his friend?

That Leonardo sent word to him instead of his own father could not be judged a bad decision, but the reason Leonardo called on him settled unwell as a poor man's distressed humors. "On the Virgin's grave," cursed Matteo. He and Ser Piero must work together for the greater good.

The bells rang.

***

"Please, tell Ser Piero Matteo Attaviano requests an urgent word with him."

The housemaid lowered her head under orders. "Yes, Signore. Come inside if you can wait. My maestro's not yet risen from his bedchamber. I'll send for him." She set her cloth aside and waited for him to enter. "Forgive me, Signore, but a…a man of your—any man in my maestro's house... Please—" She tucked her tail and scurried from the sala.

Damn. They didn't need to wake him. Matteo cringed. Now he had one tick against Ser Piero's good graces and hadn't spoken a word to him.

After some time, the housemaid returned and opened the shutters.

Soon, Ser Piero entered the room. He took his time seemingly unhindered by thought or deed. His hair stood afloat. His disheveled appearance lessened his usual effect, which set Matteo easier to his task. Be eloquent and polite Matteo reminded himself. "Ser Piero, forgive my early hour. I could not wait another minute to come to you with the news of Leona—"

"I know what has befallen your friend, Matteo," he said, folding his fingers together like a confident card player.

"Most excellent, Ser." Matteo cleared his throat. "I can then ask you, without further institution, to help fulfill a promise and duty to take every reasonable action that will lead to your son's release from the Stinche." Perhaps he should say please.

Ser Piero stood taller but his eyes cut downward. "As unacceptable as Leonardo's accusations are, I placed myself, shamed, in front of the city's men of law to discover the truth." He raised his voice and pointed at his chest, "I, far more than Leonardo, do not want the da Vinci name tossed about like a common whore. Leonardo should have thought of virtue before his quick whoring prick. The evidence against him is clear." Flushed, he fired, "He's guilty as charged."

Matteo should have known he'd exhaust his efforts to remain calm. "I thought that with your knowledge of these matters and your connections to the men in," he rolled his hand about, "in high places that you could find a way to help."

"You ask too much. I cannot risk my hard-won work and reputation for Leonardo's bad judgment. That is bad business and a violation of trust. A man in my position earns everything based on his integrity."

"What about the needs of your son? What about his trust?" Matteo ground his teeth together. "I pity you and your work ethics. They come on your family in cruel ways. He sent for me because he knew. He knows you." Matteo turned to leave before he did something regretful.

"You cannot enter a man's house and insult him, Matteo."

"And so I leave before my shit stains your floor."

"Your father would have never stood for such language or behavior."

"Never tell me what behaviors my father found acceptable." Now Matteo would do the pointing. "My father committed himself to telling the truth. My father believed in integrity and he lived by it."

"Judge not before you have lived. You young men, you giovani, you think you know everything. You have much to learn."

"I've learned much this morning. Don't worry yourself. I'll not set foot in your house again." Matteo yanked the door open to leave.

"You think me cruel? Would so cruel a man raise his illegitimate son? I feed him, clothe him well, educate him—I found him an apprenticeship."

Matteo opened his mouth to argue but Ser Piero continued.

"I'm not the father he wants me to be." Ser Piero hurried to an intricate table decorated with an ornamental vase. He pulled open a drawer. "Boys know nothing of fatherhood. A father says a prayer and sets the way for his son to stand on his own two feet. You want the truth? You cannot make anyone love you the way you want." Ser Piero shifted the contents of the drawer and held something in his hand. "Take it to him," he said and moved his arm to indicate Matteo should catch. The bag jangled.

Matteo caught it and stepped out of the house. "Coward," he said, "you should take it to him."

Ser Piero shut the door.

***

Heat in his blood, Matteo strode down the road following the Arno opposite the water's current. He would call it the long way. He turned on the Via de' Benci toward the Piazza di Santa Croce. Not wanting to disappoint Leonardo, he stopped in the Piazza to buy bread, a flask of wine for himself, a handful of dried figs, and some honeyed almonds. "More of those," he told the man scooping the nuts. "Fill the bag to the top."

"No half-measures for this one," an all to familiar Guido said. "He always wants more than everyone else."

"And you don't think the same for yourself?" When Guido smiled, his oversized upper lip resembled a duckbill, which fit his animal likeness more so with his too small eyes. Matteo smiled back. Guido's kind would freeze in iced waters if not for the call of his brothers. "What? Guido Bartoli is lonely? Your purse ran dry and suddenly you lost your servants, err, I mean friends? You must need money."

Guido's smile flattened.

"Maybe you should run to your moneyed Uncle. Everyone knows he's the man of substance. Here, you've come to the wrong man. I have better things to do with my time these days."

"I presume you do given your absence in the alleys. Not that we can forget your last visit. Did your beating scare you off so easily?"

"No. Not that we could forget yours. I can see that it did nothing to improve the look of your face." Matteo glared at Guido. "Some people have more pressing matters to tend to beyond kicking around the womanly feelings of Guido's lost love affairs." Matteo lifted the sack of almonds and paid.

Guido's eyes sparked. "Love affairs you say? I'd venture to say you denied your tall, blonde lover and moved to easier methods. Nobody sees you walking together in the piazzas anymore. The whores are easier, I'd agree."

Matteo swung around. He struggled to keep a straight face. Guido got lucky. Plenty of young men visited prostitutes. He wouldn't let Guido see he'd sunk his teeth in. The morning took enough of a toll on Matteo. "I don't want to make an effort to insult you, Guido. I owe you nothing. Move on and find something of interest in your own life."

Guido spit. "You're an ass."

"That's why you came for the abuse?" Matteo shrugged him off. He continued on foot to the Stinche. Several times he turned to check the road behind him.

***

"Untuck your camicia please, Signore."

Matteo did.

The guard lifted his flask. "You can't bring this inside."

Matteo removed it.

"Grazie, here you'll find it when you leave." The guard checked his food and patted down his back, sides, chest, and waist. He nodded and waved Matteo in. "Find a seat."

Matteo sat and put all thoughts of Guido away. Soon a door opened to the cramped room and a guard entered followed by a handful of prisoners. He spotted Leonardo before Leonardo saw him.

"Over here," Matteo said.

Leonardo's chin whipped right at the sound of his voice.

Matteo stood.

In two elongated steps Leonardo reached him and scooped him into an embrace. Leonardo said nothing but held on tight. Matteo hugged him back, but his efforts soon turned powerless. Leonardo's size and enthusiasm swallowed him up in a mangle of arms and tensed muscles. His face smashed against Leonardo, whose hold lodged his nose near an armpit that could wake a man twice over in the morning. His friend's face buried into his hair and brushed against his neck.

Matteo tapped him on the back. "I've brought you something," he said clear as possible from his strangulated state.

"Bedding?" Leonardo said releasing Matteo, his blue eyes expectant except for the darkened spots beneath them.

"Bedding? Uh, no." Matteo slowed his words, "I can bring some next time?" Matteo retrieved a bundle from the bench. "I didn't want to be a disappointment. Sit."

"A disappointment?" Leonardo opened the bundle. He smiled. "Bread. Figs. Grazie, Matteo. What's in this?"

"Not bedding." Matteo grinned and flicked his hand for him to continue.

Leonardo lifted the bag to his nose and closed his eyes. He tore his fingers through the ties. "Honeyed almonds." He shoved some into his mouth then offered the bag to Matteo.

"They're for you. Have you eaten at all since you arrived?"

Leonardo slowed his eating. "I ate some bread and drank terrible, watered wine last night."

Matteo looked him over and watched him eat. "Maybe I've not brought enough." Do they treat you well? Tell me what you need?"

Leonardo chewed a fig and swallowed. "It's no way to live, but I've not been mistreated. It's the dark. Some light enters in the morning, some in the afternoon. They let us walk in the courtyard each morning for air."

Leonardo stole glances between bites of bread. "Needless to say, I could use bedding if you're so inclined to bring it." He ate another handful of nuts. "The food tastes better than I've ever eaten, grazie." He seemed more than grateful. "Matteo, you, here, I could wish for no more under the circumstances. Please, don't be afraid when I say that you are my only hope. I know I can't expect you to come everyday. But I beg you, please don't forget me."

To think himself Leonardo's champion sat ill-fitted. Matteo knocked his elbow into Leonardo's side. "If ever there's a way to free you from this place, I'll be the first to pursue it."

Matteo stood when the interior door opened to take the prisoners away. "I have to go, but not before I give you this." He held Ser Piero's bag of money. "I'll not deny it's from your father."

Leonardo's face paled. "You shouldn't have."

"I thought—you know what I thought. Nothing's changed. Blame me for trying if you must. Your father knew before I went to his door this morning to tell him your fate." Matteo prodded Leonardo. "Take it. I'm not convinced there'll be more from him."

Leonardo nodded. His refreshed demeanor sunk inward. He stopped listening.

Matteo took hold of him and caught his eye. "I'll not let you down. Do you hear me? Today a meal and tomorrow bedding—think of what you might need after. This will see us through."

43

Piero needed an escape from the sickly feeling that overtook him when he learned of Leonardo's sin. The cries of his infant son filled the house. "Too much, too much," he wanted to cry back, but his drunkenness made him mute. He unlatched the rickety door near the kitchen, but hesitated entering the closet. He leaned against the door and extended his candle to light the dark place. Large enough to take three steps forward, and narrow enough his hands could touch the walls, he stepped inside. Hot wax dribbled on his hand when he staggered. He needed to hide awhile and calm himself.

Piero closed the door. He stared at the crimson in his cup. Crimson like blood—his blood let by the man who abused him. Wine swished in his cup. The warmth of it snaked down his throat. Piero swallowed the color of anger, the color of blood. Drink filled him up and took him further away in his hiding place where he hoped to remember nothing.

"Wah, neh, wah, neh," came the distant newborn cries. A son. News to send every proud father out in the streets, "My son is born. Yes, I have a son."

But Ser, you have two. Blood of his loins.

"Leo—" a sob stifled Piero's call. "Not sodomy."

Cobwebs strung across Piero's eyes, brushed his lips, and stuck to his chin. He slumped onto a stool and set the candle aside. Crimson colored his clothes. Never tell. He stared into his cup.

As a boy of ten, he should have known better, but a stupid secret, a boyhood dream made him go. "Help. Make him stop," he had cried, but no one came. They were alone.

"I want to be a knight," Piero admitted so long ago. "Can you make my sword?" he asked the blacksmith. But the man laughed to shame his dream.

"Raise a sword I've made with those tiny arms of yours? That wouldn't be knightly," the blacksmith told him, amused.

"I knew I should wait until my father took me to the city where the blacksmiths know how to make marvelous swords," Piero said.

"Then bring it and show me once you have one. We can test its strength against one of my own." He shook his head. "Every man knows a sword doesn't make a knight. You're not of noble birth, boy."

"I will be a knight," Piero said in all seriousness.

The blacksmith lifted his tools. Sparks flecked on his anvil. "I'll make your sword the day you prove yourself noble as a knight." He swatted his hand for Piero to leave.

To prove his worth, Piero returned many times, but the blacksmith kept him waiting.

Months later, the blacksmith said, "I've grown used to your visits. Might we call ourselves friends, young knight?"

"Did you? Did you call me a knight?"

The blacksmith nodded. "Come. Tell me about your sword. I have a few inside," he said leading Piero into a storage house behind the stable where he shoed the horses. "Let's find the best fit for your cross-guard and hilt."

The blacksmith showed him several swords and let him hold one in his hands. Piero lifted the sword with effort, and the blacksmith came up behind him and placed his hands on Piero's. They swung together.

"Once you get the feel for it, a sword moves at ease under your command." The blacksmith slid his hands from

Piero's, down his arms, and onto his shoulders. "Now we need to discuss payment."

Piero set the blade aside and cleared a table full of tools in need of repair. "It's all I have," he said rushing to open his purse.

The blacksmith wiped his hands and drank what remained of an opened bottle of wine. He offered Piero a bite of his bread and cheese, ate some, and shook his head. "You haven't enough money to buy a sword." He fingered the money and pushed it back. "A knight places honesty and duty in greater regard than his sword, yes? Good, we agree. We can help each other. We'll both get what we want." He reached for olive oil and poured a little over his bread. "But there's a problem with your plan," he said, patting Piero above his knee, "You cannot be a knight when you tell lies."

"I am no liar, Signore."

The blacksmith sucked his breath in. "Uh ho?" he asked, his hand climbing higher on Piero's leg.

Piero's stomach hollowed and his chest hammered. "Signore, I have to go before my father notices I've been gone too long." He stood to leave.

The blacksmith pulled Piero against his huge chest. "I like you. I'll not judge you for your secrets," he said. Softly he continued, "Your father made a beautiful boy." He kissed Piero and forced his arms behind his back. "You have more to offer than a purse. I'll give you a sword," he said humored.

"Stop. Please," Piero said, struggling to get away.

The blacksmith stood and slid Piero from the bench.

Piero kicked and twisted. His wrists hurt under the man's strength. But the blacksmith didn't give up. He hoisted Piero's weak arms above his head with one hand, and shoved the other past his waist and down his backside. "Help," Piero called, "Make him stop." A horse neighed in response.

"Be a good boy, and we won't have to tell your father what you've done," the blacksmith said. "You have the voice of an angel and the face of a cherub. Don't make me cover them to quiet you." He fondled Piero's buttocks and yanked down his hose. "Shhh, now. Quiet. I'll let you loose if you sit on my lap like a good boy."

"No." Piero shook his head again. He breathed so hard he thought he would fall. Too small to get away, he closed his eyes. "Please. No."

"Then we'll do it your way. Secret-like." Clothes fumbled against his back. Piero knew what fumbled next and he tried his best to scoot away from it. The blacksmith made it slippery and dropped his bottle on the floor.

Piero stared at the crack in the wall that smashed against the side of his face.

The man tried to push into him.

Piero shrieked.

The blacksmith did it again.

Piero shrieked again and couldn't stand on his feet.

"Young knight, it pains me to hear you cry," he said without letting go. "I'll not do it again." The man pulled Piero between his thick legs and rubbed himself between Piero's thighs until he shuddered. Done, he said, "You made me do it."

The blacksmith carried Piero and laid him down behind some old crates. "I know more than one of your secrets, boy. And we both know that no one believes liars. Now, once you've licked your sores, leave."

Piero stared at the wall and wished he never wanted a sword. He squeezed his eyes shut and waited for the man to go away. The blacksmith was right. He would never be a knight.

Piero touched his buttocks. Blood colored his fingers. He wiped his eyes and moved his shaking hands to pull up his hose—torn and useless. He slipped off his shoes and yanked. The pull made him squeak, so he tenderly pulled his other foot out and tossed his hose into the corner. His shoes back on, he pulled his tunic down, but a trickle crept down his leg. Carefully he got to his feet and found the hose to wrap the way he once watched the ladies change his baby brother's linens.

Before he left, he stopped to wash. He slapped his hands into the water trough and said, "Hide the tears, unworthy knight."

Father wanted him to be a man. Piero licked the tears on his lips.

Once home, he would say he fell. Yes, he said he rolled down the hill into a thicket and told his parents nothing more. Never tell.

Piero hated blood. He drank what remained in his cup and tossed it with all his strength to hear it shatter.

44
May 1476

Matteo hurried into the crowded Mercato toward the peddler pulling his handcart filled with household trinkets. He ducked behind the far side of the cart and matched the footfalls of the peddler until he could get a better position. Damn you, Guido Bartoli, sport had a time and place. Guido burrowed under Matteo's skin like blisters of a plague. As for Guido's motivations, that was a different matter. Guido didn't take hints, and now Matteo got sucked into his childish game.

Matteo, the Great Maestro of Civettino in all of the Greve Valley, dodged and parried every boy, and once a girl, willing to try and smack him. He stood center with both feet on a boy's foot to his left and to his right. They tried to strike him, the owl. Learning the game, he took a few hits, but from then on his opponents failed. They said he moved too fast. They asked if he had eyes in the back of his head. He answered with taunts and always made hits against players less skilled than him.

In the market he'd blend much like an owl in the trees. He tried to avoid Guido, but the ass thought him a shiny plaything. First he ignored Guido's taunts, but now Guido's habit turned into more than annoyance. Matteo would put an end to the game by leading the scrawny mouse into a trap. How long did Guido think he could play and why did he think it wise to follow him? More troublesome, how long did Matteo sit in the center of the game without realizing he played?

Matteo worried he'd lost his speed and awareness when he realized Guido did catch him unaware that day in the piazza. Guido's slip of the tongue? Intentional. Come to me my prey. Oh how Matteo could play once he knew the game. Trap the mouse. Make him squeak until the truth came out. Devour him. A satisfied smile stretched Matteo's lips wide.

Once Matteo reached the stall where the man sold pots and bowls, he paused to let the mouse catch up. A corner merchant's stacked nets and cages provided room enough to strike. The mockery of the hunter becoming the hunted nearly satiated Matteo's hunger. Cage upon cage, stacked taller than the tallest of men, formed a wall to block the view of the other side. Matteo waited for Guido to spot him again then hurried into position. He rushed past the wall, straightened himself up against the edge, and waited where the late afternoon sun hadn't reached.

Guido crossed his line of sight and turned his head to the right. He twisted to the left...

Strike! Matteo slammed into Guido before he knew what hit him. Matteo used his head as a ram against Guido's chest and hooked his arms behind his knees to take him down. Guido hit the road with a satisfying crack.

Guido tried to fend off the attack by aiming a punch at Matteo's face. He missed.

"It's not so amusing when on the receiving end is it, you foul little shit?"

Guido growled and tried kneeing Matteo in the groin.

Matteo growled back and punched him in the soft part of his side and heard a grunt. He slid his knee forward against Guido's groin and pressed up. He'd make him sing.

"Agggh huuuuh," came the falsetto. Guido slackened his fight.

"I know not what you play at, but your games grow old. Now answer me," Matteo said, "Why do you follow me?"

Guido coughed then laughed and spit in Matteo's face. He tried to push Matteo off him.

Matteo shook his head and punched Guido in the face. "Wrong answer."

Guido's fists beat against Matteo in no aimed manner; he battered them right and left and did his best to try to make contact with Matteo's face.

"Wrong answer." Another punch hit its mark. This time blood bubbled from Guido's lips.

Guido bucked like a spurned horse, but Matteo rode on. They rolled a few times.

Matteo took an elbow to the face, which enraged him further. He righted himself and cracked Guido's head on the street. "Tell me why you follow me."

Guido made another attempt to get free, but Matteo looped an arm under his leg and pinned the other behind his waist. "If you don't answer, I plan to plant my elbow so far up your cock hole you'll become a woman."

Guido stopped moving when the elbow pressed in. "For the money. The money is all."

"What money? Someone is paying you to follow me? Who, why?"

"Gold coin. I don't know," Guido said. "I'm paid to follow you. I'm in the middle." He kneed Matteo in the chin and kicked his legs in attempt to crawl away. "I don't know his name you ignorant ass."

Matteo snatched Guido by his feet, dragged him back, bent his leg, and leaned into it with all his weight so he could punch the bastard in his ugly face. "Wrong answ—"

"No," Guido said planting his head against the stone road in attempt to save his face. "It was a deal in the alley. You know how it is. A man states his request and holds out the coin. The first one who grabs it gets it and the promise for a bigger portion once his work's done." Guido tried lifting Matteo off him.

"You cheap bastard. Why follow me? When are you done?" Matteo didn't like how long Guido waited to answer. "Tell me." His clawed a hand into his hair and lifted his sorry head, "Tell me before I beat—"

"They want you gone. They wait for you to make a mistake. Something that will cost you—cost more than you can pay. Then my work is done. Now let me go."

None of it made sense. Matteo worked to make his father proud. "Not a man in the alley gives half a shit about you, Guido. They'll gather round when you fall and pick you apart piece by bloody piece." His hold on Guido loosened. "You don't need the money. You come from a good family, so give the gold back. No more of these childish games."

Guido wiped his mouth on his sleeve. "I can't help a target lands on your back. You have no father, no heirs. Nothing but your holdings. And you're young," he said, hate-filled. "Don't you know how many men work until they straddle middle age and still have less to show? They say you're not worthy."

Matteo now knew the pain caused from a trampling horse. His chest heaved, but he willed his panic down. "I'll not take these ideas and think them sensible. Piss off. All of you," he said to everyone around him. His thoughts turned to his mother. He couldn't live this way. "Go." He shoved Guido hard before he beat him to death. "Get out of my way before I kick your balls off and send them back to the alley for the foulest beggar. If I catch you again, I swear I'll cut them off." For good measure he gave Guido a kick in his seat.

He made no effort to dust himself off. People gave him a wide girth on his way out of the market, and good, God help the one who laid a finger against him.

Anger Matteo understood, but jealousy drove men to the worst of evils. He wasn't rich, and herein he found his problem. A rich man sat above common contempt because people feared him, and a poor man kept well enough to himself without the luxury of waiting for better days, but the men in the middle, bit and kicked, scratched and punched. They found a way to reach for the lowest rung of a palace tower so far above them that they couldn't see it clearly yet knew it must be there. Before, Matteo displayed his confident hand and swung around a bit, but now, he didn't dare. His own kind wanted to devour him.

***

A visit to his mother turned necessary for their survival. He hoped Guido felt twice the worse for wear on principle, for he'd rather not return home in a battered body. Matteo's swollen knuckles made for a difficult hold on horse reins, and he couldn't forget the bruising up his arms, the egg on his cheek, or the tweak in his back. Mother may not get past his appearance long enough to listen to the words she longed to hear. No, she would hear him, and rush through the house like a nun who'd seen a miracle. Then she'd chide him for his appearance.

He couldn't remove the target off his back, but he could make safe the Attaviano name.

"Mother?" Matteo couldn't force his body to move any further, but he made it home, where the hills stretched out like a quilt. Soon he could lie his head down to rest.

Cook's head popped out the kitchen doorway. "Matteo? Signore, I knew nothing of your arrival." He wiped his hands on a cloth and drew closer. "Maestro, I—what's happened to you?"

"I'd be no happier saying I look far worse than I feel." Matteo tried to smile. "Nothing good wine and a warm bed can't heal."

Cook rushed ahead and pulled up a chair. "Sit. I'll bring you drink straight away."

Matteo sat. The familiar scents of orange and cypress soothed him.

"Matteo? Son? Did I hear my son?"

Mother's steps quickened once she turned the corner and saw him.

"Matteo." She hugged him and kissed the top of his head. "Holy Mary Mother of God," she said crossing herself. "You're beaten, son. How could this happen?" She wiped his hair from his eyes and held his face at an angle to get a better look. "It's blue." Her fingers pressed around his swollen eye.

"Ow." He pulled her hand away. "It's blue because it's hurt, Mother. Don't press it."

"Psh, I touched it tender as when you were a babe." She took his hand and set it across her open palm. "And this? What sort of fight did you tangle yourself in this time? Look at it, would you?" She moved all of his fingers and made him wince. "They're not broken, but this one," she ran the tip of her finger from his middle knuckle to fingernail. "Yes, I am certain. It's not in place if not broken."

"It hurts like hell."

She popped him one on the ear. "None of that."

"You'll hit your only son when he's already blue?"

Mother held her hand just begging him to watch her do it.

"Forgive me, Mother, I'm home. That has to be worth something?"

Her eyes sparkled. "You can't play the innocent. I hope that whomever did this to my boy feels no better."

"He doesn't. I assure you."

She tucked a long tendril of white-streaked hair behind her ear and called for her ladies. "You'll not like what I have to do." She waved her ladies over. "We have to set your finger right. I need two pieces of wood about this long." Mother lifted the finger for them to estimate size.

"Mamma!" Matteo pulled his finger from her reach. "No more until you're ready." Given his mother's hands-on approach, there was no way he would he tell her the reason for his visit until she finished torturing him.

"And bring some linen strips too to wrap the mess he's made," Mother said.

Cook offered wine. "Drink. I can bring more to dull the pain."

"Finally, someone sensible. Grazie, Matteo said," and Cook nodded in manly accord.

Once the ladies returned, Matteo downed his second glass of wine.

"Need I ask how this happened? I think of you everyday, Matteo. I worry, and look at you. You have to find a different way to solve your problems. Before you know it, a morning will come when you wake and discover youth escaped your body."

Mother caught hold of his wrist unaware. "Mmm," Matteo said, biting back his pain and sharp words.

Mother pinched his middle finger tight between her fingers and tugged.

"Son of a whore." He slapped his good hand against his thigh.

"Matteo di Lapo Attaviano, you're mouth is filthy," Mother said wrapping his finger. "Think about this pain the next time you think it wise to fight. One month at the least. Take it off no earlier."

He waited for her to finish her work then offered half a grin. "Shall I tell you the reason I came without notice? It wasn't for your tender care."

Mother stood patient, curious.

"It's not as simple as it sounds, but I'll tell you the rest after I've gotten some food and sleep." His throat turned dry. "Mother, you will let me sleep?"

She leaned forward in anticipation. "Of course. Why would I not let you sleep?"

Matteo paused the way he his father would when he weighed a decision of great importance. He followed in his father's shadow until he could forge his own path, and though they traveled a common road, he now reached the fork that would separate them. Everything would change. He must trust his instincts and protect his family, ensure their survival by numbers.

"Son, I can see you carry a burden on your lips, but I swear that if you don't speak I'll beat it out of you after that introduction."

Matteo swallowed. "I want the dowry and birthing hips. Now. As soon as possible."

Mother's eyes and mouth formed perfect circles. She hollered for her ladies and smashed him in her arms. "You little devil." She rushed out of the room. "A wife, a wife. My son wants a wife." She ran into the kitchen and told Cook.

"There are a few suitable girls," she said. She jumped in surprise. "I'll have a daughter." The ladies and his mother nestled close, clasped their hands, and squealed in delight.

"And the babies, Mona Serena. The babies," said her women.

Matteo stood to leave. Mother's response scared him more than his own. Sweat formed under his arms knowing what he'd say next. "Not any wife, mother. I have one in mind. I—"

"Oh, son. I can tell by the look on your face. Lucrezia is suitable and she always caught your eye."

Matteo nodded, relieved he need not say more.

Mother's face went from joy to sympathy. "Come. Sit. We have to talk." She shushed everyone out of the room.

"Don't you approve, Mother? You said she's suitable. We agree." He wouldn't sit. "What's happened to her? What? Is she...dead?"

"No, nothing that tragic. She's to marry Antonmaria Gherardini." Mother reached out to him. "You would make a better match. It could have been a first marriage for you both. But don't lose hope."

"The contract is signed?" His finger set, it would be a shame to punch something.

"I'm certain of it."

He turned away. "Leave me for the night. I'm going to bed." He didn't love Lucrezia, but he did know her. And he worried for her. She was different, like him. Also like him, place her in the wrong hands, and she walked herself straight into trouble.

45

Leonardo shouted into the darkness and he shouted into the light, but his cage absorbed men's cries like raindrops fading on stones. A prisoner breathed, no more, no less, for this was his curse. He opened his eyes, smelled fear, and waited for the hunger pangs to stab his gut. He saw flecks of his likeness in those nearby; they knew his secret. He could scream and carry on like a madman and no one batted an eye. Rest, the faces urged with their looks of too much understanding. You'll never be good enough, the faces told him.

Rest, but how? He thought he knew what it meant to be alone, but he was wrong. Time in the Stinche made man know solitude. Here a prisoner stood motionless in time. The darkness dissipated none because it would control him, bend him, work to break him. Harder it pulled until he lost the will to overcome it. It lulled him with the promise of sleep. Yes, sleep clouded the mind from life in a pit. Time passed unaware in sleep. If he closed his eyes, he could escape.

Leonardo woke with damp skin and shouted to pierce the darkness. "Ser? Please, I need you. Don't abandon me." Leonardo wiped his forehead and listened, certain he'd woken from his bad dream. A nightmare, he told himself, nothing more, but a voice boomed past the thundering of his heart and told him he belonged here, forgotten. He shook his head to disagree. "My father will come," he whispered, "be patient."

But the nights pressed on and on.

Leonardo clawed his bed in fear of the dark—the dark that told him Ser wouldn't come. "Don't forget me." He clung to his blanket in wait.

"You're not yet awake," he said realizing no one would come if they couldn't hear him. "Wake, wake." But no one heard him in this muted place. No one answered. The darkness lied.

He clawed his hands in his hair and tugged back and forth. Snags caught between his fingers. A voice shushed him and told him to quiet.

Wait no longer his mind told his heart. Ser's not coming. Accept the truth. He held his head firm in his hands and trembled.

***

Leonardo rolled the charcoal between his fingers and stared at the void. His time in nothing honed his vision to the darkness like a wild animal too cautious to enter the light. Every morning he woke to the splatting sound of water from the well, to a dry tongue and damp body, to the fetid smells of human waste, or the scratching of rock on rock, the clanking of chains, voices snoring, grunting, crying, spitting, or arguing. He began Dante's La Commedia to help pass the time until he reached The Gate of Hell. "Abandon all hope ye who enter here," he read, and returned it to Papi unwilling to devote more effort to hopelessness.

Once the short-lived sunlight reached through the barred windows, Leonardo rose from bed.

Papi sprawled flat on his bed and played like he had no knowledge of anyone's movements.

Because Papi watched, Leonardo marked another day on the wall above his bed. He refused to keep actual count though and stretched out to stare at nothing.

"Please, Leonardo. I need water," Papi's voice rasped in the dark.

"How did you get water before I became your servant?"

Papi hacked and cursed him under his breath. "By the good grace of the Friar, my one friend who hasn't forgotten me. Since you have much to do, I'll wait for him."

"You damned malcontent," Leonardo said, and willed himself out of his stupor to help a forsaken man chained to a wall.

Many uncounted marks later, Leonardo found himself waiting, ready, for Papi's call.

"Water."

Leonardo rose from bed, made his mark on the wall, and brought his washbasin to the well near the window to fill it.

"Papi," Leonardo set the basin on the floor, "your water." He helped him sit-up and grabbed a bundle from his shelf. "Have some of my bread."

Papi cupped his hands and drank, waited for Leonardo's bread, and nodded in thanks. They drank and washed, then ate to hold them over until the Friar came with better food.

"I know why you do it."

Papi looked him over.

Leonardo tipped his head toward the man the prisoners named Tartaruga, the turtle. "Rarely does he wake."

"No man wants to sleep with the dead. That's why they prod him. When he cries, they know he draws breath." Papi scratched his wiry chin. "It's about choice. Bring him water."

"Him?"

"Or don't. You choose. How's Tartaruga different than me?" Papi grumbled, "You're afraid of a man who stares at a wall?" He shoved the washbasin in Leonardo's chest. "Move. I don't want to watch the young man next to me turn to stone. Choose better." Papi's chest heaved and he dropped back to his bed, winded.

Leonardo collected water and slowed his approach. Tartaruga faced the wall. His legs curled near his chest. Leonardo spoke gently, "I may not know your name, Signore. I'll call you by none. I've brought you water." He bent down, eyes locked on the man, and watched for any sign of movement when he pulled the empty basin from beneath Tartaruga's bed. No movement. He hurried to pour the water in and slid the basin back in place. "I'll go now."

Leonardo returned and put his basin away. "He didn't know I was there."

"My boy, that's his choice. While you're moving, I say, keep going."

"I have time, Papi. I'm ready to talk. Will you hear me?"

Chains rattled. "You're in luck. I have time yet."

Leonardo sat on his bed and searched for where to begin. Many could call him a blasphemer, but some matters of the heart refused spoken words to remain sacred. Leonardo would not taint them with further villainy. The rest he told. He started at the beginning. Flashes of his childhood formed a patchwork. Everything began and ended with Ser.

***

Leonardo stopped talking and waited for Papi to respond. "Papi, are you awake?"

Papi grunted in answer.

"Have you nothing to say?"

"Calm yourself. You alone can tell your story." Papi made a humming sound. "You've been in the Stinche fifty-two days. Where can a man find goodness in the Stinche? Where can he find hope in the dark? Once I was young and believed in something." He moved to light his lamp, which lit only from their strict rationing of oil from the food given to them by the Friar. "Remembering brings pain."

"Why listen then if you want to suffer—if you want to die?"

Papi thought a moment. "These old eyes have begged to see goodness in the world before they close forever."

Papi wrapped his hands around Leonardo's face. His soft gaze held them eye-to-eye. "I'm satisfied. Here." He shook his hands, "Here I see goodness. Here I remember love. Never give up when you've only begun. Some things are done to you. Some are done for you."

Unable to look into Papi's moist eyes, Leonardo reached his hand around to palm the back of his head.

"You came to me because I forgot how to be free from my chains." Papi pointed between them. "We're not accidental in this place. I've lived. I remember."

"Papi, you above all people shouldn't be chained. Tell me why. Tell me how. I have to know."

"One's man blessing is another man's curse. I'm in chains because I have ears to hear and a tongue to speak." He held his hand up for Leonardo to wait while he coughed. "Surely you know de' Pazzi family. Jacopo, the family head? Your eyes view his forgotten Chancellor. I sat like a dog at Maestro's feet until the tight-fisted, old turd grew suspicious. Here, there, men filed in and out of his office. As Chancellor, his business was my business. That's how we worked for years, but he changed. Held secrets. One morning, as I attended to my duties, what I heard sealed my fate."

"What did you hear?"

Papi lowered his voice. "That's what Jacopo and his cohorts wanted to know. He cared not for the trust we forged over the years. He couldn't risk his compromised position. It takes few words to know an evil plot when you hear one. I cannot speak it out of respect for dangerous information. So, they put me to the strappato each day of that first week in the Stinche. I hung there, my shoulders out of place, and refused to tell Jacopo's secret, which became my burden. I lied and claimed I knew nothing. They added weights to my feet and hoisted again and again, and I maintained my resolve thinking an innocent man goes free." Papi growled. "Pahhh, innocence."

"He sent you here? How long?"

Papi shrugged. "Until everyone's forgotten I exist."

"You have no one else?"

Papi hung his head in his hands and delayed his answer. "I had a daughter. The comeliest one you've ever seen." His voice cracked. "Liviana. She's all I had when they dragged me into this hole. Twelve years to her name and she'd already lost her mother, and I, her father made her an orphan. I sent letters until my ink ran dry. Now I've lost her forever. The Ospedale degli Innocenti took her in. Then the letters stopped. They told me she'd gone. No one could tell me what happened to her, and here I sat, chained to a cursed wall."

Leonardo reached for him.

"Who enters the Stinche without a curse on their head?" He thought a moment. "I'm tired and want to suffer no more. When I say I want to die, leave me."

***

Two days later, Leonardo woke and marked his fifty-fourth day. "Papi, your water."

Papi moaned.

"Papi?" Leonardo shook him.

Papi stirred in bed. He drank and coughed up his water. "An ulcer," he said. "I dreamt of grand stairs. Sunlight streamed down brighter than we've ever seen. And I heard her. My wife called to me. Her voice carried like a song on a breeze so sweet I wanted to go to her. I tasted the thyme and basil on her skin and smelled her fresh bread. But I'm afraid."

"I dreamt of you, Papi. There's a way to bend the bars in this prison. I've thought on this. I know how to do it. First we broke your chain, and Papi, you walked beside me. We left this place together. The sun shone warm on our faces, blinding bright."

"First walk the courtyard and tell me all you see. I have to picture the light before I can accept it. Can you do this? Tell me the colors of the sky. I want to know how many birds fly above."

Leonardo refused. "You'll go while I'm gone," he said. He crouched on the stone floor to yank Papi's chain. He placed his feet against the wall and leaned back with all his power. "You believe I came to you—you came to me. Help me!" Leonardo called to anyone who would listen. "Help me free this man from the walls that close us in." He called on the one indebted to Matteo for sparing his humiliation. "Baccino, help."

Baccino refused, but another man approached.

"Help me pull if you love anything. He can't run away even once we free him. Tartaruga?" Tartaruga rushed past them and set himself to the task. The other, a man built like a stonemason, joined them. He pushed Baccino out of his way.

"My time draws near," Papi said, "I have no more fight. Dare you ask me to hold on?" Papi slumped on his bed. "Leave me, Leonardo."

"No, Papi, we'll free you. Not long. Hold on." Leonardo turned his attention to the chain and pulled.

"On the count of three, pull together," the big man said a second time.

They pulled and pulled. "One more," they chanted, and the bar slid free.

Leonardo scrambled to his feet. "Papi, you're free. Walk with me to the window. See the sky with a friend."

"Help me."

Leonardo got Papi standing and held the bar in his hand.

Papi staggered unable to stay on his feet.

"Waste none of the light. I'll carry you." Leonardo picked him up.

Papi shielded his eyes at first. "Once I'm gone, put me in my bed. None of you know how I broke free." Papi cried, "I'm ready, but," he begged, "Don't let them bury me in my chains."

They agreed and sat in the light of the window until the sun reached beyond the bars that held them.

46
July 1476

Leonardo marked his fifty-seventh day in the Stinche and went to collect his water. He poured half for the sleeping Tartaruga, returned to his bed, and drank. The life that once resided in the empty space beside him existed no more. All that remained were some light colored scratches on the wall and the joyful thought of Papi's freedom.

"Prisoners step away from the door," a guard announced in a crisp voice.

Too early for the walk in the courtyard, the prisoners turned their attention to discover the purpose of his visit.

The guard unlocked the cell door. He called for Baccino and waited for him. "Leonardo da Vinci."

Leonardo turned his attention to the crumbling hole in the wall. The hole, discovered during inspection, roused suspicion. Did someone, maybe Baccino tell what he'd done—he and Tartaruga, and the big man? Guards called on the big man a day ago and he'd not returned. The guards came and went, but sometimes they took men to the infirmary, others they put to the Rackmaster's questions.

"Leonardo da Vinci," the guard called again in a booming voice.

Blood beating in his ears, Leonardo rose from his bed.

"He comes," a voice said somewhere in the darkness.

Leonardo ambled out. He willed himself not to think more on those who preceded him. He squinted in the daylight. "Follow him," the guard said clanging the door shut and locking it.

Sweat dripped from Baccino's face. "Where do you take us?"

Through a gate, they entered a narrow walkway that opened into another room. "Signori, the Officer of the Treasury requires debts paid in full before transferring you to the holding cells."

"Holding cells?" Leonardo said.

The officer told his companion to bring their records. "You will transfer to the Captain of Justice's holding cells immediately." He turned his attention to open the records. "However, no man leaves the Stinche if he retains debt. I see you've paid two florins of your fines." The officer read the record and leaned back in his chair. "The cost of your stay plus another…" he looked at them, "It is neither here nor there." He ran his hands along the front panel of his desk and tapped them with finality.

"I don't understand," Leonardo said. "We're going back to the Officer's of the Night?" The Podestà held those awaiting execution in the tower Volognana. He didn't want to burn! Breathing hard, Leonardo pulled back and bumped into the guard. "I'm to serve my sentence in the Stinche."

"Signore da Vinci," said the impetuous Officer, "this is no means of deceit. You have fallen and will continue to fall under the mercy of the Podestà." He wrote in his record book. "Have you anything to retrieve from the malevato?"

"No. I have nothing."

Another guard entered—the Captain. Leonardo didn't forget the one who delivered him to the Stinche.

"I transferred the other two yesterd—"

The officer slapped the signed papers into the Captain's chest.

Lionardo Tornabuoni and Jacopo Saltarelli? "The others charged with us are there?"

The officer heard Leonardo yet made no reply. "Be on your way, Captain. These men are no longer under our charge." He addressed Leonardo and Baccino," It's not my place to inquire on your behalf. Perhaps you can find your answer with the Podestà." He stood from his seat. "Bind them for transfer."

***

Bound in ropes, Leonardo trailed Baccino. They exited the same way they entered. Leonardo hesitated stepping into the unknown, but each step delivered him back into the light.

The officer brought his horse round and led them away.

People watched them pass on the streets; some with jeers much like the noble towers looming from above, others looked on in pity like the Virgin tabernacles below.

In the courtyard of the Podestà, the Captain read their names again and continued, "You await an audience with the Justices, who have called you back under," he read from his document, "unnamed occurrence." He opened the holding cell door, untied them, locked them in, and departed.

"A new trial?" Leonardo shouted after the Captain, "How long must we wait?"

The Captain held his hands up in answer.

The holding cell, tiny compared to the room in the Stinche, had more light due to the position of the door that opened into the courtyard of the Podestà. It lacked the massive walls of the Stinche but did enclose them in another cavern of stone. A bench carved from the stone centered the back wall. Two men could lay the cell's width hand to foot across the floor.

"Leonardo, Leonardo da Vinci," called a voice outside their walls. Leonardo and Baccino looked to each other and listened.

"Baccino? Leonardo?" the voice said again.

Leonardo and Baccino went to the barred door. "Yes?" Baccino said.

A hand popped out. "It's Lionardo and Jacopo."

Baccino put his arm out. "What's happened?"

"Our way out, so Lionardo thinks."

"Yes," added the confident voice of Il Teri. "My family has the ears of Il Magnifico thanks to his Tournabuoni mother. Sleep well. We are saved."

"How fortuitous for you Il Teri, you're saved. You alone," Baccino said.

"Fool. If I walk free, we all walk free. How could they release one when three others are accused on the same charges at the same time and place? We know the truth. One of us spent the night with Jacopo, not all—not that night. The harlot holds quite a reputation."

Leonardo listened but said nothing in his defense. A clunk followed by grumbles sounded. "Harlot, damned harlot! You're the reason we're here and I cannot be rid of you."

"Fuck you," Jacopo said.

Il Teri thrust back, "Not a good suggestion given our condition, you fool."

Jacopo's voice carried over, "Don't play the innocent. Giorgio's ass is well-worn with your efforts, oh righteous one."

Leonardo retreated from the door. He could listen to no more of their insults. But he hoped Il Teri's claim rang true.

***

Leonardo woke from Baccino's moaning. "Quiet. I can't sleep and I don't want to listen to your abuse." He rose from his stone bed and went to look out the door.

"Quiet? All we have is quiet. We've nothing to do but stare at the walls and each other. We're dirty and you smell." Baccino angled himself away from Leonardo.

Their close confinement pared them to days of petty insults. Leonardo roared. One time, one mistake, and he paid a steep price, but these others repeated their vices without remorse.

The way Baccino grunted like a pig when he fondled himself made Leonardo's skin crawl. He tried not to listen. "I never want to see you again if we ever should leave here."

"Leonardo," Baccino said, "Leonardo?"

"What?"

"As you can see, I have no desire to see you." Baccino wiped his hand on the wall. He sat with his legs apart to display his limp, used sex, and held a grotesque grin on his sweaty face.

"You're a wretched little man. I know your kind— proud of the way you force people to see you though you're limp and weak. Pull down your tunic you foul shit. I've seen enough." Leonardo would punch him if he didn't have to place his hands on the swine. "My friend granted a wasted courtesy on you." He refused to give Baccino anymore power. He sat on the gritty floor and watched the birds in the courtyard.

Later, the Captain approached. "Clean yourselves well, giovani. By mid-day you stand before the Podestà."A guard followed behind him with bread and water.

Leonardo drank before Baccino's hands fouled his water. He couldn't eat, but watched that his portion remained while Baccino ate. Leonardo washed and kept an eye on Baccino.

Baccino finished his food portion and eyed Leonardo's.

Leonardo shook his head and snapped up his bread. "This is mine."

Baccino pulled his legs in. "I wasn't going to eat it."

Leonardo took it knowing Baccino would eat it. He stepped to the door and chucked it for the birds.

Baccino gasped. "The last words I will ever say to you are: You deserve to starve, Leonardo." Baccino pulled the bucket in and mumbled to himself.

The Captain returned. He bound the four and walked them to their audience with the Justices.

Leonardo cared not that his hands were bound at the thought of his possible release. They entered through double doors. To the side of the courtroom, a notary sat at his desk. A bar divided the room with the accused on one side and two Judges on the other. The Judges sat on a raised platform. They wore black hats and full-length robes lined with fur of gray and white. Above them a statue stood depicting Justice.

The Captain waited for the prisoners to line up before the Judges and removed the rope from their hands. "Bow before them," he said, and stepped aside.

A Judge read their names. "This the ninth day of June, 1476, before the Podestà, you come under review for your offenses against God and man. Signori, upon a second review of your sentences, we have found no record of any man to come forth against you. Thus, the Justices find the tamburo accusations hold little weight without further evidence." The judge stopped to allow the other to speak.

He read from a document. "Leonardo da Vinci, a denunciation arrived to the Officer's of the Night on the seventh of June, 1476 accusing you of sodomy for the second time."

What? Leonardo couldn't hear what the man said. His mind screamed out in protest.

"The Officer's of the Night seek the truth before persecuting any man. The court requested your papers and determined that the accusation has no bearing on your sentence since you were found to reside within the Stinche on the date listed on the second denunciation."

The first Judge continued, "Signori, we find no further reason to detain you. But heed your God and the People of Florence. Pray for your sins. Lead lives of humility and righteousness, which will give no man reason to accuse you. As your city absolves you of your crime, so you should live a life of honor to thank her." He stood. "Report to the cancelleria." He gave the documents to the notary, who made his annotations, stood, and escorted them to obtain their release.

As soon as the administrator said he was free to go, Leonardo thought of Papi, and Matteo, of his Maestro, and of Ser. He rushed out of the Palazzo.

Free air smelled of cut herbs, straw, and fresh water; it caressed Leonardo's hair and goose-fleshed his skin like a gentle lover. He stood in the summer sun then sat on a bench bordering the piazza until his stomach grumbled. He'd use his last coin for food.

He thought of Ser when he passed the doors of the notaries that worked as Podestà henchmen. All men had a price. Could he look down on them when he benefited from their avarice? Temptation harassed Leonardo from within the dark place he visited far too many days in prison. As much as Ser worked on his image, the thought of appearing before the man and his companions, the reality of Ser's family, the truth of Ser's denials—all would spill forth if only Leonardo stepped inside to speak them aloud.

"Move out my way, rat," said a peddler pulling his cart.

Leonardo searched for the man undeserving of the peddler's discourtesy.

"Move, I say," he shouted again, nudging Leonardo out of his way.

Leonardo reached his hand to his unshaven face and considered his clothes, faded, stained, and worn. "I'm no rat." He grabbed the cart and held it tight. "Wait." He looked again to be sure his eyes didn't trick him. Tucked in a sack tied to the side of the cart, he saw the buckler. "Where did you get this?" He pulled it free.

"I sell it if you have money," the man said. He held his hands out for Leonardo to return his item. "Give it back."

"I made it. You have stolen property."

"No, I trade," the peddler claimed, yanking on it. He squinted and examined Leonardo. "I bought it from a man. He look like you. He took my money. It's mine."

The peddler patted him. "If you need money, make more. I buy." He admired the buckler and waited for response.

"Take it else I'll burn it," Leonardo said turning away. He stormed down the street and swung Ser's workplace door open.

A notary sat at a long counter dividing the room in half. "Buongiorno, Signo—" He peered up and dropped his quill.

"Buongiorno," Leonardo said. "I'm here to speak with Ser Piero da Vinci."

The notary held his palms out in surrender, or perhaps surprise. "Ser Piero is not currently in. Would you…I can…allow me to…" He fumbled on, "May I ask your name Signore?"

"Ser Piero's not expecting me. I'll not leave a message. I can wait."

"No, no, you cannot wait. Not here, Signore. He should meet you. Pardon me, but this is a respectable place. I—"

"You have issue with poor men who come through your door?"

The notary crossed the length of the counter to the end where it opened. "Of course not," he said sounding offended. "Tell me how we can help you. I should not expect Ser Piero's return until the afternoon. What can I do for you?"

"I've been in prison." Leonardo slammed Ser's empty purse on the counter. "Give him this."

The notary moved no closer but stretched his neck to view the bag.

"A token of his betrayal."

47

Matteo slept little the entire summer. His day labors distracted him, but during times like these, one word swirled in his mind: Engaged. Outside his room, doors opened and closed. Clink, his door latch gave way. "I'm not awake."

"A sleeping man doesn't answer," Mother said. "I'm coming in."

Matteo pulled a pillow over his head. He made his play too late, so he protested on. He always considered Lucrezia his since the day he tossed dirt over her head. She didn't cry, but spit and clunked his shin with a stone.

Mother yanked his pillow away.

"Another swooped in and stole Lucrezia from me. I'm left with no desirable choices." He tossed his blankets off. "She promised many strong qualities." And an even stronger will. Matteo smiled. Signore Gherardini would soon discover the prickle of his "docile" bride. The fight in her did things to him, but thoughts of her betrothed's possible response chilled him.

"She was not stolen. Her father waited for the right offer." Mother clapped her hands to snap him out of his mood. Her voice grew coarser. "No need to make a fuss over what can't be undone."

"She'll be his third bride. Lucrezia can't be a third bride. She's not a…a usual girl."

Mother held her hands on her hips. "Right yourself and stop playing the child." She bustled about the room tossing clothes strewn about over her arm. "The intention, your affections…" she exhaled, "They send this old woman's heart aflutter, but you make it more difficult than necessary." She grasped his arm. "Son, I know what this is if not love. Go on. Harden your face at me. I know that once we crack it, what we find beneath is the spirited boy, who became a man and kept his tender heart."

"Hardly. I'm not weak."

"I said nothing of weakness, it's a strength. You have to understand you can't save her, Matteo."

"Save her?"

"Let the idea of her go." Mother's eyes narrowed and she angled her head as if searching for heavenly intervention. "There's Garbina, Lydia, Ferra, Da—"

"Stop." The thought of rushing to marry a suitable lady for the sake of securing his patrimony appeared a noble cause until he considered the acts required. He couldn't marry a stranger—even if she looked worthy of a tumble. "I'll not marry a second, third, or tenth choice. Mother, stop spewing names." Rather than do what his father did, and his father's father and so on, he refused them all.

Mother painted her list with sweet words, but he cared little for sweets unless he'd first filled himself on a hardy supper. He rushed forth from bed and gripped his mother's arms. "Stop. No, I say. Enough."

Startled, she stopped speaking. Tears filled her eyes.

"Mamma, I'm sorry." He tried to embrace her but she slipped away. Throughout the day he returned to her door but she kept herself behind lock and key.

Matteo studied the ledgers and sent his men to take the horses to the farrier for new shoes. He didn't tell Mother about the enemy that surrounded them. A few days later, he packed his horse for travel and tried to be happy for Lucrezia. Every girl became a woman the day of her marriage, so too did every girl wish to marry a man of good means. With no other choice, he released the idea of Lucrezia and returned to Florence without a plan.

***

"Leonardo's released from prison?" Matteo clasped his housemaid's elbows. "When, Joanna?"

"Not but four or five days since your return."

"Excellent news. I'll clean up a bit. Bring me the green hose and set out a pair of shoes. I'm off to visit him."

Matteo arrived at Verrocchio's workshop within the hour before closing.

"Matteo Attaviano," said a boy Matteo had met before.

The place smelled bitter and stung Matteo's eyes. Before he knew what hit him, Leonardo crushed him. Maestro Verrocchio nodded and grinned at them. "Leonardo, this is the best part of my day. The best part of my month." He nudged him with his elbow. "Tell me of your release."

"I may never know the truth of it, but we don't look a given horse in the mouth." Leonardo's tone turned more serious. "I can't thank you enough for your visits and your gifts, brother."

"We're brothers. I take care of you, you take care of me." Matteo stepped sideways to clear a way for passing boys. Matteo rubbed his hands together. They stood in awkward silence. "You're free," he stated like a halfwit. He cleared his throat. "Did you pick up where you left off?"

Leonardo rubbed his fingers together. His eyes darted around the bottega until he finally fixed onto Matteo's questioning look. His pained eyes worked with an intensity that forced Matteo to look away.

"Your work, Leonardo," Matteo said, realizing Leonardo misjudged his question. A couple of the older boys stifled their laughs, which caused their bodies to jerk about in fits.

"Let's go in the back?"

"Sure."

Leonardo brushed a stump of wood off used as a seat and offered it.

Matteo sat expecting that Leonardo would sit, but Leonardo remained standing. His attention floated from point to point through the air as if he meant to harvest his thoughts but found no way to hold them.

"Maestro welcomed me back like I'd never been gone." His eyes flashed Matteo's way then his voice thickened. "He put no other in my room."

"Not long, and you'll be a Maestro. He knows you could manage the place, but greater than that, he knew you'd return."

They turned their attentions to a burst of noise from the center of the bottega. Curses flew through the air. Maestro Verrocchio, assisted by several boys, wrapped a statue of Leonardo's likeness with cloth. The maestro caught the statue before it fell against the wall.

"He goes on display in the Palazzo tomorrow. On Christ's unbroken bones, don't drop it now," Leonardo's maestro said. "Careful now. Wrap it well for transport."

Leonardo swiped his hand across his mouth. "Maestro has a commission at the cathedral in Pistoia. He requires several assistants. I leave soon." His gaze traveled across Matteo's face. He rubbed the back of his neck and appeared sick.

"How long will you be gone?"

"A year…as long as it takes."

"It's one day of travel. Not far."

"I need the money. I need the distance. How can I walk without suspicion on the streets when I'm not above condemnation in the place I call home?"

Matteo shrugged and straightened his shoulders. The mockers could call him whatever they wanted, but it didn't make it so. "When you return over holidays or for any reason, you can stay in my house, Leonardo. It too is your home."

Leonardo bit his lip and gave a pathetic nod.

"Let's go for a drink—let's celebrate your freedom."

"No. Have one for me." Leonardo's face twisted. He clawed at his neckline to loosen it.

Matteo couldn't determine if Leonardo was sick, angry, hurt, or what, but he knew his method. "You're walking away. Don't look at me like that! I'm not a lame horse in need of your merciful blade. Your charges, the days you spent in prison—they change nothing. Let them look."

Leonardo yanked Matteo's sleeves. "Can't you see?"

"I can see that you're saying goodbye."

Leonardo's hands trembled and his face turned red. He turned his back to the onlookers. "This can't be. Me. You." He lowered his voice. "I'm in love with you, Matteo. For years I've hidden it. I've lied. I've tried to bury it. I've feared. It's not fair to you. I want your friendship to be enough, but it's not. Always I want more, and I know it's too much to ask. We can't change who we are."

Matteo's mouth dropped open and he could make no sound. He waited for a clearer explanation.

Leonardo waited for a better response. He threw his hands up and retreated in the stairwell until his shadow faded.

Matteo stayed where Leonardo left him—like a dog that lost his way home. When Matteo came to his senses, he made to depart before he boiled over. So help him, if anyone in the bottega curled a lip wrong he'd bloody it. He fought the urge to throttle Giorgio, the coward, tucked in the corner of the bottega. The boys must have caught scent of bloodlust since they worked like irksome innocents when Matteo passed them on his way out.

48
April 1477

The mid-morning sun illuminated Pistoia Cathedral through her upper windows and washed the cream-colored walls in a soft, golden glow. Leonardo and Lorenzo cut across to the arched, right side aisle, which repeated the same form in line with many rows of columns. A sharp, sweet incense lingered in the air from the morning mass.

"Leonardo," Maestro called in a hushed tone. He pointed toward the vaulted ceiling, "God himself knows I haven't the patience of a saint, but I could rival the best of the parish priests. I return to Florence tomorrow, and you'll ride with me. Nine months gone and you've not returned. We must go. If ever there were a time to return, why not during Lent and Carnival?" Maestro's thick hand squeezed the meaty part of Leonardo's shoulder. He whispered louder, "I'll not plead with you a moment longer. You know that my earlier demands were all pretense, but this is not about what I want. This is what you must do."

"What I must do?" Leonardo chose to live better even if it meant a piece of him died. Matteo's name cut him. His thoughts jumped back to his work. He kept his head down and stayed away, no contact with Florence, his father, Matteo. At first it was difficult, but with time it came easier. Plus, an occupied mind prevented erroneous emotions. "I must work. And Lorenzo? What of his work?"

"You've earned your pay. Both of you."

Leonardo pulled a loose paper from his notebook. "While I finished the little Madonna for Bishop Pandolfini,

I thought of this arrangement for the Donato altarpiece, Maestro. Then there's Cardinal Forteguerri's monument. Look at us. We're prepared and more than eager to begin." Lorenzo nodded in agreement.

Maestro mumbled something under his breath.

"Maestro, I chose to leave for you, for Ma—friends, and for myself. Anger towards my father lights a flame that will burn me to ash no matter the words I use against him. Blame as we may, much of our suffering comes from within. My pains will follow me forever unless I can find a way to set them free."

"How can I argue against you?" Maestro asked tucking the paper between his plans.

"Go Maestro. This is good business."

"This is rebellion. Give them a finger and they take an arm." Maestro tossed his hat to the floor for emphasis.

Leonardo tried not to smile. Maestro's infirm request didn't compel him. "Have I not proven that my duties to you come before all other work? If you won't have me continue work on your commissions, perhaps you would regard another proposition?" Leonardo proceeded without giving his Maestro time to answer. "I sent Fioravanti back to Florence with my money since I couldn't leave with the Bishop's demands hooked around my neck."

"Yes?" Maestro said.

"I got the commission at San Gennaro. Any day Fioravanti should return with my supplies." Satisfied, Leonardo retrieved Maestro's hat from the floor, brushed it off, and handed it to him.

Maestro took his hat and wrung it about in his hands. He nudged Leonardo's shoulder. A look of pride set on his worn face. "And when did you plan to tell me?" He shook his head and hands to say don't answer. "Well done, Leonardo." His exhale suggested a sure sign of forthcoming consent.

Maestro stood tall and focused on Lorenzo, whose eyes lit-up while listening to the exchange. "Don't you get any ideas, boy. You're no chief assistant. Not yet." Shaking his fist at them both, Maestro's resolve dispersed like the dust Leonardo brushed from his hat. He locked his students under stern eyes. "Only because you have a commission do you stay. I'll not tolerate discord from any of you, understood?"

"Yes, Maestro," they replied in a unified echo that carried through the Cathedral.

A priest, his robes flapping like wings, shot out of the farside nave and down the aisle toward them. He held his fingers out to say, I see you and know what you've done.

Maestro's hands fluttered to show that they knew their voices broke the heavenly accord within the church walls. He lowered his voice, "You've not more than two months to finish your work, Leonardo, and then we meet here and return to Florence before The Feast of Saint John no matter the condition. On this I'm firm," he said to impress them with his authority.

"Grazie, Maestro."

"Grazie, grazie, they say." Maestro smirked. "My joy will come the day you feel the same pains of indulging your students far too much."

Leonardo continued, focused, and made-up for the coin he lost while imprisoned. He calculated his return and formulated plans for his own bottega. Life in the country came easier; here he lived only by necessity.

Two months passed in a blink.

Leonardo added his last touches of paint on the life-sized terracotta angel at San Gennaro, and the following morning he received the final payment. His return, now real in his mind, made him ill. But Maestro gave him the gift of time away and he wouldn't sidestep the last of his duties.

***

The countryside pathway, lined by a palette of uncountable greens and golds, scrolled out before Leonardo. Here he'd found solace amongst the lowest valleys and the highest peaks of nature, the great mother. His coin purse heavier, and his body spent, he watched the sun lower over the nest-like ring of purpled hills where beams slipped across the land like brushstrokes.

His long walk served good purpose and paved his journey back. He opened his notebook to studies of plants, faces, and his months old sketches for the terracotta angel he left in San Gennaro hours ago. "Nothing is hidden under the sun," he read for reassurance. Nature revealed her secrets to those who took the time to search for them, and here among them he found reason. He could see it in his eye, hear it in the crescendo of the cicadas' song, and smell it in the lavender crushed firm beneath his feet.

But pages of unfinished letters, purposely drawn over, pulled him from his reverie. Nature whispered on the wind. She brushed her fingered grasses gently against his legs in constant reassurance: Here I've been, and here I shall remain.

49

Matteo's visits to Vanni's tavern conflicted with finding a wife, but he felt more alone than ever. He fought his sinful urges to be with women by wandering through the city's piazzas. His wanderings led him into Il Duomo Cathedral, which consummated in, what Father Enrico termed, "A new calling for a young man rightly devoted to God."

"Father, you think too well of me." He played along for more than a week now and finally admitted, "I search for a wife."

"Oh?" the priest said puckering his lips together.

Matteo knew bitter words would squirt forth.

"That may be, but the Church is not a market."

"No, Father. I—where does one find a good wife if not here?" Matteo waited for a helpful response. He meant not to offend, but where else could a man expect to gain a glimpse of the good ladies eligible for marriage?

"Many girls come here with their fathers and brothers," Father Enrico said. "They dress in gowns with trims and jewels, silk veils adorn their bound hair and drape across their low necklines all as if attending a spectacle. Dare they think their God fails to notice their vain and lustful displays?" The Father crossed himself, and recited, "Beati mundo corde, quonium ipsi Deum videbunt." He jabbed Matteo with his bony finger. "And you cannot see Him when you seek to please yourself." He added, "This is a venial sin. Your flesh desires flesh, but your soul hungers for God." He urged Matteo toward confession before continuing down the aisle.

"Father, you have it wrong," Matteo said after him. Matteo wouldn't deny the appealing physical nature of marriage, but God knew this wasn't his prime purpose. Matteo turned and thought to follow Father Enrico and ask another question, one a priest could better answer. He hesitated.

Before the worst of his anger burned out months ago, Matteo truly thanked God that Leonardo had gone so they wouldn't say or do something they'd later regret. Leonardo left him with the last word. Their mutual silence dragged on. Matteo's lingering loss prodded him toward forgiveness. A man's problem was never a question of love, but desire. Desire distracted the fragile child locked within a man until he weakened from its demands. Leonardo's desire weakened him, yet he never did he ruin them. Matteo questioned if he could forgive him, trust him, look at him the same.

Matteo sucked in his lips to avoid the bitter taste of abandonment. He could offer Leonardo no more than he'd already given. Damn them both. Brotherhood never died. Their friendship may not be enough for Leonardo, but their bond endured.

Matteo left without lighting a candle or saying a prayer, and he could not confess any wrong in wanting a wife or his friend back.

The afternoon sun baked the ground and thinned the crowd in the piazza outside the Il Duomo. People flocked to shady streets that branched out and away from the heat. Matteo flowed with them down one of the narrow roads tucked away by those who desired not to see the dishonorable parts of their city. He knew better than to visit the Malacucina. True to reputation, from what he could tell, the place brimmed with prostitutes and panderers, questionable inns, foreigners, pickpockets, cheaters, beggars, and decrepit workshops and homes.

Matteo wiped damp hair from his face. He pressed forward when little bells chimed in rhythm to feminine steps. A group of old men speaking in a foreign tongue stepped from the street into a tavern. Two prostitutes walked arm in arm in front of him. Their siren's call chimed louder until he reached close enough to gag on the waft of their over-spiced sweat. Too cheap, which was why he should return to the two he knew at Vanni's.

He glanced at the whores gathered in the entrances of the botteghe. The diversity of the women kindled the hunter within. Some of the whores had light skin with light hair; others were dark with deep black hair, and the rest fell somewhere in between. Their dresses colored their already bold appearances. Those having the greatest allure sat street side. They wore high shoes, gloves, and bells on their hats in accordance with the law. Humored by the law, Matteo concluded the city fathers must believe a man could easily mistake a virtuous woman for a prostitute without her dress. He pulled the purse strings at his waist and weighed the bag of coins in his palm.

A dark haired woman came out from the shadows, put her hands on him, and spoke in broken Italian. Her eyes locked on his purse. "Love," she whistled through a few missing teeth, "I give you…" She squeezed her breasts between her arms, "you hold in two hands." She reached for his money.

Matteo caught her by the wrists before she could snatch anything of value. "No, dark one." He snapped in repulsion, "your proposition holds no charm. Take your hands off me."

She fussed at him and twisted about. "No hands on you?" She snorted and spit at his feet. "You pay my fee. You touch me."

"I've not touched you."

She widened her eyes for emphasis at the way he cuffed her wrists.

"No," he shouted and shook her, "No."

Her face snarled. "My prick shove in your balls. No fee." She shoved her claws at him.

He cut sideways and twisted her around to pin her against his chest and maintain control. "Go," he said. She looked unconvinced, so he imitated those horrible men who abused women by raising his hand to strike.

She flinched and moved to the next man.

Matteo backed himself against the nearest wall for protection. His hands trembled a bit. He needed to find the closest way out of this piss hole he'd floated into.

He looked for a way out until a screech sounded from above. The people around him paused—probably trying to determine whether they should run or watch. Matteo pressed his purse against his leg. The screech of a woman sounded again.

"Michele, I need cool water if you make me work through the heat," a prostitute said hanging halfway out a window. Her bulging breasts threatened to pop out the top of her neckline. Given the heat, most of the windows on the upper levels were open, and work happened as witnessed by the amorous sounds.

Not far down, Matteo caught the flutter of a pink ribbon streaming down from a corner window. Graceful arms and a ruffle of hair dipped out in attempt to catch it.

He wound his way closer, dodged an oncoming horse, and searched the ground. "Signorina, I've found it," he said standing under the window. He brushed it off and lifted it to his nose. Sweet as honey. He must know how it came to rest in a nest of wasps.

A lock of golden hair fluttered on the sill. "Your ribbon," he called again. The woman sat alone and showed no interest in business on the street. He could see a faint outline of her shadowed face. That she didn't walk the street given the location, she must be hideous with a missing eye or some such defect to be alone. He tried to convince himself to go, but the fool in him wouldn't leave until he discovered her full impression.

He tucked the ribbon inside his purse. The innkeeper may scorn him and follow through with a generous lump on his head, or worse if he made the wrong assumption, but why shouldn't he assume her a prostitute? No man with any sense would bring his wife to stay here, would he? Then again, if they came from a far-off place, the Malacucina housed those looking for work but still wanting to commune with brethren from their homelands. Matteo turned back on his steps to locate the entrance to the inn where she stayed.

***

A couple of men stepped forward. "I'm looking for the innkeeper," Matteo said, "about a woman."

"No need to make your deal with him," a wiry man rolling a barrel across the floor toward the kitchen said. "A few soldi if you're quick. Five if you need more time." He laughed and his companion joined him. Another man wiped his hands and eyed Matteo hard. "You're too dark for a Vlach, and you're Italian's too good for a German. What do you want with the innkeeper?"

"I saw a woman in your maestro's window. Tell me, who stays in the corner room facing toward the road?"

The sturdy man swiped his chin. "Corrado has many rooms and women."

"All prostitutes then?"

"You want to do business or you don't. We don't tolerate questioners well."

Matteo untied his purse and plopped it on a nearby barrel. "I'm interested in the woman on the far end. She has golden hair and fair skin. I want to see her before I decide to stay."

The man tipped his wide head back to laugh without sound. "You pay first. No free peeks."

Matteo lifted his purse and made to retie it. "I've no interest in a whore with a beastly face, one leg, anything of that sort. Buongiorno."

A thick hand clutched his forearm. "She's upmarket for the Malacucina. Touched little. When good men like you come, you pay a handsome price. Use her too much and she'll be loose. Your kind won't brave the scum if not for such treasure."

Treasure? "How much, Signore?"

"You pay for one day including the night. She's not a street dog's bitch turning them in and out. If you damage her in anyway, I'll damage you forever." He flexed the muscles in his neck. "Twenty soldi."

Matteo sucked back surprise at the price. Skilled workers earned less in a day. "In the upmarket, Signore, men spend as much. I'll give you fifteen, which is fair, and still well above what the other women must bring in for five times the effort—if they can find that many to pay." Matteo straightened his back. "If you want me to return, you will accept, Signore Corrado." When the man's eyes flashed, Matteo knew he dealt with the owner. Foolish he may be, but he was no idiot.

"I accept your fifteen soldi."

***

"Rosa," the man named Corrado said with a knock on the woman's door.

Matteo closed an eye to soften what he might see in case he was cheated.

Corrado swung the door in, "You have company."

"Maestro Corrado?" a voice said from behind them. "I went to find you. You see?" the curvaceous goddess standing before Matteo said. She lifted her fair hand to smooth her waist long hair. "My ribbon slipped from the window."

"Have you another?"

"No, Maestro."

Matteo waited for her to notice him, but Rosa's attention focused on the wall, her feet, her hands, or her open door—she didn't address Corrado to his face.

"Serve him well, girl, and you'll have a new ribbon." Corrado crossed his arms and eyed Matteo again. "You like her I can see. Our deal is one day, Signore." Corrado continued, amusement in his eyes. "You'll get your money's worth." He gave Rosa a kiss on her shoulder and left them.

"Rosa," Matteo said opening his purse. "I think I found your ribbon."

Cautious, she watched his hands.

Matteo held it out for her. He tried not to focus on the fullness of her breasts.

She stepped forward, lifted her green eyes to his, and brushed the ribbon from his hand gentle as a butterfly. He'd grown to know a more forceful approach upon first meeting prostitutes of the past. Rosa the gentle. Unexpected. Her delicate face held the power to drag him anywhere she wished to go. She made him hard as a rock and thankful as a prayer. He held her door open and waited for her to enter.

"How did you know?" she asked streaming the ribbon through her fingers.

"Call it fate if you will. I saw it drop from the window, my lady." He grinned and shied away from saying what he truly thought of her. Then he said it anyway. "You're exquisite."

Rosa twisted her hair and tied it up with the ribbon.

She seemed not to take a compliment well, but the nape of her neck begged for him to reach out and stroke it with his fingers and lips. Corrado was right. She was different—upmarket.

"This will have to do," she said adding a couple pins to hold her hair. Flicking open a fan, she lifted her chin to the air and asked, "How did you come to this place?" She played modest, but eyed him top to bottom. "You're not like the others, Signore."

Matteo didn't answer. He wished only to watch her, to worship her, and he couldn't remember her question when focused on her narrow waist. He may have the day and night, but his cock would not stop humming. Wait...

Her head made a quarter turn his direction. Her nose turned up in a little bump at the tip and mocked him when she said, "Signore?"

Everything about this meeting was too easy. He couldn't understand how she lived here. It all felt wrong. He'd nearly fallen headlong into a trap. They may think they would trick him, but he wouldn't be deceived. "I could ask you how you came to this place, whore." He sprang toward her *innocent* window and searched her room.

"What?" she barked like an angry dog. She pulled his tunic and did her best to hold him back.

Matteo dragged her with him and lifted the lid of her wooden chest to be sure no one hid inside.

"What is this madness, man? Stop. This is my room." She hit him with her fan.

He jabbed his foot along the length of both sides of her straw-filled bed, and pressed down in the middle waiting for a lump or a noise." Nothing.

Rosa's fists pounded his back.

Matteo continued undeterred by her fit. He removed bunched-up clothing hanging from a hook on the wall to see behind it. "You're the madness," he said with a snarl.

"You're out of place, Rosa. This a jest meant to thieve my money."

She fell off Matteo's back. "I know not what you say, I swear I know not. Can you not see that I get little of the money that men like you spend to walk through my door? Look. Where are my jewels? Where are my veils? Do I sleep in a noble bed? I'm a whore," she shouted, "and I follow the rules of my maestro. I have nothing, you bastard." She got up and cleared her path. "I'll not have you disrespect what little I do have."

"You act the part of a well-bred woman with great delicacy. Still, your clothes are made of cloths and trims far beyond a woman of your station."

Rosa shoved her clothing into a chest and glared at him full in the face. "A whore's money goes toward her appearance, you ass. How else will she hook a fool?"

"Fool?" Matteo did see her logic. He righted an overturned chair at her rickety table. "Never have I met an honest whore."

"Never have I met an honest man," she said staring into his eyes, challenging him.

He always admired a spirited woman. And her appearance did things to him. "Then the greatest fool will apologize and send for wine." He sat and made it obvious he wasn't leaving.

"You'll stay?"

"If you wish." He'd stay and give her control, which would inflame his desire more.

Rosa unlatched her belt and snapped it. "There are no wishes for a whore."

Excited by her force but confused, Matteo asked, "Men would pay so much and not stay long?"

She shrugged. "I'm a fantasy, a means to one end. Don't worry. I'll see you get your end. Few want to stay with a barbed whore—yes, barbed was the word a man once used."

Matteo grinned and covered his cock. "Sounds painful."

She smiled. "I'll think no less of you if you quit before you start. Men don't stay longer than necessary. Not with a woman who flatters them none."

"We've met and fought, Rosa. Now I'm comfortable in my seat. I think you could ask my name."

She mocked him with her surprised look, and then turned serious. "Don't think me yours. I'll not think you mine." She bent halfway over and pulled a green over gown over her head. "I may have the look you desire, Signore, but I'm not a kind person. I don't encourage or tell lies to add to masculine pomp. We both know you have a prick." Her eyes landed on target. "How fortunate."

Matteo laughed. Yes, he did, and he was glad she took a moment to notice. He removed his belt and dropped it to the floor.

"You wear fine clothes, Signore." She held an arm out. "Shall I hang them?"

Matteo scrambled to his feet and removed his tunic.

She nodded her head and used a stool to hang their clothes on the line. When she stretched, the linen cupped her ass the way he wanted to. He never thought it becoming for a man to sit about in hose, so he removed them.

Rosa glanced over her shoulder at him and finished hanging the clothes. She faced him and freed her smooth, creamy body from her camisa.

Matteo met her before she stepped down, but her face turned blank. He nudged her chin to meet him. "This face could make me weep. I'll give you no reason to sadden." He moved to kiss her lips, but thought it too predictable. Instead, he found the long bone running from her shoulder to neck. The rise and fall of her chest quickened and he moaned when she traced her fingers down the crevice running from his neck to waist. He continued his exploration until mad. "Rosa, I—"

She pressed her fingers on his lips and led him to her bed.

"What do you want?"

She shook her head to say he shouldn't speak, and spoke firm and feverous by taking him.

50
June 1477

This Leonardo couldn't hide: His mind chose to neglect his heart. And the closer he moved to Florence, the tighter his chest became. He couldn't belong to himself when he strained in want of belonging to another. It festered as a life-long sore that wouldn't heal.

Leonardo traveled the road back with Maestro, but split off from the group riding east to Maestro's bottega. He rode down the via Ghibbelina toward Ser's house. The Stinche walls stretched before him, long and imposing. He slowed to pass the entrance and halted his horse. He spit.

How many true crimes went unpunished? Ser let circumstance accomplish his work. The Stinche was a convenience, a means to hide Ser's greatest shame, and Ser succeeded for some time. But his unpunished crimes were no lesser than those of his punished son.

Leonardo worked his horse up to a trot on the widening road. He couldn't rest until he found justice. He had to know why. Too long he searched for the right words and hid behind the proverbial bush. "Out of my way," he shouted. He entered the narrow road leading to Ser's house at full trot. Men yelled, curses flew through the air, carts bumped against walls, and people and horses stumbled out of his way. If he could no longer hide, then he wouldn't allow Ser to hide either. He clipped his heels against his horse and felt each quickening footfall a blood promise.

***

"Ser Piero's not in," the house servant told him. She scrunched her eyes up at Leonardo and gnawed her lip. "You have the look of my maestro." Resemblance or none, she straightened her back taller and set her jaw firm and ready to defend the house from a stranger. "You must be family, Signore?"

Leonardo snorted in mockery, which made the woman glare at him. "Yes, I'm family."

She shook her head no in a sort of self-protestation. She'd be wise to listen to it. "He went with his son to the piazza."

"His son?" Leonardo tasted blood in his mouth. He left the servant without further question, took a few steps, and peered back. Her watchful eyes targeted on him.

Noticing him noticing her, she scrambled inside.

Leonardo stood to the side of the Loggia dei Lanzi and spotted Ser in the uncrowded center of the square. Ser spun around with the child facing his chest. Massive smiles spread across both their faces. Ser squatted to set his son down and pointed at the pigeons nearby.

Convinced of the greater importance of his business, Leonardo strode forward prepared to frighten the pigeons into flight. But the scene before him froze his feet to the ground.

In one hand Ser grasped a chunk of bread; in the other he held the hand of his barely toddling child. Leonardo remembered Ser's hands smooth as the parchment he handled daily. Father and son watched the pigeons bob their heads and peck at crumbs on the ground. Do you see them, *Leonardo*? They follow the one that holds the bread. The child pulled bread free with his tiny fingers and the pigeons rushed forward in anticipation. The child tossed the bread quickly, and leaned back into his waiting father's arms. *My brave, Leonardo.* The boy squealed as his legs worked up and down. Ser kissed his fat cheeks and sprinkled the last of the bread on the ground. The son shrieked in panic, so Ser stood to escape the rush of the pigeons. Ser playfully ran while his son delighted in the show of flapping wings. They turned toward the Loggia, the way home.

Leonardo lifted his empty hand and backed into the shadows. His hot blood turned cold. He wouldn't do anything to hurt the child. How could he take that moment away from the boy? He swallowed hard and closed his eyes. Accept the truth: you've exerted too much effort holding on. Let it go. "Release it," he whispered. "Release this burden and set it free," he said loud enough to hear the power of his words.

He turned away from the scene that didn't belong to him and took the first step that would lead down a new path.

51
February 1478

Matteo's appetite grew larger than his coin, so perhaps he should thank Corrado for allowing him to stay with Rosa twice a week and no more. He found some satisfaction in knowing he consumed all her active time.

He couldn't remember when or how his protectiveness began, but everyday he wasn't with Rosa he endured the Malacucina to stand watch within view of her window. Some days he watched and lusted for a short while. Other days he lingered from the end of the workday until dusk.

At first, he thought of romance and the songs suitors sung with hopes of returned affections. He stood below Rosa's window and called her name. Passersby looked on in great interest, made poor suggestions, and mocked him when she made no answer. Any displays of sophistication threatened places that prized villainy and could get a man beaten and robbed. Soon the inn across the street became Matteo's watch place. Here he found a view of Rosa's window.

The gangly young man that served Matteo's drinks nudged him, "When will you learn? She answers no call until you pay your cunt coin."

Matteo lunged, his face so close to the little weasel he could smell his rotten breath. "Your expression burns my ears, foul man. This is no concern of yours." He wanted no one to take part in his fixation nor he didn't want to talk about it.

"Swallow it down," the man said. He mocked him more with a laugh. "If I have it wrong, let us see you get at her then." He circled his hand about and waited for Matteo to finish his drink and rise from his stool.

Matteo did his best to ignore the man and the scene around him until he could go. The wait chaffed him. Whatever the reason, Corrado told him he couldn't arrive before the nones bell. He waited long enough. But the piece of shit knew he had him by the balls. An elbow nudged Matteo's side.

"You used to order our best wine, Signore, but now we water it down for you." The gangly one's dark eyes twinkled. "I'd say Corrado's prick shoves well in the depths of your purse."

Matteo caught his strangle positioned hand before it made contact with the man.

"Tsk. I tell you," the man said shaking his head. "Do you see it? Can you smell it? Women from top to bottom. Any of them can be yours for less. Why wait?" He set his hands on his knees and bent closer. "Oh, look. There's your man." He arched his fist upward like a cheer.

Corrado entered his tavern.

Matteo stood, straightened his tunic, and realigned his belt.

"You go. I'll keep watch," the serving man said.

"No. Mind your work. Leave me to mine." Matteo rushed across the street.

***

Matteo identified Corrado by the width of his back. He stood at the foot of the stairs in conversation. Matteo hung back to wait his turn while the man did his business. No one appreciated prying eyes or ears, but Matteo stole glances.

Corrado's patron stepped out of the stairwell.

Matteo blinked hard. Did his eyes trick him? How, why? Guido? Matteo breathed deep. It wasn't like he laid a claim to the whole of Corrado's prostitutes, but he'd rather not see Guido. Nor should Guido see him else they'd continue their competitive match.

Matteo turned away, sat at an open stool, and slumped his head and shoulders low. How Guido came to know of the place he wouldn't guess. He hoped the experience left no lasting impression so Guido would find no desire to return.

"What will you have?" a passing worker asked Matteo.

Matteo shook his head.

"No pay, no sit."

"I wait on Corrado." Matteo thumbed over his shoulder. "We have business."

The man's face brightened when he recognized Matteo. "Very good, Signore. Here he comes."

Matteo turned in his seat. Corrado walked behind the counter. He swung his head around to the entry and watched Guido depart.

Corrado's man pointed to Matteo.

While Corrado downed some wine, Matteo approached the counter. He set his money out.

Corrado crossed his arms at his chest. "No. You have to wait."

Matteo scoot his coin forward to freshen Corrado's sight.

Corrado stared him down. "She's done no more than a few times a week, greedy one. You see, my women tell all to their maestro. You'll have my best woman loose as the two soldi hovels if you keep at your pace."

Matteo thrust his finger between them. "I pay your price. I've followed your rules."

"Take your money and spend it on another." Corrado stretched his arms out and cracked his fingers. "When Rosa's paid her dues, I've no need to work her."

You cocksucker. "I've never abused her." Ever since his first walk down the Malacucina, he carried his sling and a blade for protection. He thumbed the blade's pommel.

Corrado poured a goblet of wine for Matteo. "On me." He topped his goblet off. "Choose another at a special price." He took his time and drank a little. "I like you. Your word spreads to higher places. Keep them coming, and you may find me generous enough to offer," his eyes flickered like flames, "special services."

Matteo shoved his money back into his purse. He told no one about his visits. His gut turned to stone. He hoped Corrado could tell he wanted to crush him.

"Ah, now you catch on," Corrado said with a sick grin. "A man not unlike you graced the inn this morning."

"The asshole that just left?"

"A friend?"

Matteo knocked the goblet over in haste. He raced around the tables and knocked over a stool or two to get after Guido. He would kill him. He ran out on the street. "Guido Bartoli," he roared again and again. He ran to the other inn across the way and rushed through the door looking for the gangly one who served his drinks.

"You," he shouted shooting forward and yanking the man's clothes. "There was a man dressed in an embroidered brown tunic, belt of black. He has big lips. He left Corrado's soon after I entered." Matteo tugged his clothes again. "Tell me you saw which way he went."

The man tried to snub him but his eyes tracked his purse.

"Tell me." Matteo pulled out a soldi.

"West."

Matteo released him, returned to the street, and ran fast as he could through the crowd.

"Guido Bartoli," he shouted. An unmanned horse and cart presented a perfect pedestal for a better view. Matteo climbed up and searched. Not more than five cart lengths in front of him he found his target. He'd hit Guido before the shit turned the corner. Matteo placed a stone in the sling and waited for the rhythm to course down his arm. He released.

The stone cracked Guido's back forcing him forward.

Guido hunched over, hands on the ground, and turned to search for what hit him.

"Guido Bartoli!" Matteo hopped from the cart and plowed a path forward, but Guido was gone. Matteo growled and tossed his sling to the ground. "You followed me. You better run."

52
March 1478

Leonardo found living across from the Sant'Egidio convent made for a quieter street and fair rent. Ample sunlight drew him to the location more than anything else; it entered the front of the bottega in the mornings and lit his room in the back at day's end. Few were his belongings, and fewer would be his coins if he didn't soon get the advance for his commission of the Vision of St. Bernard. Once he needed to worry about himself, but now his boys depended on him.

Leonardo passed the convent and walked up the street to the hospital Santa Maria Nuova. He visited workshops here and there to watch the work and hear the latest word on rivalries, commissions, and competitions.

Domenico spotted Leonardo outside his bottega and invited him in. Leonardo jumped at the opportunity to join a friend. Boys cut wood, sanded, stained, glued, and inlaid panels. Domenico wore sawdust like sleeves on his arms. He made another pass to smooth a panel of wood, straightened his back, and set the hand plane to rest.

"Leonardo, my friend, come and sit. Have some wine," Domenico said offering him a seat. "How's business?" He pulled a rag from a hook on the worktable and brushed off his arms.

"Not as profitable as yours, but growing." Any day now he should receive the promised twenty-five Florins advance.

"I heard of your commission for the Signoria altarpiece."

They conversed about their work until calls for "Maestro" demanded Domenico's attention.

"Give me a moment, Leonardo. Help yourself to the wine."

Leonardo sat in admiration of the busy workshop.

Domenico returned. "Three brothers come by the bottega every day. They're looking for work for the youngest. I've given him small tasks for small pay, but I can take no more in. Would you have use of a set of hands?" Domenico's bottega could burst with another body to house and feed.

"You're a good man, my friend," Leonardo said in gentle decline. Domenico would house every boy if he could. For him it wasn't about money, but a giving spirit. Leonardo wouldn't take from another man's workshop.

"Look, I may have use of him in the future, but now I have little to offer him."

Leonardo tipped his head side-to-side.

"I'll send him your way next time I see him," Domenico said. "Don't feel forced. If he's not to your liking, I'll take no offense. Think on this: you can mold him the way you want. He'll learn your ways, and most of all, the boy will be so grateful he'll offer unrivaled loyalty." He refilled Leonardo's cup. "You can't place a price on loyalty."

The following day, two boys having close to twenty years and their younger brother of perhaps fifteen entered Leonardo's bottega. They dressed well and displayed the vigor of polished breeding. The older boys sent the youngest in ahead of them. All three removed their hats.

"Good morning, Signore," the youngest said, "Domenico da Michele Corso sent me to seek Maestro Leonardo da Vinci. I'm Paolo, Signore. I've come with my brothers." He introduced them and held his hand out to shake Leonardo's.

"Pleased to meet you Paolo. Domenico didn't say the nature of your work. Have you any inclinations?"

Paolo's eyes widened. "Signore?"

One of his brothers said, "What can you do, fool?" He flicked his finger at the back of Paolo's hair.

"Don't worry about talents, Paolo. Most things in this world can be learned. What I need is a garzone that's willing to work and learn. Some days the work will be long, other days, slower."

"No matter, Maestro." Paolo did his best to smooth his dark, curled hair away from his face and approached closer. "Tell me where to start and I'll not cause you regret."

Leonardo cared little for flatterers, but the boy's way was pure. Paolo may have been desperate for work, but no one would know given the way the boy turned his introduction into a delight. Leonardo understood why Domenico remembered Paolo. Amused, Leonardo tried not to reveal his easy willingness to take him on.

"I've learned marquetry." Paolo bounced back, his attention on his brothers. "Maestro, you want to see my work? I've done larger pieces, but brought a small box." The brothers looked on in encouragement. One handed him a bundle. Paolo unwrapped the box.

Leonardo took it. "You've spent time in the gardens or outside the city gates to make this."

"Yes, Maestro."

"Come." Leonardo led the boy to a makeshift desk and flipped through pages in a little notebook he often hung on his belt. He held the page open and tipped his head forward encouraging Paolo to look.

"A lily. Le Fleur-de-lis, or Florentia," Paolo said.

"Yes." Leonardo held the box proud as a father.

"Good." He'd be a fool not to take him. "Let me draw-up a

contract. Return in three or four days with your father to sign the agreement."

Paolo's bright face dimmed.

"Have you no father?"

"No, Maestro. Only my brothers."

Leonardo handed him his box. "I'll not slight you for it. I have half a father on good days and a brother I've never met. I'll not let it stop me, nor should you let it stop you."

The boy grinned at his brothers.

"Let me show you around."

Paolo thrived on challenges and led the other boys to strive for turning out better work. In less than a month, Leonardo's fondness for him deepened more when the boy decided to take the da Vinci name as his own.

Leonardo's gaze wandered and fixated on his young apprentice, the boy who lit dark places. The gardens and Paolo in mind, Leonardo wrote: *All things in nature are dark except where exposed by light.* How he needed light. Leonardo marveled over the boy and drank in his beauty in search of his light source.

Paolo crooked his head of ringlet hair and smiled back at him.

A maestro did well not to set his affections different between the boys in his bottega. Leonardo turned from his amorous thoughts. He loved best as a maestro, a chaste one. He heard whispers that the innocent Paolo met with men in the alleys, but the boy in the bottega gave no indication of bad living. How could he believe it?

At the end of the workday, he would finally know the truth. So he followed Paolo. Perhaps he had no right, but he must keep the boy from ruin.

Paolo entered an alleyway.

Leonardo kept distance enough that by the time he reached the entryway, he lost sight of him. He waited and listened for some time while ducking away from men coming and going in the cramped passage and made no eye contact. He should leave before discovering truths he didn't want to find. But bent on knowing the truth, he turned right into the L-shaped alcove.

In a corner of crates, stood a man with his hose around his ankles curved over Paolo. Paolo begged him for more.

Leonardo closed his eyes. He backed out of the alcove.

The next morning he approached the boy. "Do I not pay you enough, Paolo?"

"How do you mean, Maestro?"

"What does your lover in the alley offer?"

Paolo's face blushed. He made no answer.

"You're young and promising." Leonardo swallowed hard, "What you're doing is none of my business, but I care for you…just don't sell yourself."

Paolo snubbed him.

Leonardo worked Paolo past dark to keep him out of the alleys. He would do his best to keep the boy from straying.

53

"Come to me," Rosa said waving her finger at Matteo. Her face, rigid as her body, signified that he'd done something wrong.

Matteo latched Rosa's door shut without taking his eyes off her. "You're upset. Let us waste none of our time together." He untucked his clothes.

"Tell me what you're doing?" She moved close enough that her nose almost touched his chin.

Her rosewater scent taunted him. He dipped his head to kiss her, but she swerved away.

"Can you not remember the day we first met and I—"

"I remember," Matteo said and grinned.

"I said don't think me yours as I'll not think you mine." She waited for the smile to slip from his face before looking away. "I'm Corrado's, Matteo, and you'd do well to remember it. No more blaming or fights. No more watching me from across the way. Don't you understand what a prostitute is?" She fought back tears.

He reached for her. "I've done nothing to hurt you, have I? Look at me, Rosa. I come to you because we have something between us."

She recoiled from his touch.

"I don't understand." He tried pulling her toward him. "Please, Rosa."

"Don't call me Rosa," she said and tore herself from his grasp. "Go away." She pushed him back. "Please go."

"I'm not leaving. I can't bear the thought of you with another man." Matteo reached for her again. She covered her face and her body shook, so he hugged her against him. "I offered your maestro money. I offered him a holding of a small land that was a favorite of my father's if he would set you free. All he refused. Corrado says there's nothing I can pay or offer that will bring him equal return. He has me by the balls."

"You don't want to keep company with a used woman…" Her muffled voice stifled her words.

He sniffed her hair. "Rosa," he whispered to calm her, but she jabbed her elbows into his chest and stood red-faced.

"My name is a whore's name—a maestro's first gift," she said, full of spite. "Oh yes, now you act surprised? How could you not assume my name one men use for sport? Who is this woman, you ask? One you cared not to know so long as she satisfied your desire." Her eyes blazed with condemnation. "Go."

Matteo's innards clenched at the thought of leaving. "What do you know of truth? Who are you? Tell me your name for God's sake." Matteo paced unable to stay and unwilling to go. "Why would you need to lie? I can understand before we knew each other, but why continue?" His voice caught, "This is no game, woman."

"Not a game, you hypocrite? I'm a dream, Matteo. Your fantasy. I give you what you desire. Was it not my body that brought you to me?"

He didn't like this kind of question because he knew his answer would be wrong. He wouldn't admit that he wanted a wife but was too depraved to get one by custom. This she didn't know, but she did have it right. "Yes?"

Her nostrils flared and she stared at him and his poor answer.

He pressed back, "Your body beguiled me. You used it well."

She stared at him with a condescending eye.

"Did it buy you a sumptuous dress, beast, devil, liar?"

Her back straightened. She swung around ready to kill. "Have you not gotten what you paid for? That you can decide for yourself is not enough? You have a cock so you're free to do as you wish. Men think their stick gives them a longer reach." She jabbed him in the chest; her force pushed him back. "And I'd say you're right. The only power a woman holds is what lies between her legs, and men can't help but take it too. They take everything and violate her again and again until she has nothing." Her eyes widened. "A prostitute learns many lessons in the brothel, but the one that injures her most is that she enters in shame and remains in shame. She's powerless, hopeless, and cursed. These are her true names. And this is no lie."

Matteo shook his head. "Can you not understand that I meant you no harm?" He dropped to his knees.

"Ha," she said, "You meant only to use me."

He wanted to cover his ears. "I took advantage because I couldn't see. Forgive my ignorance. Don't do this. I was wrong. Let me make it right."

The woman he knew as Rosa left him begging and sat in the window chair.

"I'll not leave until you swear you feel nothing between us. I know we have something no matter how it began." He crawled to her and took her hand. "The shame you feel should be mine alone," he said and kissed each finger. "I take it and swear I'll do everything I can to protect you though your power overwhelms me. I'm hopeless without you. I'll remain cursed all my life if you cannot return my affections though I don't even know your name." He held her hands against his cheek.

"Matteo, you have to play by the rules. There can be no us. You know this."

The vacant face she wore when her maestro stood near surfaced and pierced Matteo making him desperate.

"I beg you, spend no more effort."

"If you know anything about me, you know I don't quit. The rules exist until I find a way to bend them." Matteo's panic rose. How could he leave her? "Look at me." Her dewy eyes penetrated his and softened him until he thought she'd break him apart. "Please, tell me your name."

She turned her face from him. "Remember the fantasy." She lifted her skirts and pulled him to her. "Have me one last time. Then go and don't look back."

"I'll not!" He looked away from her glorious thighs, scandalized. *God in heaven, please forgive me.* He couldn't feel his feet. "I love you."

But the woman before him held no expression.

"Did you hear me? I love you."

She blinked a few times.

Her unmoved response cut him. Now he felt her barbs. He could shake her for forcing his confession out and making him suffer. He retrieved his belt, pulled the sheathed blade from it, and tossed it at her feet. "Then finish your work."

She pulled her feet from the blade. "What can't you understand? Stop this madness. Walk away. Spare us further humiliation." She shoved her skirts down. "Please, Matteo," she said, lips trembling.

"Take my hand. Give me time. I promise I'll devise a plan to take you from this place. Once you're free, we'll bide our time until we can flee from the city." He told her about his home in Chianti. "I'll bring you there to live with me. Never again will you have to set foot in Florence. None of your abusers will find you. I know you love me and I will make you my wife."

She stared at him speechless.

Matteo pulled her firm against him and kissed her.

Her mouth opened to receive him.

Finally they found understanding. "Ow! You bit me?"

"It's all so easy when living in a dream." Rosa thrashed her arms and legs at him. "I don't want you. I don't love you." Her fists beat against his chest. "I wish you never set foot in my door."

"You lie." Matteo held her arms while she fought against herself. A few hits, and she went limp. Too easily she gave up. He waited for her to admit that she wanted him. "You have no heart when it counts. You lie and make me bleed for you, woman."

She collapsed to the floor.

"Perhaps you're not the person I thought." He tossed his mantello over his arm and stormed out before she could see him weep. He staggered down the hall and slumped into a dark, recessed area next to the stairs. He sat in his miserable state long enough for his tears to dry. More beast than man, rightly scorned, lost, and broken, he didn't want to live forever alone. He felt too tired to leave, he convinced himself. Get up and be a man! Don't let a woman beat you. Beast that you are, invite the anger—it will show you the way. If he could, he'd beat his weak skull in; better, he would beat Corrado's.

Feminine whimpers drew near.

Matteo backed deeper into his hiding place.

"What have I done?" sounded his nameless love's voice. She rushed forward in a mess of knotted hair and bare feet tangled in rumpled clothes. Crouching down, she peered into the stairwell. "Matteo?" she called hardly above a whisper. "Oh no, I've done it. He's gone. Please, come back. Turn around, come back."

The sight of her compelled him to act on the madness that possessed him since the day they met. A damned glutton for punishment, he stepped out. "I can't bring myself to leave."

She rushed to him. "Oh, Matteo. I'm sorry. I'm afraid, so afraid." She wrapped herself around him. "I love you. I want to be your wife. I want you and no other." She kissed his cheeks and his neck. "I love you and thought I'd lost you. I waited for you to pass on the street—you didn't look into my window. Say you'll always be at my window."

Matteo nodded and buried himself in her neck. "I'll be there until I no longer draw breath."

"I felt your dream gathering and found myself building a hopeless dream of my own. I don't now how we can be together—especially not as husband and wife. Oh, what have I done to you?" She held his face in her hands and kissed the tracks his tears had taken. "No matter the cost, I'll no longer live without you."

Matteo gripped her tight.

The most beautiful woman whispered, "I'm Liviana di Alesso." She caught the o on her fingers to conceal the words.

He whispered to savor the name, "Li-vi-an-a. It's beautiful."

"Swear you'll not speak my name in the open until we're free."

"I swear," he said parting strands of hair from her face. He prized the way her lips glistened pink and plump after they tasted each other. "I'm broken yet whole. You killed me and brought me back to life."

She kissed him again in a way they'd never kissed before. "I want you. Now." She lifted his tunic.

Matteo moaned. "I swear one thing more. This is the last time I'll return you to Corrado's room." He lifted her in his arms and carried her there.

***

The next morning Matteo woke to Liviana's soft lips trailing along his neck. "The day we first met, you said I didn't belong. Few women choose to be whores. I had a good life once. I can be a good wife."

"Liviana, I have no doubts about your—"

"But I want you to understand."

"Then tell me, but don't think anything you say will change how I feel."

Liviana smiled and tucked herself into the crook of his arm. "I don't remember my mother, but I do remember my father. He was a good, respected man and worked in a palazzo. My thirteenth year, Father said he intended a fine dowry for his only daughter. One night not but a few weeks later, he never returned home. I waited and feared and went to my neighbors. No one heard anything of what happened to him."

Matteo sat up in bed. "You were a child."

"As you say," she said and ran her fingers on his chest to quiet him. "A kind woman took me in for a few weeks while the men searched. Good as friends can be, the arrangement came to an end and I found myself in Ospedale, an orphan. I stayed there four and a half years, Matteo. They were gentle, loving people, but there were so many young children and few people to tend them." She glanced away. "Once a girl reaches eighteen, she can no longer stay. They found me work in a wool shop for little pay…until the day my maestro got an offer he couldn't refuse from Signore Corrado. That day, men seized what was not theirs. They made me what I am today."

"Shh, you're safe now."

"No, not here." She wiped her wet eyes. "How can we do it? I warned you, but you, stubborn man, you don't listen. Now you're my only hope. Please, don't hurt me. The hope you've given turns me against my maestro and this wretched life. If you fail, I'll die whether by my maestro's hands or another's. My life is in your hands."

"I'll find a way for us, Liviana. I'll not hurt you. Your last day in this hovel draws near. Make yourself ready for my return. Pack the essentials. I'll buy you new dresses—anything, as long as you leave with me and we're together. Hand-in-hand."

Liviana threaded her fingers in his. They sat together in silence.

"I'll play sick to keep Corrado from bringing another man to me. But don't make me wait so long he becomes suspicious."

"Crafty," Matteo said in admiration. "However you can keep his business from you and all matters of temptation, the less either of us need worry."

"And what of my temptation?" she asked rolling her naked body on top of him.

She discovered his answer. "Make no hesitation," he said gripping her hips.

***

"Massimo, recite the plan once more before we go tonight."

"Yes, got it. "It's very important." I'm not an idiot boy, you know? The emphasis of your request makes me think I deserve better payment."

Matteo held a finger like a viper ready to strike. "Do all I ask and I'll bring your father an entire barrel of wine on top of your pay."

Massimo's lips twitched. "Deal," he said offering a hand to seal their agreement. "Must I wear such sloppy clothes and this old man's hat? You tell me I'm to have my first night with a woman and you want me to dress in a sack."

Matteo whacked him half-heartedly upside his head. "What you wear matters not when you'll remove your sack." Matteo couldn't help but tease him, "If you have more than a little sack beneath your sack."

Massimo gave him a dirty look. He walked beside Matteo and made an obvious attempt to imitate him.

Matteo enjoyed the boy and found him amusing. "A whore doesn't care. Even if you want to look at her breasts and find you've spilled your seed. You can wait until night falls if you lack confidence. Talk to her until you build yourself up. Now, recite before we get there."

"But if she's old—"

Matteo ruffled his hair. "She'll be older than you, but not old."

Massimo stretched then recited. He reached in his bag. "I have the rope." He pulled it out. "Of course, it's sturdy as they come since my father made it himself."

Matteo agreed until the end pulled free. "What are you thinking?" He stopped walking and looked back. "It's a hangman's rope."

"I have fourteen years. I know what it is. It was the longest one Father had, and if you don't pay me my promised money, he'll take it out on my hide."

"I know I'm putting you at great risk. I thank you and wouldn't have asked for your help if I thought you unable."

Massimo smirked. "I like you enough to help. And your promises, I like them."

They approached the Malacucina. "Listen to me, Massimo. Don't dally else someone takes advantage, and once we're done, get out fast. The crowd will help you blend. Remember, I'll be across the hall should you need anything until we make the exchange at your door. And once done, I'll be waiting for you back in the last stable stall. Let me do the talking to get us inside."

Matteo entered Corrado's tavern with his arm over Massimo's shoulder. "Buongiorno, Signori," he said addressing a few of the usual faces. "I require a woman for my friend."

Corrado set aside his drink and took interest in the boy.

Matteo opened his purse. "His first time. Make her a sweet one."

"You're later than usual. Not so impatient today?" Corrado asked.

"I had to instruct the nervous boy a bit." Massimo's pinch stung Matteo'd back. "You know."

Corrado laughed. "He's staying as long as you?"

Matteo nodded.

Corrado laughed hard. "You'll kill the boy. His little prick won't know what to do past the first stroke." Corrado took the money and led them up the dark stairwell to the rooms.

Massimo's pale face gave all the sincerity needed.

Corrado opened a door. "Worry not, boy. She can sing you a lullaby." A woman with hair dark as night stood in the center of the room. She was no goddess, but handsome enough not to scar the boy.

Matteo massaged Massimo's shoulders for encouragement while Corrado made his way back down the stairs. "You see her?" Matteo said loud enough for the whore to hear, "She'll treat your virginity gently. I'll be across the hall all night." Matteo pulled him close and lowered his voice. "Don't become overeager and forget yourself. You must hear my knock." He closed the door.

Hours after dark, Matteo laid next to Liviana. Ears tuned to the room across the hall, neither he nor Liviana heard anything afoul and she fell asleep. Matteo slept little and decided to check on Massimo. He crept into the hallway and cupped his ear to the door. The inn creaked from the wind. "Son of a," he said jumping halfway to the roof. He held his fists ready to knock out the person who startled him. Shaking his head and withdrawing his fists, he grabbed Liviana's hand. "You scared me half to death," he said in a low voice.

Liviana giggled. "You'd make a good father. Look at your concern for the boy."

Matteo shook his head. "I'll never forgive myself if something should happen to him."

"I agree," she said far more serious. "You've got to settle down. All these ideas in your head strain your nerves. And mine." She pulled him back to bed. "Come and sleep."

Morning came. Matteo dressed and woke Liviana, who dressed and opened the window. He clasped her hands. "You do know you can trust me?"

"Yes. You're making me nervous."

"Have no fear," he said to her and himself. He took a deep breath before he set the plan in motion. "Liviana, take off your clothes."

She looked at him offended. "That's original as Adam's sin."

"No jests. I'm going to knock. The sooner we leave, the sooner this is over. Old Corrado has to be sleeping. No man can drink so much wine and rise this early."

Matteo went across the hall with a bundle in his arms. He checked to make sure no one stirred and gave the door three good knocks.

The handle jiggled. Massimo peeped the door open. He held a finger to his lips.

Matteo pushed the door open wider.

"Ready?" Massimo whispered.

Matteo nodded and set Liviana's dress and shoes alongside the inside wall next to the door and tiptoed to collect Massimo's hat, clothes, hose, and boots. The boy's head rocked side-to-side and he tried to pull them away.

Unsuccessful, Massimo pointed at the neatly folded dress and a pair of ankle boots, "No." He whacked Matteo's arm and shook his head in continued protest.

"Yes," Matteo insisted quiet as possible. The whore slept without notice.

"You didn't tell me about this. Don't make me do it."

Matteo scuffled his hair. "Shh. Once dressed, meet us across the hall." He stepped into the hallway. "Hurry."

No sooner than Liviana pinned-up her hair and placed the hat on her head Massimo appeared, ill-tempered.

"You're a ball kissing, ass licking son of a goat."

"Lively." Matteo disregarded him and looked to Liviana. "She's bound her breasts tight, and you," Matteo balled unused linen and shoved it in place, "now you have breasts at a glance."

Matteo and Massimo made a couple passes so Liviana could practice her walk. "No hip rolling," Matteo said.

Liviana tried again. "Like this?" They thought it acceptable. "I got it. If someone shoved a stick up my…" She laughed nervously and held her hands up in response to Matteo's scowl.

"She has it easy," Massimo said. "How am I to escape out the window with a skirt bunching in my hands and face? You wanted to make me a man. And now you make me a woman."

"You did figure it out last night?" Matteo handled Massimo's misshapen breasts again to form them better. When Massimo's face reddened, Matteo winked and tied a band at the boy's waist. "They'll not recognize you in the Malacucina since they'll look for a man and boy in the company of a woman. Now get the rope."

They pulled Liviana's seat away from the window. Matteo punched out the bottom slat of the shutter and fed the end of the rope through.

"Let me do it," Massimo said pushing Matteo away. He looked out the window and to the ground. "I'm to put my trust in the knot."

Matteo helped him tighten it.

"Go. Don't forget to send your signal once you're out." The boy wiped sweat from his face. "I'm watching."

Matteo kissed his head. "Liviana, follow close. I swear you'll get out." She pulled the hat tight over her head. They walked down the hall and stairs like they had nowhere else they'd rather be. Liviana ran into his back from moving too fast. Matteo steadied her.

Corrado's deliverymen acknowledged them with a tip of their hats.

Corrado, Matteo hoped, would make no appearance.

They stepped onto the street. A few paces from the inn, Matteo led Liviana into the alley between two buildings, kept her in range of his sight, and rushed behind the birds that gathered near the men selling bread. Arms wide, he ran into the flock and shouted, "Go boy." The mass of wings took to the sky. He waited long enough to see the noose drop out the window. "Quickly my love," Matteo said pulling Liviana along.

***

Massimo met them in the stable according to plan. He slipped Liviana's dress off and tossed it at Matteo. "They're looking for us." He shifted direction. "Horrible dresses. I flipped my legs over the windowsill and about broke my neck. I abandoned the shoes." He caught his breath. "The people on the street gathered near to watch me. They were loud and drew too much attention. Once I got my feet to the noose hole, the crowd shouted. And that's when Corrado pulled the rope. I jumped, and everyone knew I wasn't a woman. I ran and ducked into the Mercato." Massimo stood in his mutande and glared at Matteo. "I hold you to your promise, but you better go if you mean to hide."

54
April 26, 1478

Warning bells clanged across the city. Leonardo set his quill aside and went to view the street. "Are we under siege?" Past midday, activity on the via Sant'Egidio slowed, but today it stalled. The priests withdrew inside their monastery and the nuns slapped their convent shutters closed. Until Leonardo could discover the source of the disturbance, he would follow their lead. "Boys," he called, "close all the shutters and fasten the bars."

The two jumped from their seats to do what he asked, all too eager to discover the reason for the warning before closing them inside.

Leonardo unfolded the hinged panels of the bottega entrance, latched the top, middle, and bottom tight, and went to the smaller entrance door. Halfway out the doorway, he waited. Where was his garzone? The boy could've purchased ink twice over. Then he saw him.

Paolo passed the hospital and ran forward gesturing his arms wildly.

Leonardo stepped onto the street to wait for him and waved for him to move faster, which he did.

"Maestro, we must go. People are pouring into the streets. They carry weapons. You know the warning toll. It's for all the citizens."

Leonardo reached out to guide the boy inside. He backed into his other two apprentices gathered behind him. "What's happened?" he asked closing the door and sliding the top latch in place.

"Murder and deception against the Medici. Palle, palle shout the people in the piazza." One of the boys held a lantern between them so they could see Paolo's excited face. "It happened during the mass. Men attacked our princes in Santa Croce cathedral," he said wide-eyed.

"The intruders are known?"

Paolo set his purchase down. "They're Florentine, Maestro." For further dramatic effect, he opened his mouth allowing his audience to hang on his telling before saying, "De' Pazzi and the Archbishop Salviati are the traitors, among others."

Leonardo shook his head from displeasure, not disbelief. He noted the faces of his boy's expressions, an unveiling of innocence amidst confusion. They watched him locate his blade and string it on his belt, which motivated them to ready themselves to follow. Leonardo reached for his hat and turned back. "Your city calls you citizens?"

Their shoulders slumped and their heads drooped at his tone.

Leonardo bent to meet Paolo eye-to-eye. "No boy learns his duties, nor can he be wise if denied access to political matters." He addressed them all, "We go to learn what's happened. Any man who's done what Paolo said would surely hide, but stay close and keep quiet. I wish not to risk your father's or brother's wrath upon on my head." The boys grinned and bumped each other. Leonardo led them outside, closed his door, and turned both locks.

They walked to reach the via Proconsolo, which led them to the center of the city. Leonardo's company caught up with a group of men who'd left their work and homes for the streets; some took their women and children with them afraid to leave them home. Each man told his interpretation of what happened. A son walking with his father suggested that the Medici brothers brought the noble de' Pazzi low and lifted common men above them, and this was why they met a sharp end. Leonardo shook his head in agreement of his sound take on events. The common people did gather at de' Medici bosoms like lost sheep. Another man, quite wise, admitted to knowing nothing. Others and their companions decided that both princes were dead from loving the same secreted woman, and another said Giuliano refused to hand over his purse filled with gold he meant to give in offering to the church. Leonardo nodded without stating their ideas should earn them a fool's crown.

People filled the narrow roads leading into the Piazza della Signoria. Bell tolls equaled the power of the citizen's shouts and everyone pushed to enter.

A man near the piazza entrance raised himself high and spoke loud for all nearby to hear. "For the people and freedom, shouted that de' Pazzi traitor. He thinks we're not free?" The man received response, so he continued, "Christians spilled out of the cathedral to flee from the evil that bloodied their consecrated ground." He thrust his arms up and yelled, "Will we watch traitors within our own city kill the Medici, our brothers, friends of the common people?" The crowd reacted with an astounding, "No". The announcer continued, "Now we'll have the conspirators by their necks."

"Who, Signore? What men do they search for?" a voice in the crowd asked.

The man waited for a pause between pealing bells. "Francesco de' Pazzi and Bandino Baroncelli, the assassins. Curse them and their armed riders. The two sent Giuliano de'Medici to his death on the cathedral floor. And Lorenzo bleeds from his neck. God help our prince!"

The crowd let out a gasp and the announcer continued, "Jacopo de'Pazzi and the Archbishop Salviati rode about the piazza calling for the people to unseat our leaders. We will answer by cutting them down. Cut all the conspirators down," he charged in equal sentiment to the crowd.

How easily people found themselves curved to impassioned senses. People spoke few words against de' Medici's above a whisper, but Leonardo knew how little more than a whisper held the power to destroy. Lorenzo toyed with the Pope and lacked consideration for Florence and her people; worse, he meddled tediously in their lives for his own benefit. He'd ruin anyone who dared stand in his way, and he changed laws, many said, to thwart de' Pazzi family succession of well-placed daughters in favor of nephews. And now? He ruled the day by drawing breath. How easy the people of Florence crossed back over to his side. And if they should see Lorenzo, the sun would certainly shine out his ass.

Angered roars continued to fly through the air until the people began flowing freely into the piazza. One man held a flag with the herald of the Medici's recognizable five balls, the palle, and waved it high into the air continuing shouts of, "Palle, palle, cut the assassins down." Citizens banded together chanting, "Search for the Pazzi. Find the conspirators. Bring them to justice." The people stepped around strewn rocks that were hurled at the plotters in the piazza while more men gathered for pursuit with spears, blades, swords, bows, shovels—anything with a pointed end.

Pazzi, de' Pazzi, rang in Leonardo's head. Papi spoke the name. Yes, Jacopo de' Pazzi removed Papi to the Stinche. The treachery, insult, the pain, these devoured the old man. Leonardo thirsted for revenge—if not his own, then Papi's. His boys tugged on his sleeves while the scene unfolded. Evil men tied Papi to a wall, and they would meet their ends bounded by the laws of eternal justice. Never had Leonardo found entertainment in torture or death, but this time he would bear witness.

While hot-blooded men took to the streets, others found their positions to be prime spots for viewing the captured enemies, who, no doubt, would see the fruits of their labors dispensed. Leonardo joined them with his boys to wait for the spectacle to come.

***

Word came on wings of the wind to announce that Lorenzo de' Medici made an appearance in the window of his palace. When he showed the people that he lived, the determination of Florentines set them to impassioned revenge. Soon the first of the plotters arrived. Priest to the Bishop, the man fell under the full wrath of vengeance. Leonardo found cause to look away when they put their blades to him.

The priest shrieked until distinct cracks silenced him. His quartered body bloodied the cobblestones so thick they turned black. One man began another chant that called for "Death to the traitors." He chopped off the priest's head, tossed aside his axe, stuck the head on the tip of a lance, and led the swarm to hunt for more blood. Bodies flowed beaten and battered into the piazza—some half-dead, some lively. None named Jacopo arrived.

Late in the day, bodies dropped out the Signoria and Bargello windows. The latest swung and twitched on foul display. Leonardo looked away unable to watch another man fight for breath. Those who'd gone before were cut down from the Signoria windows to make room for those to follow. The terrible thuds of bones dropping to the ground landing dead body on top of dead body left Leonardo the stomach for no more. The greatest offense anyone could count was the loss of life where neither side could claim absolute right or wrong.

Boys, not his, pounced after the dead kicking, pulling, and dragging the corpses through the streets. Sickened, Leonardo knew they should have left sooner. "Boy's, come," he said leading his apprentices across the piazza, "This is no longer justice. We've seen more than enough." They parted a way through the people to cross the piazza on the bloodless end.

A familiar figure observed the Bargello bodies. He talked to men beside him and swept hair from his eyes.

"Maestro? Are you coming?" Paolo asked.

Leonardo nodded to indicate that he followed though he didn't move. Should he call his friend's name, keep walking? Surely not stand motionless and dull-witted.

Matteo peered over his shoulder and saw him. He strolled over seemingly less affected than Leonardo by their chance meeting.

Matteo hadn't changed his direct approach, nor did he regard those on his receiving end with less than a firm handshake. A double-handed arm grip would determine friend from foe.

Leonardo's heart pounded though the blood in his hands, arms, and legs waned. He signaled for his boys to wait. He couldn't let chance pass him by, but a punch to the face, he supposed, would mean he should have kept walking. Before he could think of what he should say, Matteo stood close.

"Been back long enough?" Matteo said crossing his arms at his chest.

"Too long." Groping, groping for words. Leonardo indicated the scene around them as reason for his answer. So, Matteo knew he stayed away.

The side of Matteo's mouth twitched. He dodged a group of clumsy men. "Will it never end?"

Leonardo shrugged. He could think of nothing but closing the gulf between them. "God, Matteo, you've been my best friend since we were snot-nosed, piss-in-the-dirt boys." Leonardo embraced him.

Matteo gripped Leonardo on the meaty part of his shoulder. He laughed. "You had the only snot-nose."

Leonardo laughed. His blood reached numbed places. Matteo's familiar lemon scent brought him comfort and relief, not torture. "Tell me how you've been," he said, his voice easier now.

Matteo's bright face faded to regret. "Here we are, and I'm leaving in two days, but," he ran his hand down the back of his head and neck, "not alone. There's someone you should meet before I leave. We're to marry once we go to Mother."

"What?" Leonardo said. "Married?" He gave Matteo a spirited punch in the arm. "Not Lucrezia? How can I believe it?"

Matteo shrugged. "I didn't know what would please me until I did. I care not for a dowry or a name. Father's gone. I'm the one left to arrange my marriage. I'll carry my family forward." He grinned like he'd won a prize. "Never say never. Life has a way of taking us unexpected places."

Unexpected places? "Then I'm happy for you." What did this mean for their saved friendship? "You'll return to Florence after your nuptials?"

Matteo nudged Leonardo's arm. "Damn, it's good to see you. Come by my house tomorrow and we'll catch up on lost time."

Leonardo's chest seized. He'd lost him…"Wait, before we part, you should meet my boys." Leonardo waved them over and introduced them. "My bottega's on the Sant'Egidio across from Santa Maria Nuova."

"What, a bottega?" Matteo asked in good humor. He nudged Paolo's shoulder, "I'm not surprised. I've seen your maestro's work." Matteo clasped his hands together and made to walk away.

"Look for the sign with vines," Leonardo said wanting to follow.

"We've two days to cover almost two years," Matteo said. He took a few steps, and turned back. "I'll see the place before I go." Matteo hid the hint of sadness in his eyes with a grin. "What are we waiting for? Let's go to your bottega now."

***

The next day, outside Matteo's house, Leonardo combed his fingers through his hair and placed his hat back on his head. A few steps later he realigned his belt and smoothed his new and favorite rosato colored tunic. Though he'd wiped down his leather boots before he left, street dust collected on the toes. He wanted to make the right impression on behalf of his friend and Matteo's future wife and family. He tried not to focus on what Matteo may have told her about him.

Matteo met him mid-street. The honor bestowed by the greeting caused people to take notice.

"Leonardo," he said embracing him. Matteo looked him over. "Are you trying to make my woman question her choice?" He laughed and gave Leonardo a pat on his back. "Grazie for coming." His eyes danced. They walked inside together. "Now, my friend," he said, taking Leonardo's hat, "I'm pleased to introduce Liviana."

Liviana stepped forward and tipped her head. "Welcome, Signore. I'm pleased to finally meet you."

Smaller than expected, but not too thin, Liviana's well endowed…not the breasts, don't dwell…yes, she had what Matteo liked. Her lovely face didn't hurt her cause. Her eyes, green as spring grass, locked onto his. In that moment he knew Matteo saw her as bold and worthy of his effort.

"I'm pleased to meet you." Leoanrdo bent to kiss her cheeks.

"Matteo's told me all about you. Please, call me Liviana."

"I heed your warning, Liviana," Leonardo said and grinned. He glanced around the room for her father, possibly her mother, saw none, and turned his head to Matteo in question.

Matteo slipped into place without explanation and set an arm at their backs to guide them. "He does come with a warning, or he should." Liviana laughed.

Leonardo didn't miss her questioning look at her betrothed. They waited for Matteo to speak.

"We have much to discuss given our time apart." Matteo sat beside Liviana. "Bellisima, you have no reason to worry."

The house servants removed themselves from the room so Matteo went to find one.

Liviana fidgeted in her seat. "Forgive me. I've not been outside these walls for weeks. It makes one forget how to talk to people. Matteo calmed my fears saying we can trust you. Because of your friendship—and discretion."

Matteo's request echoed down the hall, "We'll have the wine and morning meal."

Leonardo twisted the ring on his finger and fought the urge to storm from his seat. Perhaps he made a mistake coming here. "I don't understand what you mean." He glared at Matteo, who joined his bride silent as his sealed lips.

"I'll not play your fool, Matteo. Not yours or hers, not anyone's." Leonardo stood to gain advantage. "You're here. Living together. Where's her father? We know all of Florence would tear you apart for your...arrangement."

Leonardo knew condemnation and punishment, and he would keep Matteo from it. "I'll take no part in your game. Do what you must, but don't pull me into your troubles. I've had enough and need no more. Now I know why you leave for the country. Go. Go and marry. Once you've made yourselves right, invite me beneath your roof. Until then, I'll not be more abused by scandal." He reached the door in three strides.

Matteo rushed at him and held his arms out to block him. "Stop. You don't understand. What in hell do you think I'd do to you?"

Leonardo shook his head. "Move or I'll make you."

"Damn it, Leonardo, I'm on your side. It's been nearly two years. Sit. I'll explain." He moved close keeping his hands up in the air. "Liviana lives with me because she has to stay hidden for her protection. That's why we need to go to the country. I want to marry her, but she's not met my mother because we've waited to make our travels safe."

Liviana brought herself between them and faced Leonardo. "I'll not be what comes between you. Please understand. I've lost my father. I love your friend. Don't make him choose." She moved slow and steady, and took Leonardo by the hand. Firm, yet gentle, she led him to sit beside her. "Please, don't make him choose. A whore has few she can trust."

"You're a prostitute?" Leonardo looked back and forth between her and Matteo. "I'm going to beat sense into you—" he growled after Matteo.

Liviana gripped Leonardo's hands tight when he moved to get at Matteo.

Leonardo pulled harder in repulsion. Liviana's strength unsettled him. He stopped when she scowled. "Liviana?" He knew her—the squared shape of her hands, the length of her fingers, the slope of her nose—how could he miss those same penetrating eyes? He clasped both her hands in his.

Her look intensified and Matteo pressed in on them.

"I know you." Though Leonardo had no doubt, he wished he knew Papi's true name so he could ask for certainty.

Liviana's grip slacked. She closed her eyes.

Matteo jumped in prepared to strangle him.

"Stop." Leonardo lifted his arm to block any forthcoming blows. "I don't know her that way, you fool." He turned his attention to Liviana. "You have the look of a man I knew." A knot formed in his throat. "I know what happened to your father. We were in the Stinche together. He, a political prisoner…" his voice cracked. "He told me about you. He never forgot you and you must know he did all he could to find you. The guards read all his letters and

withheld some too. He knew you lived in the orphanage."
Leonardo swallowed.

Liviana's nails dug into his hands. "But he's not living,
is he?" She cried. "You, a criminal saw my father and I
couldn't." She stood and shouted, "What did he do to be
tossed away like rubbish? What did I do to earn my vile
life?"

Matteo tried to calm her.

"My father was no criminal." Frantic, she shouted, "It's
not fair."

"He saved me," Leonardo said loud enough for her to
hear. "My bed beside his was no accident. He saved me, I
believe, so I could save him." Leonardo offered his hand.
"I'm sorry. He was a great man and I'll never forget him."

"Did he suffer?"

Leonardo hesitated.

Liviana came at him and clutched his clothes. "Did he
suffer in the end?"

"I carried his frail body to the window. We sat together
until his spirit flew free." With that finality, they sat in
silence. Matteo held Liviana.

Leonardo viewed the couple. His breath caught and he
placed his hand over his heart to keep it in. "You don't
need my blessing. You have your father's. Both of you."

"Thank you, for loving my father, Signore." Liviana
wrapped her arms around Leonardo's chest.

Leonardo breathed again. "You're going to marry my
best friend. Please, call me by my name." Leonardo
motioned for Matteo to come closer, which he did. He
smothered Matteo's head at his chest and breathed him in.
"Liviana, make an honest man of him." He squeezed to
muffle Matteo's mouth.

"I will," she said.

Matteo mumbled from beneath Leonardo's hand, "I'm
honest as they come."

Leonardo stifled a laugh. "You're probably right."

Liviana's face softened into a warm glow when she fixed on Matteo. No stranger to the feeling, Leonardo could choose no better match for his friend. He let a ragged breath out.

"Say you'll visit," Liviana said. "This can't be goodbye."

Leonardo nodded though he questioned his ability to visit. "I know the way."

55

Matteo thought he put his difficulties behind him, but now that he arrived home, well, he never brought a woman home, and for good reason. He violated custom in every way. Who found a wife in a brothel? What man brought a woman beneath his roof before sealing the nuptial agreement? Bringing Liviana into his house acted as much a marital agreement as any document. Mother wouldn't like it, but he found no other choice. Liviana lessened the sting in telling him no custom or ring proved his fidelity more than the day he sealed his pledge by saving her. He would do right by her and his mother.

One of Matteo's men dismounted and came to take Liviana's reins. He offered an arm to help her down. "Forgive me," she said scooting from the saddle, "My leg has gone to sleep." She wiggled her leg on the foot platform, stepped down, and walked a little with Matteo at her side. "Thankfully I wore the lily green dress," she said in complaint of her soiled clothes. She shook her skirt, wiped at her face, and felt her hair lacing. "The ribbon is in place?" She frowned. "I'm a mess."

"You're beautiful." She felt around her hair again. Her wide-banded braid held all in place. Matteo moved her hand from her head. "It's looks the same as when we left. Don't worry."

"What if she finds me lacking?"

"Then she must open her eyes wider to see you through mine. My mother's a practiced woman. Her critical eye comes from the tasks she does in my stead. How can I blame her?" He softened his look. "Her approach may be coarse but she has a gentle heart." Mother would understand. She knew the family line ended with him. She knew the pangs of loneliness. He would present Liviana's ring in Mother's presence to honor her as a witness to the completion of his union.

Liviana's hand fidgeted until Matteo wrapped his fingers tight around it. As much as he wanted to calm her fears, he wanted to smooth the transition with his mother first. He kissed Liviana's forehead. "Welcome home." Liviana's breaths came shallow while Matteo's drew deep. Ripening mulberry trees led a straight path to the threshold. Hands woven together, they approached the house to the songs of birds above and the crunching of gravel under their feet.

He led Liviana inside. She stood in the doorway and peered around the open room. Her attention moved to the depiction of the Golden Fleece on the floor, Father's showpiece and vision of their trade. Matteo rubbed his thumb across Liviana's hand.

Long blocks of the late day sunlight angled a harsh path across the sala floor. Glad they arrived with the light on their side, Matteo wished to give his mother no reason to think him suspicious and hiding under cover of darkness. A grin pulled across his face. Here he had the women he loved at his side, the comfort and safety of home, and soon he would be married, children would run down these halls, and the Attaviano family would thrive. They passed a servant woman he'd never met. She gaped at them. "Buongiorno, I'm your maestro come home," he said.

Cook came out of the kitchen wiping his hands on a cloth. "Maestro Matteo?" He smiled. His eyes trailed from Matteo's face, down his arm, to his hand that connected to Liviana's. Cook's head drew back.

"Cook," Matteo said with a kind slap on the back, "I've brought you another lady of the house." Matteo lifted his clasped hand. "This is Liviana," he said urging her into the kitchen while he excused himself a moment to look for his mother. "Mother?" he called up the stairway.

"My lady?" Cook said, not two steps away.

Matteo nodded and put a finger to his lips when he heard his mother.

The sound of her skirts rustled. She turned the top stair corner. "Cook, men stir outside our stable," she said. "Two approach the house."

Matteo hurried to meet her before she charged down and scared his beloved half to death. Mother gained some weight. Grey overwhelmed her hair. Her brows pinched together in a scowl when she saw him. "Matteo, son of Lapo di Attaviano," she said. "You've been gone too long for a poor, widowed woman. Letters alone do not bring a mother peace."

He shook his head. "Look me over then. I'm well, Mother. I never forget you." He bent forward to kiss her. He kissed one cheek and skipped the second when two of his men barged into the sala carrying Liviana's new chest. They stood awaiting direction. "Signore, Signoria," they said, their voices echoing. Matteo asked them to set the chest aside. He focused back on his mother. Liviana waited near the kitchen doorway.

"Beautiful. Oh, son."

He agreed and joined her in praise of the view. But she focused on the chest. "Oh no." Not Liviana. She must have thought the chest he'd given Liviana a gift.

Liviana, pale and damp, stepped out to meet his mother. Cook followed close behind with a raised brow and a sudden need to gnaw his lips.

"What's this?" Mother said curving her head around.

"This," Matteo said, "is Livian—"

"Liviana di Alesso. I'm pleased to meet you, Signoria." Liviana gently kissed Matteo's stunned mother on her cheeks. "You're lovelier than Matteo led me to believe."

Matteo took each woman's hand. He smiled at them and waited for his Mother to rejoice—once she swallowed.

But confusion set on her brow. Her eyes bounced between him and Liviana. She rushed into the sala. When no one entered, she opened the door and peered out.

"What are you doing?" Matteo asked. Never did she act so strange. He shrugged apologetically at his mother's erratic behavior.

Mother rushed back. Except for the frown on her face, she spoke not a word. She ran her fingers along the fabric of Liviana's dress, turned her hands to view Liviana's nails and palms, and raised the hem of his beloved's skirts to examine her feet.

"Stop," Matteo said. He reached for his mother when he saw how Liviana turned to stone. "Don't be rude, Mother. She's no slave. Please, she's my—"

"Quiet." Mother swatted him off then plucked at Liviana's hair to examine the light color. She fingered the thin gold chain around Liviana's neck, which completed her predatory circle. Her lips twisted then burst, "You've ruined us. Who saw you enter my house?" She reached for her forehead and turned white. "One memorable as her will have our neighbors talking. Tell them she's a friend from afar brought to visit me. Oh, they'll think her some kind of vile woman keeping company with my unbridled son. They'll think me wretched." She tried to catch her breath. "This is what happens when a family loses its head."

Liviana reached for Matteo, teary-eyed.

"No, mother." He pulled Liviana to his chest. "I'll have her as my wife."

Mother staggered back, her face went blank, and she lost her feet.

Matteo sprang forward to catch her before she dropped, but Cook caught her first.

"My lady. Quiet now. Breathe," Cook said. He rested her head on his knees and smoothed hair from her face.

Matteo kneeled to reach her. "Mother. Mamma? What's wrong with her, Cook?"

"She's done it before when your father passed. The doctor's say it's from a rush of blood to an inner affliction, an apoplexy. You've bled her heart, this I know. You'd know if ever you were home. You distress the poor woman. She needs rest."

Mother woke, fear on her face. She took in her position on the floor and tried to stand like nothing happened. Color blushed her cheeks; whether in embarrassment or a sign of regained strength, Matteo didn't know. He could see how Cook stepped in where he failed. Mother calmed when Cook soothed her. "Never do I forget my mother. You both know it," Matteo said. "I left for the good of this family. I've tried to fill my father's shoes. I do my best for you, Mother, and like you, I don't want to be alone. Neither does she," he said pulling Liviana to him. "All will be well for us."

Cook held Mother upright and tried to lead her away, but Mother insisted she remain.

Matteo wrapped his arms around Liviana. Mother would not have her way.

Mother stared at Liviana's face, then at Liviana's hands against Matteo's chest.

"When I need you, you hold her. You're my son."

"I'll always be your son, Mother. I love you both. You want happiness, you want me to marry, and you want grandchildren."

Mother surveyed the room and shouted, "Out. All of you." Her hands swung in the air to make the curious house servants looking from above and across the room leave. Cook left on the same request. She turned to Matteo. "How dare you come into the house of your birth and defile it. Tell me you've already married though you'll break my heart." She paced and mumbled to herself to the point of not hearing Matteo's calls to her. "Remove your hands from each other. This is no brothel. We go to mass tomorrow to beg for forgiveness. Oh my God, they've sinned against you and against their families."

"Mother. Will you listen? We're not married."

"That's why she wears no ring! You love her?" She stabbed her hand between them. "This is no way to show it." She took hold of his face. "You look at me." Her fingers dug in hard. "You've taken advantage in the worst way. How dare you. People will talk. Your family, Matteo! Why didn't you think of the Attaviano name?"

"All I've done is think of my family."

"No. You think of yourself. You brought her under our roof without one to escort her. Everyone will think her unchaste." She let go of his face and shook her head hard as if she could make the situation dissolve. "Her family is dishonored. Her parents care not if you love her anymore than I do. They want your name—your influence—all part of the web we spin. If you fall, you break the strands we've worked so hard to build. And if they saw you with your hands on each other." She looked into the sala again. "Oh Saintly Mother, is she? They don't want your name. They sent her away." Mother turned bright red and spittle shot from her mouth, "She's with child."

"No, mother," Matteo shouted. He reached his arm back to block Liviana from her. Now he'd have to withhold information. They could admit she'd lost her parents, but never could his mother know she was a prostitute. "She has nowhere else to go. She's lost her parents. She has no one but me, and she's come to live with us. She'll be my wife."

"As lady of this household, I forbid it."

Liviana's gasps turned to tears.

Filled beyond what he could tolerate, Matteo stood firm to face his mother. "As Maestro of this household, woman, I will decide who stays and who goes."

Mother winced. "All I've done for you, thankless child. You'll be rid of me?"

Her look pained him, but he couldn't take her side. "Never. I love you, Mother though I make my own decisions. Let us not be against each other."

Mother fled from him. Her stumbling footsteps traveled up the stairs and faded into a sharp silence.

***

For most of the next week, Matteo went from Liviana's door to his mother's and back again, but both refused to chance an encounter with the other. Liviana let him enter; his mother didn't. Others in the house kept him company.

No more, Matteo said upon waking. He committed to finally doing away with the exhausted, fruitless battle. He waited until the morning meal when Liviana and Mother opened their doors for food and drink. He stood in the hallway and spoke loud enough for all to hear, "A week's gone by and though you live together but separate, you do live together, beneath the same roof, right or wrong, no matter who has seen or not, my marriage stands consummated by tradition in leading Liviana through my door. I'm going now for my wife's ring and the notary. When I return, you'll be dressed and prepared to meet me in the sala. We'll proceed to the mass, for you Mother, once the papers are complete. And when we return, we'll live together in peace."

Liviana's door opened. "I'd like to sit outside and await your return. I've been closed-up too long." She looked down the hallway, saw no one but him, and pulled him in for a kiss. "I'm sorry."

Matteo shrugged. "Mother will come around. I should apologize."

"She's been through her share of loss. I see her fight in you. She protests because she fears losing you. Be gentle with her."

**

Awake, Matteo kept his eyes closed but fanned his arm across his bed to locate Liviana. He couldn't feel her. A hard, ball-shaped lump rolled under his finger. He popped an eye open. Liviana kept the shutters closed, but shafts of light squeezed through the cracks. He pinched the tiny stone between his fingers. Was this some kind of wives' tale to make her fertile, or perhaps similar to those horn pins attached to the clothes of infant sons for protection from the evil eye?

He washed, dressed, and went to find his wife. "Liviana? Mother?" he called downstairs.

"They're outside. Together," Cook said. "Your ladies await the morning meal. Will you join them?"

Matteo smiled. "I'm no longer a child, Cook. I need no early morning meal with the women."

Cook squeezed Matteo's shoulder. "You're just wed. A married man can use his daily bread, huh?" He waggled his eyebrows. "Keep your vigor up?"

Matteo laughed along. "I suppose I should follow sound advice."

Cook handed him a chunk of bread and offered apricots and cherries. "Eat, young Maestro, eat."

Matteo paused mid-chew. "My daily bread, ha." He finished his bite. His stomach flipped. "You didn't hear— you—no one—we disturbed your sleep?"

Cook laughed. "Maestro goes rosy? No, no." Cook whistled and busied himself.

Matteo finished his bread in the kitchen and watched his women seated and facing each other in peaceful conversation. Liviana dressed in a yellow gown with white sleeves that matched her beaming face and golden hair. His mother dressed in sky blue, which never failed to receive compliments. They seemed relaxed and attentive. He couldn't be more thankful. Mother said something and smiled. Liviana gave a little laugh.

"Maestro," the house servants said, passing him to bring the ladies their food.

Best to let them be. Matteo stole another glance and went to his father's office to go over the ledgers. He took his time walking along the hall, running his hands across the books, the trinkets, the memories. He felt closest to his father when he sat in his chair. If only Father were here. He could find no better happiness than gaining Father's approval, but Mother took his place. He hoped she could find comfort now.

"Matteo? Are you there?" Liviana said sometime later.

"Done so soon? I'm here," he said, "and I have a question for you."

"Will I have an answer?" She sat.

Matteo caught himself smiling again. "I woke this morning without you in my bed."

"That's not a question, but I'm sad for you and for me."

He tipped his head and continued, "My hand ran across a rounded stone in our bedding."

Liviana stood. Her hands ran repeatedly over her stomach. "I didn't know I lost it. Oh no."

He held his arms out. "Stop worrying. It's a stone."

Liviana's eyes widened. "A mere stone? It's been weeks since I used the honey-paste to keep it in place. I was fortunate to learn the old ways, but I've failed you. There are wise whores who know a woman should go no more than a few days without pessary and paste else she find herself sick with bile and ripe with child." She searched his face. "You couldn't have thought me barren?"

"No, my love." He placed his hand on her stomach. Heat snaked down his spine. "Forget the old ways," he said freeing his erection and sliding his hand up her skirts, "I'll have sons."

56
May 1478

"Papapapapa," called the sweet voice of Piero's son down the hallway from the bedroom. The boy and his mother entered Piero's office.

Piero set the papers aside on his desk and rose from his seat. "Come to me, Antonio. Come to Papa." He bent to his son's level and held his arms out. Antonio ran into them. Spittle glistened on the boy's lips and chin.

"There's your Papa," Margherita said in a singsong voice. Bent at the waist, her breasts hung like summer squash beneath the camisa that hugged her round figure. She gave Antonio's little hands a shake. "Your son called for his Papa while Diana changed his soiled cloths. We've come to say goodnight."

Piero scooped Antonio up and lifted him so he could fly. Candlelight flickered when the boy flew high and low through the air.

"Mow, mow," Antonio said rowing his arms.

"He must sleep soon, Piero. Not too much." Antonio giggled then fussed after her. She sighed. "He doesn't want me. He wants into everything. When anyone holds him still, he cries."

Piero smiled in pride. "And you'll deny his determination?"

"No, husband. I would deny him nothing."

Piero held his son facing outward toward his mother. He waited for her to say more but she admired them together. He set the boy down.

Antonio headed to a stool to climb. He looked at them. When Margherita moved to pick him up, his bottom lip quivered.

Piero stopped her. "He will never learn if someone is always there to stop him. He needs no spoiling."

"He's a baby," she said as their son teetered on the stool. "His father, then, will be the one to deny him."

Piero wriggled his fingers at Antonio. "He will have all he needs." Antonio climbed down. He stepped toward his father, but his gown pulled at his neck and thrust him face down onto the floor. Spoiled cries turned to wails. Piero lifted him and tried to calm him, but his son's shrieks pierced his ears. He handed him to his mother. "Tell Diana he no longer wears cradle gowns. This is women's business, a mother's best judgment. I should not be the one to make these demands."

***

Piero waited until the house quieted to go to bed. He removed his clothes, pulled the drapery shut, and slid beneath the light blankets. Margherita's foot touched his. She nuzzled against his side and kissed his shoulder.

In the beginning, she came to their bed timid and quiet, but now he reminded her of all religious holidays—even the minor ones—to call for her restraint. Healthy and demanding, her youth lent her far more than his fifty some years of spent vigor. He could seed a child but his force was not always thorough enough to sap Margherita's speech.

"I would deny you nothing, Piero," Margherita whispered in his ear.

He held her hand on his chest. "Kind of you, gracious woman." He closed his eyes and exhaled loud and deep.

"You love us."

"Mmmhmm." Piero lifted his arms behind his head.

"You love Antonio as a first son?" She asked glancing at the sleeping boy not far from her side.

"You know I love him. He bears my father's name."

"Rightly so. And I know you'll grant his birthright."

Familiar words. She never let them rest. "He is young."

Margherita sucked in a sharp breath. "He's your first legitimate son. Why would you refuse his claim?"

"I will tell you true. Many times my sons have been taken from me." Piero turned to face her. "Pray he lives long. If my love were enough, he would never die."

She cupped her hand against his face. "I pray he lives long and well as you. He's strong and determined. While God smiles upon us should we not then embrace His gifts and shower our son with all we can offer him?"

Margherita cupped his manhood in her hand and stroked the way he liked.

He nodded in compliance to her convincing hand, but soon sucked back his desire. He would not let her play him tonight.

"Plentiful are the gifts we can give," she added working him rigid. "His father has plenty to offer."

Piero would grant Antonio's birthright at the right time. He turned on his side and parted his wife's legs. Using her method against her, he let his fingers do the talking. Ah, the music of hushed petitions.

57
June 1478

Leonardo would have gone to the near abandoned military camp for news, but the soldiers and mounted cavalry left for Chianti with guns, carts burdened with barrel upon barrel of powder, spears and crossbows, and other uncountable munitions and supplies. At the Porta S. Piero Gattolino, he approached the now familiar gate guard, young Fino, who saw him coming.

"Leonardo."

"Fino, anything new?"

Fino offered him drink. "Come stand under the arch for shade. It's damn hot today." He drank deep. "Better them than me. No way you'd find me fighting those Aragonese dogs or their Sienese bitches. I hope the sun cooks those bastards in their armor."

Leonardo turned an eye to the road leading away from the city. The rivalry between Florence and her choleric neighbor, bolstered by the King of Aragon's Neapolitan army, and now the Pope and his murderers, found no rest. "What have we come to when the Pope, of all people, thinks of vengeance and treasure first? He and his Pazzi lapdogs failed their plot, but his eye for power and revenue will not rest until he crushes us." Leonardo asked Fino, "Have any couriers come?"

"Not since first of the month. Where's your friend from again?"

"Monteficalle near the town of Greve. I care not if the courier returns my correspondence, only that he delivered my plea for Matteo to return to Florence." And if Matteo did read his letter would he act with forethought other than defense?

A fellow guard elbowed Fino. "Idiot. Remember the man who rode through these gates not three days ago? From Panzano?"

Fino hit him back. "What of it?"

"Panzano's at the center of Chianti—near our friend, yes?"

"Yes," Leonardo said with bite.

"Our men find themselves backing further up the Valley to Panzano's doorstep. Not far south, the man said the towns are good as gone. They disabled the mills and burnt the crops before any provisions can fall into enemy hands." He placed a hand on Leonardo's shoulder. "Our countrymen should be along shortly I think."

Leonardo offered him his flask in thanks. He glanced back once more in hopes of witnessing a miracle. If marriage did tame a man, Matteo would surely heed the danger and lead his household to safety. "I thank you. Our countrymen seek protection, but goodness will not follow on their heels. We'll have famine. And Plague."

***

Two days later, Florentines greeted battle-weary family, friends, and neighbors. The city gates churned and choked on the flood of citizens seeking safety within the great walls. They arrived on well-lathered horses, over-burdened mules, and oxen pulling hastily packed carts stuffed with as much as they could move from their homes. Entire households, many on foot, arrived dirty and exhausted. Women and capable children carried babies, lanterns, foodstuffs, earthenware and platters, baskets filled with assorted valuables, small animals, and anything else they could move of value.

Leonardo crossed the river to the Oltrarno side to locate Matteo. He listened to the people recount how the skies to the south thickened dark with smoke. Few knew if it came from the Florentine army or the enemy, but they warned their brethren as they passed through towns along the valley roads.

A man asked an arriving family for news. "Leave now while you can, they told us," he said. "We've made it. But to move my family, leave our home, our crops, our livestock," his lips trembled, "we held out with our men. Panzano became the forward line of our city's defense. You know there's no more time when you see soldiers pack and flee north. They poisoned the wells, led off the cattle, chopped down the vines—all to break our enemies. Three days we've carted from Panzano—slow, painful, praying as we looked over our shoulders. All's lost." He removed his hat to cover his face.

Leonardo went to the care-worn woman trailing behind the man's cart pulled by a single mule. He offered to carry her bawling baby. "Grazie, Signore," she said crying. The mother's trembling arms couldn't lift her little girl who cried and clawed at her skirts.

Leonardo bent low holding a free arm out to her, "Here child." He lifted her to his hip. "Rest now," he told her and the baby while her two bigger brothers fell further behind. They walked not too far to the San Frediano quarter where the family planned to stay with the wife's cousin. Leonardo placed the children back in their care, wished them well, and made for the gates.

Matteo's able-bodied household and all his men should fare better than many of the people passing through the gates, but no longer could Leonardo tolerate helplessness. He hurried to the stables, tacked up his horse, and rode to the gates.

Fino's companion recognized him and reached for his reins. "Signore, you'd be advised not to venture beyond the city walls."

"Yes I would," Leonardo said. "People I love are out there somewhere and I can't sit idle wondering when or if they might appear."

Fino's jaw tightened and he nodded. "But Signore, you have no protection." He unbuckled his belt and removed his dagger. "In good conscience I can't watch you ride away without defense," he said extending the dagger for Leonardo to take. "I'll pray for you and your loved ones. God's speed."

"Grazie. When I return, you'll have it back." Leonardo strung the dagger around his belt, waved, and kicked his horse to a canter. He skimmed the incoming countrymen on his way out. If he had to travel the full way to Monteficalle, he'd be more lethal than any inferno or poisoned well.

***

Leonardo rode to the mouth of the via Chiantigiana and worried he may miss the turn-off concealed by brush and trees, but fresh cart tracks, hoof prints, shit, and trampled grasses cut the path wider than he'd ever seen it before. He gave his horse its head and looked out to the expanse before him. If Matteo had the sense to flee, he could take no better road under the burden of heavy carts.

Some time later, loosened dust swirled on a ridge nearby. Leonardo could see no riders, but he led his horse off the road to wait. He dismounted, unclasped his dagger and moved behind a group of trees. To calm his horse, he rubbed her withers. "Shh."

First he heard gnaws and creaks of a cart. Then hoof beats, followed by snorting and neighs. Horses never lied. Theirs sensed him near. He mounted his horse and edged near the road. Horse and cart lacked speed or surprise, but still he kept his hand on the dagger. His horse turned its ears forward and swished its tail. "Easy," he told her hearing the cart slow.

"Buongiorno," a male voice said, and made a brief pause for response.

Leonardo tried to make out bodies to go with the voices concealed by the trees, but before he called back, rapid hoof beats thundered his direction. A group of seven or eight men shot down the road with bows, swords, and axes drawn.

Leonardo centered himself on the road and made an effort not to squeeze his legs against his horse and send her running at them. "Single-rider," he shouted hoping they'd slow. He lifted his open hands high into the air.

The riders encircled him in a cloud of dust.

"Leonardo? Damn the devil. It's Leonardo."

"Matteo?" Leonardo steadied his horse. "I've come for you. I sent a courier two weeks ago."

Matteo whistled at his men. "He's friend, not foe. Bring the carts forward." Matteo held an arm out and grasped Leonardo the old way of the Roman's. "You look like hell."

"As do you. Why wait until your ass catches fire before leaving? Don't risk your family, Matteo. Don't risk yourself."

Matteo's face went dark. "How do I choose what stays and what goes? Everything's there, Leonardo—my father's house, all I have left of him. We left in a vicious calm where everything looked the same, and I could only stare knowing we may return to ruins. These faces tell the truth of madness." Hands shaking, he lifted a flask to his lips. "My neighbors, my friends, they all worked fervent as my household to gather as much and the best of what we have. Leave no one behind, we all agreed. People are what we have in the end."

"And so I came," Leonardo said.

"I'm sorry, I saw no courier."

"Forget it. What can I do?"

Matteos' forlorn face offered a weak grin. "Ride beside us, brother."

Matteo's men, his household, and many familiar people continued forward. Glad to see the women and children off their feet, Leonardo turned his horse to join them. When he sidled up to the line, he caught sight of Lucrezia's mother, who sat next to her father. Her father held the reins of their stuffed mule cart and tipped his head. Her mother lifted a hand in greeting.

Leonardo recognized Lucrezia by the intensity of her gaze and the upturn in her lips—always she seemed amused. No amount of affliction dimmed her appearance. He looked for her husband, curious, but she rode sidesaddle alongside her parents. When he caught her eye, she lowered her face.

58

Matteo held pink roses at his chest and arranged himself square with Liviana's window. "Madonna," he called, "Mona Liviana."

She peered out the window, her face surprised to see him.

"I'll always be outside your window," he said, hoping she'd smile.

"Bah," said a passing old widow named Bona, who let him snip from her flowerbox.

Liviana waved her hand for him to come up.

Matteo rushed through the sala and ran up the stairs to meet her. "For me?" she asked holding the flowers close to smell them.

"No other," he said kissing her forehead. "My heart breaks when you carry a sad face, my love." He brushed his thumb over Liviana's bottom lip. They'd not made love since they arrived back in Florence. "Tell me what hurts you."

Liviana sat in her window seat. "To have a new life with you…our time in Chianti was beautiful. More than a woman like me could ever hope for."

Matteo opened his mouth to protest.

"But here I'm shackled. What would happen if I go beyond these same four walls?" She bit her lip. "Do you think Corrado and his men still search for us? Who might see me and know what I've done? What we've done?"

"Once the battle ends, I'll return us home. We'll live free."

"You believe it possible?"

"I do."

"But Corrado doesn't forget. Shadows of the past rise too large and keep me locked away."

Matteo lowered himself to look in her eyes. "Corrado's trade requires his meddling attentions. His men have more interest in drinks, dice, and cheap whores. What we've done holds no comparison to what they've done and continue to do to you. No one knows who's come or gone, or where he or she may be. I say we take advantage of the chaos." He took her hands. "If you stepped out the door, without fear, tell me, where would you want to go?"

Liviana shook her head unwilling to consider his suggestion.

"You could go to the women's baths. We could walk the piazza and make up stories about the people who pass by and eat every sweet we see. Would you like a new dress? Shoes, ribbons?" He stopped and smiled. "Choose one, of course," he said with a laugh.

Her face withdrew more.

"I'll stay in tomorrow, with you. There's nothing I'll not give to see you happy again."

"Stop," she said when he attempted to pull her to her feet. "Out my window near midday, I saw proof enough for caution." She twisted her figure to show him. "Guido Bartoli stood there, beneath the jetty right before the alley across the way. He knows we're here. He watched Cook and Luca roll the wine barrels in. There'll be no free day for me."

Matteo ground his teeth. "You're certain it was Guido?"

She nodded. "Will it never end? The shame of him in my bed—I can't look at him, but I must watch for him. I fight against myself and I hate him for it. I hate them all." Tears welled in her eyes. She held her hands to her belly as if to protect herself.

"I hate them too."

"Now, I must find escape from within," she said guiding his hand on her belly. "Matteo, promise me you'll cast them away from your thoughts. We must find a way."

He shrugged.

"Promise us," she said and pressed on his hand. "Promise you'll not seek them out."

"I promise."

Liviana set her head against his chest and locked her fingers in his. "Do you feel how my heart races?"

Matteo shook his head. "Fear not. You're safe with me." He glanced at their conjoined hands against her belly and jerked his head up in wonder. "Us?"

She nodded at his questioning face. "I'm with child."

He blinked and blinked again to be sure he heard her right.

Liviana lifted his face to hers. "I've not bled since before we left Chianti. I feel terrible day and night."

"My love." He kissed her and her belly. "A child." He lifted Liviana in his arms, spun her around, and kissed her again.

Liviana covered her mouth. "I'm going to be sick."

"This is good," Matteo said, and ran for a basin. "Let us tell the others the good news."

***

Not two months later, Matteo sold the last of the silk they brought when they fled the countryside. Numbers from the ledger ran through his head. Without the crops, livestock, and grazing land, the size of his household sucked money out of his purse faster than he could put coin in. Men do with less, he knew, and his men would think no less of him if he told them true. One need only look around to see a neighbor's losses. Wise families rationed food and supplies. All tightened their purse strings. Every day

Matteo conversed with people in the market or the piazzas in search of information about the battle that already took so much. No one knew of any changes.

Returning from the piazza, he ran to his wife squatted on the ground outside his home. The widow Bona held Liviana's bowed head. "Oh God, what's happened? Liviana?" Matteo's bowels could give. He tipped Liviana forward in his arms expecting to see the worst, her bloodied skirts. Where's Mother—any woman under his roof? "My son, my son?"

Liviana clamped her nails into Matteo's arms and labored to catch her breath.

Matteo could find no blood on her. "What's happened?"

Liviana's eyes bulged in her head and she pointed at the house. "She'll kkkill me."

Bona excused herself and left.

Matteo pulled his wife to her feet. "I don't understand, damn it. Who?"

"Your mother," Liviana said. "Her ladies. They..." she lowered herself to the ground. "Ladies kept her back. Told me to run." She heaved and heaved and vomited. "Guido came. Told her," she said gagging. Liviana held her hands to her belly. Her eyes pleaded with him. "What if I birth a monstrous child? My worries. My sins."

Matteo let her loose. His anger burned in his chest. He growled loud enough it echoed. "I say who stays and who goes. Get on your feet," he said. "I'll beat my mother and kill that fucking bastard."

"Serena Attaviano," he roared entering the house. Liviana cowered in the corner by the door. He left her to bring his mother in-line. He called again.

Cook rushed down the corridor. He looked at him and held his arms out. "No Maestro. You can't go to her in your state."

"Move out of my way, Cook, or I'll toss you aside."

Cook lowered his arms. "This is a misunderstanding. I'm certain of it."

"Go to your lady who's been abused and abandoned." He said referring to his wife, but Cook's eyes turned toward Mother's room. "What kind of woman threatens the mother of my child? No mother of mine." Matteo grabbed Cook by his collar and shoved him the right direction.

He rattled Mother's door handle. "Women, open the door."

Mother shouted commands at her ladies.

Matteo thrust the door with the side of his body. He tried again, feet first. His foot landed forceful against the jamb and the door swung open with a crash. He unbuckled the belt at his waist. "Everyone out."

Mother's face snarled in reproach. "You'll beat me, child?" She strode straight to face him. "You lied. We raised you better than you act." She swung her arm out to slap him.

Matteo caught her arm and snapped his belt free. "I'm no child, Mother."

"She's a prostitute," Mother said, "and the world knows it. This is more than any mother can bear. Think of your father, Matteo, your poor dead father. This is beyond scandalous. It's the worst I've ever heard."

"You've crossed a line. You want to kill the woman who carries my child? You force my hand." He tightened his hold and cracked the belt on her backside.

Mother yipped. "In anger I said I'd kill her. Everything's lost." She held her hand out eyeing the belt. "You're father would have beaten you. This marriage, this child, they're unacceptable. He would never allow it. Nor will I."

"I'm sick, Mother. Sick on how you betray me." He swung the belt again. "How can I trust you?"

Mother turned to stone. "Betray you? I'm going home to Lucca where I belong. Where I had proper respect. I have no son." She yanked herself free.

Matteo buckled his belt and searched for a response. "I never meant to disrespect you, Mother. I wanted our family to prosper. Liviana's had a hard life. If you would sit and listen. Try to understand. Open your heart."

"No." Mother winced when she touched her backside. She tossed clothing into a chest. "You force me to do the unthinkable. Leave me to my packing. Pestilence and heartache fill this foul city and I'll not feed on another of your same portions."

Matteo returned to Liviana and led her to the horses.

"Guido sneered at your mother and proclaimed his work done once he told her of my past," Liviana said. "'Excuse me, Signora,' he said, 'I must go north to the lands where the harvest awaits. A place known for respectable families.'" He shook his apologetic head at your mother, Matteo. His soul is black. He stayed until your mother threatened me."

***

"We ride," Matteo said. He and Liviana cut across the city center. "You'll stay with one I can trust while I end this. Guido's pushed too far."

"But you promised," she said.

"I'll break any promise that threatens my family. Guido's torn us apart. I fear for you and the child," he said tying the horses in front of Leonardo's bottega. He swallowed to fight his fear away. "I thought we'd lost our son today. Here you'll be safe until I return." He'd find Guido. No man worth his weight would do less under such insult. "I'll send Guido straight to hell where he belongs."

They entered the bottega. Leonardo sprang from his chair. Before he could respond, Matteo crossed half the room. "I apologize, my friend, but we've nowhere safer to go. Will you keep her awhile?"

"Of course," Leonardo said, concerned. "You look like a madman, and she's worn thin. What's this about?"

"I've no time to explain. I must go. Latch your doors once I've gone. Do not answer even for my mother. When I return, I'll knock three rapid beats three times followed by two singles."

Leonardo's large hand cupped the thick of Matteo's arm. He said nothing yet everything then let him go.

Not far away, Matteo jumped from his horse and pounded on the Bartoli residence door. An elderly woman answered.

"I'm looking for Guido."

"Yes, Signore. He's not here. They left for the Vicchio del Mugello up north," she said pointing west.

Do not abandon Liviana, Matteo told himself. He'd never make it to Guido before dark. "And when do you expect his return?"

She held up her hands unsure. "Should we tell him you called?"

"Yes. He knows where to find me. Tell him Matteo Attaviano awaits him." Once she closed the door, he spit and kicked and cursed the air. The piece of shit would have him eaten from the inside out before he showed his ugly face.

59
August 1478

Leonardo leaned against the far wall of the hospital to sketch anyone who caught his eye. He'd seen the man with the misshapen head come and go and waited for him. How he pitied the grotesques who lived on the edge of society yet found themselves smothered within it, for they lacked much but found redress in wisdom. The grotesques gave up on vanity and pretense and appreciated beauty with a tender eye.

Today Leonardo followed the man whose head cramped at the curl of his nose and pointed into a twisted, upturned chin. The man shuffled and labored with a cane that strengthened each step of his weak leg. The mysteries of the grotesque drew Leonardo in with every line and shade, and he decided the face not cursed, for within every body such a creature hid, but the beautiful flung their abuses on the few who had no choice but to display their ugliness.

The man looked at him with suspicion when they turned the same corner into the market. He hobbled away into the crowd. No matter, the rare face Leonardo could remember without difficulty.

Leonardo walked to the corner of the Mercato past the seller who stacked a wall of wicker baskets, nets, and caged songbirds. "Two birds, Signore."

"What birds d'you want?" The gauntly bearded man lifted cages with his calloused, cracked hands awaiting his decision.

"Those will do."

"He doesn't give a friar's fart," the seller spoke to a man of his likeness. "Watch what he thinks of our birds."

Leonardo paid the man and took the cages. He passed the man selling pots and bowls and the woman and her husband selling second-pickings vegetables. In front of the Column of Abundance where the pillory ring held two chains, and above the platform on which an accused person would stand, Leonardo set the cages down. This reserved spot offered open space.

"Lovely songbirds."

Leonardo turned to see who noticed his birds. Lucrezia's father gave a cordial greeting. Lucrezia wore her hair in a spiral braid on her crown and her hair flowed in small ripples over her ears. A ribbon centered a set of pearls adorned with wings at her forehead and held a length of veil cascading over waves past her shoulders. She viewed the birds and burrowed her bronze eyes into his. She blinked, and for a second, her eyes opened to the creature she locked deep inside.

Leonardo spoke before he revealed too much notice. "They sing caged or free. But if you open the door, they take to the sky." Leonardo untied the door of the first cage. Before he opened it, he turned to Lucrezia, who cocked her head, captivated. The bird seller's son stood behind them. Leonardo opened the door and held out the cage. The swallow gave a chirp, hopped to the door, and took flight.

The seller's son clapped sarcastically. "Set them free and I'll catch them again."

"I know you will, but the bird would take a few moments of flight over a lifetime in a cage."

The seller's son waved Leonardo off and walked away.

Leonardo lifted the remaining bird and held it out for Lucrezia.

She looked first to her father, who shook his head refusing to indulge her.

"Come, Lucrezia, your husband awaits us. We can't be late when his associate expects us to attend the baptismal festa." His large hand clamped across her shoulder.

She clenched her jaw and took the cage in her hands.

Leonardo worked the tie undone and glimpsed at her, searching—he knew nothing, as she once told him, but some things a person couldn't hide. "When you're ready, open the door," he told her stepping out of the way.

She wasted no time. They watched her bird soar over the rooftops.

When Leonardo turned back toward them, the cage rested on the ground and Lucrezia's father led her away firmly under his grasp.

The cages Leonardo used for kindling, but today he abandoned them for greater pursuit. He trailed far enough behind to remain unnoticed. Lucrezia and her father arrived in time to join others gathered at a home near the Strozzi Palazzo. The procession ran a good length of the street. Visitors held boxed biscotti, wine, and other gifts. They filed inside behind a father carrying his newborn child.

Leonardo tucked himself in a doorway, pulled out his stub of charcoal, and lifted his notebook. He made fast his sketch to catch Lucrezia's essence. When she turned away from her father her hair fluttered in the breeze. She closed her eyes as if sleeping and bowed her head in what he thought may be a prayer. This moment he captured on the page and thought sufficient to take back and detail in ink.

60

"Lucrezia?" Matteo said like an explosion.

"Yes?" she said raising her chin and eyebrows daring him to ask why she'd come to his house. She stood outside his door and waved off her escort. "Where my husband finds himself preoccupied by all matters, we find his cousin," she said holding a hand out to the man, "Michele." She stepped closer to Matteo. "You see. He's quite fitting an escort." She twisted something in her hands, looked up, and added, "Never did one find a better eunuch for the guarding of honor."

The man appeared unaffected by her statement. Matteo stifled a laugh. Perhaps the man was a eunuch. Matteo refocused. Lucrezia was the last person he thought he'd see.

"I've come to return this to your mother," she said holding out a small, beaded purse for Michele to give him, "Before she departs." Lucrezia bit her lip.

It seemed that word spread about his Mother leaving. Matteo took the purse by the strings to avoid the temptation of digging his fingers in to determine the contents.

"Thank her for me," she said turning her attentions away for a moment while Michele took his position a step behind her. Lucrezia set her shoulders straight. "If there's anything I might do in repayment for her kindness…much as the day in the piazza. Signore, do you remember our friend, Gaddea?"

Lucrezia's words always did hook his ears. Matteo nodded. How could he forget? He wiped hair from his brow, and signaled without trying to make it obvious, that they shouldn't converse about it. "I'll see my mother gets her purse."

She nodded, eyes wide and blinking in the most unnatural way. "Let no debt go unpaid." She gathered her hands at her waist and jerked her thumbs outward.

Matteo didn't catch her meaning until he read her lips, which mouthed: Open. "Very well, Signoria Gherardini," he said, "Buongiorno."

Matteo shut his door and opened the purse. A rosary wrapped around a piece of paper with a dangling crucifix— a jest? He worked the paper free and read.

"What do you have there?" Liviana said running her hand across his back.

He crumpled the note. "A debt to repay." Damn her! He tossed the note.

"If you can't pay, you can find another way." Liviana retrieved the note from the floor.

"It's not that I can't pay. It's that I question the wisdom of stretching my neck out for another man's woman. Lucrezia del Caccia kept me out of the fire once, and now she asks me to walk into it blind. I know not what she plays at, but it settles smooth as boils." He stretched his neck until it cracked. "She wants to meet with you in two days "to talk of womanly things" before she calls on me to cancel my debt." He scratched his chin. "What do you make of womanly things? She's a married woman."

"You think she knows?"

Matteo plucked the note from her hand. "I do know my debt need not include you." He palmed her belly and tried to think of any reason Lucrezia may have come to him. "Perhaps she wants a child? She's been married long enough." He suddenly choked on the air.

Liviana whacked his arm. "She, you…you once loved her?"

He flung his hands in the air. "Not love. We grew up together with a good prospect of marriage. Our families matched. I took to thinking of her that way."

Liviana lowered her face.

"I'll not lie. Affection I felt. I could trust her." He reached for his wife and kissed her. "You I love and no other. As for these womanly things—"

Liviana took his hands and searched his face. "You trust me?"

He knew Lucrezia would cause his head to ache. "Yes, you know I do, my love. I trust you."

"Then let us do this and free you from the past."

***

Matteo's men loaded food and belongings into Mother's cart. The moment Matteo feared had come. He could watch from his window no longer.

Mother placed her hat on her head and snapped her fingers at the ties so one of her ladies would do them up.

"Don't do this, Mother. This is your home. Father's home."

She glared at him and shook her head forcing her lady to redo the ties. "My home is the lands of my father. There I have my rightful place."

Matteo stepped forward. He should toss her belongings from the cart to take charge, but he wanted her to choose to stay. What point could he achieve by forcing her? He moved to embrace her.

She refused him and set her shoulders. "I'll have none of this and no more of you. My dowry," she said, a demand. "I know what your father received from mine."

"Don't deny what's true, Mother." He gave her the purse holding her substantial request and clasped her hand. "No matter the words you speak, nothing can change that

I'm your son. Every son needs his mother as much as his father."

She wouldn't look at him, but her ladies snuffled and snorted in tears.

"I love you. If you desire to return or if you need help, or anything Mother..." he stammered, "Anything you need, you send for me."

She turned and drifted out the door like a stranger. Her ladies trailed behind.

Matteo followed. "I did it for us," he shouted in front of everyone. "We have nothing if we don't have family." How could she walk away so cold? He grabbed Cook who tucked his mother's foot into the cart. They stared at each other.

"Cook," Mother said, moving her hand for him to hurry.

"Forgive me, Matteo. She's my life. I love your mother. I can't abandon her." Cook tucked the edge of his lady's dress in.

"I'm sorry, Mamma. Don't go."

Cook's head hung low. He shrank from Matteo when the men brought his horse around.

"Cook," Matteo said. He moved his hands to speak where his throat squeezed shut. "Send word of your safe arrival?" Could a man feel the weight of his failures more than when his mother chose to abandon him? "I did it for the life of our family," he said again.

The party rode away without further word, but Matteo watched and waited for the cart to return. He stood unwavering in his hope. He willed them back. Failure meant giving up, and he refused. His mother shut the door many times before, but she always opened it. They would return. He had to believe it. Here he would stand.

***

Matteo regretted his family's dishonor though he'd apologize no more for love. Every day brought him a little closer to frenzy, slipping as if on thin ice. He fought to maintain control but lost his footing. He needed to anchor himself, so he worked to make good on all his debts and bonds, but desperation and rage infected his efforts.

He tried to bury his anger for Liviana's peace and health. A man needed his family and his friends, but he had little if he couldn't protect and provide for them, as a man should. Beasts of cursed hell, how much longer until he could return to Chianti?

When his feet seemed to lose ground he remembered his wife and his unborn child and what they needed from him: make safe their home, tend to the trees and silk worms, the gardens, the fields, get an ox or two, some mules, and harvest as much food as possible. He and his remaining household would gather what they could to get through the winter. But did their home stand secure in the battle lands? He thought it possible, but wouldn't know until he could see it with his own eyes.

A feeling—the knot in his gut—he should listen to it. Move or die. It tugged at him and told him to go. Go where? In another month, he'd have little for trade and naught but a few, pitiful coins in his purse. He had no means to leave Florence. Weeks gone by, no one had given a reliable report from the south. He waited too long. Mother kept him lingering. While he remained motionless, Guido's snare ripped his flesh away and gnawed at the bone.

61
September 1478

Leonardo knew he failed Paolo when the Medici banished the boy from Florence. The loss of Paolo crushed him. At a disadvantage to help, Leonardo listened only to the artful boasts on his way to Domenico's bottega. He avoided the usual, evil gossip—the kind that sent Paolo away from him.

As soon as Paolo set foot in Bologna, he found himself arrested, as reported in his letter sent to Leonardo. Paolo said he wasn't worthy to keep the da Vinci name and asked only for forgiveness.

"My friend," Domenico said. He sat beside Leonardo.

"Paolo's gone. Banished," Leonardo said. "He wrote me from prison. As his maestro, is it not my responsibility to go to Il Magnifico and plead his case?"

"Perhaps. Go on," Domenico said.

"He's accused of living a wicked life. I have reason to believe his exile comes hard on him because I am marked by de' Medici. My name reaches Lorenzo's ears with scorn and suspicion." Leonardo added, "We were never lovers, but my name they remember from Il Teri." People knew Domenico had boy lovers. Maybe he'd understand. "You know the boy. Would you help me in this matter? For Paolo's sake."

Domenico poured wine and drained his cup. He lifted his hands they way he always did when he wanted to help but didn't know how.

"Anything you can do. You could write a letter and vouch for his good character. This way you don't have to leave your bottega nor would you have to present yourself in the lion's den."

"I'm sorry to hear what's happened." Domenico nodded. "I'll write a letter though I doubt it will serve a great purpose."

"Grazie. He's only a boy." Leonardo could think of no better way to help Paolo. The problem with people was that they reveled in and remembered another's worst moments. Was it not payment enough for a person to live with regret?

62

Leonardo pulled the key ring on his belt forward, fingered through the keys, missed the one to unlock the rear door of his room, and searched again for the one with the short teeth. He glanced over his shoulder to view the street. How could he loose a key? It slipped free or a pickpocket stole it. Now he'd never sleep. Mumbling under his breath, he walked the longer way down the road to the v-split of the Sant' Egidio and around to the front entrance of his bottega.

"Rafaello," he said in greeting to the boy who continued grinding colors with his pestle. Leonardo removed his hat and set his new parchment on the nearest table. "Where are the others?"

"Uhh, they left."

"Where did they go?" Leonardo waited, but his garzone placed his obvious frustration on the pestle. As the newest and the youngest in the bottega, he suffered from the exclusionary games the older boys played.

"Maestro, my work is simple. I grind your pigments, do this and that, and clean the bottega. I'm not their keeper."

"You're right. Your bottega brothers have responsibilities and they'll take your cleaning duties until they can remember the efforts of a full day's work."

Rafaello's face brightened.

"Rafaello, take some time," Leonardo said. "Riposo. No need to work while we're all away. I'll see you in the sixth hour. Here," he said pulling a quattrino from his purse. He peered into the finely ground pigment and squeezed the boy's shoulder. "You've done fine work."

Rafaello sprang from his seat. "Grazie, Maestro."

"Go on," Leonardo said with a flick of his head. "And Rafaello, if you find a key lying around, would you bring it to me?"

Leonardo opened the door to his dark room. He stepped inside, closed it, and removed the key ring from his belt. The nail on the hinged side of the door he found without effort. He hung his key ring.

A rustle sounded near his bed. He clicked his tongue to call to the cat. "I'm sorry I closed you in old boy." He waited for the meow or a rub against his leg. "Orso?"

The air smelled different, sweet. "Orso?" Leonardo froze in place. He extended an arm to feel into the black. Nothing. No, something. He held both his arms out to skim the darkness. A breath. Did he hear a breath? He tasted floral on his tongue and his hair stood on end. He raced to the door, fumbled with the latch, and thrust it open.

"Shh, Leonardo," a female voice said. "If I meant you harm, I would've attacked. Shh, it's Lucrezia."

"What?" He pushed the door open wide to peer deeper into his room. Still he couldn't see her. He heard rustling and the sliding free of the window latch.

"Please," the voice that might be Lucrezia's said. "Come inside. I have your key." She cracked the window open enough for a narrow sliver of light to cut a line across the floor and stepped into it. Her hands she held well away from her skirts and she splayed them out at her sides to calm him. His key dangled from her wrist.

"What—why—" Leonardo shook his head to clear the confusion. "How did you get my key?" he asked, his voice rising.

"Send a man to make noise over here while a woman slips in over there." She held his key out for him. "Don't fault your boys for my plan."

His head swung back to be sure that no one in his bottega saw or heard them. Blood pounded in his head. "What man helped you? I'll take this up with him as soon as you depart." He pointed an accusatory finger. "I'll not partake of men's wicked devices or women's."

"Listen for a moment," she told him, "I pulled Matteo in. Now we're even. I kept his secret, so he'll keep mine. No one will know I've come," she said undisturbed.

"This," he held his finger up, "this thing you two do…" Leonardo shook his head with a solid no. They both took advantage. He kicked the door. "What honeyed words did you have to inflict on him?" He thought of Liviana. "He's married! And you're a woman—where's your escort?" He went to peer out the window then another realization struck him, "You're a married woman! You mustn't be here." He pressed his fingers against his temples and paced. "Go now. Go," he said in a flurry, but she didn't move. "Don't tell me how you came to be here. You must leave before we're found."

Lucrezia watched and listened but made no effort to leave.

"Can you not hear me?" Leonardo thought the conditions an exception for him to take hold of her and steer her out of his room, out of his bottega, out of her folly. First he pressed his forefingers on her back with minimal force and to no effect. "I want no more distress." He looked to Heaven and took hold of her shoulders to force her out.

"No," she said digging in her heels. She twisted to gain a foothold, handhold, anything. When that failed, she yelled, "You don't know the efforts I've made—"

Leonardo covered her mouth with his hand. He stretched out his other arm and slammed his door shut. "Quiet, for both our sakes."

She nodded beneath his grasp and mumbled.

"Quiet," he reminded, and let her loose.

"I wanted to come to speak freely."

"Nothing's free, Lucrezia."

"Please, don't be angry. Matteo wanted to see me no more than you." She slumped to the end of his bed where the shaft of light from the window illuminated her from behind.

Leonardo slid the door lock in place and held his hand out indicating she needed to speak lower. "Tell me why you're here, Lucrezia. Tell me what you want so you can be on your way."

She wrapped her arms around herself, her face stayed hidden in the dark. "Am I such a burden?" Her voice strained. "Everyone would be rid of me."

He sighed and waited for her to say what she found so vitally important to risk telling him, privately, in his room, which she gained entrance by trickery. She seemed frail, desperate, and if he rejected her, she may collapse, and then what would he do with her? "You're not a burden," he told her, questioning his judgment.

"You saved me once, Leonardo," she said lifting her hands to her chest. "And your birds—they take flight with my unspoken desires. You know. You see. They say what we cannot. When the songbird took to the sky I drew breath so deep, so light, it burned my fear away enough to step out."

Leonardo said nothing. How steep a price he paid for stepping out. In unspoken reply, Lucrezia's body shrank at his silence that shamed her. He sighed again, unbuckled his belt, and unstrung his notebook. He flipped through a few pages to the drawing of her.

She ran her finger along the paper's edge, looked at the drawing, him, then the drawing again.

He stared at her knowing he couldn't help her anymore than he could help himself. "This is what I see," he said turning the page to the drawing he touched with ink.

She gasped. "You made me beautiful."

Leonardo turned from her to his tableside lantern, flint, and steel. After a few strikes, a spark smoked on the small tray of tinder. He put the flame to the candle, closed the calf-parchment door, and held the light between them. "I can't free you," he said moving to the window. He looked for anyone who may have heard them, saw none, and closed the shutter tight.

"I have no one," Lucrezia said. "My father was my friend. He truly loved me. Perhaps he wished I were a son, but never did he speak of regret." Her eyes traveled over him. "Time has its way with us. My father's abandoned me. My family's money has dwindled. Strange men trample father's lands. There may be nothing left. Father says we no longer have the prosperity to choose."

"Your father loves you. Though you think he's abandoned you, you're mistaken. You can't live with him forever. He's given you much. You have a husban—"

"I have nothing if I can't breathe," she said lowering her head. Her lips trembled. "Ever since we surfaced from the river, I saw my reflection in your face. Can you breathe, Leonardo?"

Her prying question stunned the breath from him.

She nodded her head gently in understanding. "We strain and gasp. No matter what we've done or not done, the blade of rejection slices deeper."

Leonardo held a hand up to make her stop.

She covered his hand with her own. "I understand your pain, Leonardo, believe that I do, but you have a blessing. You've not lost the father you thought you had."

She told him true and also crushed him. God he knew. How he knew. Setting it loose, though, made it alive. He wanted to curse her. He wanted to curse his father. He wanted no more of this conversation, but her bloodletting reopened his scabbed wounds. He dropped beside her and gaped at them.

"You can trust I've told no one what I've seen. But there's more." She shifted her position. "I'm a married woman, yet my marriage is incomplete. My dowry's not fully paid. My husband refuses to take me under his roof until he has surety of payment. As long as he's waited, he may be a saint. Not once has he done what most would— move on to one whose father could pay her dowry." She dropped her head. "I've heard the rumors…that I'm a blemish upon women. Do you think Antonmaria listens to them? He may be too decent a man to step away." She started to cry. "I'll make no bride for Christ blemished or married, nor can I be a woman under my father's roof. What's left for me? I'll not remain a child in my father's eyes as the years pass me by and I grow embittered by the waste I'll become."

Leonardo stood to fetch her a spare piece of cloth to dry her eyes. He offered it. "Lucrezia, there are more questions than answers. We do the best we can."

Her face drew back from him, hurt, disappointed. She embraced herself. "I've nothing left."

Leonardo lifted her chin. "Listen to me. Don't loose sight. You keep your eyes to the sky."

She looked up at him. "You saved me once. You pulled my head above the water that would take me, but I'm drowning again."

Silence filled the gap between them.

"He's never touched me the way a husband should," she said with a sniffle. "I'm not worthy. I'm done with waiting." She pointed to the drawing on the end of his bed. "Am I truly beautiful?"

"Your husband is a fool, Lucrezia."

She reached for him. "Maybe I'm not worth so great a dowry in my father's eyes." Her hand curled around his arm. "Am I beautiful?"

Leonardo didn't answer, but felt her tremble. Yes, you're beautiful.

"Please," she said, "you see me better than anyone." She pushed her gown off her shoulders.

Leonardo shook his head and lifted the gown back into place, his hands now trembling. He unclasped the top of his farsetto and gasped. "You're beautiful," he told her so she felt no need to show more for his approval. He stood and turned his back to her.

"I love you as my friend, Leonardo. As the boy who saved me. As a woman to a man," she said in an unsteady voice.

"Lucrezia, you have it wrong. Think of what could happen to us if we we're discovered right here, right now?" He had to act to save himself. "I don't know how you think this conversation wise. It's injurious. I can't let you harm yourself any further, nor can I save you."

"You already have," she answered and moved about.

He stood and held his hand out to show her to the door. But her voice grew desperate.

"How am I lacking?"

Leonardo's stomach clenched and he turned to her. "We're all lacking." The blacks of her eyes glowed with something large and unbroken. He paused. "You go places others lack the courage to visit, Lucrezia. You frighten people."

"I frighten you?"

He persisted in turning away from her. "You frighten me."

The sound of fabric rustled again. He peered over his shoulder, her over gown pooled onto the floor. When he moved to lift it, she stopped him. Her small, warm hands cupped the back of his head. A faint wash of jasmine filled his nostrils.

"Let us bury all things that tell us we're not worthy— that tell us we should be afraid. Forget them," she said. Her warm breath caressed his face, "I want you," she whispered, "I'll fly free, if only for a moment. Come with me." Her lips found his.

He would allow her a parting kiss and walk away. But her hands moved over him as if she couldn't pull him close enough. "I want you," she said again, steady and determined. She beckoned with such force he closed his eyes and lost himself by kissing her back.

His hands found her skin. Whatever the force, she wanted him. He needed to absorb her desire and allow it to fill him up. How he needed saving. He could become a man Ser would welcome. He needed to feel what she offered. Lucrezia held him close. She understood. Her lips grazed his midsection while her hands slipped his tunic up to his shoulders.

He removed it and tipped her back to lie on his bed.

In the shadows, they joined together until he woke from his trance. "Lucrezia," he whimpered, feeling sick, "forgive me." He pulled free from her. "Forgive me," he said in panic. He reached for his discarded tunic and pulled it over his head.

"You've done nothing wrong," she said, her hand on his back. "You didn't hurt me. There's only a little blood. I'll clean it."

He looked her over and located the spot. "There's no time for that," he said tossing a cover over it. He sat on the edge of his bed, elbows on his knees, his hands in his hair, grasping for a way to send her from him without hurting her. What have I done? He rocked back and forth.

"I'll go. Quietly. No one will know, Leonardo," she said reaching out to him. "There's no shame in love."

He couldn't face her after what he'd done.

She dressed. "Say nothing then. But when you can speak, don't tell me that you're sorry."

63
October 1478

Leonardo sat at his desk and held his quill midair. *Don't tell me that you're sorry.* Ink blotted his parchment. Damn. He poured sand over it. Lucrezia's parting words twisted and hooked deeper.

They should be sorry. After their swift amore, they should be sorry! She came without restraint or regard. He gave audience to a distraught woman in the shadows of his own room, despoiled her, a virgin, cuckolded a man, violated his own better judgment, and much more. Cite these things no more, he ordered, and poured the sand from the page to continue his studies.

He made a couple more annotations and flicked the quill from his fingers. He held his head and pressed his temples. Lucrezia came uninvited. No, she came unsought and turned him so he welcomed her. If anyone discovered them... The sweat on his tunic didn't come from the October heat.

He ventured out little these last weeks and found fitful rest when he tried to sleep. He waited for Matteo to come to him, to explain, to somehow make things right. Matteo had done him wrong.

"Signore Leonardo da Vinci?" a courier said. He held a letter.

Leonardo pushed his chair back and rose from his seat. Matteo. It had to be Matteo, finally. He took the letter and paid the man. The writing came from no hand he recognized.

"Boys, you stay here. I have immediate business." He reached for his keys first, counted them, strung his purse to his waist, and shoved the letter in it.

He moved brisk to be unhindered in pursuit of the snake, Matteo. The name grated on his tongue. How useful his friend must have found Lucrezia's request. She cancelled his debt, and Matteo stuffed her away to let him—oh yes, he could hear Matteo say his name, the sound warm and innocent—acquaint with her at your will, good friend. He pictured Matteo's likely grin as he helped Lucrezia hide. How convenient Matteo must have found his deed as he washed his hands clean of her.

***

Leonardo fisted the scruff of Matteo's tailored neckline. "You meddling snake." He yanked Matteo's body from his seat in the small garden at the back of his house. The stool crashed into the dirt next to a lemon tree. Matteo's legs thumped over it.

"Get off." Matteo swung around. His fist shot out and skimmed Leonardo's ear. "What's wrong with you?"

"Crafty speaks the devil. What's wrong with me?" Leonardo lifted Matteo high enough his toes dangled in the dirt. "You cleared your debt by tossing that woman my way." The sight of Matteo rankled him more. Leonardo tightened his fist. "I've sinned against nature." He clenched his teeth and rammed Matteo's back against the tree. "And you can't live with it."

"Down," Matteo said. His face snarled and his body hardened in warning. He gripped Leonardo at the shoulder and clawed his neck.

"Admit it," Leonardo said like a growl. Matteo's face reddened in his grasp.

"I stood at your side," Matteo said. He tightened his hands.

From under the branch Leonardo considered pinning Matteo to, he saw Liviana running toward them. He tried to shout but his throat choked off.

"Stop," Matteo said with effort.

Unable to draw adequate breath, Leonardo let go.

Matteo dropped to the ground and waved Liviana off.

They both coughed and caught their breath. Glares shot both directions.

"You shit," Leonardo said, expending all his air. After a few more breaths he spoke. "You asked what I thought you'd do to me. Well, now we have our answer. I never would have guessed the way of it." He cleared his throat and pushed Matteo back. "Did you take a single moment of consideration?" He shook his head. "How could you have when what you've done could end one, two, all of us? You don't decide my fate."

Matteo righted his fallen stool. "It was a debt. I have to take Liviana out of the city as soon as the way is safe." He sat. "Lucrezia called. How could I refuse her? She saved me. Remember? I'll not go when I owe."

Leonardo stood prepared to choke Matteo again before he could dig his hole deeper and ruin any fondness Leonardo had left for him.

"Don't lay a finger against me," Matteo said. "You're my friend, but I've reached my last thread to hold life together here. Don't push it, Leonardo. I'm not proud of what I've done. Push too far, and I will break." Matteo's face went hard but sunk into dark circles that rounded the pits of his eyes.

"No more then. You don't know me. You're dangerous and put everyone around you at risk." Without further measure, they were done. Leonardo flung his hand out. "Goodbye Matteo." He turned to depart.

"She said she wanted to talk with you. She came to us with her plan. The woman spared no effort, I tell you."

He heard Matteo but kept walking.

"Leonardo," Matteo said tenderly to urge him back. "It's not easy for me to understand your nature. But I try. Who else can say as much?" his voice trailed off. "I know nothing of your conversation with Lucrezia." Matteo tried again, "But she convinced me when she said, no one should be alone."

His words, her words, whoever lay claim to them—they surfaced like a bubble on the frothy edge of turbulent waters. Leonardo cursed.

"Come back, Leonardo. How could I say no? You're always alone. You deserve better than that. How could I say no when I have to leave? I have to for my family. We have no life here. We're pawns in a terrible game."

Matteo's brows furrowed together. He closed his eyes and hung his head back tired, limp. "You're right. It's all my doing. Forgive me," he said, "I meant you no harm."

Leonardo leaned in. "Because you believe yourself a pawn, I too should be one in your game?"

Matteo shook his head. "I didn't mean to lead you to think that. Please, sit. I'll tell you the worse of it."

Matteo told him about Guido and his mother. "He'd see me writhe in the dirt with nothing left before he stops his madness. Few are the moments I feel more man than beast."

Leonardo covered his lips and shifted in his seat. For the first time in a long time, his words could form a prayer. "The things desperate men do confound all. Can we get nothing right?" My God, what can we do? He dropped his shoulders. The fight flowed out of him; he wished to float away with it.

Matteo exhaled. "Lucrezia wanted to talk. I thought it a simple request. Not entirely pure, truth told, but simple. How could I know her effect?" Something in his face shifted briefly. He curled a finger over his mouth and his eyes lit with a sort of revelation.

Leonardo found a knick on the table to pick. No, no, he'd give nothing away. On what remained of Lucrezia's honor and his own, he couldn't speak of what happened. He squashed any ideas Matteo might entertain by making eye contact and squaring his jaw for emphasis.

64

Matteo pressed his back hard against the jagged stone of the Podestà wall. It bit into his skin. The sting quieted him while he waited for the city's announcements. Rumors traveled fast, and if he could find any truth in them, he hoped today would be a day of good news. A group of soldiers, he'd heard, rode into the camp outside the city gates not two days ago.

Hoofbeats clacked on the cobblestones as the city Bannitore rode across the piazza. He dressed in red and white and wore a silver chain around his neck. People evaluated him looking for an apologetic eye, or better, a brightened smile he might show toward the news he'd tell them, but the man showed the mastery of a practiced gambler.

The Bannitore dismounted his horse and stepped onto the platform of the loggia. He lifted his horn adorned with a banner, which hung to his ankles and displayed a fleur-de-lis at the center. He played his fanfare in three bursts to prepare the people for forthcoming announcements. "Attention, attention," he called in a clear voice. The crier read all matters of law and proclamations before the people:

Good citizens of Florence, this, the eighth day of October, the year of our Lord, Fourteen-Hundred and Seventy-Eight...

Matteo prayed for patience while the crier rambled over the refined points.

The Bannitore continued:

Word from the south: Signori, the castle Brolio fell to our enemy the Thirteenth day of September before nightfall. The enemy presses northward and overruns the soldiers of Florence with great force. Commanders declare the earth scorched, the crops now turned to ash, the waters diverted, and the towns abandoned but for the remaining homes that provide shelter for our men, many who wane in the heat and at the sight of their homeland's destruction. Citizens be warned: The battle continues. The Sienese and Aragonese armies push north and now possess greater Chianti.

The Bannitore went on but Matteo could listen no more. He wandered from the crowd sick at heart. He'd have to tell Liviana they couldn't leave, that they must ration their kitchen stores, live simply, and accept their God-forsaken fate.

Matteo sifted to the outskirts of the crowd and noticed a boy up to no good. The boy, aware of Matteo's watchfulness, bounded up and ran. The imp circled behind a man pushing a handcart of manure, which nearly tipped onto Matteo's shoes. "Excuse me," Matteo said. Shit on his shoes would complete his day. He took care to avoid soiled feet and arched around the cart while trying to keep an eye on the little deceiver. He'd let no innocent man's purse empty under his watch.

When clear of the shit, he turned his focus back to the boy. He couldn't have gone far. A shove lurched him forward. He spun around. "Little bastard spying a mark," he said, and struck fast. He caught the cheat by his scrawny arm. "What have you taken, thief?"

"Nothing. Unhand me," the boy said swatting at him. Matteo let him flail and waited for him to tire and realize he couldn't escape. "You're not my mark." The boy held out his dirty hands to show them empty.

Matteo jerked him close to his face and ran his free hand over his purse and along his belt. He didn't like the way the boy played innocent or the mocking tone that rolled so easy off his tongue.

"Let me loose or I'll scream you want to take me, you Florenzer."

"Take you? Do you know what happens to lying, thieving boys?" He pictured the boy's bare ass, which could use a massive ripping from a lash. Matteo gave him a look to suggest the boy should scream.

The boy flinched.

Matteo breathed out. He'd let him go after dragging him to the Popolo and giving him a proper scare. But the jangle of coins in the boy's purse he couldn't ignore. No boy of his lot had such money. His matted hair, faded tunic, old shoes didn't add up—even if he worked as a rent boy. "Reckless and running through the streets. Where did you get that money?"

"My purse is my business," the boy said protectively clutching it in his fist. He twisted in attempt to get away.

Holding tight, Matteo scanned the piazza in the direction the boy wanted to flee. If not a thief, then a bribe filled the purse. He was no rent boy.

"You're hurting me, Signore," the boy shrieked loud enough to gather attention. "I have to return to my sick mother." People turned toward the disturbance. "This man is trying to take me. Help before he rapes me and steals my money."

"Liar."

The people eyed Matteo and waited for his proper response.

They'd believe a boy before they'd believe him? The boy pitched forward on his hands at Matteo's sudden release. Matteo could do nothing but set him free. No need to drag him. Watch and let the imp lead.

The boy ran and signaled at a candle maker's shop cast in the shadows of the towering buildings across from Orsanmichele.

Grazie boy, betrayed are the indebted. A familiar voice said Matteo's name. Matteo licked his lips and flexed his hands. "Guido," he said, full of venom. He squinted and searched until he stepped into the shade and locked onto the slippery provoker.

Guido and his companion laughed. Guido leaned against a wall slicing fruit. A poisonous smirk stretched across his foul face. He picked his teeth with a knife and held the tip outward to acknowledge Matteo.

Fire raged on Matteo's skin. I'll shove my fist so hard up the butt of that blade it'll part your teeth and slice out your tongue.

Guido made a lazy glance his way.

Matteo broke into a run.

The pompous look slid from Guido's face. He chucked the fruit Matteo's direction and took off with his companion.

Matteo sprinted and gained on them. "Meet me like a man, Guido. You miserable piece of shit." His words vibrated down the passage.

They turned left past the church. The heat of Matteo's blood swelled with each footfall. It urged him on. Faster. He turned a tight corner and freed the strap of his dagger.

Soon the three stood in a triangular pattern in an alley that ended short from a wall of stone. Guido and his companion found themselves trapped. The companion appeared a nervous sort ready to flee at the first blow, but Guido held his blade and waved it around.

"You mean to butter your bread with that?" How Matteo hated him. He laughed like a madman.

Guido stopped waving his blade. "You're still angry about our whore, oh yes," he said with a lewd snarl, "I mean your wife—"

"Shut your mouth." Matteo pulled his dagger free, ready to strike. He caught his breath at the thought of Liviana. If he killed a man, he could be taken from her and the child. "This is between us. Leave my family alone."

Guido and his companion closed in. They eyed each other and signaled their moves by the movements of their heads. "You earn nothing, Matteo, but you get everything. First fruits for a first son. What do I get?"

"Piss off. You're alone in these unfound grievances." Matteo loosened the upper clasps of his shirt. Breathe. Reclaim your family's honor and bring them peace. You have no other choice. He kept his eye on both men.

"We're no different, Matteo, but you make me a fool. You think me weak."

Matteo lifted his dagger point at Guido in return courtesy and agreement. "You're nothing more than a cunt posing as a man of worth."

Guido spit. He jabbed his knife and sliced the air.

Matteo lunged back. He flicked his head back to determine his distance from the wall behind him.

"You have no respect," Guido complained, red-faced.

Matteo's heart battered against his chest. "I care not as much as a flea on a rat's ass." He swung a fist at the companion, who tried to catch him off guard.

"Once you're gone, I'll take her again, and again. I'll take it all." Guido rushed forward, his blade aimed at Matteo's gut.

Matteo held his dagger at both ends like a shield. He blocked the hit. It forced him back. He maintained his balance and extended his arm in attempt to slice Guido. He missed and ducked before Guido's companion got hold of him.

The companion held his arms up ready to protect his body or strike.

The three maneuvered and feigned. They tried to decide their best move.

Every wrong Matteo knew bubbled to the surface. All the frustrations and errors he made, he channeled into the arm that would end Guido. His target stood in front, ready for the taking. But the nuisance sucking at Guido's teat must go.

Matteo stepped in and thrust at Guido, but Guido's second-hand man cut from behind.

Matteo grazed Guido's shirt. "Fight you twittering bitches." Matteo twisted and sliced the nuisance across his arm. He thrust again and slashed his chest. A blood streaked shirt forced the surprised man back.

"Forget you," Guido's bitch said, and ran away.

Matteo spun back to face Guido before he could strike from behind. He caught a flash of Guido's blade half an arm's length from his chest. His arm cut across and deflected the force down toward Guido's knee. Matteo's dagger hand lined with Guido's belly.

Aware of his position, Guido dropped back on his ass.

Undeterred, Matteo pressed in. Stick Guido to his resting place. He plunged his dagger down.

Guido's leg shot out and sent Matteo tumbling to the ground.

Matteo tasted the salt of his sweat and the sting of it in his eyes. His lungs filled with the musk of men bent on killing. He rolled, and got to his feet. Drunk on revenge, he rushed to seize his advantage.

His blade slowed. It opened flesh.

Guido howled at the wound across his forearm. If he hadn't lifted it, Matteo knew he would have sliced his neck. He had him now. A roar escaped from Matteo's chest.

Guido charged. He slashed his knife left and right until their arms clashed together, steel cutting against their wrists. They pushed the other's forearm for leverage.

Guido's knife-edge pierced Matteo's forearm.

Matteo punched Guido in the face until he fell back.

Guido sprang forward to serve a return blow.

Blood beaded down Matteo's arm. Before it weakened, he knew he must strike. Hard.

Guido wiped his face and shifted his feet. The tell of Guido's tightening hand gave away his intent to strike. He came at Matteo, his knife drawn up by his ear.

Matteo waited. He drew his life's breath in and exhaled. He twisted to block Guido's killing blow, gripped Guido's arm, and struck his elbow with the pommel of his blade. A crunch gave him satisfaction.

Guido's knife skittered across the ground. He howled in pain and dropped like a sack of stones. "You broke my arm!"

Matteo's chest stung above his nipple. He found a finger's length cut that bled. Restore your honor, hummed every urge in his body. He switched the dagger to his left hand, wiped his sweaty face with the right, and switched it back again. Make it stick. He forced all his weight behind the blade.

But Guido rolled away with no more than a tear on his tunic.

Clang. Pain shot up Matteo's arm. Hitting solid ground made the dagger topple. He fumbled for his blade, but lost all feeling in his hand.

A solid punch to Matteo's back forced him down. "Hu ugh," he heard spill from his lips. The dagger. He gripped it in his good hand and got to his feet.

Guido clutched his useless arm. "You're done Attavaino. I plucked your Rosa and now I fucked you. Delicious. So delicious."

Matteo pictured his future with clarity. He roared and gripped his dagger tight and plunged it into Guido's soft belly. Locked on Guido's eyes, Matteo held his dagger firm in place. He had to see Guido's pain and fear. "Now you can die."

Matteo tried to catch his breath. He tasted blood.

Guido's wide eyes held him in disbelief. Guido held the blade Matteo lacked the strength or willingness to pull free.

Matteo took a few labored steps back and spit red. A searing heat pierced the left side of his chest. He found a wall for support. It moved, or was it his eyes? He ran his shoulder along the wall to guide him and keep him standing.

He tried straightening but couldn't catch his breath. Liviana. The child. No matter the distance or how long it would take, he'd get back to them. He staggered out of the alley. Once on the main street, he studied his surroundings. Through the waves of movement, he identified the Silk Guild house down the road. Move. Every effort exhausted him. He couldn't make it far.

He stumbled into a man and his children and dropped to his knees. "You." He pointed at them. Then remembered the stables nearby. He pointed up the road the opposite direction. "Stables." He wiped his mouth with the back of his hand. Blood. "Call on Massimo. Come—with cart." He pointed again. The man nodded and sent the boys to run the way he indicated.

He closed his eyes and thought he'd rest a bit before Massimo came for him.

"Matteo?"

Matteo jumped once again aware of his pain.

"It's Massimo, Matteo. You, uh, you're injured. Come. I'll help you stand. Three steps to the cart and I'll take you to the Ospedale."

Massimo hooked his arms under Matteo's from the front. "Come, Matteo. We must hurry."

Matteo shook his head and willed his legs to take every torturous step. "Bad?"

"You have a knife in your back."

Matteo cringed. "Take it out."

"No." Massimo yanked his hands away.

"Please."

"I'll try," Massimo said, pulling slowly.

"Stooooop!"

"Wait for the healers at Santa Maria Nuova. Lay here." Massimo did his best to position Matteo and worked the horses as fast as they could go.

Every sway of the cart, every bump, each turn, twisted the blade. Matteo focused on thoughts of his wife and child to keep him strong.

Soon Massimo halted the cart. He returned with three men; one priest, a nurse dressed in long robes with an apron, and a doctor identifiable in a red robe. They held a length of linen in their hands. "You," the doctor said addressing Massimo and the priest. "Stretch it out while we help position him."

They placed him in the center of the cloth.

The doctor took the corner at the afflicted side. "Take a corner and carry him inside."

Massimo took a corner near Matteo's head.

Matteo gritted his teeth and wound his hand around Massimo's forearm. "Leonardo. That way," he said pointing southeast from the direction they carried him. "Walk or ride." He squeezed his eyes together when they jostled him.

"Careful," the doctor told them.

Matteo tightened his hand. "Sign with vines," he said and gasped for air.

65

Massimo burst into Leonardo's bottega. "Matteo's wounded." He rushed to Leonardo's desk. Papers fluttered to the floor.

Leonardo caught one in midair. "What are you saying?"

The boy moved about in a distressed state.

Leonardo gathered the papers. He shook his head in agitation. "I just saw him. Tell him to come himself."

Massimo shook his head. "Are you not his friend?" The boy seemed offended. "You must come right away, Signore. He asked me to come here." He grabbed Leonardo's elbow to steer him out of the bottega. Sweat trickled down the boy's face.

Leonardo's stomach flipped. This was no trick. "You mean he's wounded?"

The boy let out a frustrated sigh. "I said, wou-n-ded. Now come."

Leonardo vaulted to his feet. "Where? When?" He looked about in a stupor for what to bring with him.

"Leave it." Massimo wiped his hand over his forehead and pulled his hair back from his face. "He could die. He took a knife in his back."

Leonardo's stomach twisted. "Where is he?"

"The hospital. Go. Tell him I've gone for his wife." Massimo turned to the bottega boys. "Pray for him."

Leonardo pulled Massimo out the door and ran. He turned at the piazza of the Ospedale where the off-centered double doors opened beneath a pitched roof with covered entry. He doubled the stairs leading in.

"Buongiornio, Signore," addressed a low, calm voice.

Leonardo forced the door closed and turned his head toward the soft-spoken man.

"How can I help you?" The short man seemed to evaluate his wellness.

"My friend, Matteo Attaviano." He caught his breath, "I'm told he's here. Where can I find him?" His pulse quickened while the man checked the register. "Please, Signore. There's no time to spare."

"I understand." With an apologetic tip of the head, he said, "A moment, please." He held his hand out at Leonardo, who tried to follow. "Wait here. We must be sure he's received confession." He left his post, curved the corner, and walked down the long corridor.

Leonardo wanted to yell to set him faster to his task. "Hurry," he called to spurn the man forward before he charged down the rows of beds. A whiff of stagnant air mixed into a stench of sour bodies and sickness. He paced in and out of the sunlit window feeling more ill with each pass.

Certain he'd waited long enough, Leonardo scanned the corridor for the admission man before he disregarded his request to wait. Light from the large, glass window centered down the length of the ward illuminating an aisle walkway that led to a chapel. The beam stretched a portion of the way down. Half the length of the ward, he located the man. A priest sat on a stool bedside. Another man wearing brown, an infirmarer, took the place of the departing priest while a nurse carried a basin that he set at the foot of the bed. The admissions man started back. Faster, Leonardo repeated until he returned.

"Yes. Signore Attaviano is in bed sixteen."

Leonardo hurried down the corridor. The headboards of each bed had a number. Bed XIV, XV, Matteo. Matteo's back faced Leonardo. He wore a sleeveless hospital tunic and sat with his head resting on his hand. Matteo shook his head to refuse the offered drink. The nurse tucked Matteo's shoes under the bed and stood to check his bandages, which wrapped around his middle. A mound of cloth marked where the stab must have occurred. The cloths were clean and dry.

His friend had a swollen eyebrow cut, cleaned and salved, and a bandaged forearm. The Matteo Leonardo knew slumped weak and broken. His frailty took such a hold that Leonardo's own knees weakened. Leonardo stood, though, in silence for them to finish.

The nurse lifted Matteo's legs gently. He whimpered as the nurse eased him back onto pillows. Matteo's eyes squeezed shut in a look of agony.

"The wine has medicine to help the pain." The nurse adjusted his pillows. "Drink, then I'll leave you with your visitor."

"Matteo?"

Matteo squinted at Leonardo and clawed his hand out to bid him closer.

"Ehm, ehm. Drink first," the nurse said. He held the cup to Matteo's lips.

Matteo swallowed, turned his nose, and swallowed again. He pulled off his cap to protest. The nurse covered him with a blanket and put the cap back on his head. "It's good you've come to be with him."

Matteo waved his hand at the nurse in an angry way.

"Grazie," Leonardo said. If Matteo had fight left in him... His skin looked waxy and blue. Leonardo extended a trembling hand. "What happened?"

Matteo's cool arm and fingers colored white. He worked harder than he should for breath, and answered, "Guido." His voice wheezed. He drew another breath in, "No choice." His lips turned darker blue.

"He stabbed you?" Leonardo covered his own mouth with a finger. "No, don't answer. Don't speak, Matteo." His friend seemed a stranger. The bed next to Matteo's held an old man who slept. He looked so peaceful and content. Would it be wicked to ask God to take the man in Matteo's place?

Matteo gave Leonardo's hand a weak squeeze. "My family." He wheezed and closed his eyes, "Safe."

"I know." Leonardo caressed his arm. But you're not. "They need you. I, I…" Leonardo's voice cracked. They both turned their heads toward the commotion at the entrance to the corridor.

"This is the men's ward," echoed down the corridor.

Four infirmarers and the doctor, all marked with the image of crutch and wreath on their robes, rushed down the men's ward after Liviana. "You cannot be in here without consent, woman. Show respect for God and the sick."

Massimo rushed on their heels. "She wants to see her husband. He's not well, Signori."

Liviana tried to keep her momentum while searching. She recognized Leonardo and slowed when she reached Matteo's bed. "Matteo? Oh no." A terrified look set upon her face. She palmed Matteo's face with both hands and kissed him. "You're cold. Bring more blankets." Her tears dripped onto Matteo's neck. She took his hand and curved it over the delicate swell of her belly. "Stay with me. With us."

Matteo used his uninjured arm to stroke her face and hair.

The hospital workers gathered around Matteo's bed while Massimo made them wait. They turned their hardened faces the other way and allowed husband and wife a moment.

Leonardo considered doing the same, but he couldn't look away. Offering a minor consolation would not make them well.

Matteo pulled the cap off his head and covered his face. His chest heaved and his breaths labored. He slid the cap away. His eyes bulged. He stretched his neck gulping for air.

"Help him," Leonardo said rushing to his side.

Matteo's body stiffened. He fought too hard for air.

"Out of the way," the doctor said pushing his way through the group to his patient. "Step aside. Bring more dwale wine." He took Matteo by his shoulders and sat him upright. He held the drink to Matteo's lips.

Matteo refused him.

"It will calm you as will rest. There's nothing more we can do."

Matteo refused.

The doctor sloshed the cup and found his apron splotched with burgundy. He set the drink aside. "Then breathe. Deep as you can." The doctor kept breathing time with him.

Liviana tried pushing her way toward Matteo, but Leonardo embraced her to keep her back. Her frightened sobs helped no one. "Shh. You have to calm." He said to her, but gave as his own command. When she cried out he felt the vibration of her tortured voice against his chest. He pulled her closer and let her pain speak for them both.

"Take her out," the doctor said. "This is no place for a wailing woman, wife or otherwise."

Matteo followed her with his eyes while he focused on his breathing.

The infirmarers took hold of Liviana. "Let her loose," one infirmarer with the bearings of a bull said.

Leonardo made no move to release her. "You will quiet, won't you, gentle woman?" She nodded as he held her against him. "There you see. Take your hands from her and she'll make no disturbance."

"Yes," Massimo said, "She'll do as you ask." He pressed on the chest of the bullish infirmarer.

Leonardo released her but the bull did not. Two infirmarers seized her arms. The others went for Massimo.

"I love him." Liviana pushed against them and tried shaking them away. "He's my husband. He's fading. Don't take me from him."

Matteo attempted to rise from bed, but the doctor held him down easily. Matteo closed his eyes and shook his head.

The doctor thrust his hand out and pointed at the entrance. "Take her to the women's ward. Treat her for suffocation of the womb. She's not well."

"Bastards. How dare you! I hope the consciences God gave you keep you awake every night the rest of your arrogant lives."

"Out now," the doctor said, "Both of them."

Liviana stilled. "Remove your hands from me and I'll go." Her face hollowed. She turned and did as she said. The Ospedale men trailed behind her.

"I'm going with her. I require no force," Massimo said loud enough for all to hear though he directed it at Matteo.

Leonardo swallowed hard. Should he go with them? He watched only Matteo. They stared at each other. The creases at Matteo's brown eyes smoothed and his breath slowed. His body relaxed and he held his hand out for Leonardo.

The doctor called for more pillows, and propped him upright in bed. "He needs to rest." A nurse came requesting the doctor's immediate assistance. "Stay with him," he told the nurse. His lips pinched together in a frown. "And bring out the image of the crucified Christ."

Matteo wasted no time. "Forgive. Me."

"Always." Leonardo wiped tears from his eyes.

"My will," Matteo wheezed. "Desk chest. Key here." He pointed at Leonardo's purse.

"No, Matteo." Leonardo squeezed his hand. "You can heal. Try. Do what they ask."

"Livi—chil." Though Matteo made great effort, his voice faded. "You care…for them." He drew in several breaths.

Leonardo shook his head. Living alone took all his strength. And he had his boys, which he couldn't afford to keep.

Christ hung above them. "…He humbled himself, becoming obedient to the point of death," recited the nurse.

Leonardo covered his face in fear and shame. He couldn't be the person Matteo wanted him to be.

The nurse's voice continued, "Jesus cried out again in a loud voice, and gave up his spirit."

A tear ran down Matteo's nose. "Nothing to. Give you." His breath labored again. "Please."

"Give me? I need you. Nothing more. Keep breathing, Matteo." Leonardo bowed his head. How could he do it? How could he promise to take Matteo's place? He had nothing to offer.

Matteo squeezed his hand again. "Please."

Leonardo inhaled deep. Moments came when a man had one chance to make the right decision. He looked Matteo in the eye. "I will." How could he not? Leonardo cleared his throat. "I will take them as my sister and son."

Matteo sucked in air, the pain of sustaining life unmistakable. "Name. My son. Massim." His voice cut-off. "M—"

Leonardo filled-in, "Massimo?"

Matteo nodded. "Lapo di."

"Massimo Lapo di Attaviano."

Matteo nodded and closed his eyes. His head dropped back onto his pillow.

"A good name. Matteo?" Leonardo nudged his shoulder but he didn't answer. "Matteo?" He turned his chin to face him and rubbed his hands along Matteo's arms to stir him, to warm him. "There's more to say. Matteo?"

Matteo's head turned and his mouth curved into the grin Leonardo lived for. "Remember the child," he whispered in a perfect voice. He opened his eyes wide as if he recognized himself in the sound. He tried grasping Leonardo's hand, but his weak fingers failed him.

Leonardo did the work for him. He bent forward and placed his head on Matteo's chest to listen to the sound of his heart. Slow and faint. Thump. Thump.

The nurse called for the priest.

Matteo's head sank deeper into his pillow. Thump, beat his heart. Uneven. Fainter and fainter. Until it stopped.

Leonardo pressed his ear harder against his friend's chest. He listened. He shook him and turned Matteo's face to see his eyes reopen.

No.

Come back.

He fisted Matteo's hair. "Breathe."

"Matteo?"

He pulled his limp body into his arms and kissed him. "Come back. Don't leave me."

***

"Signore, you have to let him go," the nurse said.

"I cannot."

"I'm sorry, but you must." The nurse's warm hand rested on his shoulder. "The priest has come, gone, and returned again. Your friend suffers no more. Now we must tend to his soul."

Leonardo pulled Matteo's head into his chest and inhaled his scent one last time. Gently he lowered him onto the bed half hoping he'd fight back. But his body had no more fight.

The nurses wrapped Matteo in linen. They lifted his body and placed it on a waiting bier. Leonardo helped them carry Matteo to the center of the hospital. They set him down in front of the altar and lit a consecrated candle to set at his head and placed an oil lamp at his feet.

Leonardo searched the quiet room for direction. "His family and friends. Wait until tomorrow. They will come for the funeral."

"As you request." The nurse led Leonardo away to tend to the details.

"Can I provide you an escort home, Signore da Vinci?"

Leonardo stared into the man's face then remembered what he needed to do. "No, grazie." He scanned the piazza for Liviana and Massimo. He swallowed hard. "I have to tell his wife."

66

Matteo's front door stood like a battle-worn shield, tall and harsh, and Leonardo wanted none of the other side. He could smell the ash in the hearth, feel the knick on the rim of Matteo's favorite wine cup, and picture the indented cushion of his desk chair. What of the clothing Matteo draped over chairs, or the scent that held him to this place? How could these things remain while a living, breathing man ceased? Leonardo's hand paused unable to knock.

He tried standing straight to deliver the blow with compassion, as he should, but he had to brace himself against the doorframe for strength. Matteo's purse. He opened it, found the key to the chest that held his will, and cinched it closed. Searching for the right words, he found none.

The door creaked open and a woman peeked through the crack. "Buongiorno, Signore," she said with a curious lift of the brow. "My Maestro is not in."

Leonardo bowed his head. "No, Signorina. I bring terrible news."

The servant opened to door wide. "Please, come in, Signore."

"No." He couldn't break apart now. "Where's the lady of the house?"

"Not here, Signore." She held a hand at her chest, her fear unmistakable. "My lady left with fire on her feet some time ago," she said.

"Then call on your maestro's head man. I'll wait here." Leonardo turned and faced the street. He stretched his sore neck. His head ached. He wanted to go home.

Matteo's man, Nicco, staggered backward when Leonardo told him what happened. Nicco stroked his cheeks and chin more than necessary but maintained a good face. "I'll tell the others," he said.

Leonardo nodded his thanks for Nicco's help as much as for his fortitude, which made his task easier. "Again, I'm sorry. Can you tell me where I can find his wife?"

"I don't know, but we'll help our lady, not abandon her," he said. "I can do what needs doing, but" Nicco breathed out, "Maestro, rest his soul, he has no father, no brother."

Leonardo closed his eyes to find strength.

"Ah, Signore, Nicco asked, "Who do we wait for?"

Leonardo held up Matteo's purse. "Matteo gave me this. I know where to find his will. First, I must find Mona Attaviano." Leonardo gathered his thoughts. "Call for a notary. Tell him and the household what happened, for the day after tomorrow their maestro finds his resting place. Santa Maria Nuova has begun the funeral preparations."

He shot more instructions out before the task overwhelmed him. "Members of his guild's confraternity will come to assist the family. Accept their help and contributions with thanks. I'll pay every servant in this house as they're owed and marked in your maestro's ledger. Once the will is read, you all shall be granted accordingly, to include a period of grace to make arrangements from the dissolved household."

"Household dissolved, Signore?"

"I'll not deceive you. To pay what's owed to everyone, this house can be no more. Understand, I'll not see a widowed woman bear any greater a burden."

Nicco staggered back but thanked him for his honesty. "We'll help search for our lady." His discomfort showed as he treaded carefully around his words. "What will become of her and…" his face flushed when mentioning Liviana's condition, "the child?"

Leonardo barely swallowed. "I vowed to protect and keep them in my care." The man made not a questionable blink. "We have much to do, but first we must find lady Attaviano."

Leonardo took no more than a few steps from Matteo's house when he heard his name. A horse with cart charged up the street.

"Leonardo da Vinci," Massimo called. He jumped from the cart before it came to a complete stop. "I've lost her. Liviana ran from the hospital and from me when I went to bring up the cart to take her home." He wiped his dusty sleeve and waited for Leonardo to say something helpful. "I meant to stay with her."

"Liviana knew he wouldn't make it." Leonardo drew in breath. "They forced her out." He rested a hand on the boy's shoulder. "Matteo's gone."

"Gone?"

Leonardo didn't want to say it again.

The boy's head dropped. He spit. "I'm glad he gutted that cazzo in the alley," he said, his cheeks streaked with tears. "I saw the man who did this. If Matteo hadn't killed him, I would."

"Massimo, I need your help. Where would Liviana go?"

Massimo made no answer while he punched a fist repeatedly into his palm.

Leonardo shook the boy. "You know where Matteo found her?"

"Yes."

"Take me there."

"Why would she go back to that place?"

Leonardo trusted his instinct. "Because she has nothing else. Because everything seems hopeless."

***

They rode down the street lined with brothels, businesses, travelers, men, prostitutes, and other questionable scenes. Massimo's horse frothed at the mouth. What could have driven Matteo to such a place? Leonardo grew angrier and more confused.

A crowd blocked their progress when they neared the far end of the street. People shouted and pointed. Leonardo followed their outstretched hands. A woman.

"God have mercy!" He leaped from the cart. Liviana. He was sure. The thickest part of the rope gathered under her chin and forced her face to the sky. Leonardo swallowed back bile.

He tossed people out of his way until he reached the front of the crowd. "Help me." He tried to set her hanging weight on his shoulders. Her foot grazed his ear. The rope frayed where it rubbed the window's edge. Leonardo's head went dizzy.

"Massimo," Leonardo called, but the boy refused to come closer.

A man answered Leonardo's call for help. He steadied Liviana's swaying body. "The poor wretch jumped. Before anyone could help, she went still. 'Tis a fair drop. It pleases me none to say it, but she's dead."

"Cut the rope." Leonardo said, searching the crowd.

Massimo buried his face in his lap.

A big, visibly drunk man worked with another. They sawed at the rope to cut Liviana free. Each cut strand lowered her enough that the men could guide her body down.

The last braid broke free and Leonardo steadied his hand to remove the noose.

Liviana's head cocked back on his forearm. All her life had gone. All of it. And he held the result in blue and black bruising, a pale face, a slackened body, and an unfulfilled vow.

Leonardo lowered her onto the cart. What happened here, unforgiveable—he failed them—all of them. He dropped to his knees.

"Signore, called the man who cut the rope, "Here." He handed him a bed sheet. "In respect for the dead." They covered the body.

***

"You will go the way I say," Leonardo told Massimo again.

"No. We have to take her to be with her husband." Massimo flicked the reins of his horse with one hand and pushed Leonardo with the other.

Leonardo scruffed the boy and pulled him close. "He can help her no more than anyone else now. You make for the eastern gate or I will."

Massimo's lip curled. "I'll toss you from my cart."

"Try it and you'll be relieved of your cart, boy."

Massimo dropped the reins and threw himself on Leonardo. "I hate you," he said punching him hard.

Leonardo blocked the next couple of blows.

Massimo tried to push him off the cart without success. The boy's fight didn't last. He tired, his arms wrapped around Leonardo.

The horse halted.

"There's no other way, Massimo. The body won't keep. We have nowhere else to take her. Can you understand?" Leonardo kept the boy tight against him.

"But the priest won't come. He won't say any prayers or mass or bless the grave the way he did for my mother. She'll be outside the gates. Alone."

"You're right, but there's nothing we can do for that now. It's between her and God, but no one can stop your prayers. Let us give her rest." Leonardo fingered Matteo's purse. "He pulled a coin for the burial and asked Massimo to stop for lilies, which Massimo would place in the ground with Liviana and the unborn child.

67

Leonardo scratched the hairline on his forehead, which felt almost as hairy as his tongue. A cool hand wrapped around his forearm.

"Awake? Bring the man a bite of bread and some watered wine," a woman said somewhere beyond the floating clouds in Leonardo's head.

He wouldn't sleep for fear of things that would haunt him in the night, but somewhere in his cups he must have nodded off. Slowly, Leonardo turned his head to peer out the window. Sunlight, like lightning, shot in his eyes. He rubbed them and leaned back.

"Watch it, dear," the woman said catching him before he fell off his stool. She waved her request away. "No watered wine. Bring the ginger, lemon, and honey cure."

The woman held a cup beneath his nose. "Drink before you get on with your day."

Leonardo tried to remember when he arrived in the tavern—after he returned from the reading of Matteo's will. He sipped his remedy. A day ago. He sprang up and held his pounding head.

"I have to go." He downed his warm drink and hurried outside clutching a lump of bread. The sun cast his shadow long. If he hurried, he could get home in time to wash and change his clothes.

At the appointed time, the chapel bells rang, and two priests in black cassocks came with a large cross before the gathering of people. Two lay brothers lit torches and sang while Leonardo, friends, and many members of the Silk

Guild Confraternity, carried Matteo. The altar glowed with
the light of perhaps forty candles.

Leonardo recognized many from Matteo's household,
some of his friends, men from the silk guild, the old woman
neighbor, and Massimo, who sat in the back with a man
similar in appearance—likely his father. In the opposite
aisle many gathered; among them, Lucrezia's mother and
father, and beside him, Lucrezia, whose mournful face
stared hard upon him and made him look away.

The Virgin looked down on the living and the dead.
Incense burned too sweet and wafted thick in the air. The
sounds of women's cries blended with the Requiem and
carried beyond the walls of stone.

Leonardo took his seat. Too many eyes scrutinized him,
judged him. Perhaps they could read the hurt and guilt
written across his face. How could they know the worst of
what happened? Who knew the magnitude of this loss?
None could know his. He'd find no favor. Not from
anyone. Not in the eyes of Ser, whose head protruded
above the rest and examined him from the back row.

The funeral party left the chapel and entered the
Cloister of Bones.

The servants placed Matteo's covered body in its
resting place. People paid their respects and departed.

Leonardo waited until alone and took out the lock of
Liviana's golden hair he tied with her pink ribbon.

"Matteo." He cried and crumpled to the floor. "I'm
sorry, my friend." He pressed his head against the chilled
bed of the crypt and placed the token on Matteo's chest.

"Matteo," he said, his voice echoing. A single,
remaining lantern flickered in the silence for a long while.
Unable to remain any longer, Leonardo ran.

Leonardo staggered into his bottega. His boys watched
him, their faces curious and concerned. Oh, they should be
concerned. He had no money to support them. "I don't
know what you're looking at, but find something to do," he

snapped. *While you have pay*, he prepared to say but tossed the thought away and wished he'd spoken lighter for the comfort of his pounding head.

Rafaello stood and approached. "Maestro?"

Leonardo ignored the boy. He wanted no sympathy. What he wanted was wine. He rifled through the kitchen for every bottle and flask he could find, bunched his collection into his arms, and retreated into his room where he locked the door. He bit the cork free from a flask and drank to soothe his aches.

Shutters closed, and a flask later, he could no longer differentiate between day and night. He stripped off his belt, vest, tunic, and hose, and tossed them to the floor. In nothing but his camicia, he curled up on his bed and wept. The terrors of the night could take him.

68

Piero shook his head. "He's been locked in there since the funeral?" He couldn't help his criticizing tone. Four day past they attended Matteo's funeral.

The boy, Rafaello answered, "Yes, Ser da Vinci. That's why we asked around for you. We knock day and night, but Leonardo will not come out." He diverted his eyes. "Not even to eat. Light shines under the door here or there. He tossed a bottle to send us away once."

Piero removed his hat and unclasped his robe. He hung them and took a quick account of the boys.

"Grazie, Signore for coming," the boy said. The three boys swarmed together awaiting direction.

"Have you any food?"

"Not much, Ser," the oldest boy said. "A bit of bread, some grapes, onions, beans. May we offer you some?"

"No, no," Piero said having found an opportunity to bring order back to the place. He would provide Leonardo room to display a good face before his students while also clearing the bottega of intrusive ears. He gave the boys money. "Off with you to market. Your maestro will be hungry once you return." He waved his hands to send them to their task.

Piero turned on his heels and surveyed the bottega. Barren and quiet, the place held a few worktables devoid of the usual sights and smells that seeped out of such buildings when one passed them on the street. Leonardo's boys did keep it clean considering they had an absent maestro. He spotted Leonardo's desk by the flood of papers that lay jumbled and spilled over onto an adjoining table used as a desktop. Piero shook his head. Anyone could surmise that Leonardo needed work. Keeping the boys seemed an unnecessary strain. Piero shook any speculation of wicked possibilities away.

He approached Leonardo's room. A slight orange-tinged glow shined through the crack under the door—unnecessary if Leonardo would open his windows to the bright and cloudless day. He knocked but received no answer. "Leonardo. It's your father. Open the door."

Piero listened for the slightest response. The sound of shuffling feet and creaking old planks alerted him to life inside the room.

"Matteo was your companion, a brother. His tragic passing is not lost on me. But you cannot hide yourself away."

"I want no visitors." Grumbling and muddled speech followed.

"You think this the best way to honor him?"

"Leave me alone," Leonardo said.

"I'm not leaving until you come out." Piero banged on the door. "Your boys came for me, Leonardo. They have concern for you. Come out and face the world. Come out now." He jiggled the lock.

The silence Leonardo served only made him bristle. The state of the bottega triggered greater annoyance though Piero found no precise reason why. An unfinished painting sat askew nearby. Perhaps the greater absence of signs denoting work and effort pressed on him. "Open the damned door or I'll break it down."

Piero went to the hearth. He lifted the fire fork with its hooked end, certain he could force it past the doorframe. He shoved it hard near the lock, found leverage, and pulled. The wood cracked. "You have been running away," he said between grunts, "ever since you were a child." A few bits of wood splintered to the floor.

The lock clicked and Leonardo yanked the door open with such force it crashed into him. His matted hair strewed about his shoulders, and his clothes, discolored with stains, made Piero think of a madman.

"I've been running away?" Leonardo said in more an accusation than a question. His blood-shot eyes and tight lips set ready to strike. "You do mean in the same way you so prudently tucked away my mother so you could run into the waiting arms of your father? To please him? To marry another?" He glanced at the damage to his door. "You left a poor woman who carried your child."

Piero stepped through the door to grab him. Clothes littered the room. The chamber pot brimmed with piss. Broken pottery speckled the floor near the door.

Leonardo backed up. "Don't touch me." His bare foot rattled an empty wine bottle. "What do you know of love? You've come for what? To console me? Ha. My loss, my love, these keep me in this room. I'll leave when I am ready, as I always have, like you, father."

Piero reached Leonardo in two strides. He came out of concern, not for abuse. His breath came in short bursts and he fisted Leonardo's soiled gown. Their eyes met. "How dare you bring your mother into this outrage. That was long ago." Spittle sprayed from his mouth, "Life is full of difficult choices, you…" he yanked and tore Leonardo's neckline, "you bastard. We all make mistakes."

"Fine choice of words." Leonardo made no further move to yield his ground. "The first mistake was never my own. It was yours, you damned hypocrite. You left me then. Worse, you took me back and made me long for what could never be mine." Leonardo shoved him. "Oh but you'll be saved from the misery of one son by giving all your warmth to another."

Piero held a hand between them and braced himself against the bed.

"We can never change that I'm your firstborn son." Leonardo's hand swung out ready to strike. "You've broken me. Tell me why you would take me in only to deny me later."

Piero spoke quickly. "As a firstborn son, as any son, every time I look at you, I see myself—all the good and the bad. You were better, Leonardo. No matter your position or grievances toward me or anyone else, you cast light out before you, unfettered by others. You showed me my wrongs." Piero choked back tears. "You were better because you were not me." Piero hit his fists on the bed. "I had hopes for you. I believed you could do right where I turned wrong."

"No, Ser. I want the yoke of your mistakes on me no longer." He hit his chest. "Look now. This is me and no other. See me."

He couldn't look on him long. "Why could you not find a young woman to love?" Piero's voice boomed.

Leonardo echoed back, "Why could you not love a son?"

69

Leonardo closed his eyes to remove Ser from view. He let unanswered questions hang in the air. Searching for something he could grasp in his hands, he found a couple of empty bottles, but knew he'd find no answers in them.

Why couldn't he love a woman? He did love a woman though he knew his actions came in a moment of weakness, perhaps not unlike what happened between Ser and his mother long ago. The act, called love, was not good love at all.

He accepted his desperate acts, his choices, his perversions built on years of frustration. He could tell Ser and purge the deeds, the guilt, and prove himself equal to the difficult man before him. Say it, you have loved a woman, and sit aright with him, the desperation told him, but he knew it folly to build a fire near the sea at low tide. He'd not make another suffer to give his father an answer. He agreed with one thing, he was better. Love he knew.

Ser stood. "I will give you an answer." He avoided Leonardo's face. "I wanted to give you what a father should, and I was prepared to grant you as my firstborn but," Ser struggled, "I cannot. I will not concede my love to a sodomite son."

"The truth comes out." Though the sting never lessened. "You wanted an easier choice," Leonardo said, "but there are none." He tossed his torn garment off and slipped a fresh one over his head. "What more is there to say?" Leonardo could do nothing more. "It's time for you to go." He picked up the fire fork for reinforcement.

Ser retreated without force.

Leonardo's breath came sharp, but he breathed. Before his boys returned, he collected the bottles and flasks, swept shards from behind his door, made his bed, cracked open his shutters, snuffed his lamp, and gathered his clothes from the floor.

When he lifted his belt, his purse fell loose. A couple of coins, a piece of charcoal, and a crumpled letter slipped out. He'd forgotten about the letter. He smoothed it out and read through a dated list of household items, some crossed out, others had tallies beside them. He considered the letter came into his possession by error, until he found writing scrolled across the page in a different hand from the rest. It read:

Meet me at Santa Spirito church in the Oltrarno. Every Tuesday during the third hour I pray alone. This is the only way. Do not make light of my request, I beseech you.

No closing salutation showed on the page. Leonardo pinched a rumpled white feather folded in the crevice of the letter and twisted it in his fingers. After everything, he must meet her.

Letter. The letter made him remember what he'd forgotten. He wrote a letter of condolence to Matteo's mother.

***

Leonardo's legs quivered in every drawn-out step he took down the church aisle. He couldn't make a habit of secret meetings, but he owed Lucrezia this if not more. She said she'd tell no one. Would her promise hold true under all circumstances? He did wrong, but thought telling the clergy remiss, for they wished to purge all evil to the greatest degree.

She may have changed her mind after all. He retraced his footsteps to wait in the back for visibility when she arrived.

But Lucrezia knelt beside the middlemost white column in the nave. Her covered hair, bound in lacing and beretta, caused him not to recognize her from behind at first pass. Eyes closed, she held a rosary between her folded hands, and her lips moved to form silent prayers.

Leonardo approached slowly to evaluate the number of people sitting close enough to see them as well as the distance he should properly keep from her. He knelt behind her and waited for her to lift her head. He whispered, "Lucrezia?"

Her head made a slight turn his direction and stopped. "Thank you for coming," she whispered back. "Say three rosaries then meet me in the back by the statue of the Virgin." She stood, quickly, glanced at him, and made for her location.

Chanting from a private chapel filled Leonardo's ears. "Convertat Dominus vultum suum ad te et det tibi pacem," came a priests echoes through the expansive church.

Lucrezia lit a candle at the Virgin's feet.

Leonardo fumbled for coin and bought a candle to do the same. Alone with her, he knelt beside her.

She snuffled.

"Lucrezia," he said soft enough she alone could hear.

She wiped her eyes. "I'm sorry. So sorry." She covered her face with her hands then whispered, "I could find no other way. But you must know." She gave a weary glance his way. "I'm with child."

Leonardo dropped his candle.

Before anyone found anything amiss, he scooped it up and quickly placed it unlit at the Virgin's feet. "You're certain?" he asked from a voice that seemed outside of his body.

"Yes. I've been with no other."

"No," rushed from his lips. His heart beat in his ears. "I mean you've not miscounted?"

An embroidered handkerchief fell from Lucrezia's hand. "No."

He picked it up and held it out for her but her shoulders shook and she dropped back on her heels.

She wiped her eyes and stifled her cries when a husband and wife came to kneel beside them.

Each sat alone in their tortured minds. Leonardo bowed his head. What curse marked him with such hatred? His conversation with Ser ran through his head and he thought he might burst before the interrupting couple left. "Lucrezia," Leonardo said, her name a plea. He did damn himself straight to hell. If he would be damned, what hell would she endure, and the child?

She spoke through her hiccupping cries. "Tell me what you want."

"What I want?" It was too late to consider what he or she wanted; they had to consider what must be done. His mind raced for an answer. Without question, he'd never choose to send a bastardized child into the world.

An answer. And it didn't take a lifetime of searching to find it. Part of him fought against what he knew would pass from his lips, but he shoved those worries aside.

"Lucrezia, if you value more than one life you'll agree to what I say." He trembled at the words. "How can I keep silent and allow another man to shoulder my responsibilities?" He wiped perspiration from his upper lip.

Lucrezia's eyes rounded in fright, panic, surprise? Leonardo tried to swallow the ball in his throat. He held Lucrezia firm in his sight. "I forfeit my rights. To give you a life," he said to her and the life growing inside her. "A good life free of blemish." He had nothing else to give them. He grasped her arm. "None of this is as it should be," he said, voice raised.

They looked to be sure he caused no attention. He continued, "But it's right."

Lucrezia's eyes closed and opened; she held him in their reflection.

"Then give us your silence," she said without flinching. She covered her mouth for a moment then dropped her hand. "My husband will have his full dowry not a week from now. I'll go to his bed and give him the rest."

Leonardo looked on her in respect and concern. He dropped his gaze and shook his head. He could find nothing more to say.

"Shh, you've lost so much. Go on with your life. Give us hope, Leonardo. It's all we have to sustain us." Lucrezia kissed her fingers and touched them to his hand. "Let it be enough."

70
June 1479

Leonardo kept his silence and his distance, for never did Lucrezia know he watched from afar. Her time should arrive soon. He ducked under the long arm of the mature oak tree near a row of houses on the Oltrarno side of the city. Hidden in the shade, he sketched parts of a wing for a machine that would fly. His attentions floated away from his work while he waited for Lucrezia's servants to depart for the market.

A man came out. The old woman followed behind. She shut the door, tugged on her apron, and tied up her skirts so as not to tangle in them.

Leonardo closed his notebook and followed.

In the market, the servants parted, each to their own tasks.

"Signorina," Leonardo said eyeing her heavy basket, "May I help you with that?"

The woman's lips upturned at his flattery. She raised her head to look at him. "Young man, this old woman will take any help she can get."

"Old?" Leonardo said, feigning surprise. He took hold of the overfilled basket. "Your household must be quite large. That or your maestro has a hearty appetite."

They both laughed and walked out the way they entered.

" 'Tis in celebration. My maestro called for the festa on the occasion of his firstborn child," she said beaming. "A girl. Born midday yesterday."

"A girl?" Leonardo's heart fluttered. The fifteenth of June. "A healthy child? Congratulations to you and to her father. Your lady must be well, up, content, and recovered?"

The woman gave him a wary look, but nodded. "Yes, Signore. Now I must hurry. The Baptismal procession begins soon and I must get back to prepare. Thank you for your help."

"Yes, to the baptism."

***

Antonmaria, his family, and friends soon gathered at the doors of the Baptistery. He cradled the bound bambina in his arms. Onlookers in the piazza gathered in. Leonardo joined them.

Antonmaria unwrapped the child dressed in a gown of pure white that draped over his forearm. The man the child would call father held her out to receive the blessing.

Leonardo marveled at her tiny, fisted hands that startled like new wings when dedicated to the open air. Her dark hair and attentive eyes, so like her mother's, drew him in, charmed him—a perfect little girl.

The priest cupped water in his hand and lifted it. Droplets fell onto the bambina's head but she made no cries. Everyone delighted in her smile. "I baptize you in the name of the Father, the Son, and the Holy Spirit, Lisa Gherardini."

"Lisa," Leonardo whispered to speak the name of his treasure. She, his masterpiece, he knew he would someday paint.

J.A.Burton graduated from Methodist University as an

english major.

She lives in Colorado and is a lover of animals, the arts,

and travel.

Connect Online:

www.jaburton.com

Made in the USA
Middletown, DE
16 December 2020

28243970R00274